PURSUIT

PURSUIT

A NOVEL

STEVE MONROE

ISBN: 978-1-5040-1262-1

Distributed by Open Road Distribution
345 Hudson Street
New York, NY 10014
www.openroadmedia.com

PURSUIT

Aupie -
Keep Rockin'
Best Wishes !

[signature]

He escapes who is not pursued.
Sophocles

Thursday

3:54 P.M.

Jules set the last bag of groceries on the floor, turned and closed the front door. As the door swung shut, she got a final glimpse of the SOLD sign in the front yard and, again, her heart leaped. She sat down on the brown paper runner the movers had left just inside the door and kicked off her boots. Snow melted on the paper and as she took off her coat, she noticed how filthy the runner had become and decided she'd take it up before James arrived at their new home for the first time. She stood up, hung her coat on the banister and bounded up the carpeted stairs, two at a time. She returned moments later, slippers added to her blue jeans and red sweater.

Jules picked up two bags of groceries from the floor, took them to the kitchen, and then returned to get the final bag. As she walked back through the front room, she noticed the movers had unpacked the pictures and mirror from the dining room at the old place and had simply leaned them against the wall outside the kitchen door. And they'd left the couch and overstuffed chairs wrapped in plastic. Yeah, there was plenty of work to do and she was beat. But she laughed at her reflection in the mirror; her long auburn hair spilled out from underneath the knit stocking hat, cheeks and nose red from the cold,

5

sweater dotted with bits of brown packing paper and cardboard. She stepped into the kitchen, put the bags on the counter and sighed. She looked every bit as tired as she felt.

It was her first day of real freedom, she thought, as she took off the hat and tossed it onto the kitchen table. She picked up her iPod, slipped the ear buds into her ears, flipped through her playlists and selected "Workout Tunes." The Pussycat Dolls blasted as she sashayed toward the counter and began putting away the groceries.

First day of real freedom. First day in her new home. A home she owned. It had been her signature and her money. True, it had taken longer for the divorce to be finalized and to sell the old house than she'd anticipated, but she was finally free of Rod. No more of his ego, his ridiculous narcissism. No more late nights lying awake until he came home, reeking of booze, babbling lies. She'd never have to go to another party with him and listen to him talk to his colleagues about the latest tenant they represented or building that was being developed. No more real estate talk, no more being ignored while he read his BlackBerry and soon, she'd be rid of his last name and then that would be it—no more Rod. Thirty-two years old and starting her life all over. She felt good, really good, as she put the last can of soup in the cupboard, opened the refrigerator and took out a pitcher of water.

She filled a glass and drained it almost as quickly. She was tired from all of the unpacking and pushing furniture around, but the membership Rod had paid for at the East Bank Club hadn't gone for naught. Although she knew she would always be described as "short and busty," she was in great shape and, if the movers' glances could be believed, still pretty darn sexy. She sighed again as she realized there was no more East Bank Club for her; she'd be lucky to find any gym she could afford, or even find time to visit, now that she was a single working mother. The thought startled her, momentarily, but then she smiled. She pulled her iPod out of its holster, switched on her new theme song and listened to the group No Doubt sing "It's My Life." And it was her life, she thought, as she ran back up the stairs. But it was also a new life for James and she wanted her ten-year-old son's new room to be unpacked and in perfect condition before he arrived. And that, she realized as she saw the single mattress and box springs leaning against the wall of his room, floor nearly covered in boxes, was no small task. Jules had less than an hour.

Thirty minutes later, Jules finished in her son's room. She'd unpacked most of the boxes, put the bed frame together and made the bed. There was nothing more she wanted than a long bath, but she didn't think she had enough time before James would arrive, so, instead, she crossed the hall and walked through her bedroom to the private bathroom. There were several boxes stacked in the tub, each marked "Master bathroom" with a short list of items packed inside. She picked up the top box from the stack, set it aside and opened the next box. She rummaged through the contents, then triumphantly plucked out her hair dryer. No one was laughing at her sense of order now!

Jules pulled the earbuds from her ears, turned off her iPod and set it on the bathroom counter. She turned on the faucet, cupped a handful of cold water and splashed it across her face. Then she wet her hands and wove them through her hair. It was matted from wearing the stocking hat but it would take only a minute to add some body, so she plugged in the hair dryer, clicked it on and . . . the lights went off in the bathroom.

"You've got to be kidding me," she muttered. She flipped the light switch but nothing happened and when she looked back into the bedroom she saw that the lights were off there, too, as well as in the hall.

Jules walked through the bedroom, back into the hall and made her way to the stairs. Her mind raced as she carefully made her way down the steps. The electrical panel, she knew, was in the garage. She'd made a point to ask about it, as it was one of the things her father had reminded her to check when she'd told him she was purchasing a house. She silently thanked him as she reached the first level, noted that the lights were on in the front room and made her way to the door to the garage.

The garage was dark when she opened the door but when she reached across the wall and flicked the light switch, the garage lit up. Jules looked at the filthy garage floor, then simply shook her head as she set a slippered foot onto the concrete and made her way toward the electrical panel.

It was cold in the garage and Jules saw through the garage door windows that it was already pitch dark outside. She shivered a bit as she opened the gray electrical panel door. Two columns of black switches stared back at her. The switches bore the numbers 15, 20 and 30 in no apparent order and she didn't know the significance of the designations. She felt her arms tense as she stared at the switches but then she looked at the inside of the panel door and saw an inspection form and underneath the form, a wiring diagram and to the right of the diagram, a circuit breaker directory. She calmed herself with a deep breath and said, out loud, "You can do this."

Jules looked at the switches and saw that four were in the "off" position. She then glanced at the diagram and directory and noted that most of the spaces on the directory that were to have been used to fill in the name of the room corresponding to a specific switch had been left blank. The switches for the kitchen, laundry room and back porch had been identified and someone had used a magic marker to write, "Spare bedroom" next to one switch and "East garage wall" next to another. But, as luck would have it, the four that were off hadn't been marked.

Jules thought of her father again. If he'd been there, he'd have taken care of everything for her. This was the kind of thing that he could fix in his sleep. But he wasn't there and suddenly she felt very alone as she realized she couldn't yell inside to anyone as she flipped a switch, ask them if the lights had come on. No, there was no one inside at all.

"Here goes," said Jules. She flipped the two switches on the left side of the panel to the "On" position and headed back inside.

The door to the garage closed behind her as she reached the staircase, took the first few steps. She was lost in thought, wondering why four circuits had been off, when a flash of light caught her eye. She stopped, poised to take another step and looked toward the light.

A desk lamp dimly lit the front room and cast a dagger of light up the curtains. But on the far side of the room, in the open area used as a dining room, a light suddenly flashed again, then disappeared. Jules caught her breath. The previous owner had taken the chandelier from the dining room so that couldn't be it. Was it a flashlight? Someone coming in the back door? She gazed across the dining area, strained to see through the darkness when suddenly the light came on again and this time it stayed on long enough so that she could make out the source of the confusing light.

"Oh, my God," muttered Jules. She chuckled as she slipped back down the steps. One of the movers must have plugged in a floor lamp as he'd fastened the legs on the wooden dining room table. But the cord lay over the lid of a box, which flapped ever so slightly, driven by the stream of warm air from the furnace vent. And as the lid flapped, it jostled the cord, which, in turn, rhythmically moved the plug in the wall socket. Finally, as if to illustrate the effect, the plug began to wiggle in the socket and the light from the lamp pulsed on and off like it was following a mad beat.

Before Jules could take a step across the room, a bell chimed. She was confused, momentarily, but then realized it was the doorbell. She'd been so focused on the odd light that she'd jumped at the sound but she quickly gathered herself, self-consciously ran a hand through her hair and strode to the front door. She touched the brass doorknob, then leaned forward and looked out the peephole. She saw nothing but darkness, but then a figure pulled back and she realized it was a man in a dark overcoat. A black knit hat covered most of his gray hair and when he turned his hulking body and his face appeared in front of the peephole, she saw that tiny icicles hung from his thick gray eyebrows. His face was a deep red. The blood vessels in his nose were broken and when he cupped his hands in front of his face and exhaled, two huge puffs of breath billowed around his head. He leaned into the door and a yellow, red-streaked eyeball searched the peephole expectantly. He blinked, then pulled back, shivered and blew into his cupped hands.

Jules stood for a moment, not sure she should open the door. But it was an old man. And if he was lost or wandering . . . She gently unlocked the door and opened it a crack.

"Can I . . ."

The door blew open. She tumbled, fell back onto the stairs. The old man hauled her to her feet, thrust a hand over her mouth. He pushed her, slammed the side of her head into the banister. He stepped away, kicked the door shut as she fell to the floor. Her mind spun. Instinct; she rose to her knees, tried to crawl away. Her slippers caught in the runner and she kicked them off, scrambled drunkenly, but the old man reached for her. She fell on her side, kicked at him, screamed. But he grabbed her by the hair, lifted her as she shook, veins popping out of her neck, hollering at the top of her lungs, "No!" He wrapped an arm around her neck, choked her quiet, pushed her forward, across the front room. Her vision blurred, head jerked. Her knees gave out but she was yanked upright, pushed forward.

"Oh my God!" She heard a voice but it wasn't a man's voice. It was shrill and high pitched. The strong arms spun her. The man's eyes went wide. The shrill voice screeched, "Oh, my God! I'm hurt! I'm hurt! What do I do? Where do I go?" He spun her. She saw the bathroom door on the right and the couch to the left and a chair and boxes, then the bathroom and then the couch and the chair and then the bathroom and then she was moving forward . . . The shrill voice screamed, "Oh God! I need help!" The old man kicked open the bathroom door. She saw her blurred reflection in the mirror. Blood covered the right side of her head and face. Her head lolled. There was a pounding behind her right eye. She felt nauseous. Something grabbed her hair, drew her head back. She saw her eyes descend the mirror, the old man behind her, screaming, falsetto: "I've tripped again!" as her head shot down, hit the edge of the sink mid-scream.

A deep voice, awful, hoarse . . . "Christ. These lights. Reminds me of Faces, over on Rush Street. You know, I was a pretty good dancer back in the day."

The man pushed her away from his body, spun her. She only saw shapes and colors, blurs, then his face. His eyes were wide, face caught in a delirious grin. She felt herself being flung around the room, strong arms holding her up, swinging her. She was on her heels; her head hung to the side. She felt like she was on a merry-go-round and the only thing that stopped her from flying out of control was the old man's grip as he spun her. "Yeah," he said. "I was a pretty good dancer."

She felt him drag her across the room; her toes scraped the floor. He stood her upright, took her hand and wrapped it around the portable phone. But then he let go of her hand and the phone dropped to the floor. He put a towel in her hand, lifted it to her head and then stepped back. Jules's eyes rolled back in her head as she fell forward. Her knees buckled, hit the floor. The towel fell at her side as the floor came straight at her face. She felt her nose and lips explode. Something pushed deep into her head. A warm liquid filled her pant leg. And then there was hot breath at her cheek. And a deep, low, rumbling voice as his lips neared her cheek.

"Back in the day."

5:15 P.M.

Wally stared at the computer screen. He rubbed his brow with both hands, then over his short hair, and finally rested his elbows on the desk, leaned forward and stared even more intently. Nothing came to him. But that was nothing new. He'd never considered himself the brightest bulb in the shed, but his parents were farmers and like them, he knew success came through hard work. *Work, work, work*, he repeated the word in his head, concentrated on the pictures. He heard a knock at the door and turned as his wife peeked into the study.

"What do you want for dinner, Wallace?" she asked.

He took off the headset, set it on the desk, minimized the window on his computer and spun the chair to face her. The casters moved easily across the hardwood floor and he lifted his feet, like a little kid, he thought, as he planted his heels, looked up at Theresa. "What did you say, baby?"

Theresa smiled, obviously amused. Her dark eyes rested on him and he felt his heart jolt as he looked up at her. "I asked," she said, like she was playing with one of her students, "what you would like for dinner."

Wally clapped at his belly. "I shoulda worked out tonight," he said. "Second time I missed this week and it's only Thursday. You wanna have salads and a yogurt dessert?"

"I'll make you a salad," said Theresa. "The thing is, there's two pieces of pizza left from last night, so if you want one, tell me now. I don't want you grabbing one from my plate after you eat your salad."

It was Wally's turn to smile. He liked his wife's slight accent, noticeable only on occasion, like when she pronounced the last letter in *thing* with a hard *g* sound. "No pizza for me," he said. "But if you want to go out, I could do that."

"I don't want to go out until May, at the earliest," she said. She pushed the door open further, stepped into the room. "Working on your book?"

"Uh, yep. I want to get it done so I can figure out the course work."

Theresa nodded at the headphones and her dark hair fell over her brow. She scooped it over the shoulder of her sweatshirt and Wally smiled again as he noted the puffy red slippers that peered out from the bottom of her blue sweatpants.

"I thought you needed total silence when you wrote," said Theresa.

"Mood music," said Wally as he stood up. He was nearly a foot taller than his wife but they shared a squat build. He was lucky enough to combat it with a thick neck and barrel chest and Theresa had been blessed with great looks, as far as he was concerned. He pulled her to his chest and hugged her, kissed her cheek. "Why don't you make my salad and heat up your pizza? I'll finish up here and then after dinner we can play some gin."

He turned from her, expected her to start out the door, but she didn't move. "Did you think about what we talked about last night?" she asked.

Wally sat down, turned back toward his computer. "Last night and every night? Yes, dear, I did." He heard the sarcasm in his voice, so stopped and turned to face her. "I know you want your sister close by, but there's a lot to think about. First of all, you'd have to find a place for her, here—"

Theresa interrupted. "I did. I can talk to her doctors and the insurance company and start filling out the paperwork, but I want to know I have your support." Her voice echoed in the hall. "I'd visit my sister more and she'd join us for holidays and, well, you know, it'd be a lot more responsibility. But it would be great for her and we'd have a lot of fun. What do you think?"

"Oh, boy," he sighed. He regretted his tone immediately. "I mean, we . . . Have you talked to your brother-in-law about it?"

"No," said Theresa. "That's why I want to make sure you agree with me that it'd be best for Maria. If you agree, we can talk to Jesus about it. I think he'd love the help and I'm sure he could find work here. And with his military benefits, you'd think they'd be covered in Illinois."

Wally smiled. His brother-in-law was a good guy, pretty simple but kindhearted. He'd stuck with his wife when she'd been diagnosed with early onset Alzheimer's. But he didn't make much money and Wally knew that, nearly every time Jesus called, the tagline would lead to another short-term loan. And the short term sure seemed to be getting longer and longer. But, it was hard to begrudge the man. "Let me think about it some more. Is it gonna cost us anything?" He cringed at the question, hoped Theresa knew it was meant to address practicality—not place a price on caring. He was relieved when she simply shook her head, continued the frank conversation.

"No," said Theresa. "And the home I found is pretty close, so I can stop in and see her when you're working late and take her to church on Sundays."

"That sounds great, hon," said Wally. He clapped his thighs. It was his way of indicating the discussion was over and he had to get back to work.

Theresa ignored the sign. "It would do her a lot of good. Maybe it would turn things around for her."

"The doctors told us there's no cure for Alzheimer's—only drugs that can kind of slow it down." Wally knew he was treading on thin ice. "Maybe being around us would be good for her, but it's not gonna make her better."

"Those doctors don't know everything," said Theresa. Her eyes flashed for a moment, but then softened. "Just promise me you'll think about it."

Wally sighed. No use fighting her. "I promise."

He returned to his computer, slipped on the headset and barely heard Theresa whisper, "You've got to believe, Wallace. You've got to believe."

"I believe," he mumbled to himself as he heard the door close behind him. "I believe in osmosis, or I'd better if I want to learn Spanish."

He moved the mouse over the play symbol, left clicked and the program started playing, again. A woman's voice came from the computer, said, "I'd like to order a cup of coffee, please. Me gustaria pedir una taza de cafe, por favor."

"I'd like to order a cup of coffee, please. Me gustaria pedir una taza de cafe, por favor," repeated Wally.

5:47 P.M.

James peered out the passenger window, into the darkness, while his dad read from his BlackBerry, talked out of the side of his mouth. "Remember, start out by telling her you're mad at me for getting you here late. That puts you on her side, shows you're not biased toward me."

The dome light flicked on and when James turned, he saw his dad staring at him, the BlackBerry in his lap. "I'm listening," said James.

His father flipped James's long bangs off his forehead, leaned over and rested a hand on his shoulder. "Then, you tell her you saw a movie at school about fishing. Get her involved, ask her if she's ever been fishing. Ask her if her dad ever took her fishing when she was growing up in Iowa. Then, when she gets into it, you've got to say, 'Well, ironically,' and the key word is *ironically*, so she thinks it's a coincidence . . ."

James rolled his eyes, scrunched his chubby face, stared up at his father from under his knit Bears hat. "Dad, she's gonna know you told me to say all this stuff."

His dad snorted. "No, she isn't. You give her way too much credit for perception. She couldn't make the connection if she was led by GPS."

"Aren't you supposed to leave me out of it," said James. He turned to look out the passenger window again. His hair was nearly as long as his dad's and he stuck out his lower lip and blew it away from his eyes. "Edgar's dad told him he wouldn't ever talk bad about his mother in front of her children."

"Edgar's dad gets paid every Friday. He offers any kind of opinion, he's afraid they'll pull the crack pipe."

"What does that mean?"

"It means I'm paid for my opinions, whether it's at work or in my home. Somebody doesn't want to be there, there's no dog collar around their neck."

"Mom never tells me anything bad about you."

"There you go. Even your mom knows she screwed up." James watched his dad's eyes as they noted the light on the BlackBerry go red. "So draw out the word, *i-ron-ic-ly* so it sounds like you're really mulling the coincidence. Then say, 'Ironically, dad asked me to go to fishing with him in Florida tomorrow morning.' Now, she's going to throw her little hissy, tell you it's your first weekend in her new garbage dump, but play up the fact you'll be back Sunday night."

"But you said we wouldn't be back until Wednesday."

"That's another call," said his dad. Then, he reached over again and yanked the knit hat down over James's eyes. He pulled it up quickly and said, "You've got to sell it, slugger. If push comes to shove, don't be afraid to use some tears, remind her she wouldn't let you go to the Super Bowl and watch your Chicago Bears."

"You didn't have tickets or a hotel room, Dad."

The red light blinked again. "I'm resourceful. We had our choice between a houseboat or a condo." His dad reached across his lap, jerked the door handle, pushed the door open. Cold air filled the SUV and his dad unsnapped his seat belt, nudged him out of the vehicle. "Sell it, boy. You're a born salesman."

"Whatever," said James as he slid off the seat, stepped out into the darkness.

Ice crunched beneath his feet and his snow pants made a funny sound as the legs rubbed together. His mom's new place looked weird, he thought as he trudged across the yard. It was a lot smaller than their old place. It looked older, too. No light came from the windows and she hadn't even bothered to turn on the porch light. Some dang welcome.

He heard his dad yell, "You want to go, don't you, slugger? Tell your mom I'll pick you up at seven in the morning and I'm out tonight, so she won't be able to get hold of me." He heard his dad's laugh, then, "Tell her I've got a date."

James stepped out of the yard, onto the porch and stomped his boots on the concrete. He reached up with a mitten and hit the doorbell. His face was cold and he resisted licking his lips. He waited a moment, wondered if he should just open the door and walk in, then rang the doorbell again. Nothing happened. He turned, looked for his dad but saw that he was hunched over the steering wheel, dome light off, the tiny red light methodically illuminating in the dark car. He was about to make his way back across the yard when he heard a sound at the door. He stepped toward it but when he saw nothing but darkness, he stopped.

Then, the door cracked open.

Rod stared at the Sold sign in the front yard, pictured Jules microwaving hot chocolate, a plate of cookies waiting for James. He lifted his eyes toward his son, but James was barely visible in the fresh night. He felt a jolt as he hoped his son could sell the lie because Sheila, his admin, said she wouldn't go unless they brought a playmate for her daughter.

He threw the gear shift into drive, was about to take off when he realized the porch light wasn't on so he figured he'd better wait until James got inside. He waited for a moment as he saw his son reach, again, for the doorbell. James turned and looked at him, but Rod couldn't make out the expression on his face and James turned away, back toward the door.

Rod put his foot to the gas pedal. The SUV crept forward. He nosed under a streetlight, wondered if should just go ask Jules himself. But he glanced in the rearview mirror, quickly changed his mind.

Rod's nose crinkled, eyes spat disgust as he sped off. Fucking bitch walked out on him!

And look at the way she just yanked their son inside.

Friday

4:30 A.M.

Theresa heard the alarm, felt Wallace roll over. Instinctively, she pulled her feet out from underneath the covers, sat up and stepped into her slippers. She heard Wallace say, "Don't get up, honey," as she tied her housecoat and walked out into the hall.

"Come on, go back to bed," she heard him say as he lumbered across the bedroom floor, opened the closet door.

"I'm making your oatmeal," she said as she hurried down the hall.

"Can't, I'm working out," he yelled behind her.

She stopped at the refrigerator, yelled back down the hall. "I'll make you a shake." She opened the refrigerator, took out the vanilla yogurt and chilled coffee. She set them on the counter, filled a plastic White Hen cup with ice, then peeled a banana and dropped it in the blender. She spooned yogurt over the banana, then took half of a cup of dry oatmeal from the box and sprinkled it over the yogurt. Finally, she dumped the ice into the blender, poured in the coffee and hit blend. The kitchen filled with the sound of the blender mixing Wallace's shake. It may not have been the ideal thing for him to take on a cold winter day, but it was better than doughnuts or a breakfast sandwich.

Theresa filled the plastic White Hen cup with the shake, set it on the counter and then opened the refrigerator door and took out the jar filled with coffee grounds.

"Don't make coffee on my account," said Wally as he entered the kitchen.

"It's for me," said Theresa. She fought a smile at the first sight of her husband dressed in tennis shoes, gray sweatpants and a warm-up jacket, with a wool sport coat completing the outfit. He kissed her cheek, walked to the laundry room and returned a moment later with a pair of slacks and a cotton dress shirt. She took the shirt from him and folded it neatly as he placed his slacks inside his gym bag, on top of his dress shoes. She handed him the shirt and he set it in the gym bag, then took his gun and holster from the counter, slipped them inside the bag and zipped it shut.

Theresa fought a yawn, scooped coffee grounds into the coffee-maker as Wally pulled his winter coat over his sport coat and warm-up jacket. He already had color in his face—a true Scot with an ever-present red hue. But he was still handsome—hair in a short business-man's cut, silver high on his temples. Only a few flecks of light brown hair remained. He had big cheeks and dark eyebrows over deep blue eyes and whenever anyone guessed at his profession, they said either football coach or cop. He was the latter and although it scared Theresa, she knew he'd always be one.

She grabbed him by the shoulder, handed him his shake. "Wallace," she said. "Drink this. We've got to lower your cholesterol."

Wally took the cup. "My dad's seventy-six years old, honey."

"He was a farmer. He didn't eat all of the junk food and processed foods."

"He moved to the city twenty years ago and ate nothing but burgers and steak." Theresa peered up at him as he lifted the cup, drank from it. "But he also said, 'Mother knows best' so who am I to disagree?" He took another swig from the cup and then leaned over and kissed her.

"Thank you, Wallace," said Theresa as she watched him bolt across the kitchen, pick up his workout bag, then open the door to the garage. He stepped out and she heard the garage door start to open.

"And thank God I put the car inside last night," said Wally as he opened the car door. "Go back to bed now, baby," he said. "I'll see you tonight."

Theresa waited as he started the car, backed out of the garage. Cold air whipped through the garage and she smelled the exhaust as the car slipped into the early morning darkness. She saw the headlights wave across the frozen driveway and when their car shot forward, she thought she saw Wally wave, so she waved back. Then, she pushed the button to close the garage door, closed the door and stepped back into the kitchen.

"Querido, Dios, por favor proteja Wallace," she whispered as she lowered her head and leaned over the counter. "Él volverá a mí."

She lifted her head, poured herself a cup of coffee and figured since she was already up, she'd finish typing her class's story. After all, the Literacy Showcase at Anixter Center was that coming Monday.

Theresa had only four days.

5:34 A.M.

Wally tried to keep his balance as he stepped across the parking lot. The wind wasn't so bad but there had been no break in the ridiculous temperatures and the dirty spots of snow and ice were treacherous. He opened the door and stepped inside and said to the gathering of cops at the Area Five front desk, "Cold enough for ya?"

A group of patrol officers surrounded the desk. One of the desk crew said, "We've got a heater."

"Good thing," said Wally.

"No, a *heater* heater. Big time crime scene. Command van's been set up since three this morning."

Guess I'll work out tomorrow, thought Wally as he strode past the officers, ran up the stairs to the Detective Division.

6:17 A.M.

Light trucks lit up the Lincolnwood address like Wrigley Field. The Detective Division Command Van sat like a mobile home for cops. Wagon men propped on two wagons, prepped with cigars. News media yacked into microphones, shot pics, *annoyed*. Wally strode through controlled chaos, signed the log, and crossed both strips of barrier tape. He stopped ten feet from the house, eyeballed it.

The house was a Cape Cod, windows jack-o'-lantern lit, dormers dark. No car in the driveway, a paved walk straight to the front door, another around the right side of the house. A cop from the district brushed by him, "Big boys all over the place."

Wally took a glove off with his teeth, pulled a pen from his pocket and jotted notes on his GPR. There were way too many people around to take his normal route and since he was probably the seventieth guy on the scene, he moved through the front door, looked for a familiar face.

"Dan," yelled Wally as he stood in the entryway, let the door shut behind him.

Dan Shepherd, a First Watch dick, tall and laidback, white haired, walked over, shook his hand. "Pretty awful."

"I could tell by the audience," said Wally. "I only got a little bit back at Division."

Shepherd's lips curled. "Victim at the dining room table, one shot to the head. Another in the basement. Female officer from District 18. Anna Rodriguez. Duct taped to a chair. Tortured. A long morning's turning into a longer day."

"Jiminy," muttered Wally. "Fill me in. The homeowner the vic in the kitchen?"

"Yep. Phillip Costa."

Wally caught Shepherd's stare, said, "I got it."

"Figured," said Shepherd. "The Feds have already weighed in and it's gonna get worse."

Wally shook his head. "No wonder all the press. They love Outfit stuff. Who called it in?"

Shepherd said, "Neighbor. Says he was a friend of the deceased.

The deceased and his family were supposed to be away on vacation. Seems the neighbor came home from a night in the Viagra Triangle, saw the night lights weren't on and decided to check it out. His son was supposed to feed the Costas' fish, so he had a key. The neighbor opened the front door, turned on the lights, took a few steps inside and saw Mr. Costa at the dining room table. He hightailed it out of there and called 911 from his home. Responding officers had to knock on his door to get him out. Guess he was worried whoever did this might've still been around."

"The rest of the family been accounted for?"

"Yep. Wife and two daughters. They're in Mexico. Gerin got their hotel info, called the local authorities . . . Some vacation."

"What time did the neighbor open that door?" asked Wally, pointing at the front door.

Shepherd caught it, nodded, "Yeah, front door. Little after 2 a.m. We've got the time from his call and he's got a receipt from Tavern on Rush that shows 12:53."

Wally looked past Shepherd, said, "Let me review the reports. I'm done with that, I'll check back with you, okay?"

Shepherd said, "Okay," turned and walked toward the dining room.

Wally watched crime lab techs dust *everywhere*. He looked past them, through the living room, up a bloody rug at two lab men hunched over something. One stepped to the side, spray bottle in hand. Wally got a full look at the dining room—a body slumped dead, hands nailed to the table.

6:58 A.M.

"What a piece of shit!" hissed Rod. He banged on the front door, again, stepped back and looked for any movement. The curtains didn't rustle. He looked up at the second story, gray siding nearly indistinguishable from the white trim around the windows. There were three small windows but all of the curtains were drawn and no light eked out. Rod slipped off a glove, pulled his BlackBerry from his coat pocket and hit the call button, again. He lifted it to his ear and listened to the ring.

"Son of a bitch!" yelled Rod. He lifted the BlackBerry as if he was about to slam it into snow piled against the house when he heard something. It was a song. That stupid song Jules had on her phone. He lifted the phone to his ear but got her voice mail, so he hung up and dialed again. Now it was unmistakable. He heard the song again and pushed his ear against the front door. It was louder. Her phone was somewhere just inside the front door!

"Jules!" he yelled. "Open the door. This is ridiculous!"

A sound from the back of the house jarred him—a screen door! He sprinted around the corner, saw a figure dash from the house toward the unattached garage. "Jules!" yelled Rod as he sprinted down the driveway. "Jules! You can't do this!"

He nearly slipped on the icy driveway, caught his balance and stopped on the walkway from the house to the garage. He reached toward the door to the garage and tried to turn the brass handle. It was locked. He raised a fist, beat on the door and a motor whirred, the garage light came on and the overhead door began to lift. Rod stepped onto the driveway. He smelled the exhaust, tried to see through the smoke. He heard the car's engine rev. He stepped back and yelled, "Jules. Let James out of the car. You're acting like an infant!"

He moved back further, saw the garage door finish its ascent, watched as the smoke cleared and the car started to back out. He waved his hands in front of his face, coughed through the exhaust as he heard tires spin on ice. The garage light gave him a brief view: a head of gray hair, visible over the driver's headrest, turned. One eye peered at him over a huge shoulder and he thought he saw teeth and a smile. He got a sick feeling in his stomach. His legs felt weak. He wanted to run but the car shot backward, hit him thigh level and launched him into the air. He landed on his back, felt his head hit concrete as the first tire rolled up his leg.

7:44 A.M.

Wally parked his dark blue Impala behind a squad car, noted the ambulance and another squad car parked in the street. He smiled, glad they'd left the driveway free. Thirty minutes removed from what he was sure would be one of Chicago's hottest crime scenes, but he didn't mind. The murder of a police officer and the brother of the head of Chicago's mob meant a lot of attention and pressure. And since he'd been late to the scene, he couldn't approach it his way. A fluke call took him out; Deputy Superintendent Allen Yates had said, "A homicide reported in Edgebrook. Near here. It's yours."

The ambulance blocked the driveway, stretcher in the drive. Three EMTs worked on a man on the stretcher. A uniformed cop interviewed a woman in a parka; her housecoat fluttered underneath. Another cop stood guard near the back door of the house. Wally tugged at a cop standing near the stretcher. "You first responder?"

"Yep," said the cop. He looked late twenties, dark hair, brows. He nodded toward the cop near the house. "My partner and I answered a major accident scene call. The guy on the stretcher got run over in the driveway. The witness over there got a quick look under the streetlight, said it was a gray-haired man, big guy with a dark coat. Driving a white Mazda Six. We already called it in. My partner went in the front door, saw a body and made the call."

Wally leaned into the EMTs. "How is he?"

One said, "Not good. We're out of here in thirty seconds." On cue, his partners lifted the stretcher, moved toward the back of the ambulance. Wally leaned in, got a good look: male, mid-thirties, long light brown hair, slender, black cashmere-looking turtleneck, designer jeans, boots, ski jacket, black winter gloves.

"Officer," said Wally, turning toward the cop. "Ride with 'em. He expires I want a dying declaration. Can you do that for me?" The cop nodded, Wally continued. "Did you check him for identification?"

"Yep. None. I'd bet the SUV here is his," said the cop, pointing at a vehicle parked a few yards in front of the ambulance. "Want me to check it out?"

"No, we'll handle it," said Wally. He heard the ambulance driver slam his door shut, said, "You'd better hop in." He handed the cop a card. "My card with my cell. Call me with anything."

The cop hopped into the ambulance. The doors shut. Wally jogged toward the house, heard the cop yell, "Jeez, everyone knows you, Principal!"

"I, uh, I rang the doorbell and knocked several times," said the cop near the back of the house. He tugged his stocking hat down on his forehead. "I didn't get a response, so I walked around back and saw that the back door wasn't shut."

"Did you touch the screen door?" asked Wally.

"I had on gloves. I thought I was alerting someone inside or . . . I didn't expect to find a dead . . ."

"So . . ."

"So I stood inside the screen door, pushed the back door open and yelled for anyone inside. I didn't get a response, but since the door had been open, I got kind of worried. I mean it's freezing outside and people don't just . . ." He let out a deep breath. "So I walked through the kitchen, into the dining room and living room. I was just going to yell up the stairs but when I saw over the couch, there was a body on the floor. She was just lying there—definitely dead. So now I figured there was a dead woman in the living room, and somebody else in the driveway, and somebody that had left in a hurry, so I figured I'd better make sure there wasn't anyone else in the house. I mean I had to weigh it out. I didn't want to disturb the scene, but I had to make sure there wasn't anyone else in the house."

Wally raised both eyebrows, kept him going, "And?"

"And there wasn't. I didn't touch anything. I had my gloves on, pushed doors open without touching the knobs and didn't close them. Believe you me, I got in and out of there as fast as I could."

"You did right," said Wally. "I'm on my way in. Start a log. I want your name and badge number as well as the other two cops'. I called my partner, Detective Jones, so when he gets here, tell him I'm inside. I want yellow barrier tape all the way out to the street, then follow the lot line. Give me red tape from the driveway in. Start a scene sup and I want that witness back in her home." He glanced at the witness, saw her flailing her arms, heard her shriek, "And he ran toward the garage screaming, 'Jews! No Jews!' I couldn't believe my ears!"

Wally shook his head, sighed, "No more questions. Someone stay with her until I send a detective over."

"She's from—"

"The house across the street," said Wally. "See the green trash bin still lying in the middle of the drive? Must've scared the bejeezus out of her."

Wally counted ten footprints in the snow leading from the back door to the garage. He twisted the knob on the screen door—not the side someone would use on their way out—pushed the back door open and stepped inside. A small kitchen, linoleum floor dirty with tracked mud. A glass pitcher of water and a knit hat with a couple of loose red hairs sat on a wooden kitchen table. A woman's purse sat on the counter, multiple plastic grocery bags sporting big yellow smiley faces piled on the counter next to the refrigerator. Two boxes, opened, dishes visible—still packed. Two dish packs, still taped shut, held open the door from the kitchen to the dining room. Wally stood in the kitchen, thought.

First responder said the front door is locked. The back door was open. Whoever left this house exited the back door. Obvious. But important. See what's in the next room.

Wally entered the dining room, looked ahead and then, left, right. The table was already set up; a cheap lamp plugged into the wall. Four chairs were tucked under the table, boxes lined the perimeter. A mirror and some pictures leaned against the wall. Wally fought an anxious feeling, glanced at the pictures. One was black and white; an old couple face-pressed. Another was a landscape—an Ansel Adams snow-dusted forest. One more, tucked between the others—a young couple and a little boy, family picture smiles flashed for the camera.

He mentally recorded, fought thought, observed. Eight steps and around the couch, the body lay on the floor, full rigor. Wally stood and stared, embarrassed by the intimacy. "Jeez, I'm sorry," he said to himself. "I don't want to see you this way."

He saw a phone, towel, bare feet. He moved toward the stairs, saw two red slippers on dirty brown paper—the slippers sent acid to his stomach. He saw blood on the banister, paper and floor. He huffed up the stairs, saw two bedrooms, a den and a bathroom. He saw one bedroom unpacked, a single bed assembled, sheeted and made. He gasped, ran back down the stairs, past the body, noted the bare left hand. He stopped in front of the dining room wall, gloved the pictures apart, focused on the one of the young couple. He sprinted into the kitchen, spilled the purse on the table, unsnapped the wallet, looked at the driver's license and ran out the back door. He barked, as he saw Romar Jones, "All call! Murder! Possible kidnapping!"

The detectives gathered in the driveway. Wally directed: "This is changing by the second. What appeared to be a hit and run became a hit and run and a murder and now it may become a hit and run, a murder and a kidnapping. It appears the deceased is the wife or ex-wife of the man run over in the driveway. Thus, both parents were on the scene but no sign of the son. We just don't know what's occurred, yet." He pointed at each man as he spoke: "Jerry, call the realtor on that sign in the front yard. Get her over here. I want to find out anything we can about Julie Patterson, including a maiden name, anything about Ms. Patterson's relationship, her parents, his parents, new relations. Roscoe, take one of the uniforms with you to that grocery store up the street and ask if anyone saw her there and saw a gray-haired man anywhere near her. There are empty bags with the store's logo on 'em, so she's been there. Also, there's a family portrait inside. Take a digital picture of it and show that." He turned to the oldest of the group. "Don, get the uniforms to start canvassing the neighborhood. You interview the witness across the street."

The men disbanded. Wally started toward the SUV, followed by his partner.

"I thought you'd be in Lincolnwood," said Romar, softly, like he always seemed to talk.

Wally glanced at his partner. Romar's brow was furrowed, like he was deep in thought, but after a while, Wally had figured out that that was how Romar always looked—serious. He looked that way because he had dark eyes under a thick brow that looked like it had been molded by the pad of a football helmet. He had a broad nose and short-cropped black hair, and when he smiled, it was kind of startling. In fact, although Wally would never tell him, he'd heard a lot of women state that Detective Romar Jones was one good-looking man.

"I was there," said Wally. "I walked into the Command Van the split second the call came in about this homicide. It was like fate intervening. Yates just looked at me and basically said, 'You.'" He strode around to the SUV's driver's side, peered in the window. "We're both wearing gloves. Let's take a quick look." He lifted the door handle and the door opened. He leaned in, searched. He stood up, hit the unlock button. "Nothing. See if his wallet's in the glove."

Romar opened the door, then the glove compartment. "Yep," said Romar as he extracted the wallet. He was about to close the door when he saw an envelope. He grabbed it, shut the door, met Wally in front of the vehicle. He handed Wally the wallet and opened the envelope.

"Rodney Patterson," said Wally, reading from a driver's license. "What ya got there?"

Romar studied paper. His nostrils flared. "Two United Airlines tickets. Rodney Patterson and James Patterson. Flight to Miami leaving at 9:30 this morning."

Wally sighed. "They ain't gonna make it."

8:05 A.M.

Wally stood in the living room, back to the front door. Only moments before the crime lab had arrived. Wally surveyed the scene, jotted notes on a GPR, *studied.*

Reverse chronology: A guy run over in the driveway by someone who pulled a car out of the garage, left the house by the back door. If there hadn't been any hit and run in the driveway, what would we have found? A dead woman lying in a pool of blood in the front room of her new home. A mobile phone and bloody towel next to her. Blood on the banister; spatter on the wall by the stairs. A trail of drops from the runner in front of the stairs leading to the bathroom. Blood on the sink. Drops of blood all over the floor, surrounding the body.

Original thought? Blood on the banister, spatter on the wall, trail to the bathroom, blood on the floor, towel, phone . . . signs of an accident. The woman came down the stairs, slipped, banged her head on the banister. Dazed, she made her way to the bathroom, grabbed a towel, fell and smacked her head on the sink. Stunned even worse, she searched for the phone, bled all over the place, finally succumbed in the living room. No sign of rigor mortis subsiding, so she died late afternoon, early evening.

Add it all. The guy taking the car, blowing out of the driveway changes everything. He could've been a burglar—staking out a new home isn't original—but why would he take car keys from her purse and not her wallet, money? If he was there to take the car, he'd have taken her money. And the timing isn't right –not many burglars break in early in the morning when newspapers are delivered and the neighborhood's alive. No, this isn't a burglary and it isn't an accident.

Wally heard car doors slam, loud conversation. He heard Don Haskins talking to Fred Pence, the crime scene photographer. *Thoughts: Julie Patterson moves into a new home in the dead of winter. She wants to move. (Bad breakup? Custody battle? Boyfriend?) The paper runner's still on the floor in the entryway. Furniture Saran-wrapped. She's been to the grocery store, unpacked her groceries and left her purse on the table. The kitchen table and dining room table have been set up, but the movers would've done that. The only other thing completed is the single bed put together in a bedroom upstairs. Even the queen bed in the main bedroom hasn't been put together. So back up. Back up. She moves in. The movers leave. She goes to the store, comes home, puts away her groceries, puts on her slippers, and makes her kid's bed. She's home. She's comfortable. No stranger is there. But someone comes in (did one of the movers leave the back door open?) surprises her and whacks her head on the banister. But why parade her around the room, create the illusion of an accident? Because the killer didn't want us to search for him. When the body was found, he wanted it to look like an accident and leave it at that. But at some time, for some reason, things changed. One thing we know: Rodney Patterson ran around the side of the house, toward the garage, yelling something (alerting a neighbor) and got run over by a vehicle purportedly driven by someone with gray hair. He had airline tickets in his car for himself and his son. He never made it out of the driveway. So, a lot of questions, but the most important one, the one that has the hair on my arms standing, is "Where is the boy?"*

8:10 A.M.

The conductor sighed, stared down at the young woman. "You must give up your seat so this man can secure his bicycle," he said. He showed no emotion, kept his voice low, monotone.

The woman wouldn't back down. "We're just a couple of minutes from Union Station! He can hold the bike for two more minutes." She hugged her backpack.

"I'm sorry. It's a danger. You can see that the area is clearly marked," said the conductor. The woman looked a bit younger than him, probably a student. He started to say something but felt a hand on his shoulder and turned around. A short Asian woman looked at him, excited. She pointed to the bathroom door, motioned like she was trying to open it and shook her head. He turned away from the student, brushed past the man and his bicycle, reached out and tried the restroom door. It didn't budge.

"It's in use," he said. "We're nearing the station."

"Been in there whole ride."

The conductor looked up at a black woman leaning over from the second level. "What?"

The woman leaned down, her glasses fell toward the tip of her nose and she pulled her briefcase into her lap. "I said, he's been in there the whole ride. After you took my ticket, a man went into that bathroom and he ain't been out since."

The train started to slow. People began to button up their coats, gather their things. The conductor pounded on the bathroom door. "Sir!" he shouted, over the crowd noise. "We have reached the end of the line." He pounded a palm on the door, pulled at his keychain, searched for the bathroom key. "Sir!" he screamed again. "Unless you are unable, you must open the door and depart. We have reached the end of the line!"

8:11 A.M.

Wally watched as a woman from the crime lab examined the body. "Note the scratches on the top of her toes," said Delia Grant. "Carpet burns. You know anyone that walks on the top of their toes?"

Wally's cell phone rang. He answered it as he walked into the kitchen. "Greer."

"Principal. This is Lieutenant Dave Abel. Thirteenth district. We've found your white Mazda. It's parked at the Edgebrook train station. We are approaching the vehicle as we speak. There are two officers in front of me and they're separating, taking either side of the vehicle."

Wally gave the floor a vacant stare, hung on each word.

"The officer on the passenger side is shaking his head. So is the officer on the driver's side. That's a negative on anyone in the vehicle."

Wally heard the lieutenant spit orders. "Simmons, pop the trunk. If it doesn't spring open, use your bar. Do not contaminate the vehicle with any handprints."

Wally heard metal being pried, the trunk rush open, the pry bar clang on cement. Muted voices. An exhale. "Shit."

A pause, winter long. Finally, the lieutenant's voice came back. "The boy's in the trunk. He's dead. The son of a bitch wrapped his face in duct tape."

8:13 A.M.

The conductor pounded on the door, fumbled with his keys. Inbound passengers had nearly vacated the car. Outbounds wedged their way in. "Sir. For the last time. This is the end of the line!"

The door opened. A dark figure pushed him out of the way. The conductor stumbled, grabbed a rail. A deep voice came to him as the man glared at him, then stepped off the train. "No shit."

8:15 A.M.

Wally said, "I want the Metra police alerted that a Caucasian male—big, gray hair, possibly wearing a dark coat—is wanted for questioning in a multiple homicide. Yes, I know how that sounds but if someone fitting that description does something out of the ordinary, I want him held. Tell them to watch every platform between here and downtown and between downtown and both airports. Anyone that fits that description and even looks slightly out of place, I want 'em stopped and questioned."

Wally yelled, "Where is that realtor? What have we learned about the parents or in-laws?"

Wally looked at Romar Jones, said, "Dave Abel's checking cameras at the train station and talking to everyone at the station. I'm gonna put Don Haskins in charge of the crime scene. As soon as I talk to that real estate agent, I'm gonna head back over to the heater. The cop in the basement was duct taped and so was that boy. That's too much of a coincidence. If our killer's tied to that one, we've got a lot better chance of identifying him soon. Too much longer, he could be anywhere."

8:17 A.M.

Charlie pulled the cap down over his ears. The wind off the river seemed even colder than normal and he nearly slipped on the wood bridge. He took a left in front of the Boeing store, crossed over by Pot Belly's and walked south until he got to his spot by the CVS. The crosswalk light turned green and the crowd of businesspeople rushed north across Madison Street, passed by him like he was just another statue set out by the mayor.

Charlie took off his stocking hat, let his long gray hair fall. He held the hat in front of him, started his chant. "Good morning, young man; good morning, young man; good morning, young lady; good morning, young man; good morning, young lady . . ." He tried to catch the eye of every person who passed, intent on calling them out.

"Good morning, young man. Good morning, young lady. Good morning, young lady. Good morning, young man."

A couple of regulars dropped coins in his hat. A woman in a leather Bulls jacket set a five in his hat, said, "Good morning."

Charlie smiled, nodded at her. He thought she was a regular, but wasn't sure. Maybe he'd known her when he'd driven the bus. Or maybe it was from the days when he bartended. He just couldn't remember. Now what was he thinking about? Did Billy take his gloves last night?

The light turned red. The crowd on the other side of the street grew. He wrapped the hat around his hands, sniffed the snot back into his nose. It started to snow and he felt his hair get wet as a couple of men in suits jumped the light, started seconds before the rest of the crowd followed. The two men both dropped coins in his hat as Charlie took a deep breath, nearly sang.

"Good morning, young man. Good morning, young lady. Good morning, young man. Good morning, old man . . ."

8:55 A.M.

Martin unbuttoned his overcoat, took off his gloves and tucked them in a pocket. The men gathered around his car, awaited instructions. "Hanratty," Martin said, nodded at a red-haired man in jeans and a short pea coat. "Take three men and go around back. If we apprehend him inside, you probably won't see anything. I'll send someone to get you. If we don't apprehend him, he's likely to go out the back door and make for the forest preserve."

"He's like eighty years old," said Hanratty. "If he tries to run, I'll crawl after him."

"I'll inform the state's attorney you'd prefer to apprehend track stars. Get going."

Four men jogged around the back of the house, weapons drawn. Martin looked at Ron Melcher from the Chicago Police Department's Organized Crime Unit, said, "I'll do the talking," and trotted to the porch. He rang the doorbell as Melcher stepped up next to him, waved at five uniformed cops to spread out around the porch. Martin glanced back at the line of cars on the street, saw Terry and Bob, matching blue suits under FBI coats, kneel, handguns at their sides.

The front door opened. A short brunette in a housecoat and slippers held a baby to her chest. Her eyes were red, puffy. "Jesus Christ," she muttered. "Do we have to do this? Today of all days?"

Martin held the paper high. "This is an arrest warrant for Mr. Francis Costa. You will step aside, ma'am and let us in."

The woman turned, yelled, "Grandma, the Feds are here!"

The five uniformed cops and three agents rushed by Martin. The woman looked at Melcher yelled, "Jesus Christ, Ron. Do we really have to go through this? You should be here protecting us! My great uncle's dead!"

Martin interrupted. "I'm Martin Lowell of the Federal Bureau of Investigation. I'm assuming you are the granddaughter, Angelica Costa."

The woman snorted, said, "No kidding. Graduate top of your class?" Her thick dark hair fell over her eyes. She looked at Melcher, said, "I asked you if we really have to go through with this. You know he isn't here. You should be looking for whoever killed Uncle Phil. Some maniac is on the loose and you're here?"

"Sorry," said Melcher. "You know we have men outside protecting you. And half of Area Five's working on your uncle's murder. I'm really sorry. They'll be out of here in a few minutes."

Angelica adjusted the baby as he started to cry. "You. Lowell. Your skin's as dark as mine and your hair is jet black. My kids are in the kitchen! What kind of man can do this? Are you proud of yourself?" Her scratchy voice ratcheted up a notch. "You motherfuckers got everything you want from us and you still won't leave us alone. You go on with this charade. Anything's out of sorts, I'm calling my lawyer." She sneered at Martin, turned and walked back through the house.

Melcher stroked his thick brown handlebar mustache. "Wait 'til you meet her grandmother."

On cue, the elder Costa woman walked toward the front door. She was short and wiry and wore green sweatpants, a black and red T-shirt and carried a lit cigarette and a cup of coffee. Her white hair looked like it hadn't been combed and Martin saw the blue veins in her hand as she shook it in his face. "You didn't need to do this!" she said as she flicked ashes at Martin. "The neighbors. Christ, they'll talk. No one said anything about this to our lawyer!"

Martin looked at Melcher, quashed the question on the cop's face. "Check on the men. If he's not here, we'll get going." Melcher nodded, strode off.

"No one said anything about searching our house," said the woman. She dropped her cigarette in her coffee. "You FBI types have been in and out of here." She looked him up and down. "This family's been through hell and today Phillie's killed and you come walking up our steps like some Baird and Warner gal on a house tour? You've got some nerve."

Martin watched as she took some rosary beads from the pocket of her sweatpants, rubbed them. "You don't seem too surprised about your brother-in-law," he said. "And you haven't asked once about his family."

The old lady stopped rubbing the beads, curled her lips. "You Welch! You piece of garbage. Get out of my house!"

Melcher walked up behind the woman, peered at Martin over her shoulder. "He's not here."

Martin heard doors close; an agent yelled from upstairs, "Nothing!" A cop walked out of the living room, his arm around Angelica Costa's wrist. She writhed, shrieked. "She hit me," said the cop.

"Let her go," said Martin. He turned, walked out the front door as the women screamed.

The rear passenger window was iced. Martin blew steam, watched the window fog over, wrote the word *Fuck* with his index finger. The agent driving looked at him through the rearview mirror, said, "Is that your phone?"

Martin fished inside the breast pocket of his suit, took out his cell phone, clicked, "Talk."

"Lowell."

"Special Agent Martin Lowell?" said a voice.

"Yes."

"Special Agent Lowell, this is Officer Hanratty of the Chicago Police Department. I was just wondering, since you left the Costa residence, were you ever planning on sending someone to the backyard to tell us?"

Martin sighed, pulled the phone from his ear as Hanratty's voice registered, "Asshole."

10:30 A.M.

Wally sat in the Impala, his office away from the office. The heater blew a current of warm air, but he could still smell the realtor's perfume. She'd been terrified when he'd first started interviewing her, but by the time she left, she was somber yet calm. And Wally knew it was his voice and demeanor.

He had one of those voices that was kind of soft and reassuring—no high notes or low growls—smooth and confident. One woman he'd picked up for shoplifting on Michigan Avenue had actually given him her card and told him she could get him voice-over work. Instead, he testified against her in court and, from the look on her face, she'd no longer been so impressed with his voice.

And his demeanor? That, he knew, came from experience. The realtor had experienced something new—awful and shocking. Wally still viewed such scenes as awful, but he was no longer shocked. In fact, it was practically self-defense: A detective overcome by emotion wasn't effective; Wally knew he had to be calm, cool and focused.

Focus. He read his notes, listened as the realtor's words rang in his head. *"It was a bad marriage, but not a bad divorce. She pitied her ex.*

She wasn't bitter; she was happy! She was about to start a new job. She had a new house. She had a new life."

Facts: Her parents lived in a small town in Kansas. His parents were deceased. The couple had joint custody of their son. The son was dead, murdered like the officer from the first scene Wally had visited earlier in the day. There was no boyfriend, no angry ex (angry maybe, but he'd been carted off in an ambulance) and no easy explanation.

But there was an explanation to be found because there were two murder scenes and they were linked. If he could determine why they were linked—what a divorcée in Edgebrook had in common with the brother of a mobster and a police officer—it would go a long way toward pinpointing the killer.

Wally tossed his notebook onto the passenger seat, put the car in drive and pulled away from the curb.

11:15 A.M.

Wally stepped into the Command Van, unzipped his coat and said, "Jiminy, it's not the cold that kills a guy, it's jumping in and out of it."

Detective Superintendent Allen Yates didn't look up from the computer screen, handed Wally a sheet of paper. "Then stay outside. I thought you had another murder scene."

"I do," said Wally. "Two bodies. A little boy was duct taped, just like the officer here."

Yates's head jerked up. He spun in his chair to face Wally and when he did, his suit coat opened and Wally saw the Bigsby & Kruthers patch and fought a smile. He figured Yates for about a hundred and fifty pounds on a wet day and the suit testified he hadn't gained a pound in probably ten years. Skinny, nice threads, not a blond hair out of place and ready to kiss any keester he could to get a promotion.

"If you'll read that press release, Detective, I think you'll gather that whatever happened here is tied to an ongoing investigation into organized crime. How do the murders of a woman and her son tie into that?"

Wally knew Yates had heard about it on the radio. Sitting in the Command Van was no different than pulling your office to a crime scene. "I don't know, yet, but I don't believe in coincidence and murders in Edgebrook and Lincolnwood on the same day and both using duct tape? That tells you something, Superintendent. Have they established the time of death for the victims here?"

"Not definitively. The bodies were still in full rigor mortis. Noon, early afternoon yesterday."

"Same with the woman in Edgebrook when I got there this morning. That means she died somewhere between twelve and twenty-four hours before I saw the body. The time frame fits."

"Read," said Yates as he turned back to the computer. "Or don't . . . if you have your DVR set for now. They're having a live press conference."

Wally stepped around Yates and moved to a table that held an empty coffee cup and a printout of an aerial of the neighborhood. He saw that houses that had already been canvassed bore a red X. He pushed the paper aside, sat down, unzipped his coat and pulled his reading glasses from his shirt pocket. He put on his glasses, read the release:

U.S. Department of Justice
United States Attorney
Northern District of Illinois
Federal Building

Raymond Denton

United States Attorney

FOR IMMEDIATE RELEASE PRESS CONTACTS:

IRWIN MARTIN (312) XXX-XXXX

13 DEFENDANTS INDICTED FOR ALLEGED CONSPIRACY, MOB ACTIVITIES; CHICAGO ORGANIZED CRIME FIGURES ALLEGED TO HAVE COMMITTED 20 MURDERS.

CHICAGO A ten-count indictment was unsealed today and thirteen defendants were in the process of being picked up—ten in Illinois, two in Las Vegas and one in Memphis. All thirteen defendants are alleged members of "The Chicago Outfit." The defendants were charged with racketeering, conspiracy to commit murder and attempted murder. The indictment was announced by Raymond Denton, United States Attorney for the Northern District of Illinois and Special Agent Martin Lowell, Organized Crime Squad Supervisor of the Chicago Office of the Federal Bureau of Investigation.

"If this doesn't effectively end Outfit activity in Chicago, it nearly nails the coffin shut," said Mr. Denton. "The thirteen defendants represent the upper echelon of the Chicago mob, with the glaring exception of Francis Costa, and I have faith Mr. Costa will be apprehended soon. When that happens, mob activity will cease to exist in this city. This investigation involved crimes that are decades old and the information we have gleaned shows how this criminal machine was greased and oiled—and by whom. I guarantee tonight not a dirty politician, cop or businessman will get a second of sleep. When this case is tried in court, sunlight will shine on those who have bled this city dry for years. This may be the end of the Outfit in Chicago but it's also the beginning of the end of the corruption that runs through our government services and our politicians. We've all heard this before, but never from those who exploited this city. You're about to hear it in their own words. This is the turning point we've waited for since the days of Al Capone."

Included in the conspiracy charges is the attempted murder of legendary Chicago police officer Gus Carson. "If Officer Carson was here today, he'd be proud to see the men who attempted to kill him finally face a jury of their peers. It was the memory of Officer Carson and the innocent civilians caught up in the Outfit's web of crime that gave us the fortitude to carry on each day through a long, arduous investigation," said Special Agent Lowell. "He would also be proud of his own department's role in picking up and apprehending the defendants. This was a dangerous but vital function and we are very fortunate that no one was injured in the apprehension of these violent offenders."

The document went on to name the defendants, state the maximum sentences and penalties and detail the crimes they were alleged to have committed. It finished with the usual statements that the defendants were innocent until proven guilty and that the burden was on the government to prove guilt beyond reasonable doubt.

Wally set the paper down, tucked his reading glasses back into his shirt pocket. "Superintendent Yates. We have two murder scenes within a couple of miles of one another and it's obvious they're related. It states here these men were picked up this morning. I think one of the first things we should do is interview each of 'em and document their whereabouts for the last day or so."

"I've already spoken to the FBI," said Yates. "All of these men were under surveillance for the last forty-eight hours. Therefore, they couldn't have done it." He waved his hand dismissively, cut off Wally's interjection. "I know, that doesn't mean they couldn't have orchestrated it. I'll set up jailhouse interviews. In the meantime, we need physical evidence or a witness. Go back to your homicide, Principal. Dig up some good evidence and find your perpetrator. If you can tie him to these murders, too, that's even better."

Wally stood, zipped his coat and put on his gloves. "I'm gonna make a run through the house one more time, talk to Dan Shepherd again. I'm also gonna have the techies match the duct tape."

"Take the patience of a saint to match the strands of that tape," said Yates.

"One time I had a case where two guys were strung up with pieces of this thick old rope," said Wally. "One was in Boys Town, the other in Streeterville. This rope was nasty. Turns out it had been used to tie up a boat at Montrose Harbor for years. But just 'cause two pieces of old rope look the same, doesn't mean they are the same. Roland Brown worked for over a week to put it together. Finally, he calls me and says he can show, conclusively, that they were part of the same rope. I asked him how he proved it and he said, 'You get the hang of it.'"

Yates winced. "Call me if you get anything, Principal. There's heat all over this one already."

"Okay," said Wally. "You, too." He stepped out of the Command Van, let the door close behind him and headed toward the house. He knew the superintendent wouldn't call him, but he didn't mind Wally requesting a call. It showed him Yates might be a kiss ass, but he wanted to solve the murders. At least they had that in common.

11:50 A.M.

Back at crime scene number two: Wally parked the Impala in front of the Patterson house, started to trudge across the frozen lawn. He saw Romar step out the front door, walk through the yard to meet him. Romar splayed the fingers on each gloved hand as he walked. His hands were hip high and Wally thought he walked like an athlete, coolly rolling forward on the balls of his feet. They met in the middle of the yard, near the realtor's sign.

"Anything new?" asked Wally.

"That neighbor across the street saw the boy come home last night, around six. She thinks he got out of an SUV, but she didn't see who was driving or who answered the door. Said she'd call if she remembered more. And speaking of calls, Roscoe called," said Romar. "He ran the plates on the cars in the grocery store's parking lot. One of 'em is registered to Phillip Costa. And he placed Ms. Patterson and an old man at the store, too. He's got a sketch artist drawing up the old man and they're checking security tapes from all of the surrounding buildings."

"Hot Jesus!" said Wally. He slammed a fist into his palm. "It is all tied together. So whoever killed Costa and Officer Rodriguez ends up at the grocery store. He sees Julie Patterson and for whatever reason, decides to follow her home. So, he must've followed her in Costa's car, then taken the car back to the grocery store and walked back to her house."

"Maybe she paid with a check and he just got her address off it," said Romar.

"Maybe, but she just moved in. It's doubtful she'd have checks printed up already."

Romar said, "Probably not. But if she opened a new account around here, she'd probably use a blank check and the store might make her write her address and phone number on it."

"Have Roscoe look into it," said Wally. "I'm calling Dan Shepherd to make sure he hears this from me. And now we've got a strong tie to the heater. Romar, you ever interview a real live FBI agent?"

Romar shook his head.

"Well, you're about to . . ."

12:15 P.M.

Martin pushed his black hair off his forehead, pulled the hood of his sweatshirt up over his head, tied it tight. He slipped his hands inside brown cotton gloves, dangled them in the air and jogged in place. When the traffic heading north on Wabash cleared, he ran across the street. Moments later, he cut over Michigan Avenue then down the steps by the river. He jogged east, the river to his right. Most days, when he wasn't running with his running group, he looked at the water or just dodged people walking out the back of the Sheraton. But the river held chunks of ice that reminded him of the cold and no one else was outside, so he ran with his thoughts.

When he passed the fountain, he turned north, then minutes later ran across Lake Shore Drive, found the bike path through the snow and headed north next to the lake. He passed two men in parkas, walking on the inside lane. He was surprised he passed them so quickly; he was so tired he felt like he was barely moving. Only a mile or so into his run, North Avenue barely visible, and he felt the gray cotton from his sweatshirt and sweatpants start to moisten on the inside. His face already stung and he knew he should've wrapped it in a scarf, but he was so tired he just wasn't thinking right.

Less than thirty minutes out of the press conference, his nerves jazzed. He should have stuck around, answered questions, played the game. But he listened to his body, which practically shouted, "Run!"

It was the biggest case of his life. Jesus, it would've been the biggest case of any FBI agent's life! He could punch his own ticket, go wherever he wanted to go. He'd shared credit with the state's attorney, Denton, but that was too little to bicker over. No, the way it had fallen into his lap, he couldn't complain about anything. He'd worked hard on the case, spent years putting evidence together. But the final piece of the puzzle? No, that was damn near blind luck. So, he wouldn't complain. But now . . . Now, when he should be hammering out the last pieces of the deal, following up on new information, prepping for testimony; now, when he should be waiting those last tense moments before Denton and his men put the final touches on an airtight case . . . Now, instead of all that, he saw it all falling apart. Only, he didn't really see it, he just felt it. Because the only thing he could see was that scene in the basement. And the part of the scene that just wouldn't leave him, would keep him up at night? The part of the scene that he saw more vivid than the waves of Lake Michigan or the outline of the Hancock? The part of the scene that really made up the whole scene? Her eyes.

Martin heard his breath, wheezed as cold air hit his lungs. His legs were going and his mind was gone and he knew if he didn't concentrate, he'd veer off into the lake and never make it out. What was it his track coach at Northwestern had said? "When you're so tired you want to die? Just concentrate on taking a big step and lean forward. 'Cause if you put that foot out and lean forward, the other foot has to follow or you'll fall flat on your face."

Martin forced his left foot out, leaned forward, thought about dying.

1:28 P.M.

Wally actually heard the clock tick. He understood immediately why the woman had left him and Romar in Special Agent Lowell's office to wait—there was nothing personal to view and nothing too confidential in sight. There were some papers on the desk. Wally saw the words *Subpoena Ad Testificandum* at the top of one page and a few lines underneath it read, in bold letters, "In the name of the People of the State of Illinois." A Scales of Justice paperweight sat on top of the papers. An empty coffee cup sat on a coaster.

Romar nodded toward the wall. "Ward map."

"Always good to know what alderman's gonna be barking up your butt," said Wally. "You know, I used to . . ."

The door opened. Wally and Romar stood up.

A man in a dark blue suit, white shirt and blue tie entered. "Special Agent Martin Lowell," said the man. He was dark, but not quite handsome—stern, with a long nose and big ears. About Romar's height; just short of six feet. He looked taut, wiry. Wally guessed him for a runner.

"I'm Detective Wallace Greer and this is Detective Romar Jones. You can call me Wally." Wally offered his hand, but Lowell ignored it, moved around the desk. When he turned around, Wally saw sweat stains on the front of his shirt. Lowell caught Wally's gaze, buttoned his suit coat.

"Happens to me when I work out at lunch, too," said Wally as he sat back down. "One time, back in my single days, I went to see this state's attorney right after a workout. I don't mind telling you, she was one attractive lady. I sat in this light blue overstuffed chair in her office and when I got up to leave, you could see this dark blue silhouette." Wally laughed, slapped his knee. "It was awful."

"How'd that work out for you?" asked Romar, soft.

"Didn't," said Wally. He offered Lowell, who failed to return it, a smile.

"I don't have time much time," said Lowell. "What can I do for you?"

Wally leaned forward, folded his hands, rested his forearms on Lowell's desk. "You were at the Costa residence this morning—"

"That's the end of this conversation," said Lowell. He pushed his chair back, started to stand, but Wally waved a hand, gestured for him to sit. Lowell sat, continued, "Superintendent Yates has already been told he will receive a report with any information that we deem appropriate."

"Well," said Wally. "You see, we're not really here about the murders of Officer Rodriguez and Mr. Costa. We're working a related double homicide."

Lowell interrupted, again. "My statement regarding anything related has already been released to the public."

Wally winced. "You mean that press release about releasing the indictments? I didn't get a copy and I didn't see you on TV."

"Are you being a smart-ass, Detective?"

Wally lifted his eyebrows. "No. I really didn't see it. If there's any useful info . . ."

Romar popped a knuckle. "You never asked who got killed."

"What?" asked Lowell.

"You got up before four in the morning to visit that heater and when the Principal told you there was a related double homicide, you didn't even ask who got killed." Lowell and Wally stared at him so Romar said, "I'm just saying."

"Who got killed?" asked Martin.

Wally spoke loud, tried to break the stare-down between Romar and Lowell. "A woman and her son. Julie and James Patterson. The boy was only ten years old."

"I'm sorry," said Lowell. He leaned back in his chair. "I am."

"And we have information that a big, gray-haired man may have been the perpetrator. He also ran over Patterson's ex-husband in the drive way. He was seen by a neighbor."

"I understand," said Lowell. "Time is of the essence. Please send a copy of your General Progress Report to Special Agent Simmons. I'll have my assistant get you his contact information. So, now—"

"Detective Jones was actually asking you something, here, Marty," said Wally. "I think the murders at both scenes are connected. So far, the only common denominators are geography, duct tape . . . and you. I'd hate to think you got up that early, visited the heater and may have some thoughts that can help us but—"

Lowell interrupted Wally. "I'm an early riser. You can make your own inferences about any ties between the murder of the brother of the Chicago mob and our arrests this morning."

Wally smiled, tried to cut through the tension. "I'm an early riser, too. My dad was a farmer. He always said, 'The cows don't milk themselves.'"

Lowell feigned a smile. "My father was with the Bureau. He worked eighteen-hour days most of his professional life."

"So we got that in common. A work ethic," said Wally. "Look, I know you've got stuff to do, so we won't keep you. But throw us a bone. The guy who murdered this woman and her son is still at large. My gut tells me he's the one that killed Officer Rodriguez and Mr. Costa, too. See, the thing that's got me worried is that I think there's some kind of tie to whatever you guys have going on. And Mrs. Patterson and her son, they just happened to get in the way. And if I don't know what you've going on, there's no way for me to tell where 'in the way' is gonna be, next."

Lowell stood. "I'll be happy to get you a copy of the press release."

The answer was the answer. Wally stood, forced up a smile. "Yeah, that'd be great." Romar stood up next to him, started toward the door, so Wally said, "Could we get it, now?"

Lowell gave him a "If that gets you out of my office, now" smile, said, "Certainly," and picked up the phone. "Frasier, Lowell. I have a Detective Greer and a Detective Jones of the Chicago Police Department in my office. I'll have Maggie walk them by your office on their way out. They need a copy of the press release on today's announcement. Yes. Give them whatever they need. Thank you."

Lowell hung up. He followed them out the door, told the woman who had brought them to his office to take them to see AUSA Frasier. Wally spoke up as Lowell turned his back, walked back toward his office. "Say, Special Agent Lowell. Did I mention that the boy was only ten years old?"

Wally stopped, stared expectantly at Lowell's back. "Yes," said Lowell as he walked back into his office, pushed the door closed behind him. "Yes, you did."

1:50 P.M.

Wally took the papers from AUSA Frasier while Romar and their guide stood in the doorway. He glanced at papers, said, "Sorry, no, I need the originals."

Frasier scratched the top of his scalp through his crew cut, heavy eyelids attempted to rise. "He told me to give you the press release. Here it is." He pushed it at Wally, again.

"I was standing in his office, sir. He said, 'Give 'em anything they need.' I'm interested in one of the men that wasn't picked up today."

"I'm authorized to give you the release from this morning," said Frasier. "Anything else hasn't been released to the public, so I—"

Romar interrupted. "Just call him."

"What?" asked Frasier.

Romar leaned into the room. "Just call Special Agent Lowell. This is important. I'm sure he won't mind being interrupted."

Frasier eyed the press release. "He did say to give you everything you wanted, didn't he?"

"Yep," said Wally.

Frasier opened a drawer, sifted through a file and pulled out another set of papers. He stapled them together, handed them to Wally. "You taught that homicide class in Springfield last year, didn't you?"

Wally nodded.

"My son took it. He loved it. He's got a copy of your book in his apartment."

Wally grinned. "Updating it now for the next class. Your son Chicago PD?"

"He's a PPO in Area Two."

"That's great," said Wally. "Who's his FTO?"

"Milo Garrison."

Romar piped up. "I know him. Good man."

"Agreed," said Wally. He shook Frasier's hand, started out the door. "Tough area but he's learning from the best. Thanks for the help."

Wally slid into the passenger seat, buckled up while Romar started the car. "Crank up that heater," said Wally as he took off his gloves, reached into his pants pocket and pulled out a set of papers.

"Where are we headed?" asked Romar.

"Let it warm up a bit."

Wally studied the papers, eyes going back and forth between the press release he'd received from Frasier and the papers he'd pulled from his pocket.

"I thought you didn't see the press release," said Romar.

"Actually, I said I didn't get a copy." Wally set the papers in his lap, rubbed his hands together. "But I guess you could say I was a bit less than truthful." He leaned forward, started to compare the two releases.

"Well, you got what you wanted."

"I liked how you told him to call Lowell. Were you sure he wouldn't?"

"Man, I've only known that guy Lowell a few minutes and I don't like him. I knew he wouldn't."

"You're an astute student of human nature, Detective," cracked Wally. "I'll tell you what else I noticed about Special Agent Lowell. He's feeling some pressure. I'm guessing he went for a run over his lunch hour, but the man was still sweating when we left. He wasn't wearing a wedding ring and there were no family pictures in his office. Nothing personal. Guy lives for his work and he's obviously nervous about this case."

"He didn't seem too interested in ours."

"That was a poker face. Anybody else, you tell 'em you're working a double homicide, they ask who got killed. You tell 'em a big gray-haired man may be the perp, they ask how big and how old. That's human nature, too."

Wally picked up the set of papers he'd received from Frasier and grabbed the radio and called in. "This is Detective Greer. I need the last known addresses for the following. Mr. Henry Lopes, age seventy-three, Chicago; Mr. Vitus Gorski, seventy-five, Chicago; and Mr. Francis Costa, seventy-six, Oak Park. Right. Right." He returned the radio to its perch, took out his cell phone and dialed. "Don, yeah, Wally. Listen, I just called in looking for last known addresses for three men that may include our perp. I know. They'll be in FBI files. Tell Delia to have 'em run any prints they find on the scene against prints for the following: Henry Lopes, seventy-three, Chicago; Vitus Gorski, seventy-five, Chicago; Francis Costa, seventy-six, Oak Park. Yes, yes he is. Thanks."

Wally ended the call, dropped the cell phone in his lap, folded the papers and put them in his pocket. He turned to Romar. "The original press release said there were fifteen men picked up other than Costa. Today, there were only thirteen men. Lopes and Gorski weren't apprehended, nor was Costa. Looks like they knew they weren't gonna get Costa from the get-go."

"Did you know that about the fifteen guys? Is that why you asked for the original?" asked Romar.

"No," said Wally. "That was just a hunch. The press release said, 'in the process of being picked up,' indicating they weren't all in custody. But, I figured they didn't want to throw a number out they couldn't match—you know, have some reporter say a few days from now, 'Hey, you said you were picking up thirteen and there are only eleven guys in custody . . . ' And with all the publicity this trial will get, you know they didn't write that thing up a few minutes before the press conference. I figured they wrote it up earlier, it got blessed by all the appropriate parties and then they edited it today."

Romar revved the engine, held a hand over the vent. "What's that tell us other than that they weren't arrested?"

"They weren't picked up and the FBI doesn't anticipate picking 'em up anytime soon. Yates told me this morning that the FBI told him that every man on their list had been under surveillance. So, either those two slipped away or there just wasn't enough evidence to arrest 'em. These guys had something to do with Lowell's case and since they're all in their seventies, I imagine they've got gray hair—if they've got any hair at all. Someplace to start."

"Are you sure it's the same guy at both murder scenes? I'm not saying it isn't, but I wasn't at the heater."

"No such thing as coincidence. These were too close together. Two victims had their mouths duct taped. The time frame's right. No, I ain't bet since the Bears got seven in Super Bowl XLI, but this one's a lock. Whoever killed that young officer and the mobster's brother also killed that lady and her little boy."

"But what would that lady and her boy have to do with the Outfit?" asked Romar. He rubbed the knuckles on his right hand, like he always did when he was mad. "Why them?"

Wally sighed. "That's what scares me. Nothing. Ms. Patterson's killer tried to make it look like an accident. He didn't want us looking for him. You ready for my gut on this one, Detective?"

"Yep."

"My gut says whoever killed Phillip Costa and Officer Rodriguez saw Julie Patterson at the Happy Foods. He followed her home and when he saw the Sold sign he figured no new neighbors would be stopping by. Maybe he heard her say something in the store or maybe he saw her left ring finger was bare, but for some reason, he chose her. And he killed her. Then, instead of leaving, he stayed at the residence. At some point, the boy came home and he killed him, too. The next morning, the father surprised him and he just ran him down while he was getting away."

"You still haven't given me a motive."

"The motive?" said Wally. "You mean, 'Why did he kill her?' One of the basic needs . . . shelter."

Romar snorted. "Why wouldn't he just get a hotel room or go home?"

"Let's say he killed Costa and the officer. That's pretty high profile. If someone would've stumbled on it earlier, there would've been an All Call. You watch. It'll be on all the news shows tonight. A Chicago cop and the brother of the head of the Chicago Outfit get murdered on the same day the FBI nabs all these mobsters? That's news."

"Then why wouldn't he just skip town?"

"Now, there's the question. Maybe he was getting a flight today or maybe he had something else to do. I hope it's a flight. 'Cause if it ain't, and he has something else to do, we've got a problem. This city's nearly ten million people and some more are bound to get in his way. And you know where that's got us."

"Yep," said Romar. "Absolutely screwed."

2:38 P.M.

Martin looked out the window at Roosevelt Road, gray, slushy. Snow piled on the shoulders. Traffic moved slowly. A Pea Pod van stopped in his line of vision, stalled as its tires spun.

"Special Agent Lowell?" A woman in a blue suit pulled him from the window. "Follow me, please." They walked down the hallway, stopped in front of an unmarked door. The woman opened the door and gestured for Martin to enter, so he did.

A windowless conference room. Three people sat around the conference table—clockwise from the head of the table: Special Agent in Charge Darren Greene, State's Attorney Raymond Denton and a blond-haired woman. Greene and Denton wore power suits and red ties. Denton's silver hair looked freshly cut. The woman was a knockout with dark eyebrows and a green suit so dark it was black. Her red lips were pursed in a smile.

"Have a seat," said Greene. He took off his glasses, leaned over the table. "Please note that Special Agent Martin Lowell has entered the room."

"Are we being taped?" asked Martin.

"No," answered Greene. Martin followed his gaze toward the center of the table and noted a red light flicker on the speakerphone.

Greene pushed a set of papers in front of Martin. Denton and the blonde appeared to read copies of the set.

"Special Agent Lowell," said Greene, his Irish brogue turning *Lowell* into *Lull*. "As we work with the State's Attorney's Office to bring this most important case against Chicago's organized crime to trial, we are here today to assess any damage that may have come to the case over the past twenty four hours. You know—"

"Speed up the introductions," said Denton, his voice a deep grumble. He wrapped a fist inside a palm, leaned his huge body over the table and rested his elbows two feet apart. "Ms. Hughes is with me."

Greene blanched. Martin watched as he stared at Denton for a moment, then continued. "We're here today to assess the events of the past twenty-four hours and see how they might impact this case. As I stated, this is the most high-profile case ever brought against the Outfit and neither the FBI nor the State's Attorney's Office can afford anything but a series of convictions. As you can imagine, recent events have got us all a bit unnerved, Special Agent Lowell."

"That's an understatement," said Denton. He set the papers on the table to his right, stared at Martin. "We're going to dispense with decorum. Martin Lowell, as Organized Crime Squad Supervisor for Chicago, you have led the FBI's efforts in this case. Is that correct?"

"Yes," said Martin. He looked at Greene, who shrugged his shoulders.

"You organized and supervised the apprehension of the fugitives."

"Yes."

Denton's voice rose. "The brother of the main target of this investigation and a Chicago Police officer were murdered the day before these arrests. Is that also correct?"

"Yes," said Martin. He looked at Greene, who fiddled with his tie bar. He glanced to Denton's right and the blonde leaned back in her chair, met his gaze.

"Martin Lowell, as Organized Crime Squad Supervisor you specified the surveillance of each of the individuals that were about to be indicted. Is that correct?"

"Yes."

"You authorized around-the-clock surveillance on fifteen men, is that, too, correct?"

"No, sir, as you know, it was only thirteen."

Denton took a deep breath, exhaled. "As I know. As I know." He glanced at Greene, back at Martin. "It was your idea to pull back surveillance on two men, Mr. Lowell. After deliberation, you opted not to apprehend one, but the other escaped. Is that correct?"

"Yes. As you know, there is precedent that if a man finds himself under surveillance, he will often flee."

"If he's under surveillance, wouldn't that preclude him from fleeing?" asked Denton. He folded his hands, pulled them toward his mouth. "Wouldn't you say that it's easier to keep tabs on a man if you're watching him?"

"In this case, I thought we were too close. I thought we'd spook him."

"Spook him!" Denton slammed a fist on the table. "Spook him? We have more bodies lying around than Burr Oak Cemetery! Spook him?"

Martin felt acid hit his stomach. He ground his teeth. Greene jumped in, saved him.

"Martin, the brother of the head of the Chicago Outfit was murdered, as well as a Chicago Police Officer. Did you order surveillance on him?"

"No."

"Do you know why the officer was at his residence or why she would have been murdered?"

"No."

"The Chicago PD also believes that an innocent woman and her son were murdered by the same party that killed Costa and the police officer," said Denton. "Do you believe that?"

"No."

Denton sighed. "Well, you'd better hope not. And it better not be someone where you pulled surveillance."

"Martin," said Greene. "Your choices are starting to come under scrutiny. We don't know how these things are going to play out, but we can't have any more surprises."

"Did you learn anything at the scene of the Costa murder?" asked Denton.

"No," said Martin. "I don't have enough information to make even an educated guess as to what happened. The only thing I can say is that it can only help our case."

Denton grunted. "What leads you to that assessment?"

"I believe the brutal murder of his brother will be the final straw for Mr. Costa. His full cooperation is virtually assured."

Denton sat back in his chair, stared at Martin, didn't say a word. The blonde smiled wider, crossed her left arm over heavy breasts, rested her left hand in the crook of her right elbow and stroked her chin with her right hand. Martin took it all in, tapped his foot.

"Martin," said Greene. "You've worked on this case for eight years. Mr. Denton and I talked earlier today and agreed that, until the last twenty-four hours, this case seemed to be progressing smoothly and, frankly, with the divine intervention we've encountered, I thought it would be a fantastic success. But, this morning, I felt the familiar pang of a Cubs fan. When things seemed perfect, that damn black cat walked out and all hell has broken loose. I need your personal assurance that, until the arraignment on Monday morning, things will run smoothly. The men we have arrested have been locked up. Our witnesses are safe. We're getting the final bits of incriminating, unimpeachable testimony. So, look me in the eye and tell me that you have confidence that everything we've planned and built with Mr. Denton's office will come to fruition."

Martin folded his hands, locked eyes with Greene. "Yes, sir. It will."

"Elizabeth?"

Martin turned, followed Denton's words, eyes. The blonde stared back at him, her smile had gone straight-lipped. She spoke, her voice quiet, forceful. "He doesn't understand the situation."

Martin waited out the rising anger, kept his pace. Deadpan: "I understand the situation. You're afraid of losing and you need a scapegoat." He looked for an outside lane, instead cut inside. "Remember, you need my testimony."

Greene started to speak, but Denton pushed a palm at him. "Are you insinuating something about your testimony, Lowell?" asked Denton.

"Not at all," said Martin. "You want my testimony given with confidence and passion. Candidly, I consider this questioning not only in poor taste but misguided. It would've been far more useful simply to ask me for any pertinent facts and my opinions."

No one spoke. Martin brushed by, kicked for home. "And Ms. Hughes, if you're joining Mr. Denton in court, you shouldn't dress like a distraction."

The woman didn't bat an eyelash. The room went silent. Martin looked at Greene, Denton, Hughes, back at Denton. "Is that it?" asked Martin.

"You really don't understand the situation. It's not your competence we're questioning," said Denton. He looked at Hughes, who folded her set of papers, twice, then dropped them in the wastebasket at her side. "Elizabeth?"

Martin stared at her. Her eyes were closed. Slowly, they opened, like covers coming off coffins—the deep, unfeeling black of her eyes: "He's lying."

"About what?" asked Denton.

"Everything."

The room was silent for three minutes; Martin counted in his head. Finally, Denton stood, gathered his papers and walked out. Hughes followed, stole a glance at Martin over her shoulder as Greene caught the door, held up two fingers at Martin and mouthed, "Back in two."

The door closed with a thud. Martin fought the urge to relax, sat straight and stared. The red light glowed. Static crackled, then, "Bravo, Special Agent Lowell." The voice so recognizable. "You will continue to offer an air of confidence. But, I want to know exactly what happened at the Costa residence. Send your written report directly to me and do not leave out the tiniest bit of information. And I want our best men to join forces with the Chicago Police Department. In this day and age, we need to show that we cooperate. We share information. You have delivered an airtight case and I want to make sure it stays that way."

Martin heard the metal rollers of an office chair roll across a wood floor, two shoes flop on a glass desktop. A sigh. "The woman, Martin. Was she attractive?"

"Not to me, particularly, sir."

"Good breeding stock?"

"Sir?"

"You're a single male, Special Agent Lowell. Thirty-seven years old and healthy. Would you give it a go?"

"If you're asking me—"

"Don't play the Puritan with me. I'm asking you if you'd sleep with her."

"Yes, I'd sleep with her."

"Then, Martin, when you're lying, don't point out the props. It tells everyone you're looking for them. You should've played to her vanity. And don't let any line of questioning make you uncomfortable. Answer with crisp, clean language in brief, pointed sentences."

"Yes, sir."

"Perfect. Martin?"

"Yes, sir?"

"You're learning. Deliver this case."

"Yes, sir."

The line went dead. The glow from the red light disappeared. Martin stared at the phone, waited for his leg to stop shaking before he rose.

3:45 P.M.

Gray, cloud-filled skies blocked the sun. Wally walked across the service station's lot, the smell of chocolate rising from the Blommer factory. He stopped in front of the station, took the glove off his right hand and held it with the notebook in his left hand as he pulled a pen from his pocket. He tucked the glove in his pocket and started to take notes.

"Wonder why they don't sell gas?" asked Romar. He stepped around Wally, walked toward the corner to get a better view.

Wally jotted in his notebook: single story building—four service bays, a small convenience store with a cash register and two coolers. Six cars in the lot, all four bays full. Four mechanics at work. Male, Hispanic, all late twenties to early thirties, wearing blue coveralls.

A husky voice said, "Can I help you, Officer?"

Wally stopped writing, watched as a man approached. Wally eyeballed him at five foot eight and a buck seventy five—too small to be the "big gray-haired man." He wore the same blue coveralls but also a heavy winter jacket emblazoned with a Chicago Bears logo and a blue stocking cap. Thin gray sideburns poked out of the bottom of the hat. The skin on his face was dark and wrinkled and seemed to fall from his high cheekbones.

"We're looking for a Mr. Henry Lopes," said Wally, adding a second syllable and *z* to the last name.

"It's Lopes, as in 'jogs fast,'" said the man. "I'm Henry Lopes."

Wally asked for identification, followed Lopes back inside the convenience store and saw Romar stride toward them and step inside just before the door closed.

Lopes stepped behind the counter as Wally watched the dirty slush melt off his boots. "Here you go," said the man as he reached over the counter, handed Wally an Illinois driver's license.

Wally wrote down the driver's license number, pertinent information. He handed the card back. "Thank you, Mr. Lopes." He gestured at Romar. "This is Detective Jones and I'm Detective Greer." Wally let the hand holding the notebook fall to his side, chuckled. "I gotta ask ya. Why didn't you even ask me what this was about before you forked over your ID?"

Lopes stepped from behind the counter, leaned against the corner. "I'm seventy-three years old, Detective, and I still run this business. I don't have time for games."

"I'll bet you don't," said Wally. "At this point, we're just looking for some help. You can answer on your own, but if I don't like what I'm hearing, I'll have to bring you in. Got it?"

"I've been getting it for seventy-three years," said Lopes.

A bell rang as the door opened. Lopes looked over Wally's shoulder. "It's okay, Daniel."

Wally turned and watched as one of the mechanics brushed past Romar, who stared at Lopes, ignoring the man. The bell rang again as the door opened, closed.

"Can you prove your whereabouts for the past thirty-six hours?" asked Wally, lifting the notebook back toward his chest, pen poised.

Lopes laughed. "I can tell you where I've been the past two weeks. Right here. I've worked from five in the morning until midnight and then back again at five. I've got the cash register receipts to prove it and if you want to waste your time, you can call my customers and ask who checked them in and out. I've got a cot in the back and a space heater that blows ninety-degree heat."

"I don't care about the last two weeks," said Wally. "Just the last thirty-six hours. Let's talk for a while and I'll let you know if I need those receipts."

"Fine by me," said Lopes. "Can we go in back near the heater?"

"Sure," said Wally.

Lopes turned, stepped around a rack of maps, took a key from his pocket and opened a door. Wally and Romar followed him as he stepped into the back room.

Wally looked around as Lopes fiddled with the space heater. The room was long and narrow, just big enough for the cot and stacks of boxed candy, chips and snacks. A pile of magazines sat in the corner and a small television balanced on a folding chair. The door to a metal locker was open and Wally saw two more pairs of coveralls hanging from a metal hanger.

"I don't live here, if that's what you're thinking," said Lopes. "I just stay here when it gets too late. I don't drive in the dark anymore."

"I hear that," said Wally. "Have you really been here for two weeks?"

"Close," said Lopes. "What is this, Friday? It'll be two weeks tomorrow. But, if Red and Skinny and their cousins keep working, I'll be home tomorrow night. Listen, I gotta stay on 'em to keep working. I guess I do need to ask you what this is about."

"Have you heard about the murders of Phillip Costa and a police officer?"

"Yeah," said Lopes. "But what's that got to do with me? I'm not stupid enough to do that."

Wally took the glove off his other hand, moved in front of the space heater. "Why is the FBI interested in you?"

"They're not," said Lopes. He took off his hat, tossed it onto the cot. His thin hair stood up straight, lifted by static electricity.

"If you start lying to me, we're going to have to take you in, Mr. Lopes. I know the FBI is interested in you."

"They was, but not anymore," said Lopes. He moved to his right, put a hand on the locker to get his balance. "Did you see on the news about the guys they picked up today?"

Wally and Romar both said, "Yeah."

"Guilt by association. I used to know some of 'em a long, long time ago. But I did a stretch in Stateville. I got out, started this garage, stopped hanging around the wrong people. Now, I've been running my business here for forty-two years."

"Why don't you sell gas?" asked Romar.

"No money in it. The guys that sell gas make more money working on a guy's brakes. And it contaminates the property. Have you seen what's going on in this neighborhood? The homes? The Jewel? All the stuff east of here? I might look like just another grease monkey to you guys, but really I'm a real estate developer. Donald Trump's got nothing on me."

"Except empty retail spaces," said Romar.

Lopes grinned. Wally looked at Romar, wondered why he could never filter his questions. "Why were you in Stateville?"

Lopes's grin disappeared. "Second-degree murder. Security guard pulled his gun. It was him or me. You can check the record."

"I will. Did you work for the Outfit?"

"Now, you're getting into that FBI shit. I'm Native American. You probably thought me and my nephews were all Mexicans. We're not. We're from the Peoria tribe. If you even watch the pay television channels, you know the Outfit's not hiring Indians."

"You said guilt by association," said Wally.

"I went to grade school with some of them. Then, I knew some from the streets. Things were different in those days. I knew everybody."

"We're looking for a man who may have been involved with those murders and a related double homicide. We got your name along with a Vitus Gorski and Francis Costa. Do you know them?"

Lopes whistled. He ran a hand through his thin gray hair, scratched at the back of his scalp. "Those are two names from the past. Costa was my bookie and Gorski was muscle. That's no secret. You can read about it in the papers. But I haven't seen them in probably twenty years."

Romar moved next to Wally, said, "You said you've owned this business for forty-two years and stopped hanging around the wrong people when you started it. But, you just said you haven't seen them in twenty years."

"Figure of speech," said Lopes. "I just mean I haven't seen 'em in a long time. I don't have anything to do with them."

"When did you?" asked Wally.

"When I bet. In those days, everybody bet through a bookie. You didn't have computers."

"Mr. Lopes," said Wally. "Think about it, hard. If I find out you're involved with these guys, I'll make sure the FBI and all other interested parties know about it. If you quit with the vague answers, it might help."

"I can't help you with your murders, guys, 'cause I don't have anything to do with 'em. Now, you're asking me about people I ain't seen in a long time and I can't help you." He held out his hands. "You got to take me in, you've got to take me in, but I still won't be able to help you."

"There are plenty of prints at the scene," said Wally. "If any are yours, we'll have a match this afternoon."

"Only prints I've left are on my cash register and a '97 Honda Accord," said Lopes.

Wally saw the dead end. He eyeballed it, took another route. "What can you tell us about Gorski and Costa? Are they big guys?"

"You mean like hotshots or tall? 'Cause if you mean like hotshots, all I know is what I read in the paper, so yeah, Costa's a hotshot." Lopes looked at Romar, then Wally. "Both were taller than any of us. Gorski was always really tall and really big. Costa was about the same height, but not as big."

"What do you mean when you say, 'was always really tall'?" asked Romar.

Lopes gave a silent chuckle. "You'll find out. You shrink. Guy might've been a giant but when he gets to be our age, he's hunched over and his bones shrink. Guess I should've drank more fucking milk."

Wally said, "So, when you knew 'em, did Costa do his own work or did he leave it all to Gorski?"

"Work?" asked Lopes. "You mean working somebody over? Violence?"

"Or kill someone," said Wally.

"That's a stupid question," said Lopes. He caught himself. "Sorry, Detective. Costa was a boxer. He had problems, he'd fix 'em himself. He had this temper. Man, oh, man. One time, this Mick cop was giving him grief, on account of his name, Francis. They used to say it like a girl, with this high voice. Fraaanciiis. Well, he beat this cop and his partner near dead with his fists. The Flying Squad showed up and busted him up so bad he couldn't get outta bed for months. Then that crippled cop—Jack something or other?—choked him out in the holding cell. Lucky he didn't die."

"What about Gorski?"

Lopes shook his head. "Man, that guy's got no feelings. We used to work on cars together. He had his own garage. I worked on a lug nut for hours? He'd twist it off like taking the lid off a jar of peanut butter."

"Do you think, even at his age, he could've committed these murders?" asked Wally.

"Listen," said Lopes. "Most guys, I wouldn't speculate about what they did or would do. But this guy? He's sick. Me and him went to this small town in Kentucky one time back in the day. Gorski said it was the only time he'd ever left Illinois. Can you imagine that? Anyway, we were picking up some special car parts. We went for breakfast at this diner and some kid next to us started screaming, kind of throwin' a tantrum. The kid's mom couldn't get him to shut up and even though it was annoyin', I didn't really care, 'cause I sure wasn't having any conversation with Gorski. But all of a sudden, this kid—he's probably ten or eleven—starts spitting up blood. I mean everywhere. And Gorski? He just hands me the bill and says, 'You pay,' like there was nothing going on. A bunch of people ran over and it was pure fucking chaos and he just stood up, waited for me to leave my money, then walked out."

Wally and Romar stared, waited.

"See, this sick bastard carried around a bag of shredded glass in his pocket. Someone pissed him off, he just sprinkled a little in their drink. I only drank bottled beer when I was around him."

"What happened to the kid?" asked Romar.

"I don't know," said Lopes. "We didn't stick around to find out."

"You're a regular sweetheart," said Wally. He watched as Romar walked out the door, headed toward the service bays. "The related murders involved a young boy. I gather you think Gorski could've done it. How about Costa?"

Lopes nodded. "Like I said, I don't like to speculate on anybody, but those guys are different. Wouldn't surprise me if either one did it."

Wally closed his notebook. "I'll get back to you on those receipts." He left the back room, straight out the door to the lot, followed by Lopes. The cold cut through his jacket and he put his gloves back on as Lopes extended a hand.

"Glad I could help," said Lopes, hand stranded midair.

Wally ignored it. "You walked out on that kid."

Lopes's face went blank. His eyelids fell to half-mast. "You don't get it, Detective. You might want to sit this one out, let the FBI do its job. Those guys ain't like regular people. You know what Gorski said to me when we got in the car?"

Wally shook his head.

"He said, 'You shouldn't have tipped her.' Huh? 'You shouldn't have tipped her. My coffee was cold.' That's what you're dealing with, Detective. And God help you if those guys think you're looking for 'em. 'Cause if they find out, you won't have to look hard. They'll come looking for you."

5:03 P.M.

Wally walked north on State Street, took a left on Division. Romar followed, hands jammed in his pockets. They cut across the street, walked under a green awning and opened the door to Butch McGuire's. The doorman nodded as he tucked his white shirt back into his pants.

Wally sat down at the bar, pulled a bar stool across the wood floor, motioned for Romar to sit. Light still shone through the front window; traffic slithered across the icy street. A group of tourists ogled bar signs, split choices between Mother's and The Lodge. A squad car parked on the north side of the street and Wally laughed as two uniformed cops ran through the cold into Five Faces, eyes trained on the gyro joint.

"Man, you gonna tell me why you picked this spot for your watering hole?" asked Romar. "I know you used to work here, but now?"

Someone pushed a bill into the jukebox; Bob Seger filled the room. Wally propped his elbows on the bar. "I'm taking a liking to this gal, Stacy," he said. "She's industrious."

"She's twenty-nine," said Romar. "She's still working at a bar."

"She had it rough," said Wally. "She's in night school at DePaul now. I admire that."

One cue, the bartender set down the mugs she'd washed, dried her hands on a dish towel. "Hi!" she said. Heads jerked to Wally's left; her voice lifted eyes like the crack of a bat. Wally thought about how he'd describe her: high cheek bones, a dark complexion, dark hair and eyes. Probably five foot eight, a buck ten. Her waist was the size of one of his thighs. She smiled and he smiled back.

"How ya doing, Stacy?" asked Wally.

"I'm great, Detective."

"Not a lot of people out for a Friday night," said Wally.

"This is the after-work crowd," replied Stacy. "It'll be jammed, later. What can I get you?"

"Two Bud Lights," said Romar.

Wally interrupted. "Nah. Give me a decaf coffee and a burger, well done with jalapeños and grilled onions."

Stacy nodded, walked away; eyes followed her to the point Wally thought he could take every mug from the bar and no one would notice.

"I thought we were stopping for a beer," said Romar. "And you're not getting a beer?"

"I'm heading back to HQ after this," said Wally. "I'm gonna check on those prints, read up on Costa and Gorski, get the lay of the land. I'd be terrible company tonight anyway."

"Did you tell Theresa that? I seem to remember you bowling or playing cards most Friday nights."

Wally murmured, "Haven't called her, yet. I will."

"Well, I gotta head home soon," said Romar. "There's a party in our building tonight and I gotta work it."

"How's Lou Lou?" asked Wally. He watched as Romar cracked his knuckles, one by one, put his chin in his hands.

"She's good," said Romar. "I'm having a hard time getting her back into her walker, though. She drives her electric wheelchair at school, now, and she's getting too tall for the walker. The other night, the wheels caught in the carpet and she fell."

"Did she get hurt?"

"Nah. She got lucky. She fell on the ottoman. But, man, that place is small for the two of us and with that shitty carpet, she just don't like walking in her walker. I tell her she needs to so she can keep her legs in shape, but she ain't listening."

"How old is she, again?" asked Wally.

"Thirteen."

"I hear that's the age they all stop listening," said Wally. "She's a great kid. Consider yourself lucky."

"Not lucky enough to afford a decent place," said Romar. He rubbed his eyes. "But, I'll tell you what, we ever move, anyway, they're gonna keep my security deposit and come after me for all the scrapes on the wall from her chair."

Wally looked at Romar, shrugged. "No big deal," he said. "I'll help you with the drywall. I finished off my basement, I can repair a few walls for you."

Stacy stopped in front of them, set down their drinks. "Decaf coffee and a Bud Light," she said. She took two paper napkins from her green apron, lifted the drinks and slipped the napkins underneath.

"So, how's school going?" asked Wally as he took a sip from his cup.

Stacy set an elbow on the bar, brushed her hair off her forehead. "You know, Detective, you always ask about me." She looked at Romar. "And you never ask about anything. So it's my turn." She returned her gaze to Wally. "You told me you're from a small town in Southern Illinois. How'd you become a Chicago cop?"

"It's a long story . . ." said Wally. He bit off a smile when she told him she didn't get off 'til midnight and slipped Romar a sideways glance that had him diving into his beer.

"Okay," said Wally. He took a quick slug from his coffee, wiped his mouth with the paper napkin. "Growing up, it was me, my younger brother and two sisters. My sisters still live there. My dad was a farmer. I was a pretty decent football player and got a scholarship to U of I. I was a fullback. A guy on our team knew Butch McGuire, so after I graduated, I came here that summer to work the door while I interviewed for a job. My girlfriend went back to our hometown and I came here for what I thought was gonna be one summer and has turned out to be the rest of my life. One of the other guys working the door came from a family of cops and after I struck out interviewing a few times, I decided to follow him in. And that's how I ended up right back here."

Stacy put both elbows on the bar, leaned in like she was prying, grinned. "And, what happened to the girlfriend?"

Wally's cheeks lifted but the smile fell off his face. His voice got quiet. "She died."

Stacy shot up. "I'm sorry."

Wally felt Romar's eyes on him, avoided him. "Car accident," he said, staring at Stacy. "Long time ago."

Stacy stood up straight, ran her hands across her apron, looked like she wanted to run. "So, your sisters still live there."

"Yep," said Wally.

Stacy looked relieved. "What about your brother? Did he stay or follow you here?"

"Neither," said Wally. He offered a smile to soften the blow. "He died, too. Same accident."

Stacy gasped, covered her mouth. "I am so sorry. I—"

"You didn't know," said Wally.

"How'd it happen?" asked Romar.

Wally turned, saw Romar was diverting the attention—he'd heard the story before. "My brother's car got sideswiped. There was red paint on the side of the car. They hit a tree. Both killed instantly."

"Anyone arrested?" asked Romar.

"Nope. Unsolved. Probably some trucker who passed 'em and didn't even know he hit 'em."

Stacy jumped when one of the guys from the kitchen tapped her on the shoulder, handed her a plate. "Here's your burger," she said, setting the plate in front of Wally. She looked like she was glad to get lost in the mundane. "Ketchup, mustard, a gag for my mouth?"

Wally laughed. "Don't worry about it." He surveyed his plate, looked back up at her. "You know, the funny thing is, though, I never knew what they were doing. They didn't like each other too much. Maybe he was just giving her a ride somewhere or maybe they were on their way to pay me a surprise visit. I'll never know." He plucked lettuce off his burger, used his fork to push the jalapeños to the center of the meat. "My brother's girlfriend lost it. She just up and left town. After the funeral, I did, too. I didn't leave 'cause I couldn't bear to be there. I left because I knew if I stayed, I'd end up working the farm with my dad. So I came to Chicago. And you know what? A few years ago, he did, too. He and my mom live in a retirement home not too far from me. They're happy as larks. My sisters still live back home—one bought the farm with her husband and the other runs the local store. I always got a place to stay and can see anybody in town at my sister's store."

Someone from the end of the bar beckoned to Stacy and Wally ate his burger while she was gone. He watched as she took orders, served businessmen drinks, listened as a group of twenty-something girls offered IDs, ordered beers. She came back moments later.

She stopped in front of Wally, braced herself. "But, you're married. And happily. You act it."

Wally's cheeks went red. "I'm lucky. I met my wife when I was working the Puerto Rican Day Parade in Humboldt Park."

"You?" said Stacy, turning toward Romar.

"Bud Light," he said.

Stacy rolled her eyes, playfully. "Are you married?"

"Nah," said Romar. He fiddled with the empty bottle, pointed the mouth at her.

"Listen to the way he said, 'Gnaw', like he's chewing on some food," said Wally. "Romar here thinks he's tough 'cause he's an expert in martial arts. I tell him he'll be tough when he's an expert in marital arts!"

Stacy laughed as Wally made a funny face, slapped his knee. "Bud Light," she said, glancing at Romar. "For the karate cop."

Wally laughed, mock slapped the bar. "You're something, Romar. Why are you so nervous?"

"Huh?" asked Romar.

"Why are you so nervous? She's a pretty girl. So what? She's nice. You want to ask her out, just ask her out."

"I don't want to ask her out," said Romar. "I like to just sit back, evaluate the situation. I'm not nervous."

Wally looked at the bar in front of Romar. "Then how come you wadded up that napkin?"

Romar looked down, saw the wadded napkin in front of him. "Principal, you may think you're observant, but I've been doing that for years."

"I've never seen it before," said Wally. "It caught my attention because it's uncommon for you. It'd be like if I came in wearing a baseball hat—nothing wrong with it, but you'd notice 'cause I never wear baseball hats."

Romar scoffed. "What do I usually do with my hands?"

Wally sat up straight. "That's a loaded question, Detective. I don't want to know the answer to that."

"Cold, man," said Romar. Stacy came back with his beer and he gratefully took it from her.

"Do you want anything else?" asked Stacy, noticing Wally's empty plate. "Fries?"

Wally grinned. "Got any lamb fries?"

"No," said Stacy, knowing smile offered with light lipstick.

Wally turned to Romar. "Know what lamb fries are?"

"Nope."

"They're delicious," said Wally. "Deep fried, seasoned just right . . ."

Romar, annoyed: "You still didn't tell me what they are . . ."

"After they snip the sheep," said Wally. "They sing soprano."

Romar sighed, tilted his bottle and feigned a look inside. "Man, Principal. With you, every day is a learning experience."

Stacy leaned forward. "Why do they call you Principal?"

"I teach a class in homicide investigation in the summer."

Romar snorted, loud. "Tell me you did not just say that."

"What? It's true."

"I know it's true," said Romar. He pushed his beer to the side, leaned around Wally, looked over at Stacy. "Stacy, you've heard of 'old school'? You know, doing it the old way, like a throwback?"

Stacy nodded. "Yeah."

"Well, if there's old school, this guy's the principal."

Wally reared back. "What? You've got to be kidding me!"

"No, man. You're like Pete Rose and that detective from *Dragnet* all throwed into one."

"You've only got one chance to do it right the first time," murmured Wally. "Nothing wrong with that."

"No, nothing wrong with that," said Romar. "Like when the Bears' linemen wear short sleeves in a cold game, I can dig it. But, I just don't need to do it, myself."

Wally took a deep breath, exhaled. "Check, please."

"Oh, c'mon, man," said Romar. "I'm just clownin' you."

Wally took the check from Stacy. "I know. I've gotta get going. Things to do at the office and I want to get home at a decent hour."

Wally set bills on the bar, left a big tip. "Bye."

Stacy smiled. "Bye. See you soon, and be careful."

Wally and Romar stepped out into the cold, walked south toward Wally's car.

"I'll jump in a cab," said Romar, breath showing in the early night air.

"I'll drop you," said Wally. "I'll hop on Lake Shore. No big deal."

They climbed into Wally's car, moments later, cranked the heat. Wally flipped it to defrost, waited for the windshield to clear, then drove east and hopped on Lake Shore Drive.

"I never knew that last part about your brother and girlfriend," said Romar. "You didn't know what they were doing together. That bother you?"

"No," said Wally. "It ate at me for a while, but there are some things in life we'll never know. That's one of 'em."

"How come you never told me?" asked Romar. "And why did you tell that girl?"

Wally looked over his shoulder, signaled and moved into the center lane. He saw the lights from the Ferris wheel coming from Navy Pier, navigated the bend near Chicago Avenue. "You know," he said, irritated. "Your questioning veers off in some weird routes."

"Man."

"No, I'm serious. Like why did you ask Lopes why he doesn't sell gas? What could that possibly have to do with our case?"

Romar looked out the window, toward the city. "Man, if something doesn't seem right, I ask about it. It don't fit, how do I know what it's about? Ain't that what you've been teaching me? 'Never jump to conclusions. Keep an open mind.'"

Wally drove, quiet, finally spoke up. "She's just a nice girl. I'm making a friend. You ought to ask her out sometime. She gave you that look, you know."

"What look?"

"That 'I like your friend but he's married, so you'll have to do,' look," said Wally. He chuckled at his own joke, shoulders bobbing in the dark interior.

"You sure know how to butcher a good joke," said Romar.

"Well, look who's Mr. Sensitive now," said Wally. He exited, slipped south and turned back east. "We're in front of your place. Get out."

Romar opened the car door, started to get out. He turned back to Wally as cold air filled the car. "Work out in the morning?"

"Yeah," said Wally. "Five-thirty."

"It's Saturday, man."

"Hey, I may have loosened up a little, but we've got a ton of work to do. Four people are dead and the perp's still out there. If we lay in bed, that ain't helping anybody."

Romar slid out, started to close the car door. "Five-thirty," he said. "See you in the morning, Principal."

6:30 P.M.

Wally pulled into the Area Five parking lot, put on his gloves, grabbed his notebook and got out of the car. He started to trudge across the parking lot, saw someone approach. He couldn't make out the face, but the stocky figure, the shuffle were unmistakable.

"How goes it, Roscoe?"

Roscoe pulled a stocking cap over his ears, rolled up the sides. "Middle-aged bag boy sat for a sketch artist. The killer looks a lot like my Uncle Bernie."

"Anything else?"

Roscoe sniffled, loud. "You heard about Costa's car?"

"Yeah, nice work," said Wally.

"It ties the murders together," said Roscoe. "What kind of psycho wipes out a family like that?"

Wally started. "Family?"

"Shit, yeah. The dad just died. Looks like whoever this guy is, he's got five bodies already."

"Jeez," muttered Wally. "Jeez." He turned toward the building, took an anxious step.

"Hey," said Roscoe. He tapped Wally's shoulder. "This may not sound right, Wally, but we're heading to the High Roller for some beers. Third Watch is all over this thing. Why don't you join us? You and I ain't tipped a pint in a while."

Wally gave him a polite, "No." When he'd married Theresa, he'd realized he could either go out for drinks after work or go home to the love of his life, and he'd made the simple choice. He didn't begrudge the cops who took the edge off with their buddies and after softball, he'd still stop for an occasional beer, but tonight the choice was easy. He had work to do. And Theresa was waiting at home.

6:54 P.M.

Martin sat in his office, hunched over his desk. His right hand covered his mouth. The knot in his tie was still tight, seemed to cut off his breath. He took short, quick breaths, tried to erase nagging thoughts.

He read the General Progress Reports, made mental notes: Time of death—midafternoon, a pure guess. Officer Rodriguez was on First Watch, off at 5 p.m. Phillip Costa had gone home for lunch, missed his afternoon appointments and hadn't answered calls. His phone showed the first voice message of the day was received at 1:27 p.m., at his office, the first of many calls.

A canvass of the neighborhood had turned up crime scene witnesses—the police car had been there since midafternoon—two housewives dropping kids at the bus stop had seen the car.

Bloodstains across the carpet—*she'd* been dragged downstairs. *She'd* been tortured. But why? The killer tortured Costa, too. What did he think they knew?

Martin ran both hands over his face, rubbed his temples. His eyes felt like they'd been raked. His bones felt dry, rigid. He flipped back to the beginning of the report, started to read it, again.

One question hung like a piñata, waiting for someone to swing at it, destroy his career: Why had she been there?

The phone jarred Martin from the report. "Lowell."

The voice: familiar. "Special Agent Lowell. This is Detective Greer. We've got a match on prints from both murder scenes." A pause, Martin blank-stared air. "Looks like our guy is Vitus Gorski."

Martin squeezed the phone in a fist, hung up without responding.

7:02 P.M.

Wally surveyed: two Third Watch detectives, four men from the Chicago Police Department's Fugitive Apprehension Unit. Less than forty-five minutes after he'd been told the prints matched those of Vitus Gorski, he stood just inside the front door of Gorski's bungalow, a stone's throw from the Eisenhower in Oak Park.

Wind whistled through the splintered door frame. Cold air stung Wally's eyes. He moved to his left as the last man entered the bungalow. He reached for the light switch, snorted when the lights failed to come on. He pointed his flashlight toward the noise from the ceiling fan in the front room—broken lightbulbs hung from the sockets.

The light from a flashlight crossed Wally's face. "Clear," said a voice in the distance. Three separate voices repeated it.

Empty. Not a surprise. Wally shined a light on the two plastic-bagged newspapers in his hand: Thursday and Friday's *Tribune*. He made a mental note to ask Martin Lowell if and when the FBI had lost Gorski; guessed it was Wednesday.

Wally stepped through the house, heard one of the Third Watch dicks order portable lights over his cell phone. Wally flashlight-searched for the bathroom, found it and opened the medicine cabinet. He swept it with the light—razor blades, cologne and Q-Tips on the upper shelves, bottom shelf empty. "He knew he wasn't coming back," said Wally.

"What?" asked a cop as he walked by.

"Nothing," said Wally. Every guy over fifty takes pills. Gorski must've taken his with him. He's not coming back.

"Well, check this out, Principal," said one of the Third Watch detectives.

Wally stepped out of the bathroom, followed the detective through the kitchen, into the garage. The detective stepped to the side, aimed his flashlight at the floor. Two plastic bowls sat side-by-side, one empty, the other a water bowl turned to ice. "The guy had a dog," said the detective.

The smell in the garage confirmed it. Wally nodded. "And if our guy had a dog, and no one has reported a dog anywhere he's been seen and it's not here . . ."

"Then where is it?" asked the detective.

Wally looked around the garage, saw tools on the counters, a work bench against one wall. Rakes and shovels hung from hooks fastened to a track on the wall and two large buckets sat next to the hot water heater.

Wally walked back toward the door, stopped and hit the button to open the garage door. The motor droned as the door pulled free from the icy cement and opened. Sunlight filled the garage and Wally noticed a puddle of oil pooled near a black canvas that had been draped over something. "Snow blower," he thought as he strode toward the canvas. He stepped over the oil and when he lifted the canvas, he leaped back. "Shit!"

Cold air blew through the garage. The detective with Wally covered his nose with the crook of an arm. Wally flipped the corner of the canvas, pulled it up and away. A young Caucasian male, mid-thirties, thick black hair cropped close to his head, sat, legs extended. He wore a bib of blood. The source was obviously the hole in his throat. Wally took a gloved hand, reached toward the body, opened the leather jacket and extracted the man's wallet. He stepped away from the body, positioned himself under the garage light and opened the wallet. A driver's license was visible and he carefully lifted it by the edges.

"Charles Dragone, Chicago. He'd have been thirty-seven next week," said Wally.

"Jesus," said another cop as he stepped into the garage.

Wally ignored the cop, looked back at the body. He stared at the floor, mind working. There was only that small pool of blood, but if the body had been drug across the floor of the garage, even with the dirt and all, there ought to have been a trail of blood. Or, if the guy had been shot right there, a hell of a lot bigger pool . . .

Wally's mind jarred to a halt. He stared at the small pool of blood, let his line of vision move outward. He shook his head, echoed the cop's recent muttering. "Jesus."

"You've got to be fucking kidding me," said the detective. "Are those dog tracks in that blood?"

7:45 P.M.

Romar stood near the door in the party room, surveyed the crowd. The room was filled with tenants—old, young, black, white, Section 8 and young nurses from Northwestern Hospital. He saw two Russian hookers he'd met at the pool the previous summer. The drug dealer from the seventh floor caught his gaze, turned and walked out.

The building manager, mid-forties, chubby with pale skin, dark hair and a maroon jacket that matched her lipstick walked over with one of the maintenance men, said "Hi," then beelined toward a couple of new tenants. The maintenance man told him to try the hot beef sandwiches, pointed at a table, then sauntered back for another helping.

Romar saw his niece wheel over to her friends, Marvis and Chantel. She stopped in front of the siblings, flashed that huge smile. Her head lolled slightly to the left, big eyes wide as night. She talked to her friends and Romar could see the strain of her labored speech, watched as her friends said, "Huh?" and she repeated herself, hiding frustration. Her left arm was curled toward her chest but she laughed, loud, and her friends followed suit. Romar's nostrils flared as he smiled wide.

The maintenance man came back, handed him a hot beef sandwich on a paper plate. "Didn't think you'd want a beer," said the man.

"Want and will are two different things," said Romar. He took half of the sandwich in one bite.

"Man, your niece. She's like one of the happiest people I've ever seen," said the man. "She's always smiling."

Romar nodded, thought, Bullshit. Her grandmother, dead from diabetes, mother killed by crack. Put in special ed classes when her mind was fine. Raised by her uncle and at thirteen starting to really grasp the challenges ahead. Happy? Not necessarily. Courageous? Determined? Tougher than anyone he'd ever known? Hell yeah.

Three teens, African American, winter coats with gloves wedged in pockets, stood in front of the keg in the corner—two stood in front while one filled a big cup. Romar tossed the plate in a plastic trash can, walked over to the boys.

"You boys are gonna have to leave," said Romar. He saw the boy with the cup turn his back to him, chug the beer and toss the cup behind the keg. "This party is for residents only."

"We here with our boy Phonso," said one.

The kid that had chugged the beer said, "Lesgo." The other two followed him out the door. Romar watched 'til they got on the elevator.

"They was from our school."

Romar turned. It was Marvis. "They ever hassle you, you let me know," said Romar.

"Thanks," said Marvis. He wore jeans and a Devin Hester Bears jersey. His head bobbed near Romar's shoulders. "Do you care if we take Lou Lou up to your place and play Wii golf?"

"No," said Romar. "That's cool. I've got to stay 'til the party's over. I'll see you in a while."

Marvis waved at his sister and Lou Lou and the three of them left, Lou Lou grinning at her uncle as she wheeled by.

The building manager walked over to Romar, radio in hand. "Those boys that just left? They're causing trouble down in the lobby. Rosey just called."

Romar shook his head. "On it." He left the room, stepped into the elevator and cringed as a twentysomething blond girl yakked on her cell phone. She looked frustrated when she lost the call, looked at Romar for sympathy. He half shut his eyes, said, "You are in an elevator . . ." He shook his head as the girl ignored him, thumbed numbers on her phone.

The elevator door opened and after he held the door for the girl to pass, Romar stepped out, walked by the rows of mail slots, stepped through the glass doors into the lobby. He walked to the security counter, leaned over it and raised his eyebrows at the doorman. "S'up Rosey?"

The doorman, a short black man with close-cropped hair and a goatee, said, "Some boys ducked into the elevator lobby. I can smell the smoke. I told 'em they had to leave and they said they'd be back for my ass. They's standing outside now." He pointed out the revolving door toward the curb. "Three guys right there."

Romar shook his head, walked through the revolving door and

stepped outside. He walked slowly toward the boys and when he got a few steps away, they turned.

"What the fuck you want?" said the one who'd chugged the beer.

"You boys threaten someone?"

The three eye-fucked him. Romar returned the stares, bent down, untied his sneakers.

"What you doing, you crazy fool?" said the tallest boy.

Romar looked up. "Don't want to get any blood on my Jordans." He stood up—no coat, barefoot. The three looked at one another, back at him.

"Tyrone. That's Lou Lou's uncle" said a teen, sitting on a wall near the parking garage. "He a cop."

"So," said the tall boy.

The kid continued. "He's like MMA or something."

The tall kid shook his head like, I'm bad, too. The other two tugged at the sleeves of his jacket, whispered something.

"No, bro," said the kid on the wall. "For real."

The tall kid shrugged. "I like Lou Lou, man. She cool."

"Yeah," said the other two. "She cool."

Romar watched as the boys sauntered west, toward McClurg Court. They turned north, near the bank, so he picked up his shoes, walked over and sat down next to the kid on the wall.

"S'up?" said the kid.

"Not much," said Romar. "S'up with you?"

8:30 P.M.

Wally and Theresa sat in matching brown leather recliners. Wally's laptop lay on his stomach; Theresa had a pile of papers in her lap. Theresa held a page, face high.

"Oh, my God, Wally. You've got to read this when I'm done. It's a story one of the literacy classes wrote."

Wally looked over his shoulder. "Wrote?"

"A volunteer guides them. They created this character, Jacob

Eichelberger. He's hysterical. They discuss the situation, then outline the stories and then the volunteer transcribes as they agree on sentences. This story is wonderful!"

"Sounds good," said Wally. His eyes drifted back to his laptop.

Theresa set the page on the pile in her lap. She looked over at Wally. "I called Jesus today."

"Oh, boy," said Wally. "What did he have to say?"

Theresa sat up, preened. "It went pretty well. I coaxed him into admitting that it's getting really hard on him. The other day, when he came home from work, Maria wasn't there. He couldn't find her anywhere, but then got a call from one of the neighbors that she was at their house. They'd come home from work and she was just sitting there. Their daughter had been building a snowman in the front yard when Maria just walked up and started helping. She wasn't even wearing a coat."

"You didn't say anything, yet, did you?"

"No," said Theresa. "Well, I kind of broached the topic. I asked him if he'd thought about getting some help and he went on and on about how he was going to work another shift so he could afford to have someone stay with her all the time when he's working."

"Working?" sighed Wally. "How many jobs has he had since we've known him? You know he's going to ask you for more money before he lets you move your sister here."

"I don't know," said Theresa. She gazed thoughtfully at Wally. "It sounded like it's getting to be too much for him. He said she's fine most of the time but she's having these episodes more and more. One day she looked at the car keys and asked him what they were. She didn't ask what they were for, but what they were. She didn't recognize car keys."

Wally watched as Theresa's eyes began to well up. She closed her eyes, rubbed her eyelids with her thumb and forefinger. "It was a first step," she said. "I'll call him again this weekend and offer to come visit. Maybe you can come with me and talk some sense into him."

Wally peered over at her. "Sure. Let's talk this weekend and get our ducks in a row. If you're serious about moving her here and it's getting tough on Jesus, then maybe it'll go okay."

Theresa sniffled, smiled at Wally. "Thanks," she said. She stood up, started toward the kitchen. "Do you want some yogurt, Wally?"

"No, thanks," he said. He picked up his laptop, opened it and continued reading.

9:00 P.M.

Roscoe—two hours deep in highballs. The High Roller: Used to be *the spot*. Now, a great restaurant with a long bar for regulars and a sidecar for under-thirty–year-olds that stayed open late. Roscoe eyed two overdressed forty-year-old women at the bar, ran a finger over his thick eyebrows, then his dark mustache.

Fred Pence leaned through the crowd, announced, "Officer Hanratty here and I are going to chase some wool tonight."

Hanratty patted Pence's bald head; both men wore sport coats over collared shirts, winter coats draped over their free arms. "Please don't say that, Freddie. You date yourself."

"Who'd you think he dates?" cracked Roscoe. He looked down the bar: Pence and Hanratty. Delia Grant, looking skinny but good. Don Haskins and Jerry Grunwald—the oldest detective and the ugliest—quite a pair. Five of 'em plus himself. He turned back to the bar, leaned over and flagged down the bartender. "Six Jameson's—and make mine a double." He held up both thumbs and the four fingers of his right hand, which veered off in all directions, thanks to years of sixteen-inch softball.

"Oh, no," said Delia Grant. She stepped next to Roscoe, looped an arm over his shoulder. He felt her bony hips against his side, smelled the stuff in her hair.

"Just one," said Roscoe.

"You said that two rounds ago," said Don Haskins as he picked bar food out of his mustache.

The bartender set six shots on the bar and they each took one. Roscoe lifted his glass and the others followed suit. He quoted the line he'd seen in detective bureaus all over the country: "He who is not pursued, escapes." They drained the shots. Roscoe exhaled, loud, said, "Find 'em and grind 'em."

Delia Grant leaned against Roscoe, looked over at Don Haskins and said, "They ID'd this Vitus Gorski today for the murders. It'll be all over the news tonight. Think they'll just say he's wanted for questioning?"

Haskins stroked his 'stache. "No. They'll say he's a homicide suspect and could be considered armed and dangerous."

Hanratty leaned around Pence, said, "We're already looking for him. He's gotta have something to do with all this stuff that went down today." He set a hand on the bar, glanced over at Delia. "I was at Francis Costa's place this morning. Dickhead FBI guy left us all out in the backyard. I hadn't called him on his cell phone, we'd probably all still be back there stacking firewood."

"The Federal Bureau of Indigestion," murmured Jerry Grunwald.

"What did you say, Gruns?" asked Roscoe, leaning toward him.

Grunwald didn't turn toward Roscoe. He lifted his shot glass to his lips, sipped the tiny pool of whiskey that had been left in the bottom of the glass. "Nothing," he murmured. "Alcohol accentuates my natural pessimism."

"Pessimism's just realism's ugly sister," said Roscoe. "Ain't gonna be easy to find this guy."

Hanratty slid between Roscoe and Delia, glanced from them to Don Haskins. "So, what are you guys hearing on this?"

Roscoe curled a lip, spit air. "We're homicide dicks, kid. We're not looking to throw another governor in jail, just a murderer."

Hanratty flinched. "I'd like to know what they're saying. You know, what do they say? How things are all 'intertwined.' I'd like to know what they're saying—like what they have to do with the Outfit."

"Who's 'they'?" asked Roscoe. "'They're saying. They say.' Who's 'they'?"

Hanratty flushed, embarrassed. "You know. 'The word on the street.'"

Roscoe craned his neck, looked over his big shoulder. "No. I don't know. You keep saying 'they' like there's some group of guys that know everything. And now you're telling us there's a street where they all hang out and exchange words. Enlighten us, Officer. Make our jobs easier. If you can fill us in on who 'they' are and what street 'they' are hanging out on, we can probably catch this piece of shit Gorski."

Hanratty ignored the jabs, lifted a glass. "Amen to that, brother."

Roscoe eye-fucked him, waited 'til the guy looked embarrassed, then smiled and said, "I'm just busting your balls. Long day." He raised his glass. "Amen to that, brother."

Glasses clinked. A stuffed olive rolled down the bar and Gruns snatched it and ate it. The two women at the end of the bar stood up, glanced around the room as they put on their winter coats. Someone yelled, "Turn on the Blackhawks game."

Fred Pence set his empty glass and two twenties on the bar, clapped Hanratty on the shoulder and said, "Let's get out of here."

Hanratty said, "Okay," and held a fist toward Roscoe.

Roscoe looked at the fist, casually bumped it and watched as Hanratty followed Pence on a serpentine route through the crowd and out the door.

Delia pulled up a stool next to Roscoe. Don Haskins threw a twenty-dollar bill on the bar, headed to the bathroom. Gruns started to snore.

"Little edgy tonight?" asked Delia. She propped both elbows on the bar, folded her hands, waited for the answer.

Roscoe took a big gulp of beer, wiped his mouth with his hand. "I just hate fucking winter."

10:00 P.M.

Romar helped Lou Lou take off her shoes, slipped her under the covers, fully clothed, like she liked to sleep. He tucked her in, then plugged her wheelchair into the battery charger. He sat on the edge of her bed, leaned over and kissed her forehead.

"You know how much I love you, Lou Lou?"

Lou Lou struggled to position her head on the pillow, looked up and smiled. "Yes. I love you, too, Uncle Romar."

"Did you have fun tonight?" asked Romar.

"Yep," said Lou Lou. Her eyes grew wide. "Were you afraid of them boys you made leave?"

Romar smiled. His voice was soft. "No. They were just partying and acting tough."

"They're not so bad," said Lou Lou. "I like Dewan. He was the one in the white shirt. He's nice to me."

The big kid. "Cool," said Romar. "Hey, I gotta get up early. I'm meeting Wally for a workout."

"I'm working out tomorrow, too," said Lou Lou. "Ginny's coming here in the afternoon."

. Romar nodded. Her occupational therapist. Cool. "Mrs. Webber's gonna come say hi in the morning, stay a while."

"I don't need any help. If you just leave my meds out, I'll be fine."

"She's gonna fix you lunch." Romar stood up, started to leave the room. "I'll call you when I'm coming home. Answer the phone."

"Want me to ask Ginny to stay for dinner?" asked Lou Lou.

Romar hovered near the light switch. "Why you asking that?"

Lou Lou grinned. "You like her. I can tell. You get really quiet around her."

Romar sighed. "Man, both you and Wally."

Lou Lou giggled. "I like Wally."

"Me, too."

"Should I ask her, then?"

"Nah," said Romar. "Another time." He turned out the light, closed the door and stepped out into the front room.

There probably wouldn't be another time, thought Romar as he walked over to the couch, took the cushions off it and pulled out the hide-a-bed. He had enough responsibility as it was and, finally, there was some semblance of order in his life. Finally, he had a schedule. Nah, man, a woman in his life meant changing his schedule and more time away from Lou Lou and that just wasn't gonna happen.

He stripped down to his boxers, looked past his reflection, out the window toward Lake Michigan. He stood there for a moment, then turned around, leaned over and pulled back the covers, sat on the bed, reached over and turned off the light. He lay back, pulled the covers over him and stared up at the ceiling. He watched as the light from the window threw streaks on the ceiling. He closed his eyes, thought about Stacy and Ginny. He liked them. Both of them. But he didn't like thinking about them. Because they reminded him. He was staggeringly . . . unalterably . . . lonely.

10:15 P.M.

Wally sat in the recliner, laptop on his stomach, feet up. He glanced at the television, which Theresa had turned on to watch the weather forecast. When it had shown a five-day forecast of bitter cold and a more snow, she'd sighed and left the room.

The newscaster looked solemn and a photograph filled the screen. Wally bolted upright, cranked up the volume.

"Authorities aren't saying when Costa was taken into custody or whether it was of his own volition," said a reporter. He stood in front of the Dirksen Federal Building and despite a heavy coat, shivered. "They did say he was the fourteenth member of Chicago's Outfit in custody. Jim, Brenda, back to you."

Wally shook his head. "Jeez," he muttered. Francis Costa in custody and his buddy on the lam for the murders. What in the heck was it all about? There was something there and he had to find it. His head still shook from side to side as he lowered it, searched the internet.

"Aren't you coming to bed, Wally? It's nearly ten-thirty." Theresa stood in the hallway, terry cloth robe tied tight, red slippers on her feet.

Wally looked up. "Not yet," he said. "I've got to check some things."

"Can't you check in the morning?" asked Theresa. "You need your sleep."

"No," said Wally. "There's something nagging at me and I want to check it out."

"Wally," said Theresa.

He looked up, again, waited.

"You can't save everyone."

Wally's head dropped. He ran a finger over the keyboard. The screen lit up as a new document opened up. "But," said Wally as Theresa turned and walked down the hall, "I can try."

11:03 P.M.

Ling walked south on the west side of La Salle Street. It was freezing; her nose was cold despite the wool scarf she'd wrapped around her face. It felt like her body heat had deserted her in the fifteen minutes it had taken her to walk home from the Jewel store. Her arms ached and she switched the plastic bags of groceries from one hand to the other, shifting the weight of the heavy bag to give her right arm a rest.

She walked by a bar and rolled her eyes at the line of kids waiting in the cold. Music blared; bass pounded the walls, made her ears hurt. She scurried by the line, crossed Hubbard at the light.

It used to be so quiet! There had been no megabars in the area. No late-night music or screaming drunks. It had been peaceful, almost serene. River North had been beautiful loft buildings, some empty space and offbeat, interesting shops and businesses. But now, it was all bars and restaurants. Despite the furniture stores and an occasional adult book store, it had lost its character and color. And every morning the evidence was there when she walked west on Hubbard to the Merchandise Mart: broken beer bottles, cigarette butts, food wrappers and the contents from some kid's stomach left in a puddle on the sidewalk.

She stepped up to the rear entrance of her condominium building, took off a glove with her teeth and fished in her pocket for her keys. She found them, flashed the fob at the door and when the green light lit up, she pushed her glove in her coat pocket and reached for the door but her knuckles hit the side of the door and she dropped her keys. Ling barely caught the door and said, "Shit," as she set her grocery bags on the cement, reached for the keys.

"Let me."

Ling looked up, startled. A tall man bent over her. His face neared hers and he smiled as he picked up her keys, handed them to her. He grabbed the plastic bags and stood up and, as he did, the streetlight shone on his face and she saw that he was old. A gust of wind blew through his gray hair and he kicked a foot out, planted a boot against the door and said, "Go ahead."

"Thank you," said Ling. She entered the service hall and started to reach for her bags but the old man nearly ran into her, so she moved forward, walked past the dry cleaner's and when she reached the elevator lobby, said, "Thank you, very much." She reached for the groceries again, but the man smiled, nodded at the elevator button, so she returned his smile and hit the button. She looked at the man, again, saw that he held a bag of his own but when he saw her glance he said, "I'm okay."

Ling was quiet, by nature, but observant. Usually, she wouldn't have made small talk, even waiting for the elevator, but her curiosity got the best of her. "Your face is all red," she said. "Were you working outside?"

"No," said the man. His voice was deep, labored. "I'm visiting. It's such a big city that I started walking around and got kind of lost."

The elevator button light turned off and the elevator doors opened. The man gestured for Ling to go first, so she did. He followed her inside, and nodded when she hit the button for the thirteenth floor. "Me, too," he said.

"Oh," said Ling. "Who are you visiting?"

The man looped his fingers through a plastic bag, rested his hand on the handrail and mumbled something. Ling couldn't make out what he'd said, but it didn't matter. She was sizing him up. He was huge! Ling prided herself on her ability to see shapes and angles and this man was tall and thick, with broad shoulders but not a V frame. Rather, he was linear, with a long trunk, legs and arms. And there, cradling heavy plastic bags of groceries, were his hands—wide and thick with fingers like sausages. She was thinking about how she'd draw him when she realized the man had said something to her.

"Know many people on your floor?" asked the man as he stared at her.

"No," said Ling. She paused, studied his face. His eyebrows were gray and thick and were perched over dark eyes. His cheeks and nose showed broken blood vessels. He had a distinctive bone structure—a wide jaw, thick brow and low cheek bones. But he didn't remind her of anyone on her floor. Not that she knew any, anyway. "I guess that's sad. I've lived here seven years but most of the people on my floor are renters. They rent from investors. I'm an owner."

The man remained silent and his silence unnerved her. And what an odd question, thought Ling as she took off her other glove and stuffed it in her coat pocket next to its partner—asking if she knew anyone on her floor. She unzipped her coat, tried to stop herself, but her nerves got the better of her and she continued her awkward monologue. "That sounded awful, didn't it? All I meant was that most of the people on the floor are transient. They come and go."

The man nodded at her but it didn't put her at ease. He was simply acknowledging that, yes, people come and go. Ling closed her eyes, fought the jitters that had appeared in her stomach. She took a deep breath and gathered her thoughts. This was ridiculous! So, she was on the elevator with a big, creepy man. It was a high security building and the man knew someone on her floor and . . . But she'd let him in the back door with her fob. He didn't necessarily . . .

A loud ding! startled Ling and when the elevator stopped and the door opened, she let out a relieved, embarrassed laugh. She reached for her groceries, but the man said, "It's not a problem." He followed her out the door and when she walked east and rounded the corner south, he continued to follow.

Ling stopped in front of her door. "I can take it from here," she said.

"I'll hold them while you get the door," said the man. He glanced toward the door and as she fished the keys back out of her pocket, he said, "Besides, I never told you who I was visiting."

Ling unlocked the door, leaned against it to hold it open. She reached for the groceries and when the man handed them to her, she realized her heart had been beating hard and that made her smile. "So," she said. "Who are you visiting?"

The man's hand shot up, over her mouth, pushed her into the room. "You."

Saturday

5:32 A.M.

Gorski let go of the girl's ankle, stepped back into the hall and let the door close behind him. He walked to the elevator, pushed the button and waited.

A tone signaled the elevator's arrival and when the door opened he was glad to see the car was empty. He stepped inside, stared at the numbers on the panel. Hitting 1 meant the door would open to the lobby. They'd know about him soon enough, but no reason to announce himself. But what floor led directly to the parking garage?

"Fuck it," he muttered. He hit 1 and when the door opened moments later on the first floor, he retraced his steps from the night before, walked down the service hall and left through the back of the building. Outside, pitch dark: He walked a few steps west and slipped into the parking garage, spinning the girl's keys in his right hand.

Gorski lumbered up the parking ramp, hit the key fob periodically, watched for the car lights. His left knee throbbed by the time he got to the third floor and when he saw a car's lights flash, he winced. Fucking tiny foreign fucking car! He clicked the unlock button, opened the door and tried to slide into the front seat. He got his right leg in but the seat was too close to the steering wheel, so he had to lean across, start the car while lying on his side on the driver's seat. When the car started, he pushed the button to move the seat back, cursing under his breath as he gathered himself, slipped into the car and closed the door.

He cranked the heat and defrost, opened the glove compartment and pulled out a black case. He unzipped it, rifled through the CDs. Nothing good. Same shit as upstairs. Groups with weird names that weren't funny or anything—just plain fucking weird. He tossed them on the floorboard, turned on the radio and spun the dial until he found a sports talk show. He listened for about two seconds then turned off the radio.

It only took five minutes for the windows to clear, so he figured the foreign car wasn't so bad after all; it used to take twenty minutes to heat up the damn Tempest he'd owned back in the seventies. He looked over his shoulder, chuckled at the memory of that idiot yelling at his ex-wife as the Mazda had plowed right over him. He threw the car in reverse, backed out of the spot and followed the arrows toward the exit.

There were no overhead doors in the parking garage but as he neared the exit, he stared at the yellow and black gate arm. Wouldn't be so tough to ram it, but with his luck, someone would hear the noise, call the cops and end it all way too soon. He stared at the gate, let the car roll forward, slowly, and smiled when it made a goofy noise and the arm lifted. He glanced up as he moved past the gate and saw the parking fob attached to the sun visor.

"Thank you, honey," he said as he left the parking garage.

Gorski drove forward, slowly, toward the street. An alarm blared to alert any pedestrians on the sidewalk but no one appeared on either side of the exit. Just as he was about to make the turn onto the street, he saw a tall kid in a parka and a pair of long shorts standing next to the rear door of the building. The guy had his back to Gorski and when he stepped to his right, Gorski saw the idiot was holding a leash. A huge German shepherd took a leak in the makeshift piss plot—enough light from the garage to give Gorski a clear view of the stream.

"Jesus," said Gorski. He felt his blood start to boil. The kid must've realized the car that had just left the garage hadn't continued out onto the street so he looked up and Gorski saw his blank face and dull eyes—the look he shared with most of the idiots his age who were oblivious to the world around 'em. Gorski was surprised the kid wasn't wearing ear buds or cradling a cell phone and when the kid turned his back to him, stepped closer to the dog, Gorski touched the gas pedal and let the car slip forward, quietly.

The nose of the car was dead even with the kid and his dog when Gorski slammed the horn. The kid literally leaped into the air. The dog barked, snapped at cold air. The kid flipped the middle finger of his hand in the air and screamed as Gorski drove off.

Gorski watched the kid shake his hand in the air, middle finger still extended. "Fucking punk," said Gorski as he fiddled with the radio, again. "City's no place for a big dog."

5:43 A.M.

Wally and Romar sat, side-by-side, on the concrete floor of the workout room. Wally moved his knees up and down, caused his legs to move like a butterfly's wings. Romar took both hands, pushed them out front, leaned forward and patted the concrete. Both wore plain gray cotton shorts and gray T-shirts that read "Chicago Police."

"No," said Wally. "I gotta run first so I can stretch out. I run, then do twenty-five or thirty push-ups and then I'm ready to lift."

Romar sat up straight. "Works for you. But you only run for half an hour. When I run, I go an hour. So, when I lift with you, that means I gotta stop running thirty minutes in, then run another thirty minutes when we're done."

"Price you pay for a lifting partner like me," said Wally. He stood up, walked over to the treadmill, stepped on and tapped the display. The treadmill's belt started to move and so did Wally. He turned to Romar, who had jumped on the treadmill next to him. "You've increased your bench to 325 since we've been lifting. That's your all-time max, so I'd say this partnership is working for both of us."

"Most times, I'd take that as a compliment," said Romar. "But since I just spotted you when you put up 405, I know this is just your way of reminding me."

Wally answered, his breath already hard to come by: "You got that black belt, brother. I may have strength in my trunk but I'd trade it for a little of your athleticism. Cripes, I'm already huffing and puffing and you look like you're jogging at the beach."

"Inside, I am, baby. I am."

They both laughed. Wally leaned forward, increased the speed of the belt. He gulped breath, couldn't fight the urge to talk. "They ID'd the prints at the Patterson place. They matched prints found at the Costas'. It's Gorski. We checked his house—nothing. But, we'll find him."

"Don't make a lot of sense though, does it?" asked Romar.

"The thing that doesn't make any sense to me," said Wally, "is what that cop was doing at the Costa house and why Gorski tortured 'em." He looked over his shoulder at Romar. "Whaddaya say we run down to Area Two and ask around this morning?"

"Sounds good to me," said Romar, sounding like he was sitting with his feet up at his desk rather than damn near sprinting on his treadmill. "I've got to make a call first."

"About what?"

"Nothing yet. Just asking at this point."

Wally thought about asking more questions, figured it was time to end the conversation. Another minute or so and he wouldn't be able to answer anyway. Damn extra weight. In the old days, if he worked out like he was today, the weight would've fallen off. Now, though, it simply fell down—settled around his gut and butt.

Wally took a deep breath, raised his right hand toward Romar and flashed his index finger. One. One hour. Romar smiled, nodded back. It was just as well. Wally needed time to think. No headphones. No television. No chatter. Just good old-fashioned thinking.

5:58 A.M.

The car was quiet. He'd have to give it that. It might be a computerized piece of shit, but at least it was quiet.

Gorski drove down Post Place, took a right on Lower Wacker Drive. He pulled near some truck docks, let his lights hit the docks. Cardboard. Dirty blankets. Two small brown feet stuck out underneath. He turned, kept driving.

Fucking air freshener. The girl had an air freshener in the car and it reeked—something flowery and strong. Gorski slipped a CD into the player. Miley Cyrus? How old had the girl been, anyway? She'd looked like she was in her thirties, but with the Orientals you never knew.

Twenty minutes later, starting to feel luck-fucked. He slipped in front of another dock, saw two boots behind a Dumpster. He stopped the car, turned off the lights and walked up the steps. He nudged the boots and an old white broad showed him brown teeth. Shit. "Go back to sleep, honey," he said.

Another shoe popped out on the other side of the Dumpster and Gorski walked around to the other side, kicked the shoe. A man rolled over, yelled, "Hey!" He tore off his stocking hat. Long gray hair spilled over his cheeks. "This is my spot!"

Gorski grinned at the man, laughed. Unbelievable. Fucking bingo.

7:03 A.M.

Wally sat at his desk; sweat dotted the back of his white dress shirt. iClear was up on the computer screen; Wally searched for Gorski info. An early morning report: A Metra train conductor had identified Vitus Gorski as a passenger on Friday morning, said he carried a bag with "Lindbergh Hardware" printed on the side. The conductor had remembered the name because he was studying American history— Lucky Lindy and all. Gorski's face had made an impression, too—he'd occupied the bathroom during his ride, mouthed off to the conductor upon departure.

Wally took a call, hung up quickly and strode down the hall.

Office of the Commander of the Central Division, Barry Brooks: Brooks, suit and tie, stood behind his desk like a pit boss waiting for the last card player to take a seat.

A man and a woman sat in front of Brooks's desk. Both in their late sixties, early seventies. The woman frail, white haired. She couldn't hold Wally's gaze, dropped it as she looked at the man to her left. The man wore blue jeans and a flannel shirt; Wally saw his hunting jacket hung on Brooks's coatrack. The man's shoulders slumped like they were ready to fall out of their sockets.

"Detective Greer," said Brooks. "This is Mr. and Mrs. Winslow. Their daughter is Julie Patterson."

The man started to stand, offer Wally his hand. Wally stopped him mid-crouch, shook his hand, then took his elbow and helped him back into the chair. The man's hands were rough, age spotted, with soil under the nails. His hair was wispy and gray and his long eyebrows hung over brown eyes that seemed to bleed over the dark caverns beneath them. "Pleasedtomeetcha," muttered the man.

"The Winslows wanted to talk to you, Wally," said Brooks, offering up his first name as an icebreaker. "They've given full statements to Detective Ramirez but wanted to ask you a few questions. I told them you wouldn't mind."

"'Course not," said Wally. He searched for a chair but didn't find one and didn't think it would be right to sit casually on the corner of Brooks's desk. He was about to kneel down when Brooks pushed his own chair around the desk, toward Wally. Wally accepted the chair and sat down. He looked at the man, then his wife. "I'm really sorry about your daughter and grandson," he said.

"Thank you," said the man. He glanced at his wife, took her hand, looked back at Wally. "We heard you was the one that found her."

"It's my paper, but I didn't find her. I was second on the scene," said Wally. "You're from Stillwell, Kansas, right?" said Wally.

"Yes sir," said Mr. Winslow. "How did you know?"

"I spent the night reading, "said Wally. "I'll bet you spent the night driving."

The man's head nodded like a bobber in a still pond. "We did."

"I know you want to know everything you can about what happened," said Wally. "And in time, you will. I hate to ask you to be patient but I've got to. Area Five is the size of San Francisco. Nine-hundred and eighty-thousand people live in it. We have evidence and we will follow that evidence and make an arrest. But it's not going to come quickly and it's not going to come easily."

The woman's weak voice split the air. "You saw her. You saw what someone did to our daughter." Her eyes searched Wally's.

What could he tell them? Their daughter was spun around the room so the bloodstains would make it look like an accident? Their grandson was killed because he came home at the wrong time? The killer spent the night, then ran over their daughter's ex-husband in her driveway? It was some organized crime fiasco and her daughter was the victim of a psychopath and bad luck? Cripes, there was everything to say and nothing to say. Their grief would hang on 'em like a never-ending winter and there was nothing he could say to change that.

"Your daughter was murdered. There is nothing I can say that will make that go away. It's an awful tragedy and I can't say anything that is going to give you any solace. I've been there."

The elderly couple looked up at him, surprised at his admission.

"I lost my brother and girlfriend in an accident many years ago. It looked like they were forced off the road and we never did find out who did it or why they didn't even stop."

Mrs. Winslow trembled, started to weep. Mr. Winslow grabbed the sleeve of Wally's shirt.

"I'm going to promise you this," said Wally. "I will do everything I can to bring this killer to justice. I can't say or do anything to make this any easier on you, but I can try to make sure it never happens again."

"Thank you," said Mr. Winslow. He rocked forward but Wally put a hand on the man's arm, stood up.

"Again," said Wally. "I'm sorry for your loss. I just want you to know I'll work my tail off for you." He started for the door and then turned back to the couple. "One thing, though. Your daughter was wearing red slippers."

A confused pause, then: "We gave them to her last Christmas," said Mrs. Winslow.

"My wife wears red slippers," said Wally. He shook his head. "Sorry. I just thought you'd like to know."

7:25 A.M.

The car idled in front of the townhomes. The mayor used to live there; snow-shoveled sidewalks, black wrought-iron fences and brass door knockers. He sighed, kept his eyes trained north. He stretched, looked right and saw Soldier Field. A fucking spaceship. Everything had gone downhill since '85. Nothing ever the same.

An airport shuttle van moved by on his left, scraped the curb as it pulled up in front of one of the townhomes. He watched as the door to one of the townhomes opened. Asshole stepped out—a white robe and a pair of loafers. A figure blew by Asshole: skinny kid with a hoodie underneath a blue and red Bears coat. Asshole rubbed the kid's stocking hat, flipped open a wallet, peeled out some bills and handed them to the kid. The kid took the money, walked about fifteen feet to the black gate, opened it and moved toward the van. Asshole turned, shut the door before the kid reached the van.

Gorski shot forward, pulled alongside the van as the driver set a metal step on the ground, opened the door so the kid could climb in. Gorski rolled down the window, yelled, "Hey!"

The driver turned, pulled his hands high to protect his face. The kid spun, mid-step.

Gorski raised the pink cell phone, fired. The pic: The kid in his stocking hat, long red hair just like Asshole's. His face: shock, easily read as fear.

Cold air gushed in the open window as Gorski sped north, left the van in the slush. He laughed, loud.

Jesus, the kid looked like his old man.

7:40 A.M.

Martin sat outside Darren Greene's office, stood when the Special Agent in Charge strode by him, opened the door.

"Who authorized announcing that Costa is in custody?" asked Martin.

Greene turned. "It's not even 8 a.m. on a Saturday morning, Martin. I haven't stepped inside my office or had my first cup of coffee. Can you wait five minutes before you bust my balls?"

Greene stepped inside his office and Martin followed. "Darren, I've spent the last eight years of my life on this case! I expect to be consulted, at the very least, before something like this is announced."

Greene took off his scarf and black wool topcoat. He hung the coat on a coatrack, draped the scarf over the shoulders of the coat. "I okayed it. We don't need a surprise element. What we need is to get this situation under control." He picked up a ceramic coffee mug off his desk. "Do you know the police are floating a theory that Vitus Gorski killed Philip Costa, the cop *and* that family?"

Martin followed Greene out of the office, down the hall. "It's only a theory," said Martin. "No proof." He sped up, stepped alongside Greene. "I've read the reports. That family had nothing to do with us."

"Fingerprints at both scenes. Duct tape on the boy and Costa and the cop. I read, too, Martin."

They stepped into a small space off the hall. Two thermoses sat on a tray; someone had made coffee, already cleaned the pots. Greene put his cup under the plastic spout, pumped the thermos. "There is going to be a lot of scrutiny, Martin. Why did you pull the surveillance off Gorski?"

Martin straightened his tie, put two fingers on the bridge of his nose, tried to compose himself. "You know why!" he said, louder than he wished. "Francis Costa told us that if he went missing and Gorski saw surveillance, he'd flee. If we moved in on him early, all the others would be tipped and they'd flee! It would've been like throwing a paper cup over a group of ants. The ones that saw the shadow would just disappear."

"You could've arrested them all at the . . ." Greene recognized his error. "No, I get it. You did the best you could."

Greene turned his back toward Martin, sprinkled creamer into his coffee, stirred it with a plastic stick and started back down the hall. Martin wheeled, caught up with him.

"Nothing else on Costa will be released without consulting you, Martin," said Greene. "I talked to Denton and we agreed that if this

Gorski thing does have anything to do with Costa, once it became known Costa was already in custody, everything would calm down. We've only got until Monday and for Christ's sake, we need some peace. We've got plenty to do between now and then, as it stands."

"Gorski's not after Costa," said Martin. "He doesn't know what's going on. I can promise you that. If he had anything to do with those murders, there is some other situation we don't know about. It's got nothing to do with this case."

Greene stopped in front of his office door, put a finger on Martin's chest. "Don't fool yourself, Martin. It's all connected. Just hope they pick him up before anything else happens."

Martin thought about protesting, brushed it away. "If he stays in town, we'll get him. His picture's plastered everywhere by now. Our men, the Chicago Police, U.S. Marshals, Metra Police . . . We'll get him."

Greene's expression, read, Yeah, right. His head moved slowly back and forth, stopped when he took a sip of his coffee. "Finding one old man in this city . . ." He sighed. "On another front, I want you to call that woman from the state's attorney's office and apologize."

"What?" yelled Martin. He tugged at his tie, again.

"When you were on with the Man, Denton read me the riot act. Calling her a distraction and chastising her about how she dressed? C'mon. I put her card on your desk last night. Do it this morning. You want them protecting you on the witness stand."

Martin started to speak but Greene turned, stepped into his office and started to close the door. Martin turned to leave but Denton's voice stopped him. "And speaking of dressing . . . It's Saturday, Martin. For God's sake, lose the tie."

9:14 A.M.

Romar drove; heat cranked, both of their coats tossed in the backseat. A long drive north from the Area Two headquarters on 111th; Wally read his notes aloud.

"I'll line-item what we learned. Officer Anna Rodriguez, thirty-two years old, seven years on the force. First Watch. Puts her off at 5 p.m. She calls her supervisor for an unscheduled medical stop. Keeps her squad car and stays uniformed. Her supervisor has no idea how she ends up at the Costa residence. No phone logs, radio calls, nada." Wally stretched, cracked his back. "Jump on 55," he said. "Her gym's near your place, so head like you're going home."

"Thanks," said Romar, sarcasm dripping. "I get kinda lost, seeing how you drive so much."

"All right, smart guy," said Wally. He tapped his pen on his notebook. "So Ms. Rodriguez is single. Very attractive and single. Her partner said she didn't go on many dates but he thought she might be seeing someone from her gym. She didn't like to talk about it—to him or anyone else. But he nixed any possible romantic angle with Costa, said she'd never mess around with a married man—just wasn't in her nature."

"That could've been bull," said Romar. "Maybe her partner just didn't know . . ."

"No, I'm buying what he was selling," said Wally. "He seemed pretty certain."

"So you're eliminating any male-female relations between her and Costa?"

"Yep. I just don't think that's it. Let's follow up on this guy at her club and see where it goes."

"Is that what the police shows call a hunch?" asked Romar. "I've heard all about 'em, but I don't think I've ever really seen one being discovered before."

"Kiss my keester, Detective," said Wally. He closed his notebook, looked out at the lake as they veered north on Lake Shore Drive. Waves rose and dropped and Wally figured them for five-footers. The thought made him cold and he found himself on his couch, cuddling with his wife, the green afghan wrapped around them. Her feet in red slippers resting on the glass coffee table.

"Ain't we losing focus on our murders?" asked Romar, jarring Wally from his thoughts.

Wally waited to answer. He stared through the windshield, watched as the wipers pushed away the dark spray from the truck in front of them.

"Let me tell you something. A buddy of mine was in commercial real estate. He was pitching some big account and when he told me about it, he said there was one firm competing for the business that just didn't belong. They didn't have any experience, weren't qualified, blah, blah, yak, yak. Anyway, I told him that firm would get the work and, lo and behold, they did. So, my buddy asks me how I knew and I said, 'Since they didn't belong, there had to be a reason they were there.' I figured they knew someone up top. That turned out to be true."

"So," said Romar as he touched the brakes, moved toward the exit ramp.

"So, in our case, I'm thinking Gorski killed Costa and Officer Rodriguez, then hightailed it out of there. For some reason, he figures it might be discovered right away and he's got to stay in the area, so he goes to the local grocer, finds a single woman and follows her home. The place has just been sold, so he figures none of the new neighbors are gonna bug her—that Welcome Wagon stuff went out years ago and it's cold as hell, anyway. So he kills her. Later, the boy comes home—the movers said the boy wasn't there during the move and that neighbor across the street said she saw him trudging across the lawn on Thursday night. Gorski kills him, too. Then, in the morning, Gorski leaves and runs over the ex-husband in the driveway. Now, the woman, her son and the ex-husband are all collateral damage. They're killed because this guy needs a place to stay. It's sick but I can follow it. But when you add that scene to the Costa scene—the torture, duct tape, all that stuff—one thing still doesn't make any sense. What was the officer doing at Costa's place? That's the thing that sticks out. We fill in that piece of the puzzle, the others are gonna start falling into place. Now, park on the street. We may not be here too long."

Romar pulled the car over toward the curb, shifted into park and turned off the engine. They both reached into the backseat for their coats and their breath showed as they undid their seatbelts, put on their coats. "And there I done seen it," said Romar as he opened the door.

"What?" asked Wally as he got out on the other side, pulling on his gloves as he closed the door with his hip.

"Here I thought you just had a hunch. But all that thought you put into it? Man, you discovered that hunch and raised it all by yourself!"

"As I said before," said Wally. "Kiss my keester."

10:03 A.M.

Wally stood outside a studio near the membership office on the second floor of the building. He peered in a window and watched as a group of women and a few men contorted on blue rubber mats, sweat pouring off their bodies. The women, some wearing shorts, others in Spandex, most late twenties or early thirties. The men the same age in shorts and T-shirts.

"It's hot yoga," said a thirty-something man in slacks and a white dress shirt as he strode up to Wally.

"Seems like the only thing it'll help you do is eat a sandwich with your feet," said Wally.

"Good workout," said Romar as he joined them. "You might want to do it, Principal. Help you with stretching. Guy your age . . ."

"I'm Tony Caron," said the man. "I'm the assistant manager, here. Kristie said you wanted to see me," he said, turning to look back at a blonde at the front desk who wore a snug polo shirt that bore the name of the gym.

"I said we wanted to meet the manager," said Wally as he flashed his badge. "Detectives Greer and Jones. I'm assuming you're it today, eh?"

"I'm in charge," said Caron. He ran a hand over his short black hair, and Wally smiled as Caron slipped his hand into his pocket to wipe away some of the goop from his hair. "What can I do for you? You're not here for a membership, are you?"

"Nope," said Wally. He thought about asking to go to Caron's office, but when he looked around, he realized they had plenty of privacy. The gym was basically one big open room with several studios on the perimeter and signs that pointed toward locker rooms near the back of the gym. Free weights, weight machines and aerobic equipment were separated in three different areas and the guy closest to them looked like he was doing push-ups on a vibrating rubber pitcher's mound. Wally shook his head and sighed. "We're investigating a homicide. You had a member named Anna Rodriguez. Can you check on her, please?"

"Had? Homicide?" said Caron. "Oh, my God."

Romar reached out and touched the man's shoulder, gave him a firm pat. "We need you to check her records, see if she had a locker or anything."

"Sure," said Caron. He glanced back toward the membership office, then at the front desk. "Let's go to the front desk. Kristie can pull up her info. Have you got a picture or anything?"

"No," said Wally.

"Actually, we do," said Romar. "I got the *Trib* on my iPhone. They ran her picture this morning."

They stopped in front of the counter and Romar pulled up the picture of Officer Rodriguez, flashed it to Caron.

"Beauty," said Caron. "But we get a lot of hot girls here." He glanced at the girl behind the counter. She grinned, looked at the three men like she was waiting for instructions.

"Ever seen her before?" asked Wally.

"No," said Caron.

Romar handed the phone to the girl, Kristie. "Ever seen her before?" he asked as Caron walked behind the desk and nudged her from behind a computer.

Kristie took the phone, slid over near Romar and leaned across the counter. Her curly blond hair fell off her shoulders. "What did she do?" asked Kristie.

"Died," said Romar as he took the phone back. "Ever seen her?"

Kristie was slack-jawed. Her eyelids fluttered. "No," she said, softly.

Romar regretted his blunt answer. "Sorry. But we need any information you might have on her."

Caron leaned over the computer, spun the screen so Wally and Romar could see it. "Unfortunately, doesn't show much. She's been a member for six months. Auto debit from a Visa. No locker and no charges at the bar."

"What bar?" asked Wally.

"There's a bar downstairs, by the locker rooms," said Caron, glancing over his shoulder and nodding toward the staircase at the back of the room. "Sorry, juice bar."

"She lived on the South Side," said Wally, looking at Romar, then back toward Caron. He ignored the girl, who stared at Romar like she was trying to think of something to say. "Why would a South Sider come all the way here to work out?"

"It's a great club," said Caron, putting on his sales face. "We've got great views of Streeterville and it's an exciting place to work out. There are a lot of singles that work out here, too."

Wally looked around the room, watched the people work out. Most watched television on the screens of their respective machines, while others ran on treadmills overlooking Lake Michigan, iPod cords dangling at their sides. "Lake Michigan," muttered Wally.

"What?" asked Caron.

Wally turned back to him. "The lake. She was a runner. She came here to run by the lake. Do you have any running groups?"

Caron shook his head but Kristie stood up straight, her young breasts bouncing and she squealed as she looked at Romar. "I know a guy here that has a running club! I watched 'em at the Chicago Marathon."

"They're not affiliated with the club," said Caron.

Wally ignored Caron, looked at the girl. "Know the guy's name?"

"Sure," said Kristie. "It's Dave something. I can find it. And I've got a lot of pictures on my iPad."

"Can we see 'em?" asked Romar.

"It's at home," said Kristie. "But if you want, we can go to my place and get it. I don't live too far from here." She smiled, twisted her hair around an ear.

Wally shook his head, took out a card and handed it to the girl. "We've got a lot of running around to do today. Can you email 'em to us when you get off?"

"Sure," said Kristie. "I get off at five. I'll send them right away and if you need anything else, I'll put my phone number on my email."

"Thanks," said Romar. He handed her his card. "You can text 'em to me, too, if that's easier."

Wally thanked Caron and the girl, headed toward the elevator. He looked around, again, as Romar pushed the elevator call button. "You follow up with the girl. Get names for everyone in the pictures she sends. Come back here if you have to and get phone numbers, addresses, whatever. Only thing that makes this gym any different from one on the South Side is the location."

"Location, location, location," said Romar as they stepped into the elevator. "That and the fact that the guys here probably make a hundred grand a year more than the guys working out on the South Side."

"That too," said Wally.

11:15 A.M.

Martin felt compelled to stand up to make the call. He leaned forward, dialed, then lifted the receiver to his ear as he pushed the desk chair to the side.

One ring, then an answer: "Elizabeth Hughes."

Martin felt the acid hit his stomach. "Miss Hughes, it's Special Agent Martin Lowell of the FBI. It's Saturday; I didn't think I'd find you in."

Martin heard her exhale, like she was blowing smoke after a draw on a cigarette. Her voice was low. "So, you called hoping not to find me in? Or are you saying I'm not serious enough about my work to come in on a Saturday? I would've given you my home number if you simply wanted to insult me."

"I didn't call to insult you."

"You could've called me when I was sleeping. I'm betting it wouldn't be the first time you disappointed a woman in bed."

"You're obviously enjoying twisting my words."

"I can't reach your neck."

"Would you like to?"

"Is that an invitation to dinner or are you gauging my temper? I'm supposed to be the one that reads people, Special Agent Lowell."

Martin startled himself. "An invitation. I hear I owe you an apology."

"You hear?"

"I do. I owe you an apology. I think I was set up but—"

"You can apologize over the phone," said Elizabeth. "But you can't get flustered on the witness stand." She paused, again. "Christ, it's still morning and I could already use a drink. Meet me at Shaw's at six."

Martin stammered a quick, "See you there," and heard her breath again as she hung up. He pictured wisps of smoke rising over her hair. He wondered, for a moment, if the pressure was getting him. His blood gushed like lava.

1:30 P.M.

Albert Cordell stood in the lobby of Gibsons, stared out at the street. He slipped his arm through the sleeve of his overcoat, buttoned it and felt the weight in his stomach. He should've overruled Harry when he'd ordered the seafood platter, but something about those big fucking shrimp on a cold day got him going. Steamed broccoli the size of his head, the twice-baked potato, salad and well done Porterhouse had filled him to the point of bursting. Two dry Martinis and a bottle of beer pushed his navel toward the middle button on his coat.

Cordell turned to his left, looked into the bar and thought that if anyone was worried about the economy, they should stop by Gibsons. It was jammed on a Saturday afternoon. He glanced at the bartenders—they looked like they'd stepped out of the 1930s: heavy jowls, short gray hair and expressions that said they expected to be called "Mac." One washed glasses while two others pushed drinks across the bar. A piano player played in the corner near the entrance and Cordell saw two women seated at a high-top nearest the piano, makeup caked on like the winter freeze. He felt eyes on him and turned back toward the door.

"Aren't you . . ." said a blonde in a mink coat. A man to her left pulled her tight, caused her to rock on her heels.

Cordell yelled over the piano. "I'm Ron Santo."

The woman glanced at her date, who glared at Cordell. The man didn't say anything as Cordell strode by, stepped through the revolving door and out into the cold.

A gust of wind blew through Cordell's red hair and he paused for just a moment. He watched as women in fur coats with scarves and black gloves scurried north on Rush Street, shopping bags clutched like Depression-era groceries. His car came into view and he was about to step off the curb when he felt a hand on his sleeve.

Cordell turned and barked. "I said—"

"Hey, hey," said Harry Burton. "I'm just asking for a ride."

Cordell looked at Burton, a low-level defense attorney. He looked like a goof in his winter coat and black derby hat. His cheeks were already red and both hands were dug into coat pockets.

"Can't," said Cordell. "I'm running late."

"Jesus," shrieked Burton. "It's only three blocks."

"Take a cab," said Cordell. Burton didn't move, so Cordell lifted the back of his hand through the air, dismissive. "The walk will do you good."

Burton shook his head, muttered something.

Cordell stepped off the curb, handed the valet a fin. He was about to walk around the car to the driver's side when he felt a hand on his shoulder, again.

"Damn it, Harry . . ." he hissed.

He heard the voice before he saw him, felt his legs go weak.

"Hello, Asshole."

For just a moment, he thought of yelling or running but the stories kept him in place—the tire iron on Kels Martin, shredded glass in the kid's drink, the Bickle brothers found in the same barrel. He felt his entire body start to shake, reached his left hand toward the bumper.

"Take it easy," said Vitus Gorski. "Click that little fucker and open my door and then me and you are going to take a quick ride." Gorski patted his coat with his right hand and Cordell saw the outline of the gun.

Cordell walked around the back of the car, clicked the fob twice and opened his door. He slid into the driver's seat as Gorski moved in next to him.

"What do you want?" asked Cordell.

Gorski raised a thick eyebrow. "Close the fucking door, Asshole. It's freezing in here."

Cordell closed his door, looked at Gorski, froze until Gorski nodded. Cordell put his hands on the steering wheel, noticed them shake.

"God, it's nice to be in an American car," said Gorski. He leaned forward and cranked the heat. "Go north on Rush. I need to talk to you. Then drop me by that car dealer. I'm parked on the street."

Cordell's foot betrayed him; the car shot north, too fast.

"Slow down," said Gorski. He unbuttoned his jacket, adjusted the gun in his waist band. "Keep going, past P.J.'s"

Cordell gathered his voice. "What do you want?"

"You're a creature of habit, Asshole. You've been going there since you were a kid, sucking at your uncle's teat. You the third shyster in your family?"

"Yes. My father and uncle."

"Third asshole. I knew 'em both. So, what're you, like fifty?"

"Fifty-two. Please. Just tell me what you want. I've got a meeting shortly and if I'm not there, they'll search for me."

"Right," said Gorski. "A prick like you has a few martinis at lunch and misses a meeting. Call out the National Guard."

Cordell waited but Gorski didn't say anything, just stared through the windshield. Cordell craned his neck left, saw Harry Burton and thought of mouthing the word *help* but Burton saw him, lifted an ungloved hand, middle finger extended. He read Burton's lips: "Asshole!"

"I saw you on TV, once," said Gorski. He snickered. "It makes your head look big." He lowered the window, spit into the cold air, raised the window back up. "So how is it a shitcan lawyer like you gets a job on TV?"

"They need an expert to explain things," said Cordell. He hit a patch of ice, fought the wheel as the car swerved. He hit the brakes, straightened out the front end. "Jesus, Vitus, what do you want?"

"You know what I want," said Gorski.

"No, I don't," said Cordell. He looked over at Gorski. "Do you want me to represent you? Are you turning yourself in?"

Gorski's laughed a smoker's cackle. "Do you really think I'd do that?"

"Then what?"

"Where is he?"

Cordell had to piss. He squeezed his legs together. "Oh, God. In custody. He's going to be arraigned Monday. In court."

"Where is he, now? And don't tell me lockup."

"I don't know. I swear." The panic piss nearly shot down his leg. "When he wants to talk to me, they call with a location. I swear, I don't know where he is."

"When are you seeing him again?"

"Tomorrow night. He has papers to sign for Monday."

"When will you know the location?"

"Tonight, tomorrow . . . They're not worried about accommodating me."

"Call 'em tonight and tell 'em you need to know tonight. You've got church tomorrow and then Bulls tickets."

"I'll try. But he's in custody. What can you do?"

Gorski looked out the window, muttered. "Wish him well." He turned back to Cordell. "Give me your cell phone number."

Cordell told Gorski the number and watched as the big man used a thumb to put it into a cell phone in a pink case. When Gorski got done entering the number, he fiddled with the phone and Cordell felt his own telephone vibrating in his shirt pocket.

"Turn around here," said Gorski.

Cordell turned, drove south down State Street.

"Chuck Dragone?"

"Excuse me?" said Cordell. He gripped the steering wheel like it was ready to fall off. "What are you talking about?"

"Shit," said Gorski, no emotion. "Chuck Fucking Dragone. Twenty Chuck Dragones couldn't take me out." He turned, stared at Cordell with that big eye. "It wasn't your idea was it?"

"Jesus!" yelled Cordell. "I don't know what you're talking about!"

Gorski turned away. "What makes a man like Frank turn?" he asked. He was looking through the windshield again.

No one else calls him Frank, thought Cordell. He stammered, "Self-preservation."

"Bad choice of words," said Gorski, eerie calm. "The end is nearer than he thinks."

They drove through the light and Gorski put the phone back in a pocket, buttoned his coat and motioned for Cordell to pull over.

"I'm going to call you at nine. You'd better find out where he's at," said Gorski as the car rolled to a stop. There was a pop and Cordell jumped before he realized Gorski had simply unlocked the doors. Gorski opened the door, slid out, raised up and leaned back inside. Cordell watched as the big man's breath pooled in the air. "You know, you could never save him from me."

"I know," whimpered Cordell as the door slammed shut.

Cordell took his hands off the steering wheel, tore at the zipper on his coat. His right hand fumbled with the phone as Gorski lumbered down the street, cut down an alley.

"Jesus, Jesus, Jesus," said Cordell as he yanked the phone from his shirt pocket, clicked a button and slid the unlock symbol. He looked at the green message box, saw the number 1and touched the box. "You know . . ." Gorski's voice whispered in his head, "you could never save him from me."

The message popped up. Dear God. No.

He touched the picture.

The stocking hat.

The long red hair.

His son.

2:11 P.M.

A bell rang when Wally walked in the door. He almost laughed; the room was a throwback—wood floor, metal shelving—aisles so tight a guy could barely bend over to grab something from the bottom shelf. He looked to his left and saw the laminate countertop with an old cash register and glass change jar. A dead-eyed kid stood behind the counter, rifling through the pages of a catalog.

Wally walked up to the counter; Romar lingered behind. "Have you worked here a long time?" asked Wally.

The kid looked up. His eyelids sagged. "What?" he asked.

Wally leaned over the counter, showed his badge. "I asked if you've worked here a long time. I need to talk to someone who's been around awhile."

"What do you want?" asked the kid. Wally heard the slight accent as Russian.

"I have some questions about a bag that I believe came from your store. You look like you're still in juco, so I'm not counting on you for much help. No offense."

The kid stood up straight. He wore a name tag on the breast pocket of his light blue long-sleeved shirt. It read, "Maxwell."

"Let me get my father," said Maxwell. "I'm only in school for engineering. Maybe he can answer your juco questions."

Wally muttered to himself as Maxwell walked down an aisle. He heard the door to a back room swing open as Romar stepped up behind him.

"Nice work," said Romar. "You never taught me to piss 'em off like that. Or did I just miss that lesson?"

"Stow it," said Wally. "I don't have a patent on stupid."

Wally heard Romar chuckle, shuffle off down an aisle. Wally turned back toward the counter as an old man walked out from behind a display case, stepped behind the counter. He wore a blue shirt like the one the other guy wore and his name tag said, "Ross."

"Can I help you?" asked the man. He was short, thick and bald. Eyeglasses were perched at the end of his nose.

Wally showed his badge. "I'm Detective Greer. My partner, who's probably off looking at batteries now, and I are working a case and someone involved had a bag with your store name on the side. I looked it up on the Internet and couldn't find any other Lindbergh Hardware stores."

"This is the only one," said the man. He took off his glasses, used one of the temple arms to dig wax out of an ear. He took a Kleenex out of his pocket, cleaned the ear piece. "It's been a long time since we gave away those bags."

"How do you know which bag I'm talking about Mr. . . ."

"Rossovich," said the man, the Russian accent thick, unmistakable. "Armand Rossovich. Ross. I opened this store in 1962. I was only twenty-one years old. I'd worked for a moving and storage company since I was fifteen. How many of these young people today know what it's like to work that young? And I'd worked with my father before that."

Wally smiled, gestured toward Romar, who hovered near the door to the small store. "I know what you're talking about."

Ross shook his head. "No, he's not a young man. My son, the engineer, he's still a young man. He complains the other day because he has to work at the store after school. I tell him he goes to class four hours, works five hours, he still has fifteen hours left in the day to study and sleep. He can take his American girlfriend to the movie on Sunday. The rest of the week, he works with me."

"So, Mr. Rossovich, those bags?"

"Only one bag. Bags we use for customer were paper, now plastic. In early seventies we gave our fifty best customers canvas bag with our name on it. Man told me it was good advertising. Good advertising, bullshit. It was a lot of money for customers who came here because we have all tools."

"Do you remember a customer named Vitus Gorski?"

Wally turned as the man's son, Maxwell, strode up to the counter. "Don't say anything, Papa. I read that man's name in the paper today. He's a bad man."

"Baah," cried Ross. He swiped at the air. "You know nothing of bad men! I don't know this name, anyway, so there is nothing I can say."

Romar walked up, stepped up to the counter. "Do you recognize him?" he asked, hand held high, Gorski's picture on the screen of his phone.

Ross leaned over, put his glasses back on. "He looks like midget. I can't see him."

Romar touched the screen, spread his fingers and the picture grew. "Now?"

Ross straightened, gathered himself. He ignored Romar, looked straight at Wally. "I know this man. He come here for many years but I have not seen him in two, three years."

"What did he buy?" asked Wally.

"Tools. He worked on cars. He bought wrenches, hammers, usual things."

"Do you have an address for a garage or office for him?"

"No", said Ross. He shook his head, lips curled in a frown. "We only take cash, no customer files. I tried taking checks but deadbeats wrote bounced checks. Deadbeats."

Wally shuffled his feet, stared at the floor. The thought nagged him, so he asked, "Mr. Rossovich. This man is wanted for some very serious crimes. The only thing he seems to be carrying is a bag from your store. Now, if I was him, I'd probably have a suitcase or a duffel bag or something like that. Why would he carry a bag from your store?"

Ross scratched behind an ear, ran his hand over his chin. "Those bags were not as big as duffel bag but were bigger than bag my son takes to gymnasium. And, they are strong. They were made to carry tools. Only thing I can think of is that he carries something that is very heavy. Too big for a suitcase and too heavy for other bags."

"Like what?" muttered Wally. He pushed his card across the counter. "Please call me if you think of anything else," he said.

"No problem, Detective. I will," said Ross.

Wally turned, started to walk away, but turned back to the counter. "And hey," he said with a grin, "my partner here needs a left-handed router."

Wally laughed. Ross returned the laugh. Romar sighed as he followed Wally toward the door.

"You having computer problems?" asked Maxwell as he opened the door for Wally and Romar.

"No," said Romar. "I think that was an old man joke."

3:05 P.M.

Romar drove, shifted his eyes from the road to Wally and back. "You mind telling me what we accomplished with that?"

Wally wrote in his notebook. "It can be used to identify him. We've confirmed he got one directly from the owner. Lot of old guys walking around the streets of Chicago, but he's probably the only one carrying a Lindbergh Hardware bag."

Romar stopped the car in front of Gorski's house, parked near the curb. "Why are we here?" asked Romar as they got out of the car, both slipped on black leather gloves and walked toward the house.

"Only take five minutes," said Wally. "I want to check his closets."

Wally stepped over the barricade tape, fished a key out of his pocket and opened the door. The house was dark. The portable lights they'd used when they searched the house were gone, so Wally left the front door wide open. He followed a stream of light to the bedroom and when he found his way into the room, he opened the blinds.

"A quick search of this closet should do it," said Wally as he pulled the knob to the walk-in closet. He reached inside, found a light switch and breathed a sigh of relief when a light came on. "Probably the only bulb in the house he didn't break."

Romar's voice came from a few feet behind Wally, near the bedroom door. "Man didn't want to ruin his clothes."

Wally pushed his way through the suits and slacks that hung on each side of the closet. Near the back of the closet, on the floor, he saw a suitcase. It was a light blue, hard-shelled case and Wally had to stifle a laugh, picturing someone waiting for it at an airport carousel. "Not gonna mistake that for anyone else's bag," he muttered.

"What was that?"

"Nothing." Wally sifted through the other items on the floor and found a gym bag with a magazine's logo on the side and a white cotton laundry bag. He left them on the floor, backed out of the closet and turned off the light.

"Can you tell me what you're looking for?" asked Romar. "Or is it like the hardware store and you'll impart your wisdom when you feel like it?"

"Put some ice on your wounded feelings," said Wally. "I just wanted to see what other bags he had. I mean, why would he use a bag with a name on the side of it if he was trying to be inconspicuous? And don't tell me he wouldn't have thought of it because the two things I can see with this guy are that he's a sick SOB and he puts a lot of thought into his work."

Romar leaned against the door frame. "Like the man at the hardware store said, maybe he's carrying something heavy, like a gun."

Wally said, "Guns, plural, maybe, but he didn't use that bag just because they're heavy. He had a suitcase, gym bag and laundry bag that he could've stashed the guns in and they might've made a weird shape in the gym bag or laundry bag or been too heavy for that suitcase handle to bear, but I've got another thought and I don't like it."

"What's that?"

"If you saw a guy carrying a bag with the name of a hardware store on its side and you heard metal clanging, would you give it a second thought?"

"No."

"That's what I'm afraid of. Our boy knew he was gonna dump the car at some point and jump on a train. If he was carrying one gun, he could shove it in a gym bag or something else and no one would be the wiser. But if he was carrying a lot of guns and they were banging one another and making noise, someone might wonder what the heck was in his gym bag or whatever."

"So?"

"So, if you saw that hardware store logo, you wouldn't give it a second thought. Guy's just carrying around his tools. See, I think he's carrying a lot of guns."

"We know he's armed," said Romar. "He's killed a lot of people already."

Wally exited the room, walked toward the front door. Romar followed. "But, the only one that was shot was right here—that guy Dragone. No, whatever he's doing, he's preparing for a gun battle. He's armed for war."

Wally closed the door behind him, turned and locked it with the key. He turned to face Romar when he heard the scream.

"Bitsy!"

Wally and Romar both jerked to attention. Wally put his right arm on Romar's chest, moved in front of him, hand on his Glock. He looked past the drive, toward the sidewalk and saw a cloud of snow, blood and fur. A huge pit bull had a small white dog in its mouth. The pit bull shook the small dog like it was a weightless rag; blood and spittle dotted the snow surrounding the furor.

"Bitsy," came the high-pitched cry, again, and Wally saw an elderly woman in a gray parka with red mittens and a red stocking hat standing near the bloody battle. She seemed transfixed. She drew her mittens to her face, took a step forward, then stood up straight and took a step back.

"Don't move!" yelled Wally.

The pit bull wheeled when it heard Wally's voice. It glared at him, blood dripping through its teeth. The lifeless body of the smaller dog hung from its mouth as it opened its jaws wide, gulped air, then closed them again with a crunch.

"Do not move!" yelled Wally, again. He had his right hand on his firearm and extended his left hand like he was a traffic cop. "I'm gonna get him away from you. When I do, you hightail it away from here, okay?"

The woman nodded, then whimpered, "Okay. Please help my Bitsy."

The pit bull whirled when it heard her voice, took a step off the icy sidewalk onto the snowy lawn and moved toward her.

"Hey!" yelled Wally.

The dog turned, again, eyes fixed on Wally. It panted, heavily, and steam rose from its mouth and nostrils. Wally thought, for a moment, that the dog seemed to vibrate—the tension in its body unnerved him.

Wally unzipped his coat with his left hand, opened it and slipped his left arm and hand out. He swung the coat behind him, shook his right arm and hand free and rolled the coat around his left arm. He extended his arm, again and started to move toward the dog. After his first step, he saw Romar slide behind him, move toward the driveway, gun drawn.

The pit bull seemed confused, for a moment. It dropped the body of the smaller dog, glanced back at the woman and when she turned and ran toward Romar, it turned back to Wally and started forward.

Wally heard the dog pant as it began to trot and when it leaped through the snow and ran toward him, he took off toward the street.

He heard the snow crunch behind him. He heard the dog's heavy breath, snarls. He heard the dog's bark as its teeth flashed through the air behind him, gnashed and chomped at his heels. Just as the dog leaped, so did Wally and as he slid across the hood of his car, he heard, in rapid succession, a gunshot, yelp and the sound of the dog's body as it hit the tire and hubcap.

Wally scooted off the hood of the car. His legs felt like rubber as he stood in the street, regained his composure and walked around to the passenger door, near the curb. The dog lay next to the tire, a hole in its rib cage. Its mouth hung open, bloody tongue lying on the cold cement like a slug.

Romar strode up, stared down at the dog. "What the hell were you doing, Principal?" he asked.

"Making sure the dog didn't go near that lady," said Wally, pointing to the old woman who kneeled in the snow, crying over her dead dog.

"But what was the deal with your coat?"

Wally felt his teeth chatter, knew it wasn't the cold. "Dogs like this, the bad owners, like Gorski, train 'em by having 'em shred clothes. They're taught to rip at it. I just hoped if the dog caught me, it'd go after my coat and wouldn't tear my arm off in the process."

Romar shook his head. "Why didn't you just shoot it?"

"Are you kidding?" said Wally. "With that woman there? And a moving dog? That thing was moving so fast, I don't know what I'd have hit if I tried to shoot it."

"I hit it," said Romar as the first squad car pulled up and the woman stood up with her Bitsy in her arms and flagged down the officers. "A dog like that? Man, you just gotta kill it."

3:45

Albert Cordell sat at attention, elbows on his desk. He stared at the cell phone, thought about it one more time, realized it was his only chance. He punched the message into the phone, then reread it: "Call me at this number. Now. Asshole."

Cordell muttered, "Shit," hit send. He placed the phone on the desk in front of him, took a bottle of Blue Label out of the drawer and filled his tumbler for the second time in the past thirty minutes. He took a long drink of the whiskey, set down the glass and rubbed his eyes. He reached for the glass, but the cell phone began to vibrate so he picked it up.

"Hello."

"Asshole?"

Sigh. "Yes."

"I told you I'd call at nine. And what's this number?"

Cordell took a deep breath, prepared the rehearsed lie. "A prepaid cell phone. I got a call. My phones are tapped."

"Bullshit," said Vitus Gorski. "The Feds wouldn't do that. It's illegal."

"It's not the Feds. It's Francis."

Cordell waited for an answer, heard only Gorski's heavy breath. Thirty seconds went by before Gorski said, "Where's your meeting tomorrow night?"

"I don't know!" shrieked Cordell. "You said you were going to call at nine. I called and told them I had to know soon, that I'd be out later. So, they said they'd call right at nine. That's why I got hold of you. I want you to come here and listen when they call."

"Right," said Gorski. "I saunter into your office and you've got the Feds or Frank's guys waiting for me. Not gonna happen."

"Jesus!" yelled Cordell. "Do you think I'm stupid? I'm sure you've got someone watching my son. No, no, no. I'm not jeopardizing his life!" He fumbled with the phone. "I want you here when they call. You listen and when we find out where the meeting is, you can use my computer to look up anything you need to know about the place— directions, adjacent buildings, routes, whatever. If you're successful in whatever you mean to do and they search my computer, I can easily say the information was for me. But, I want this over with as soon as possible."

"You still in the east Loop?"

"Yes, the same building. Eighth floor. Come in the back through the parking garage. There's a keypad to get into the building. I'll text you the key code."

"Asshole, if anything goes wrong, your son dies."

Cordell didn't have to fake it, he stammered, "I understand. Nothing is going to go wrong. I just want this finished." He summoned up some courage. "I'm throwing this phone away now. Don't attempt to contact me. Get here a few minutes before nine and the minute you get everything you need, I want you to leave and swear to me you're done with me and my son."

"Once I find out where he's at, I'm done with you," said Gorski. "But do not do anything funny or I swear I will kill your son right in front of you. Do you understand me?"

"I understand," said Cordell. He hit the end button, threw the phone across the room. It shattered when it hit the wall; shards of plastic shot across the floor. He reached for the whiskey, filled the tumbler and sat back. He glanced at his watch. He had five hours.

4:15

Romar parked in the circle driveway. Wally kicked slush off his shoes as he walked through the revolving door into the condominium building. The doorman stood behind the counter, nodded when Wally flashed his badge, said, "They's in the elevator lobby and at her place on thirteen."

The doorman clicked a button and the door to the condominium units opened. Wally and Romar walked through the doorway, peeled off their gloves and stuffed them in their coat pockets.

"Not sure why they called us over here," said Wally as he passed the residents' mail slots. They turned the corner and walked into the elevator lobby and were met by two uniformed policemen and a tall gray-haired man in a sport coat and glasses.

"Ned," said Wally.

The man grasped Wally's hand, shook Romar's. "Ned French, Second Watch."

"Romar Jones."

"Look, Principal," said French. "We've got the murder of a young woman here. They found her in the trash chute this morning. She lived on the thirteenth floor and it appears she was dropped into the chute from there."

"Anyone see or hear anything?" asked Romar.

"No," replied French. He looked directly at Wally. "But we've got surveillance tape that shows her entering the building with a tall gray-haired man."

"Can you make out his face?" asked Wally.

"No," said French. "But you'll want to look at it. I called you because I read your reports. Could be your guy." He nodded at Wally, who nodded back. "Techs are already in her unit," he continued. "We've been here for an hour."

French reached forward and pushed the elevator call button. The door for one of the four cars opened and Wally and Romar followed French into the elevator. "No low- or midrise elevators here," said French. "Forty-five stories and everybody takes the same elevators. Only four ways in and out—the lobby, truck docks and service entrance on the first floor and the garage on the seventh floor."

"What about the pool deck?" asked Romar. "Lot of these buildings you can get to the truck docks or garage from another set of stairs on the pool deck."

"Not here," said French. The car stopped on the thirteenth floor and French held the door. "Go left, then right. It's at the end of the hall."

Wally and Romar followed his directions, walked toward the noise. The door to the young woman's unit was open and Wally nodded again when he saw Fred Pence and Delia Grant. Fred snapped pictures while Delia dusted for prints.

French followed Wally and Romar into the unit. They all stopped a few feet inside. "It's okay," said Delia. "Just walk a straight line down the hall and don't touch anything. We've already got the door, table in the entry way and the hall."

They walked across the hardwood floor, past the bathroom and an open closet door that showed the stackable clothes washer and dryer. Wally stopped at the entrance to the kitchen, which was only probably fifteen feet inside the front door. "Are you telling me that no one heard anything? This place is small and has hardwood floors. Everything echoes."

"No one's stepped up yet. We've canvassed the adjacent units as well as above and below." French sighed. "My guess is she was suffocated, so no noise. No blood in here. The body fell a long way so I'm not sure what the lab's going to come up with." He paused, rubbed his eyebrows. "You know, if it was your guy, it's not likely he knew her. She was a graphic designer and worked in the Merchandise Mart—not the kind of place she'd run across a guy like Vitus Gorski."

The name snapped Wally to attention. "I'm gonna look at those tapes. Did you find her cell phone?"

"They're searching the trash," said French.

Wally cringed. "Criminy. So, not here?" French didn't respond, so Wally said, "Okay. Look around for her bills. She's like most of these kids, she pays her bills online, but she might have a copy of her cell phone bill here. Let's find out which carrier she used and get a list of the recent calls, both incoming and outgoing. What about a car?"

"I just got off with the manager," said French. He leaned around and said, with an eye toward Delia Grant, "I used my cell. The manager looked it up and said she owned a parking spot. We've already checked and the car's gone."

"Check with the parking company. Find out what time her car left. They'll have a record even if it's on a pass. Get the make, model and color of the car and get it out fast."

"Gold Prius," said French. "I just called it in."

Wally watched as the evidence technicians worked the room. He turned, eyeballed the front door, vacuumed the carpet with his eyes until he saw two frayed patches. His eyes slid across the carpet, up the wall and stopped on a black mar.

"He killed her right here in the hallway," said Wally.

Romar stepped out of the kitchen, an envelope in his gloved hand. "What makes you say that?"

"Modus operandi. Same way the Patterson woman was killed. He takes 'em right inside the front door. Look at the carpet and wall," said Wally. He didn't wait for Romar to respond. "Ned, I'm gonna go check the tape. Where's the management office?"

"First floor," said French.

Wally walked out the door, started toward the elevator, saw the trash chute closet and walked toward it instead. *Fifteen steps. Another unit three steps south of the chute and another a few steps north. Any of those residents chose the wrong moment to open their door and they'd have probably joined the young lady in the trash chute.*

Wally strode back to the unit, asked Delia Grant if she'd printed the handle to the trash chute door and when he got a yes, he walked back to the chute closet. He opened the door, stepped inside and saw the chute. He reached forward, twisted the metal handle and pulled it. Inside: a black rubber cover. He pushed his hand against the cover, leaned forward as the mouth of the chute opened. *Darkness.* Noise of the search below rumbled in the chute. Wally felt the anger in his gut rise. He let the cover close, closed the metal door and stepped back out into the hall. He hit the elevator button and waited.

The manager was a sixtyish woman with close-cropped white hair. She wore a thick, green wool sweater and was hunched over her computer. Wally stood behind her and peered at the screen. She moved her mouse, clicked an icon and the tape from the service elevator lobby played.

"It's coming up, now," said the manager. "I fast forwarded for you. This was from 11:06 last night."

Wally watched as a young Asian woman rounded the corner into the elevator lobby. A tall, gray-haired man followed her. He held several large plastic grocery bags by their handles.

"Is this the only angle you have?" asked Wally.

The woman looked up, raised an eyebrow. "Yes. You could check and see if the city's cameras caught anything from the corner of Hubbard and La Salle. She probably walked back that way from the Jewel store on State Street."

Wally ignored the "Are you an idiot?" look, watched the screen as the elevator door opened and the man swung his left arm forward, gesturing for the woman to enter the elevator first.

"Pause it!" yelled Wally, a bit louder than anticipated.

The woman clicked the mouse and the picture paused.

"Look at the bag," muttered Wally. He started to read out loud. "*LIN...*"

"Ms. Lee's first name was Ling," said the manager as she offered him that same look.

"*D*," said Wally. "*LINDBE*... I can't see it all, but that's a Lindbergh Hardware bag."

"So?" asked the woman, leaning back in her chair.

Wally ignored her question, gestured for her to let the tape finish playing. She clicked the mouse again and they watched as the woman entered the elevator followed by the older man. The elevator door started to close as the older man stepped inside and turned. His head hung forward so Wally couldn't make out the face, but just as the door closed, he lifted his head slightly and the camera caught one eye as he looked straight into the lens.

"So," muttered Wally as he turned and walked out of the office. "It's him."

5:08 P.M.

Romar was waiting in the lobby. "Principal, let's go!" He rushed out the door and Wally followed him. "We got her cell phone provider. A cell tower near here was pinged at 3:45. You ain't gonna believe this, but we already found the car. It's parked on the street on Kinzie, a couple of blocks away."

They ran, tore west across Kinzie, saw two squad cars blocking the vehicle. Romar parked in the bike lane, told one of the uniformed cops to put out cones.

Wally approached the Prius, asked one of the cops, "You touch this vehicle, Officer?"

The cop shook his head. Wally put on his gloves, peered in the driver's-side window. The vehicle was empty. He took off a glove, stepped toward the front of the car and put his hand on the hood. Past the point of freezing outside and the hood was still slightly warm. Wally figured the car had probably been parked for less than twenty minutes.

"Romar," he said. "Get some of the men and check the tavern, then the restaurant. Do a walk-through and see if you spot Gorski. Check the restroom. Ask everyone there if they saw the person who parked this vehicle. Not likely he's still around, but make a thorough check."

Romar nodded, motioned toward a group of cops clustered on the north side of Kinzie, then trotted toward the restaurant. Wally gestured to another cop, told him to call Delia Grant's cell phone number and tell her to get to the vehicle, pronto. He put his glove back on, peered in through the window, again, and stared at the object protruding from under the passenger seat. He made out the pink cover, dark face. "Hello there," he said as he stared at the cell phone.

5:32 P.M.

Delia Grant finished taking prints from the cell phone. Her breath hung in clouds in the air as she spoke. "It's an unusual situation," she said. "Keep your gloves on and hold the phone around the rim. I've dusted the phone and most of the good prints will probably come from a finger on the back but be careful."

Wally smiled, said, "Thanks for getting here so quick."

"Two blocks away," said Delia. "I've got Swanson on his way to work the car. I've got to get back to the girl's apartment. Do you really think this freak is somewhere nearby?"

"I don't know. I know he took the car out this morning, then made a call late afternoon and now we find the car here. I just want to look at the phone to see if there's anything else that might lead us to him sooner rather than later." He noted the look on Delia's face, added, "I already put an All Call in with Gorski's description. There are cops all over River North right now."

Romar strode up as Delia left. "Nothing from the restaurant," he said. "Only a handful of people in there and none of 'em saw anything. We hit the tavern, too. Want us to start working our way north on Wells?"

"Yep," said Wally. He held the phone in the air. "Look what he left in the car."

"Shit," said Romar. "What's it got?"

Wally tapped the face of the phone with a gloved thumb and it came alive. He caught his breath at the screen saver: Ling and a couple of other girls. He slid the unlock button, relieved when it didn't ask for a security code. He hit the phone icon and saw only one call from the day before to a 312 number at 3:45 p.m. He looked at the voice mail folder, saw the last message was two days old. He thought for a moment and then hit the messages icon, saw the last two messages were from the same 312 number as the call. He tapped the icon for the last message and a series of numbers appeared. He tapped the icon for the message just before the last one and it read, "Call me at this number. Now. Asshole."

A truck crossed the bridge west of them, honked its horn when the driver realized they'd blocked off the street. Wally looked up for just a moment at the sound of the horn, motioned for the driver to head north, then looked back down at the phone. He stared at the column of messages for a moment, scrolled up and down the unfamiliar names and nicknames. He wasn't sure what he expected to find, then realized the second message was actually from earlier that day.

Wally clicked on the sent message from 1:39 p.m. A 773 number. It opened and he saw the single entry. There was no message, just a picture. He touched it with the thumb of his glove and it filled the screen: a teen in a stocking hat with long red hair. The kid's face registered fear. Wally stared at it, played a hunch and closed out of the messages folder. He hit the photos icon and wasn't surprised when it showed that the last picture taken was the same one that had been sent several hours after the girl's death. Wally stared at the picture of the red-haired teen, said to himself, "What the heck?"

6:00 P.M.

Martin stood in the entry way of Shaw's, looked right toward the Oyster Bar, then left toward the dining room. The hostess walked up to him, tugged at his elbow.

"Are you Mr. Lowell?"

"Yes," said Martin, surprised.

"Follow me," said the woman.

Martin followed her into the dining room. It was filled with red leather booths and white- tableclothed tables. He watched as she stopped in front of a table and Elizabeth Hughes stood up, extended a hand.

"Ms. Hughes," said Martin, as he shook her hand.

The hostess handed him a menu as he sat down. "Your waitress will be with you in a moment."

"I hate to even ask, but how did she know me?"

Elizabeth propped her elbows on the table, folded her hands and tucked them under her chin as she spoke. "I told her to look for a handsome man who looked totally lost."

"Lucky she bumped into me and not your boss," said Martin. He looked at her. She wore a gold turtleneck sweater and black slacks. Her long blond hair fell onto her shoulders. She was elegant casual— relaxed, confident. He took a deep breath, slipped off his blue suit coat and hung it on the back of his chair. "Anyway, I'm glad you could join me," he said. He rested his left arm on the table, set his right elbow in his left hand and rubbed at the stubble on his chin as he spoke. "I really am sorry if I offended you."

"It's not relevant. I'd have done the same thing if I was you. Deflect attention from yourself."

"I wasn't—"

"Please," said Elizabeth. She folded her arms, leaned forward. "I already told you I know you're lying. You can't fool me, but you could certainly fool a jury of your peers," she said, stressing the word *your*.

Martin frowned. "You're making this hard."

"Good." A salacious grin. Her eyes flickered.

Martin—no mood: "Why did you come here?"

"The wedge."

"You've got to be kidding me. The lobster, maybe, but—"

"Yours."

Martin sat up. "If you're trying to fluster me, it won't work."

Elizabeth smiled. "I've heard of fluffing. What's flustering? Is that like fluffing with a stroke?" She reached over, grabbed the Rubirosa off the table, stroked it up and down.

Martin shook his head. "You are neither flustering me nor turning me on. I'm not sure how you can be so frivolous. This case is critical to your employer and me. I agreed to come here to humor you—to be a team player so to speak."

Elizabeth let go of the peppermill. "So you're not sorry?"

She expected him to kowtow. He couldn't fake it. "No."

"Good," she replied. "Keep that tone when you testify. Serious. Unflappable. That's what a lot of people expect from the FBI, so deliver it."

"You're simply trying to gauge what my demeanor will be like on the stand?" asked Martin.

"Somewhat. I really did need a drink—do need a drink. I thought you might, too."

Elizabeth flagged down a waiter. "We haven't seen our waitress yet. You take this table. Two Bud Lights and two shots of Silver Patron, chilled."

Martin watched as the waiter scurried away. "I expected you to order a nice Pinot noir," he said.

"I'm not what you expect."

"So your job is to . . ."

"Advise on jury selection, emotional aspects of the trial. I offer my opinion on people. I read clues, verbal and nonverbal. A case can be won or lost based on jury selection alone."

"The way Denton looked at you, I imagine you give a lot more than that—advice-wise."

She blushed. Martin pounced. "So you rattle."

"Hardly," she said.

"Since I'm not on the jury, how do I fit into the emotional side of the trial? Why did they have you meet with me?"

Elizabeth unfolded her napkin, placed it in her lap. "You've been under a lot of stress. They were concerned about how you're holding up."

"What will you tell them?"

"Like I said, you're lying about something. I doubt that it's important to the trial or you would've discussed it with your supervisors. More likely, you're feeling guilty about something or you've convinced yourself you slipped up."

The beers and shots arrived. They both ordered the lobster, no sides.

"To conviction," said Elizabeth.

They toasted, shot the tequila. Both followed with a long draw off their beer.

Martin set down his bottle of beer. The shot hit him hard; he'd always gotten a buzz on the first drink. He pointed toward the lobster tank out front. "When I was in college, my buddies and I came here. One took a lobster out of the tank. He took it to a bar that used to be across the street and let it dance on the bar. He named it Larry. We sang karaoke, serenaded Larry with some Jimmy Buffet songs, then released him into the Chicago River. If you're not careful, he'll swim up your pipes and bite your ass."

"Sounds like you're testing the waters."

"I'm just trying to lighten the mood," said Martin.

"The mood is light," said Elizabeth. "I just wouldn't have marked you down as so frivolous—to use your word. If that story is true, I'll bet you came back that night and paid for the lobster."

"You don't know me as well as you think," said Martin. "I didn't go back until the next day."

Elizabeth laughed. Martin liked her laugh. He liked the pink of her tongue, the way her eyes glittered. He liked her smart mouth and taunts. He liked the hills in them thar gold and he liked the way the tequila loosened him up but gave him a shot of energy.

"I actually know you better than you realize," said Elizabeth. She ran a finger around the top of her beer bottle. "Northwestern on a cross-country scholarship. You had visions of the Olympics but ruined your knee when you fell during a race. You got up and finished second."

"More like delusions. And I'd have won if the race had gone another mile."

"Columbia for law school, after which you turned down offers from several prestigious law firms to join the FBI. Selfless instead of selfish?"

"G-spot or G-man."

"Gee, aren't we clever."

"There's right or wrong in life. I wanted to stand up for what's right. That's not selfless. I have a nice career and I can feel good about what I do for a living." He finished his beer, waved at the waiter and ordered another round, shots included.

"Are you trying to get me drunk?" asked Elizabeth, breaking his trance.

"You started it," said Martin. He loosened his tie. "If I'm trying to get anyone drunk, it's me."

The waiter came, dropped off the shots and beers. Elizabeth told him to prep the lobsters to go. "These are the last ones," she said, hoisting her shot. Martin lifted his shot glass, clinked hers and they both downed the liquor. "As soon as the food comes, let's get out of here. I'm going to see that you do not screw up your sleep pattern, now." She reached across, stroked his hand. "The trial will start soon. You need to be rested and ready. So, we'll make sure you get some exercise, go to bed early, sleep tight and get up early."

"It sounds like you have a plan," said Martin. He took a long sip of beer, pulled his hand over the white tablecloth and laced his fingers between hers. "I sleep just fine. Monday is only the arraignment. The trial may not start for quite some time."

"The attention starts Monday. You've got to get good, solid . . . sleep," said Elizabeth. "When you're tired, emotions take over."

"I'm not tired," Martin said, softly. "And I've got plenty of time to . . ."

"Martin," said Elizabeth as she took her hand from his, reached into the purse at her side and handed the waiter her credit card as he delivered the bag of food.

Martin felt the liquor wash over him. He wished she'd open the bag, eat the food at the restaurant and order a few more rounds.

"Martin," she said again.

He lifted his eyes from the table, leaned back. "Yes, Elizabeth?"

"You've only got two more nights."

7:35 P.M.

Wally stood. The other detectives sat at their desks. It was like they were playing catch with ideas; Dan Shepherd from First Watch, himself, Jerry Grunwald, Roscoe Barnes and Romar from Second Watch and Red Osburn and Jacintha Owens from Third.

"So," continued Wally. "Gorski was using the girl's cell phone. He got a text with a series of numbers. You've all got copies on your desk. They came in twenty minutes after he got a text saying, 'Call me at this number now. Asshole.'"

"It's obvious, Principal," said Roscoe Barnes. Everyone turned and looked at him and he said, "Someone wanted Gruns to call 'em."

Roscoe laughed.

Jerry Grunwald said, "Fuck you."

"There's nothing funny, here, Roscoe," said Dan Shepherd. "Stick to the point."

"Hey Shep," said Roscoe as he leaned back in his chair, stroked his mustache. "The last time there were two stashes in this room at the same time was when you busted your first pot dealer. Respect the stash."

Dan Shepherd didn't laugh. He answered, tired, solemn: "I've got a grandson the same age as that boy."

"Whoa, Dan," said Wally. "Roscoe's just being Roscoe."

Shepherd sighed. "I know."

"Go home," said Roscoe. "Have a beer." He rubbed the framed picture of Ernie Banks on his desk, said, half singing, "In fact, let's have two!"

Shepherd smiled, looked up at Wally. "I struck out Big Boy there in '87, looking. Fred Allison from Area One was umping. He looked at Roscoe and just said, kind of perplexed, 'You're out.' Know what Roscoe said?"

"'No shit,'" said Roscoe.

All the detectives laughed. Wally looked around the room, could practically see the fatigue. Shoulders drooped, coffee cups full and it was nearly eight p.m. He started to shake his head when Jazz Owens spoke up.

"Those numbers could be anything," said Jazz. "But I'm guessing they're the combination for a lock. Maybe another cell phone. My phone has a four-digit code, but maybe some other kinds have a series of numbers like this."

Red Osburn put his skinny arms on his desk, pulled the sleeves of his sport coat over his wrists. "The numbers were sent from a prepaid cell phone. We've already established that. Are you saying the originator left another phone somewhere and sent a code to use it?"

Jazz said, "Maybe. He left the other phone in his car."

Romar sat up. "I don't know, man. Sounds like a lot of work over a phone. It's probably a lock, but who knows what it's locking up."

Wally paced around the room. "What about the picture? Anyone recognize the kid?"

Blank faces. "Lab has it," said Red. "I'll follow up on it tonight. They're blowing it up, enhancing it. They might not get an address, but I'll bet they can put us in the vicinity of that townhouse. We get an area, Jazzie and I will canvass it tonight."

"That's right," said Jazz.

"Dan," said Wally, looking at Dan Shepherd. "How're you doing on Officer Rodriguez and Costa?"

Shepherd scratched the side of his nose. "It's Gorski. He left prints on the hammer. Delia said she's got nearly a dozen sets of prints. Roland Brown matched the duct tape used on Costa to the tape used on the Patterson boy."

"What about motive?" asked Wally. "Why would Gorski go after the brother of his boss?"

"Who knows," said Shepherd. "I've been on iClear patching together relationships. I've read so much that I've practically burned the pupils from my eyes. The Organized Crime Unit interviewed all the men being indicted and none of them had any clue. They won't let us talk to 'em until the trial is under way."

Romar: "Did you talk to that Fed, Lowell?"

"No," said Shepherd. "He had another guy talk to us. Everyone said Gorski and Costa were tight. The guy said most of 'em didn't believe it when he told 'em Gorski killed Phillip Costa. They said Gorski would run through a brick wall for Francis Costa—and he could."

"You're forgetting about Dragone," said Romar.

Shepherd swiveled in his chair to face Romar. "I'm not forgetting, Detective. Dragone was a burglar. He must've figured Gorski was on the run and decided to rob the place. Who knows what he thought he'd find."

"He found a hungry dog," said Roscoe.

Shepherd ignored Roscoe, continued. "Guys said they weren't surprised Dragone tried to burgle Gorski's place. He was a burglar, plain and simple."

Wally shot a finger in the air like he was casting a line. "You know, Gorski was an enforcer. He collected street tax . . . But, was he a burglar? You think he broke into Phillip Costa's house looking for something? Maybe Costa flagged down Officer Rodriguez?"

"No one offered that up," said Shepherd.

"Ah, just throwing it out there," said Wally.

"You never know," said Red.

Jazz repeated the mantra. "You never know."

Wally leaned back against the wall, moved to his left to avoid the light switch. "I just can't figure out why she was there."

Roscoe opened his desk drawer, pulled out a pair of thick gloves. "Well, I can't figure out why this sick bastard hasn't left the city. I mean, he could've taken a car or train and been in Iowa or Wisconsin. Instead, he kills a woman and her son so he can spend a night in their house one night. Then, the next night he kills a woman so he can stay in her condo. Hasn't the asshole heard of a Marriott card or something?"

"You're right, man," said Romar. "I been wondering the same thing. Maybe he's waiting on something. Could be he just needs to get to a bank. He didn't expect anyone pushing him out of the Patterson house until the dad showed up. I think he would've just waited there—"

"For what?" asked Roscoe.

"For whatever," said Romar.

No one spoke. Wally thought of Gorski, just hovering, waiting for something. He thought about the hardware bag and all of the guns it could hold. He thought about Dragone's body and the paw prints. He thought about the sound of Dave Abel's voice when he'd told Wally the boy had been found in the trunk. Wally took two steps toward the front of the room and spoke.

"Gorski's name and picture are everywhere. Let's keep buttoning up our cases so when we apprehend him he can be tried and found guilty. In the meantime, be careful, but also look for anything that may lead to this man. You never know what might seem too small or what one of your colleagues might have overlooked, me included. Let's be thorough."

"I've got my guys going through lists of known accomplices. We're locating and interviewing any and all," said Dan Shepherd.

"Red and I are going back to the girl's condo tonight," said Jazz. "We're going to talk to the night doorman and building engineers, find out if they saw anything."

Wally took a step toward them as they all got up. "Great," he said. He turned to Romar. "Romar, let's go back and see Henry Lopes tomorrow morning. He was pretty spooked by Gorski. We tell him Gorski's in the city, he might crack."

"Cool," said Romar.

"Workout at six?" asked Wally.

"Make it seven," said Romar.

Roscoe walked by, clapped Wally on the shoulder. "You should've been a coach, Wally. That speech there, just the right mix of direction and inspiration. You're a real Lee Elia."

"Thanks," said Wally.

Roscoe smiled. "Anytime. And I heard you sisters talking about a workout. I'll meet you here in the morning. Bring some extra plates in your trunk."

Wally put on his coat and gloves, followed Roscoe and Romar out the door, down the stairs and out the front door. He looked for his Impala and started to walk toward it but then turned and yelled back at Romar. "Hey, come here."

Romar stopped under a street lamp and Wally could see his displeasure at being yelled at, or maybe it was just a desire to get out of the cold, but his partner overcame it and sauntered over to the car.

"What is it, man?" asked Romar as he flipped up the collar of his coat. "It's cold out here."

Wally opened the trunk of his car, pulled out two pieces of wood, closed the trunk and walked over to Romar.

"Check this out, Detective."

Romar reached forward, looked at the two strips of wood. They were probably two and a half feet long, and six inches wide. Both were cut on some kind of slant. "What are these?" asked Romar.

"I cut 'em in my garage," said Wally. "I used my table saw on 'em. You put 'em on either side of the track for the sliding glass door going to your balcony and they form a ramp in and out. You said Lou Lou can't go out because she keeps bending the track with the wheels of her chair. I figured his might help. Next time you invite me over for beers, we can figure out how to secure 'em to the floor, but for now, if you put one on each side, she should be able to glide over the top."

"Thanks, man," said Romar.

"No problem," said Wally. He watched Romar walk back toward his own car.

The wind kicked up and when Wally got inside his car, a gust slammed the door shut. His breath fogged the windshield and he left his gloves on as he turned the temperature high, moved the knob to defrost and blasted the fan. He looked out the driver's-side window as Romar's car drifted out of the parking lot. "No problem."

Wally put the gear shift in drive and started to pull forward when he saw Roscoe a few rows back, kicking at his tire. He drove close to the big man, pulled up next to him and rolled down the window.

"Problem?"

"No," said Roscoe. Sweat poured from underneath his black stocking hat and froze on his red cheeks. "Asshole that plowed the lot left an ice drift under my tire."

"Jeez," said Wally. He peered out and saw the frozen sludge jammed under the front driver's-side tire of Roscoe's car. "Careful or you'll break your foot."

Roscoe leaned into the car. "No, I'm wearing steel-toed boots. Used to wear 'em when I worked for the railroad as a kid. Gotta wear two pairs of socks, but I can kick the shit outta this frozen slush and won't feel a thing."

"You've sure got your own logic," said Wally as he rolled up the window and watched Roscoe turn back and began to kick at the ice again.

Wally pulled forward and was about to make a left out of the lot when he saw a figure under the light near the front of the building. He squinted and saw the figure wave.

"Oh, jeesh," he muttered to himself. He thought of calling Theresa, but figured whoever it was must have a brief message because they made no move toward his car. He sighed and crept forward.

Wally stopped next to the curb and the figure moved toward the car and threw back the hood of a parka and peered over the windshield. Wally recognized the handlebar mustache immediately and hit the unlock button, leaned over and opened the passenger-side door.

"Thanks," said Ron Melcher as he slipped into the car. Ice hung from his brown mustache and he sneezed into his gloves. "What's it, fifteen degrees tonight?"

Wally looked at the dashboard. "Thirteen. Wind chill's probably ten below. You know, Ron, I haven't seen this many mustaches since Movember."

Melcher took off his gloves and rubbed his face. "I'll bet I had mine first. You know, when I saw you pull over to Roscoe's car, I almost cried." He chuckled to himself. "I just need a quick minute."

"What's up? You could've met me inside."

"No secret rendezvous, Principal. I just wanted to run something by you. It might be something, but it might not, and I don't want to run it up the flagpole only to wake up one day and find my ass up there with it."

Wally turned up the heat. "What is it? Something to do with interviewing the cons?"

"No," said Melcher. "Those have gone predictably bad. Seems a member of the Outfit gets arrested, his memory goes foggy." Melcher stared out the window for a moment, gathered his thoughts. "I was at Francis Costa's house when we went to arrest him yesterday morning."

"FBI invite you along?" asked Wally.

"Yeah. I know the wife and granddaughter and was told I'd be a calming influence. You ever meet those two, Wally, you'll see. I'm a calming influence like a bag of sand against a tidal wave. They're something."

"So, what happened?"

"Nothing, really," said Melcher. He looked out the passenger window a moment, then back at Wally. "That's kind of why I'm here. We had guys surrounding the house, guns trained down the block, the whole works. And Costa wasn't there."

"Happens," said Wally. He was hungry and ticked that Theresa was waiting. "So, anyway, Ron . . ."

"Look, Principal, this stays between me and you until it can't stay between me and you. Okay?"

"Fine."

"So, it's not unusual to have someone under surveillance but still miss 'em. I mean most of these guys have spent their lives avoiding tails. But yesterday, that wasn't it. It was the lack of expectation—the things that were said."

Wally forgot about dinner. "Whaddaya mean?"

"Do you know this Fed, Martin Lowell?"

"Met him once," said Wally. "I think I'll be seeing him again."

"He's kind of an arrogant ass," said Melcher. "But that's beside the point. What was odd was his attitude. I got the distinct impression he was just trying to make an impression. I mean, he was there because he wanted it known he'd been there."

"Ego? Playing to the papers?"

"No," said Melcher. He rubbed his temples. "It was his attitude and the things the Costa women said, like, 'You know he isn't here. Go on with this charade. No one said anything about this to our lawyer.' And she yelled 'Welch,' like someone had gone back on a promise."

"Jeez, Ron. What're you saying?"

"What I'm saying, Principal, is that I think the whole thing was a setup. I think Lowell knew Costa wasn't there. I think it was all for show."

"Well, they announced last night that he was in custody."

"That's it. I think he was already in custody when we went to his house. So, why did we go to his house? The daughter pegged it right. It was a charade."

"Why?" asked Wally.

"I have no clue," said Melcher. He put his gloves on, reached for the door but turned back toward Wally. "But we're not getting the skinny on this and that makes me nervous. I'd go to Brooks if I thought it would help, or even Yates, but with that high profile trial starting, I don't think you'll get the straight scoop. Just be careful."

"Thanks, Ron," said Wally. He watched as Melcher got out, closed the door behind him, took a few steps across the lot, then turned back around and motioned for Wally to roll down the window.

"Yeah?"

"Sorry, Principal, but I've just got to tell you one more thing. I've talked to most of the guys they're indicting. I've interviewed 'em and tried to intimidate 'em. You just can't do it. They're a sick bunch, but they're tough. But whenever I brought up the name Gorski, things changed all of a sudden. They got scared. What I'm telling you, Wally, is that the scariest sons of bitches I've ever seen locked up are scared of the guy. So, when I say be careful, I mean *be careful.*"

8:43 P.M.

You gotta be fucking kidding me. Seventy-three years old, only one real hip and two artificial knees and sitting in the front seat of an SUV with windows tinted so dark a guy couldn't see inside 'em with night-vision goggles. Fuck me.

The rim job called just after 4 p.m.: It's Gorski, he said. Fucking Gorski. Once that fucking attorney had told him it was Gorski, it didn't take much convincing. Everything had been going so great until Frank disappeared and Gorski went on the lam. And one thing was absolutely certain: Once Gorski knew, he'd be coming. The rim job's son? Whatever. He wouldn't be the first one Gorski would come after. So, a wrench had been thrown into the retirement plans. Or, actually, a Glock with a silencer.

Henry Lopes leaned back in the front seat of the SUV. Luck had been on his side; a pipe had broken and gushed water all over the parking spot that sat to his left. A sheet of ice and orange cones kept anyone from parking in it. That left him a clear sight line to the back door of the old office building. No one could get in or out without him seeing them.

The SUV Lopes had borrowed from one of his last customers—last because he was getting out, not any other fucking reason—sat in the parking garage attached to the building. He'd backed into the spot. To his right, cars came down the concrete ramp as they exited the building. To his left, cars passed him on the way in, or people passed on their way to or from the building. The door to the building was probably only fifteen feet away and, if he squinted, with his glasses on, he could see the panel Gorski would have to use to tap in the security code that the attorney had said he'd texted to him. But, that door would never open because he was gonna put a bullet in the back of Gorski's head just before he finished entering those numbers.

It was colder than shit in the SUV. He'd turned off the heat soon after he arrived around five o'clock—when most of the people from the building started to leave. He couldn't sit in the car for four hours with the engine running. That would draw attention. No, he'd just have to sit in the fucking freezing fucking vehicle until that big dumb fuck came and he could finish this once and for all. And now, Christ . . . now he had to take a leak.

He squeezed his legs together, tried to stay in the moment.

Gorski. Of all the guys left outside, it had to be Gorski. Henry Lopes wasn't afraid of many men, but Gorski was sure one of 'em. That story he'd told the cops about the shredded glass in that kid's drink? The reason he never drank anything around Gorski that had already been opened. Christ, the guy dumped some kinda poison on Touchy Capatelli's eggs. Left him facedown in an omelet. Fucking Gorski.

It had all been going so perfect. He'd finished the last car, paid the guys and sent 'em home happy. Sure, they'd be pissed, but what's a guy gonna do? You don't retire from the Outfit. So, he'd sold off nearly everything, would camp out for the duration of the trial and then head west. Cactus league baseball and a quick flight to Vegas. Sunshine year-round. None of these cold, windy, dark Chicago days. No more congestion, constant confrontation. No more traffic jams on the Kennedy at five o'clock on a Sunday evening and no more police sirens throughout the night. No more punks dropping their cars off without an appointment and bitching when they weren't fixed in twenty-four hours. No more learning computer systems on the foreign cars from the young guys or listening to their Latino rap music blare throughout the day. No more Pitbull, shit bull, snot ball, whatever. No more of that shit. All warm weather, sunshine and young broads in bikinis. Might be too old to do anything about it, but since when was looking a crime?

It had all been going so perfect . . . Until the fucking attorney called. He'd been using him 'cause he was Frank's guy. He was the guy they all used. But he never liked him. In fact, he always thought he was just an asshole. But, the asshole was right about one thing: Since Gorski was out, there was no stopping him unless you stopped him. It wasn't so much about convincing him that killing Gorski was the thing to do (in fact, it might have been his idea all along), it was convincing him that Gorski would show up at the building, on time, and that it was doable.

And now his back, hips and knees were killing him and he had to take a fucking leak. Ice had already formed on the windows, but he had to admit he was relieved when a young boy leaving the building with a woman stopped and wrote his name on the driver's-side window but still didn't see him sitting there in the driver's seat, eyes wide, thinking, "What the fuck?"

Lopes tried to stretch his legs, fiddled with the silencer. A car drove by, veered slightly to the right and disappeared down the exit ramp. He glanced at his watch: 8:53.

Perfect: A sight line directly to the building. Nobody came in or out without him noticing. Dark enough that if somebody actually got a look at him, they'd never be able to identify him. Noisy enough that a shout would get lost; the roar of the elevated train filled the garage every few minutes.

Perfect: Nobody in or out of the building in over an hour. He'd oiled the car door so it wouldn't make any noise, wore old, quiet tennis shoes. The floor of the garage between the SUV and the door of the building was clear and clean—no ice, nothing to kick like a can or a bottle. No, it was perfect. Fifteen, sixteen steps, gun drawn. Stop. Pull the trigger. Blow a round through that wild gray hair or thick, stony face. Fuck you, Gorski. Dead.

But . . . Somehow that twisted son of a bitch always survived. One jaunt to Stateville when they were kids but no serious time. Shot by Capatelli's brother—a shaving nick. Stabbed by some Micks leaving Sox park. A serious altercation with some coloreds that left two of *them* dead. And now this. Everyone arrested but him. How did he do it? How did he do it?

The size and the eyes. That's what Frank had always said. "Look at his size and his eyes." He's a gigantic motherfucker and you can see it in his eyes—he don't care.

All of 'em laughing around Vinnie Carbone's that one night. Vinnie laughing on account of he thought if he didn't, he was dead. Whadda they call that? Nervous laughter? And him and Frank laughing, staring at Gorski, asking him how he got Vinnie to pay his debt and Vinnie said, "I'll tell you how, I live on the eighth floor and when I looked out the window, he was staring in!"

The size and the eyes. The el went by. The rumble filled the parking garage. Lopes glanced down, saw a crack in the concrete. Jesus, he was glad he saw that crack! He could've tripped, lost his gun, or alerted the son of a bitch. Jesus! He looked up and down the entire path to the door, didn't see any more cracks. But that was a close one.

Suddenly, the urge to piss went from a nuisance to critical. The one thing he'd forgotten! He looked over the floorboard of the SUV. Nothing, not a bottle, bag . . . Nothing. And he couldn't slip out and take a leak. He'd sat in that godforsaken SUV for over four hours and he sure as shit wasn't gonna open that door now. Oh, Christ, hurry up, Gorski. I'll shoot you and leave a puddle by the car on my way out.

He felt his heart start to pound in his chest. His bladder felt like it was gonna burst. He leaned forward, then back. The el passed. The rumble faded. But there was a sound. A loud, buzzing sound. It seemed to come from everywhere and just when he thought it would drive him mad, he realized it was the lights. The electric current that ran the lights made a loud, steady buzz.

Reel it in. Reel it in. Oh, Christ, his bladder hurt. He squeezed his legs tight, tried to stay in the moment, but he couldn't take it anymore.

He took off his gloves, unzipped his pants and pulled it out. One quick squirt on the floorboard would be enough, but . . . Aaah, fuck. He closed his eyes. It all came out in a long gusher. He pissed all over the floorboard and when he opened his eyes, he saw it was all over his shoes. The piss ran under the seat and steam rose in the car to the point he couldn't see out the windows.

Lopes shook it, tucked it back in and zipped himself up. He took one of the gloves and wiped the steam off the driver's-side window, then the windshield. The odor in the car was awful, but Christ did he feel better. But the sound was gone.

Lopes leaned over, used the glove to wipe the steam from the passenger-side window. The garage was dark. Pitch dark. There wasn't a bit of light and the buzz was gone. It had only been like twenty seconds! It was a fucking piss! He pulled the Glock to his chest. Think. Think!

Henry Lopes held the gun to his chest like it was a newborn. He rocked back and forth, tennis shoes filling with warm urine. It had only been twenty seconds! But wait, wait. The lights had been on and he would've seen anyone coming in or out of the garage . . . wouldn't he? No one had driven in because he would've seen 'em or heard 'em, but if the lights had been out and the el was going by . . .

Oh, shit. This was bad. He looked at his watch: 9:03. Gorski was supposed to be there! He hadn't seen him and now he couldn't see him! And why were the lights out? What could . . . ?

The two lights appeared at the top of the ramp like wolves' eyes in a deep forest. Lopes hit a button on the car door and flinched when the doors unlocked. He peered through the passenger-side window. The lights started to move.

Lopes put a hand on the dash as the lights grew. He knew they were headlights but he cracked the driver's-side door and didn't hear any engine noise. But it was a car. It had to be a car. He thought about turning on his own lights, but knew that'd kill any surprise and then . . .

Oh, fuck. The lights were even bigger! He heard the sound of rubber rotating over concrete. The speed of the car increased and the lights grew and they blinded him as the car blew by, shot straight toward the door of the office building, but never veered right toward the exit. Instead, the car kept going until it crashed into the building itself—glass breaking, metal bending, bits of concrete spitting across the garage.

Lopes stared into the darkness. The cops would be there soon. Someone had to have heard the crash. Maybe somebody at the top of the ramp had backed into the space, just like he'd done with the SUV. Maybe a parking brake simply wore out. Maybe . . .

Lopes pushed the door open, slipped his left leg out of the SUV. Steam filled the air as the urine from the floorboard mixed with the cold air from the garage. He balanced himself on the concrete, pulled his right leg out and stood behind the open car door.

There was still no overhead light in the garage. The only noise was his breathing and the pounding in his ears. He stood behind the door, stared at the red glare from the wrecked car's taillights. He knew he should get back in the SUV and just drive away. He didn't need to stop for anything, didn't need to show up at court on Monday and, for Christ's sake, he didn't need to testify about anything!

One word exploded in his head like he'd stepped on a land mine: Go!

His hand shook as he drew the Glock toward his chest. He took one step forward, then stopped. Where was that crack in the cement? Go! Go!

He stepped around the driver's door, felt his left foot start to slip but then it caught on the frozen cement. He thought about crouching, but his knees wouldn't let him and he was caught in place, not sure whether to move forward or get back in the car. Go! Go!

He peered around in the darkness, looked for any sign of movement. He heard his breathing, again, as he spun, looked behind him, then spun again and saw the glow of the brake lights staring at him like embers in a fire. Go! Go! Go!

Lopes stared at the wreck, realized he couldn't move toward it. This was all a mistake. He was retiring! The past was the past! They didn't need him to nail any coffins. He took a deep breath, put the Glock in his pocket and turned back toward the SUV.

The voice came out of the darkness like the low, guttural rumble of the elevated train.

"Hello, Henry."

9:45 P.M.

The booze wore off. Martin stared at her fully clothed body, down comforter pulled up to her waist. She'd overheat in the night, probably strip. He thought about slipping her clothes off, thought better of it. He hated her for underestimating him.

He stood in the doorway, watched as her arm slid from a pillow, heard the headboard creek. Her breath was soft, rhythmic.

He'd played it well. Awkward, bordering on nervous at the restaurant. Once they'd hit his place, he'd deflected intimacy by talking shop. She responded with questions meant to provoke. *Why had he pulled back surveillance? Why was the cop at the Costa murder scene? Had he spent time going over the chronology of the case?* The final one had been the only question for which he provided an answer that she seemed to accept. He felt secluded, men were no longer under his direction so he had nothing to do but prepare for the trial.

"It is what it is," she'd said. Meaning: There is nothing but this trial for you, Martin Lowell, and you'd better not fuck it up.

He'd satisfied her without satisfying her. She'd fallen asleep on the couch, so he'd carried her to his room, placed her on his bed.

He stripped, went to the front room, stared out the window. He saw his own reflection: naked, sinewy, scrappy body. He leaned away from his bad knee, looked south, past the fountain, toward the river. Hotel lights on the south side of the river were lit. Traffic streamed on Lake Shore Drive. He sat down, did the butterfly stretch. The carpet scratched his nuts.

Martin spread his legs, leaned over his right leg and stretched. He smelled of booze and sweat. He touched the toes of his right foot, pulled them back toward him until he could feel his calf muscles stretched taut.

It was all so apparent now. The *body* guard. The mind fuck. The attention all on him. Winning was a shared experience. A loss got toe-tagged to one man—him.

He stared out the window, wished he could throw on his sweats and go for a jog. He'd head east, thread under the Drive, over the frozen sand and into Lake Michigan. The waves would slap him, cold would zap him and he'd settle at the bottom after the deep, dark descent.

10:00 P.M.

Wally sat up in bed, read from his laptop. Theresa curled up next to him, her plaid wool pajamas warmed his thigh. He sighed, leaned over and set the laptop on the nightstand. "Sorry, baby. I just don't feel like telling you about my day. Cop stuff. No need to bring both of us down." He thought for a moment. "Hey, I gave Romar the boards for the ramp."

"What'd he say?"

"Like usual. Not much. He said thanks. It's the little things, you know . . ."

Theresa wrapped an arm over his thigh, hung on like he was a lifeboat. "He's got a lot of stuff bottled up inside. So does Lou Lou. I've seen it with a lot of my students. They have so much inside that they're worried if they ever let any out, the dam will burst."

"You're probably right," said Wally. He pulled the covers up over his chest, reached over to turn off the lamp, but Theresa ran a hand over his stomach.

"Wallace, did you think any more about our conversation?"

"Not like I need to. Things just weren't right today. I got really busy."

"You're always busy. You need to devote time to it. You said you'd give it some serious thought."

"I will. I promise. I've got to work tomorrow." He looked down at Theresa, saw her big brown eyes filled with emotion. "I promise, baby. I'm gonna workout early tomorrow morning, then I've got some stuff to do for work. But, tomorrow night, we can talk about it. I swear."

"Okay. It's just that . . ."

"Te amo, Theresa."

Theresa looked up, smiled. "What did you say?"

"What I meant to say was, me alegro de que estés a mi esposa."

Theresa let out a startled laugh. She sat up, clapped her hands on his cheeks. "Wallace, have you been . . ."

"I've been studying Spanish. I bought this computer class."

Theresa kissed him full on the lips, laughed again, rolled onto her back and laughed louder. "When have you been doing this?"

"Some of the time when I told you I was working on my course book." He saw her brow furrow, so he said, "But not all the time. I'm getting 'em both done. Frankly, even though I wanted to win some points with you, Mrs. Greer, I also need to be able to understand your sister. It's getting to where she only speaks Spanish."

"I know," said Theresa. "You know, if I ever get that way, Wallace..."

Wally rolled on top of her, cut her off with a kiss. He lingered over her, brushed her hair from her face. He looked into her eyes, kissed her forehead, then the tip of her nose and, finally, her lips. He wrapped his arms around her as they kissed, pulled her toward him and ran a hand down her side and over her hip.

"Nothing's ever gonna happen to you, baby," he whispered into her ear. "Nothing."

10:30 P.M.

Lou Lou sat in her wheelchair, planted in front of the television. The tan carpet was worn from all of the times she'd pivoted on the same spot; the rubber from her wheels tore at the cheap material. She didn't even notice Romar as he passed her, set the two boards on either side of the track for the sliding glass door.

Romar walked past her again, took her winter coat from the closet and crept up behind her. He leaned down, rested his head on her shoulder. "Whatcha watching?"

Her attention never left the screen. "Disney Channel. I recorded it."

Romar reached down and gently took her right arm. He started to slip it inside the sleeve of her coat when she bolted upright. "What are you doing?" she asked.

"Going outside for a minute."

"Huh?"

"Look at the door. Wally made a kind of ramp so you can go out on the balcony without bending the tracks."

Lou Lou spun her chair, looked at the door as she leaned forward and Romar pulled her left arm back, directed it into the coat sleeve. "Wow! Oh, my gosh."

"He's gonna fasten 'em down next time he's here."

Romar strode past her, opened the sliding glass door and stepped out onto the small balcony. A cold wind made him shudder. He wore his usual night attire: a sweatshirt and gray workout shorts and a pair of flip flops. He bent down, kicked the board so it was flush against the track, then beckoned Lou Lou to join him.

Lou Lou pressed the control for her chair and it rolled forward, up and over the two boards and she made it onto the balcony with ease. "It's cold!" she screeched.

Romar kneeled down beside her and put his arm around her. "Look at the lights of the buildings," he said.

"I'm looking at you!" said Lou Lou, as she laughed, loud. "You're crazy! If you catch a cold, who is gonna take care of you?"

Romar smiled. "I'll be fine. We ain't stayin' out here long. I just wanted you to see the lights. This summer, we'll be able to see the fireworks from here."

"Cool!" said Lou Lou. Her teeth chattered. "Can we have a party?"

"Sure."

Romar looked out toward the lake, into the darkness. His mind was a whirl. He needed to tell her something, but wasn't sure how she'd respond. It was complicated. Like nearly everything involving the two of them. He glanced at her, saw the saliva gather at the corner of her mouth and reflexively he reached out and wiped it away.

"Thanks," said Lou Lou. "Are you okay out here?"

"Sure," said Romar, again.

"Can we stay one more minute?"

Romar looked at his niece, saw the flicker in her eyes. He reached out and touched her cheek. "That's cool," he said. "We got plenty of time."

11:15 P.M.

Albert Cordell woke with a start. He'd heard a noise—metal on marble. He lifted the lever on the leather recliner, sat upright. The empty glass was still in his left hand; he could still smell the scotch. He set the glass on the coffee table to his left, looked over toward the door. A piece of metal lay on the entryway floor. He stared at it, still half out of it from the liquor nap.

A voice sang, "Save big money . . ."

He turned, saw the television was still on, grabbed the remote control and turned it off halfway through the commercial. He looked back toward the entry way and watched as the door swung open.

"Easiest locks around," said Vitus Gorski as he entered the room. He seemed as casual as a man coming home from work, expecting a martini and peanuts before dinner. He set a blue bag on the floor and stepped into the living room. "Mind if I take my coat off?" he asked.

Cordell nodded. He felt his legs start to shake. He reached over, poured himself another glass of scotch, drained the entire glass and only spilled about a third of it down his chin.

Gorski folded his coat over the banister, walked past him and sat down on the couch. The big man leaned back, put his feet on the coffee table. "Why did you buy this townhouse?" he asked. "You got this tiny room on the first floor and have to take the stairs up for everything else. You got a refrigerator in the garage?"

"No," said Cordell.

Gorski looked to his left, toward the door to the garage. "And no pisser down here, either. You're watching a game, want a beer or gotta take a leak, you've got to go upstairs. Seems kinda stupid to me."

Cordell could barely think. Adrenaline shot through his body, made his legs weak and hands shake. What was happening? How could Gorski be sitting there, across from him, talking like they were old friends?

"What are you—?"

"Let's not go there tonight," said Gorski. He waved his hand, swatted away the question. He pulled his right arm from behind his back, revealed a silencer-equipped Glock. "Present from Henry. I gotta say, it's one of the few gifts I ever got that I really liked."

Cordell looked toward the glass, then back at Gorski.

"Go ahead," said Gorski. "But if that bottle leaves your hand and comes my direction, I'll squeeze this little trigger."

"I . . ." Cordell couldn't finish the sentence, leaned over, poured himself another glass of scotch. The scotch rolled over the sides of the glass before he stopped pouring. He lifted it toward his lips, spilled some in his lap. He gulped the rest from the glass, set the glass back on the coffee table and wiped at his damp suit pants.

"No coat or tie," said Gorski. "You look pretty relaxed. Must've figured it'd go okay."

"I had no choice," said Cordell. "He said no matter what, you'd kill my son."

"I told you if I got what I needed from you, I wouldn't do that," said Gorski. He sneered, looked offended. "Now, it remains to be seen. Where are they holding Frank?"

Cordell stammered. "I swear, I don't know. I was supposed to meet him tomorrow night but they canceled. That's why I . . . I just don't know. I swear on my mother's grave."

"Make it your son's grave."

Cordell leaned forward, rubbed his eyes with both hands. "Please, God. No. I can call them tomorrow, tell them—"

"There is no tomorrow for you."

Cordell jerked up, straight. "But—"

"Albert," said Gorski. "I don't really need your help. I know where he's at. But you can tell me *exactly* where they're holding him. I want the room number. Otherwise, I can figure things out on my own. I bet you didn't even know there was another staircase at that parking garage. You come in off the alley at Wabash . . . Christ, who am I talking to? A guy like you don't take the stairs."

Cordell tried to blink away the confusion. What the hell was he talking about? Stairs. And mother of God, he'd called him Albert. Desperation: "I know when you can get him. There's only one place, one time."

Gorski crossed his legs, rested the gun against his stomach and pointed the nozzle at Cordell. "I'm listening."

"Tomorrow—"

Gorski interrupted him, talked quiet. "Albert. Like I said, there is no tomorrow. Now, right now, you have to convince me you're telling the truth about where I can find Frank, or you'll die, knowing your son ain't far behind you. You make me believe you, you can die in peace."

The room spun; Cordell felt the scotch curdle in his stomach. He gulped air. He fought the dry heaves. Sweat poured off his brow. He covered his mouth with his right hand.

An automatic night light kicked on. Gorski didn't flinch. The ceiling fan turned, wheezed.

Albert Cordell told him . . . everything.

Sunday

6:15 A.M.

Elizabeth woke up, eyes to the ceiling. She'd undressed in the middle of the night; her clothes lay in a heap on the carpet next to her side of the bed. Martin slept next to her, on top of the comforter, dressed in sweatpants and a T-shirt. Quietly, she slipped her right leg out from underneath the sheet, got out of the bed and picked up her purse. Martin awoke as she hit the door. She turned and caught him staring at her as she left the room. She thought she heard him say, "Morning."

She walked down the hallway; her bare feet made almost no noise on the carpet. Just before she hit the front door, she turned to her right and entered the bathroom. She flicked the light, set her purse on the floor. She stood up, straight, didn't bother to check herself out in the full-length mirror—she knew she looked Erin Andrews–keyhole-good. Instead, she locked the door behind her, let the seat hit the toilet hard enough that Martin would hear back in the bedroom. She sat, leaned forward and took inventory. A tall rack, glass shelves full of white towels and *GQ* magazines. Toothpaste, dental floss, deodorant, shaving cream and a razor on the counter. Another white towel hung over the shower rod. She quietly peeled back the shower curtain: men's shampoo, a bar of soap and an expensive body wash.

Elizabeth flushed for effect, stood and opened the medicine cabinet. She touched, turned, lifted. Nothing, nothing and nothing. She gently closed the door, ran her eyes over every inch of the bathroom again.

She started to get nervous. It was feeling sketchy. He'd shot down her advances, but that hadn't surprised her. In fact, it played into her hunch. But, hunches without support were like weather predictions. Her career couldn't stand warm and sunny if it turned out to be cold and rainy.

She put her nose to the towel behind the door, breathed deeply. She shifted the magazines, looked behind. She opened the doors underneath the sink, squatted and rifled through the contents, tried not to scream in frustration. Shit, shit and shit.

Resigned, she turned to leave the bathroom when she noticed the green corner of something behind the can of shaving cream. She moved the can, looked at the square package. Facial wipes, cucumber and aloe. She smiled, took a plastic sandwich bag from her purse, used a square of tissue to lift the package of wipes, place it in the bag. She closed the bag, dropped it in her purse and went back to the bedroom.

A lie wasn't necessary; Martin was already up. He sat on the edge of the bed, laced his tennis shoes.

"I've got to take a run before work," he said. He stood up, walked to the window and opened the blinds and city light streamed into the room—sunrise was still half an hour away.

"We could've worked out under the sheets."

"Listen . . ." said Martin.

She pulled her panties up, sat back on the bed and waited for his act at fumbling.

"Last night was . . ."

"Was what?" asked Elizabeth. She pulled her black slacks up, over her knees, let them stop thigh high.

"Was what it was. Fun. But with the trial and all, I don't think—"

Elizabeth laughed, pulled up her slacks. She stood up, plucked her bra and sweater from the glass table near the bedroom windows, tossed the bra onto her purse and put on the sweater. "No, you don't think." She was all business. "There is no 'us' to worry about, so don't. Frankly,

I should be insulted. I've never stayed with a man who didn't at least try to screw me. I'd chock it up to an attempt at being a gentleman, but I don't think that's it." She sat back down and put on her shoes. "I think something's bothering you. But I also think you've come to the conclusion that whatever is bothering you isn't worth losing this trial over. So get your run in, prepare for the case and be ready for whatever comes your way."

She stood up, grabbed her purse and closed it, then exhaled, loud. "Now," she continued, "I'll grab my coat from the front room, you get me a stocking hat you won't miss since I didn't see a hairbrush in your bathroom and I'll walk out with you."

Martin didn't say a word, stepped behind her as she walked out of the bedroom. He opened the door to the walk-in closet, grabbed a dark blue stocking hat off the top shelf, closed the door and walked out into the front room.

Elizabeth finished buttoning her coat as he handed her the hat. She looked at it momentarily, then put it on her head. "Da Bears," she said as she tugged the hat down over her forehead, then folded it back up.

"You must be a real fan," said Martin as they walked out of the apartment.

"No," said Elizabeth. "Guess I'm just a morning person."

The elevator door was open when they stepped out into the hall and they didn't say a word as they took it to the ground floor. They walked through the lobby together and when they stepped outside, Elizabeth pulled her coat tight and Martin lifted the hood of his sweatshirt over his head, tied the drawstring under his chin.

"No cabs," said Martin. "Step back inside and the doorman will turn the cab light on for you. I'd wait with you, but I don't have much time before I have to get to the office."

She accepted the lie, didn't bother to question it. She'd been told his prep meeting was at nine and it wasn't yet seven. "Okay," she said. "I had a good time."

"Me, too," said Martin. "And tell them not to worry. I'll be fine at the trial." He leaned forward and kissed her on the cheek, then turned and jogged off.

Elizabeth watched him until he turned east, toward the Lake and disappeared. She felt his saliva freeze on her cheek. For just a moment, she wondered what it would be like for him if things went bad and she felt a flutter in her stomach. She squelched the feeling with a snort, turned around and walked back into the building.

7:08 A.M.

Wally did push-ups while Romar slipped a forty-five-pound plate onto the barbell to match the plate on the other side. When he finished his fiftieth push-up, Wally walked over, sat down on the weight bench, then lay back. He positioned each hand near the groove in the knurl, shoulder-width, then wrapped his hands around the barbell. He exhaled as he lifted the weights, took a deep breath as he lowered the bar to his chest. He exhaled again as he pressed the barbell until his elbows nearly locked, then lowered the bar toward his chest again and repeated the process. He completed fifteen repetitions, then set the barbell back onto the rack.

"No sight of Gorski, but no bodies, either," said Wally, continuing the conversation they'd started after they'd laughed at each other for both wearing blue Chicago Police Department T-shirts and gray workout shorts. "I told 'em that if there are any possible murder vics in the area that remotely match, to call me immediately. Last night it was two drive-bys on the South Side, three gang bangers on the West Side and a hit and run in the Loop—but the driver was Hispanic, so no Gorski."

Wally moved behind the weight rack, watched as Romar took his turn on the bench. Wally acted as a spotter as Romar warmed up with the barbell and two forty-five-pound weights—135 pounds. "I've been thinking," said Wally, watching the barbell move up and down in a quick, even motion. "Gorski's made his way downtown. From where we found the car yesterday in River North, he could camp out overnight and be almost anywhere downtown tomorrow. That's the only thing that makes sense to me. Maybe he just wants to get into a bank, like you said, or maybe he's waiting for the arraignment tomorrow and is gonna try to whack some witnesses."

Romar finished his reps, sat up and looked up at Wally. "I been thinking kinda the same thing. I'm wondering about witnesses. Remember that guy we went and saw, Henry Lopes?" Wally nodded, so Romar continued. "He said he'd been working two weeks straight. He made it seem like that was pretty unusual, and I'd say it is. That's something you do if you're going on vacation or something."

Wally walked over to a rack of weights and grabbed another forty-five-pound plate. Romar did the same and they slipped the plates onto either side of the barbell, pushed collars onto the bar until they fit snugly against each plate and then tightened them.

"So," continued Romar as Wally sat on the red leather bench. "I also know that's a valuable corner where his service station is sitting, especially 'cause there ain't no gas tanks there and there never was. I called a real estate guy I know and you know what? There's a closing scheduled for tomorrow at Chicago Title. Looks like somebody's fixing to leave town kind of soon."

Wally sat, transfixed. "You are turning out to be one hell of a detective, Detective Jones," he said, drawing out the *dee* in the rank.

Romar smiled. "Ain't you the guy that was giving me some grief for asking about the gas tanks and all?"

"Maybe I was," said Wally. "I've been known to be wrong before; check '84 and the Padres. I'm gonna go visit Francis Costa's wife today. Ron Melcher thinks the FBI's holding out on us. He thinks that whole thing about looking for Costa at his house the other day was a charade. I may run it up through Brooks, but I want to talk to the wife first. Maybe I can get something out of her."

"Okay," said Romar as he positioned himself behind the bar to stop Wally. "Wanna hit Lopes's place first, then Costa's?"

"No, let's split up," said Wally as he lay back and positioned his hands on the bar. "I've gotta fill out some paperwork from yesterday and I told Theresa I'd be home tonight. I want to get home early. We've got stuff to talk about and it may take a while."

Wally lifted the weights, completed five reps and re-racked the bar. He sat up, stretched his arms wide, then grabbed the crook of his left elbow and drew his bicep to his chest, then did the same with his right.

"You want to tell me what it's about, or is it like that thing with the girl at Butch's and you're gonna make me practice my detective skills?" asked Romar.

Wally ignored the rib, offered up a serious look. "Theresa wants to move her sister here."

Romar stood, silent, then said, "Man, that's something big to take on. With the Alzheimer's . . ."

"I know," said Wally. "But I can't blame her for wanting her sister nearby. It's just that I know how these things go. Once Theresa makes her mind up, she's full steam ahead. I've got to slow her down long enough to look at the insurance, check out the home . . . You know, it's a lot of stuff."

"It ain't just the clothes, today, man," said Romar as he waved Wally off the bench and sat down. "We got something else in common. I gotta tell Lou Lou something today, too." He didn't wait for Wally to ask. "Big Dog's coming home."

Wally got caught lost in thought. "You're getting her a dog?"

"No, man," said Romar. "My brother. Big Dog's coming home. His death sentence was commuted by Ryan, now they're telling us his DNA didn't match. They're saying he's innocent and letting him go. Not sure when, yet, but they say it's coming."

"Is that a good thing?"

Romar lay back on the bench, positioned his hands on the bar and looked up at Wally. "Man, he may not have killed that guy but he ain't innocent. He was a drug dealer. He ain't lived with us since I was ten years old. We just now got things going pretty good and the last thing I need is my brother coming 'round. I guess I'm glad he's getting out for his sake, but I don't want no part of him."

"He's not gonna live with you, is he?" asked Wally.

"Hell, no. But he's gonna want to see Lou Lou. He loved my sister and he's been writing to Lou Lou. I been keeping the letters. He's saying the right things but I know my brother—he always has something to say about everything. He's gonna have something to say about the way I'm raising her or what she's doing and I just don't have no time for that."

Romar did three reps, sat up, put his hands on his knees and rose. Wally watched him walk toward the rack of weights, was about to tell him to grab a twenty-five-pound plate when the door opened.

"Ladies," said Roscoe Barnes as he entered the room. He gestured around the room, which was empty save Wally and Romar. "What, you guys always wear the same Sunday-Go-to-Meeting clothes?"

Wally stared at Roscoe, shook his head. He was at a loss for words. Roscoe was breaking his balls for wearing the same T-shirt and shorts that Romar wore? Roscoe, breaking his balls, walking past him like he wasn't even standing there, lying back on the bench and lifting 225 pounds off the rack and starting to rattle off a set . . . while wearing a thermal undershirt, thermal underwear and those steel-toed work boots.

Wally looked at Romar, shook his head. "Guess he forgot to finish getting dressed."

"Blow me," said Roscoe as he exhaled, loud. He flung the barbell back onto the rack, sat up. "Stack 'em."

"Huh?" asked Romar.

"Put another forty-five on each side," said Roscoe. He stood up, walked over and grabbed a big plate.

"Two-twenty-five is your warm-up?" asked Wally. "You're gonna rip a pec."

Roscoe slipped a plate on one side of the bar while Romar slipped one on the other. "I did some heavy lifting before I left the locker room; I took a piss," said Roscoe. He laid back, gripped the bar and lowered the barbell to his chest. He quickly lifted it, repeated it four more times and re-racked the weights.

Wally stared at Roscoe, kind of ticked. The guy warmed up with 225, then ripped off a set of five at 315 pounds and it looked like it took no more effort than if the bar was empty.

"Stack 'em," said Roscoe.

"Huh?" said Romar, again.

"Four-oh-five," said Roscoe.

Wally and Romar loaded the bar, watched as Roscoe laid back down on the bench. Wally motioned Romar to stand on one side, while he spotted on the other side. Roscoe gripped the bar, took a deep breath and lifted it. He lowered it to his chest, then pushed it up. He lowered it again and lifted it. He lowered the bar for the third and fourth time and lifted it, but this time his arms trembled a bit before he locked his elbows. He held the weight in place for a second, then lowered the bar toward his chest again. Both Wally and Romar bent down, placed their hands near the bar, but Roscoe exhaled, loud, and slammed the bar up. He flung his hands back, re-racked the barbell and leaped to his feet. "Have a nice day, twinsies," he said as he left the room.

Wally stared after Roscoe, then turned and looked at Romar. They'd just seen a guy in thermal underwear and leather work boots bench press 405 pounds five times. Wally opened his eyes wide, shook his head from side to side.

"Did I just see that?" asked Wally.

"Man," said Romar. "I ain't never seen nothing like that. Guy in his underwear benching more weight than I can lift off the ground. He just ruined my day."

Wally stripped a forty-five pound plate off the bar. "He just ruined my year."

8:44 A.M.

Vitus Gorski lay on the bed, crossed one ankle over the other. The white terry cloth robe slipped open over his calf. He glanced out the window, which he'd just opened. Cold air rushed in, mixed with the smoke from his cigarette. He looked out at Soldier Field, dropped ash on the bed sheets, patted it out with his hand when the sheets smoldered.

Snow fell and he could barely see the stadium from the third floor of the townhome. He sighed, put out the cigarette on a pillow and rose. He hated to put back on his stinking clothes, but it was a necessary evil. He liked the sound of that, thought about how it would all end. The thought brought a smile to his face as he sat back on the bed, laced up his shoes.

Funny how the weirdest things made him smile, but the things that most people enjoyed, he simply observed. He'd first known it when he was just a kid. The other kids would get excited over a model airplane or a party at school. He'd see the model, study it, figure out how to put it together, but it never made him bounce around like the other kids. When they had parties, he just stood in the corner, watched, tried to figure out why everyone was so excited. After the fifth grade, he didn't have to worry about it anymore; he stopped going to school, worked for his uncle at the auto body shop. He had been big for his age, so no one ever questioned him. Christ, he was big for any age.

Over the years, he learned to fake a lot of it. Sure, he found things he liked, like big women and cigarettes, but for the most part, he just faked it. And that worked out pretty good, seeing how emotion could fuck a guy up in his line of work—like a boxer getting too amped up for a fight and wearing himself out in the first round. Like this thing with Frank—if he thought about it too much, it'd eat him alive.

Gorski walked down the stairs to the ground floor. Cordell still sat in the chair, but his face was starting to spot up, body going hard. Gorski walked over, picked up the body and threw it over his shoulder. *Ah, it wasn't so heavy—most people would've had trouble lifting it, but it was no different than lugging a couple of air hammers or a keg of beer.* He carried it to the door, twisted the knob and stepped into the cold, dark garage. He set Cordell down as he searched for the light switch, then the car keys. Then, he dragged the body over to the car, opened the trunk with one hand and dropped the body inside. "So long, asshole," he muttered. He thought about it for a moment, then put the car keys in his pocket. He shut the trunk and went back inside.

Gorski went back up the stairs to the second floor, walked into the kitchen. He made himself a bologna sandwich, ate it and washed it down with some of the coffee he'd made earlier in the morning. Funny, the things you could tell about a guy by looking in his kitchen. Like Cordell—bologna, bread, mustard and mayo in the fridge. Frozen dinners in the freezer. But a full bar with mixers and a humidor with good stogies. And two bags of ground Starbucks coffee on the counter. At least the guy had priorities.

He searched the cupboards, found a thermos and filled it with coffee. He took his coat from one of the chairs at the small kitchen table, put it on and walked back over to the stairs. He grabbed the rail, took his first step down and shifted as his foot hit the step. He was stiff from the cold and lack of a shower, but again, a guy had to have a plan and priorities. His legs ached as he walked back down the steps, hit the first floor and walked out the front door.

Lopes's SUV was already covered in snow and after Gorski set the thermos inside and wiped the windshield clean with the sleeve of his coat, he noted that he hadn't gotten a parking ticket. Lopes probably wouldn't be missed until the next morning and since he didn't have a sticker to park on the street, he figured it'd be smarter to take Lopes's SUV than Cordell's car. He climbed back into the SUV, closed the door and started the engine. He cranked the heat, took off his gloves and wrapped his hand around the thermos. One more night to go, he thought as he threw the gearshift into drive, pulled away. One more night and one place he knew would be empty. Not hard to figure out, either, since the owner's body was under a blanket in the back.

9:07 A.M.

The same windowless conference room. The director on the squawk box. Special Agent in Charge Darren Greene stared at the speaker-phone, gray hair matted, parted to the left, eyes devoid of emotion. Martin tried to read Greene, gave up when the man stifled a yawn with his fist.

"The arraignment is tomorrow, Special Agent Lowell," said Greene. "I'd say you are relieved of all other duties until the trial is over, but I'm aware of the paranoia creeping up on you, so I'll simply say that the trial and, specifically, your testimony, are the only duties for which you are responsible on a go forward basis. Are we clear?"

Martin's knee started to throb. He reached under the table, rubbed the kneecap with his fingertips. "Why have you had someone else interviewing Francis Costa?" asked Martin. "It's my case. I built it and now you're pushing me out."

"It's your testimony and your case," said Greene. "Denton believes your testimony should not be tainted by what you may or may not hear from Costa."

Martin leaned forward, spoke into the speakerphone. "I call bullshit, sir. You and Denton set me up with that Hughes woman. You need a scapegoat if this falls apart." He leaned back, gave 'em a moment to digest it. "Look, we all know what fell in our laps. It's impossible to mess this up. It's a slam dunk. This action? It's peripheral. Once the evidence is presented in court, Costa and the rest of the Outfit are done for good. I should be interviewing him myself." He tossed a hand in the air. "Christ, I've spent hours on wiretaps and now you don't want me to interview him?"

Greene looked at Martin, shook his head. "You are lax in your choice of language, Special Agent Lowell, I—"

The voice from the box cut him off. "I understand your point, Special Agent Lowell. I knew your father well. He carried the same paranoia and it was certainly justified. I give you my personal assurance that, should this trial end as we suspect, you will receive your just rewards. Should it not, your work will be reviewed like that of anyone else who failed."

The reference to his father gave Martin a jolt. For just a moment, he pictured the crew cut and horn-rim glasses over the youthful face. His father had never been paranoid. If he erred, it wasn't on the side of caution. He'd trusted. Martin vowed not to make that same mistake.

"I resent the implication," said Martin. "I've done my job and now it's up to the prosecution. If the prosecution fails to make its case, it won't be because we didn't arm them properly. Please note I said, 'we.' While I may say, sometimes, that this is my case, I fully understand that I'm just one cog in a machine. Win, lose or draw, it's a team effort."

A laugh cackled through the speakerphone. "The only way to prepare is to envision all possible outcomes, Martin. I applaud you for doing so. There are no veiled threats here. I simply want to make sure you understand the gravitas. This is an important case for the Bureau and that includes you. As a show of confidence, I'd like to give you something . . ."

Greene leaned across the table and handed Martin an unmarked manila envelope. Martin opened it, looked inside. At least two hundred pages of standard copy paper. Line after line of testimony typed in Times New Roman. Francis Costa's deposition in black and white.

The director's voice reeked of self-satisfaction. "Mr. Costa implicates police officers, politicians and has even claimed a source within the Bureau. But you won't find that name in those papers . . . yet. What do you think of that, Martin?"

Martin couldn't help himself, studied the pages while he spoke. "Regarding the police and politicians, this is Chicago, so nothing surprises me. I heard some of that on the wiretaps. In regard to his claim about the Bureau, I think he's bluffing. He needs to keep something to himself so you'll hold up your end of the bargain, play it out, so to speak."

"I'd have to agree," said Greene.

The director ignored Greene's comment. "As I said a moment ago," said the voice from the box, "the only way to prepare is to envision all possible outcomes. If Vitus Gorski killed all these people, Martin, you will be crucified for pulling back surveillance and thus aiding in his escape. You will, in effect, be considered culpable in all of the subsequent homicides. Have you thought about how you will handle that?"

Martin slipped the pages back inside the envelope, tied the clasp shut. The threat was no longer veiled, it was out there. The real question was, are you going to take responsibility for pulling back surveillance or will the spatter hit us all?

Martin rubbed his temples, leaned forward, spoke directly to the box. "You referenced my father earlier, sir, so I'd like to do the same. My father took us to a lake house when I was young. It wasn't anything fancy, but as you can attest, on Bureau pay, your vacation options are somewhat limited—"

"Yes, indeed," said the voice from the box.

Martin ignored Greene's "hurry up" look, continued: "One summer, my mother went out to the shed in the backyard to get our fishing poles and she got bitten by a rat. We had to take her to the hospital to get the wound cleaned and to make sure she was okay—"

"For God's sake, Special Agent Lowell," said Greene. "It's Sunday and we've got a busy—"

The director's voice was clipped. "Go on."

"So when we got home, my father studied that shed for a while and found out that the floor was really a false bottom. There was a good three-foot gap between the floor and the ground. It turns out that years before, when it would rain, water would seep into that shed, so the owner raised the floor. Visitors would leave their coolers and their fishing poles in the shed and it didn't take long for rats to start nesting there in that pseudo-crawlspace. My father found the hole in the floor but also three tiny holes around the bottom of the shed. He filled two of those holes with rags, then spilled a little gasoline into the hole in the floor and dropped a match inside."

"If that was a rental property," said Greene, "he could've just called the owner. The man probably would've done anything to stop from being sued."

"It wasn't as litigious a world back then," said Martin, with a smile. "His goal wasn't just to burn down that shed. He'd left that one hole open and before long, rats started streaming out."

"Your point?" said Greene as he tapped his fingers on the conference table.

"My father had soaked a twenty foot by twenty foot slice of the lawn in gasoline. When the rats came out of that shed, he lit the lawn. I don't know if you've ever seen a nest of rats, but it's made up of a lot of rats. So there were rats rushing out, others trying to rush back in and some just caught up in the commotion. And then the rats started screaming, literally, as they burned."

"Jesus," said Greene. "Disgusting. But I don't know . . ."

"Martin . . ." said the director.

Martin sighed. "They're all in the shed together, sir. The politicians, dirty cops, the crook within the Bureau, if there is one. They'll gnaw at each other and scream but in the end, they'll all burn. I'll incinerate them all."

9:28 A.M.

Vitus Gorski drove with one hand on the wheel, thermos between his legs. He turned on the wipers as the snow began to fall harder. The streets were icy and slick but he'd lived in Chicago his entire life, so driving on snow came easy. He kept his eyes on the road, fiddled with the radio.

He turned up the volume on the radio when he heard a deep, smoky voice say, "Let's take a break for the news. You're listening to the Sunday Morning Papers."

"Thanks, Rick," said the newscaster. "Chicago Police stated that the main suspect in the murder of a young River North woman, whose body was found yesterday, is the same man wanted in the slayings of a suburban woman, her young son, ex-husband and the brother of reputed Outfit leader Francis Costa and a policewoman. Detective Wallace Greer had this to say, late yesterday."

Another voice came on the radio. It was clipped and serious. "The suspect in these slayings is a Mr. Vitus Gorski. He is seventy-five years old with long gray hair. He's six feet five inches tall and weighs approximately 270 pounds, so he shouldn't be hard to spot. We've been tracking him and hope to have him in custody soon. He was last spotted in the River North area and is probably somewhere in the vicinity. He's considered armed and extremely danger-ous. The man is obviously deranged, but he's also been methodical in his planning. His picture is on our website and it's probably all over the Internet by now. If anyone sees Mr. Gorski, please dial 911 immediately."

The newscaster came back on, said that Gorski's picture was on the WGN website, too. But Gorski didn't listen. He turned off the radio, was about to slam his fist into the dash when he saw the smoke.

He glanced at the dashboard, saw the needle on the temperature gauge hover near the top. "Shit!" he muttered as he took a right turn. The wheels of the SUV spun in the snow, splashed slush into the oncoming lane. A truck passed him on his left, covered his windshield in sludge as it moved back into his lane. Gorski beat his fist on the dash until he looked to the left, over his rearview mirror and saw the sign for the service station.

Smoke filled the SUV as he glided into the lot, turned off the engine. He got out of the vehicle, slammed the door and trudged toward the office.

Deranged. The fucking cop had called him deranged. A guy couldn't be deranged and have survived this long in the Outfit. No, he wasn't deranged. Just angry. Very fucking angry.

And it was time somebody paid.

11:15 A.M.

The detective's room hummed for a Sunday. Two First Watch dicks huddled in a corner, coffee and swizzle sticks chest high. Jerry Grunwald yacked on a phone—too loud and too long. The wind rattled windows; Gruns cradled the phone under his neck, pulled on a dark blue overcoat.

Wally sat behind his desk. Romar leaned against it, faced Wally. The desk was covered in papers; a computer sat in the middle. A framed picture of Theresa stood over the desk drawers. Wally cleaned his cell phone screen with a paper towel.

"There's a lot we don't know but a lot we do," said Wally. He and Romar had both showered and changed into sport coats, slacks and dress shirts. Wally's shirt was white, Romar's a light blue. Neither wore a tie. "So, it's Wednesday night. The FBI's pulled back surveillance. Maybe Gorski notices or maybe he doesn't. Heck, we don't know if he knew he was being watched or not. But Charles Dragone notices. He probably figures the FBI dropped surveillance because Gorski flew the coop. He decides to burglarize Gorski's place, but that doesn't work out too well for him."

Romar swung his left leg back and forth. "Why would he steal from him? He'd have known the guy was mobbed up."

"Remember those guys that got killed when they stole that Outfit guy's watches? How about the guys that robbed Accardo? Found 'em with their throats cut. These guys will rob anybody—even each other."

"So," said Romar, "you're saying it started on Wednesday night."

"Yep. Gorski catches Dragone and kills him. He can't figure out what's going on. He can't get hold of Costa, so he goes to his brother's house to find him—or to find out where he can find him. Something happens there and he kills the brother. I think Officer Rodriguez was a victim of wrong place and time. So, all of a sudden, Gorski's a man without a country."

Wally leaned forward, lifted a hand in the air and waved it like he was pointing directions. "Gorski steals Costa's car and starts driving. He knows he can't keep it because once the stuff hits the fan, that car's hot. So, he drives by that grocery store and thinks, 'Voilà!' He goes inside, picks out his victim and follows her home. As luck would have it, she's close by, so he takes the car back to the store, drops it and walks back to her home. At that point, he probably didn't plan on going anywhere else anytime soon."

"Keep going," said Romar. "You look like you're feeling it."

Wally nodded. "He kills Julie Patterson, then, when her son comes home, he kills him, too. The ex surprises him Friday morning and he runs him over in the driveway. We found the car at the train station and the conductor actually came to the station and identified Gorski from the train, so we know he took the train to Union Station. Then, he hung around the downtown area until he killed Ms. Lee. At that point, he's communicating with someone. He texts a picture of a red-headed kid to somebody. What was it, a threat? Target? Witness's son? Then, he takes the car from the garage, so we can probably assume he drove somewhere Saturday morning. We found the car there later that day. So, what do we know from that?"

"Not much," said Romar. "You're on such a roll, why don't you tell me?"

"Happy to." Wally reached into the air again, jabbed a finger as he talked. "He went from Lincolnwood to Edgebrook to the train to River North. He stayed one night in Edgebrook and one night in River North. He headed that way for a reason. He didn't try to skip town. He's communicating with someone. What we know is: He's got a plan."

"Well," said Romar. "You ain't telling me a lot. But I get what you're saying. This isn't random. The FBI's after him. We're after him and in all likelihood, since he killed the brother of the head of the Outfit, the mob's after him, too. And he ain't goin', he's stayin'. He picked those places 'cause he needed somewhere to stay until he does something.

And those poor people were like Officer Rodriguez—wrong place at the wrong time."

Wally tucked his phone into the right breast pocket of his sport coat. He ran the thumb and forefinger of his right hand over his eyebrows. "Cripes. When I hear you talk in generalities like that, I realize I did the same thing. We don't know a lot, do we, Detective Jones?"

"No, Principal. We don't. But we've got a feeling and we're starting to get closer. Maybe the Costa woman or Mr. Lopes can tell us why they think he's sticking around or what he's gonna do. We figure that out, we can stop him."

"I like your optimism," said Wally.

Gruns walked by, buttoning his overcoat. When he opened the door to go out, Roscoe Barnes strode in from the hall. Gruns slipped by him as Barnes entered the room, a round plastic container in his hands.

Roscoe walked over to his desk in the far corner, set the container on it, took off his coat and gloves and slopped them over his chair. He took the top off the container, then leaned forward and took a deep breath. "Aaah," he said.

"That ain't butter," said Romar as he looked at the container.

"No," said Roscoe as he pulled out something wrapped in aluminum foil. "My Ma made runzas, so I brought some in for you weekend warriors."

Wally looked at Roscoe, who wore brown corduroy pants and a black sweater. "I'm just glad you're dressed," said Wally.

"I thought I told you to blow me, Principal," said Roscoe. He tossed Wally one of the aluminum-foil wrapped runzas and Wally caught it in his lap. It was still hot and when Wally peeled back the foil, the aroma made his stomach growl.

"What's in it?" asked Wally.

Roscoe tossed one to Romar, too. "Ground beef, spices, cabbage, pepper. The shell's homemade bread. Try it. I can promise you, you'll be begging me for another one."

Wally and Romar looked at each other, shrugged their shoulders and took a bite out of their respective runzas. Wally's mouth began to water as he tasted the spicy beef and cabbage. "Holy cow, your mom can cook," he said between bites. "Sweet Jesus is that good."

Roscoe laughed. He tore the foil off one, took half of the runza in one bite. He walked over and handed Wally and Romar each another runza. "My ma's eighty-three and she still makes me lunch on Sunday. Hard to beat that, isn't it?"

"Hard to beat that," said Wally.

The three detectives ate their food in silence, washed it down with hot coffee. A few minutes later, Wally and Romar both stood, put on their winter coats and grabbed car keys.

"Where you heading?" asked Roscoe.

"I'm going to see Francis Costa's wife," said Wally. "Maybe she can give us a little perspective on what's going on."

Roscoe laughed, belched. "From what I hear, she gives great perspective on about everything. She's a nasty old cuss." He jerked his head toward Romar. "What about you?"

"Heading to see Henry Lopes. I've got a few questions for him."

"Ain't he the gas station guy?" asked Roscoe. "I read your report."

Wally saw Romar bite his tongue, knew he was thinking, You ain't read it so well. He never sold gas. Romar remained silent.

"You ought to take someone with you," said Wally. "You never know." Wally looked over at Roscoe. "Got time to take a quick trip with my partner?"

"Sorry," said Roscoe. He put his foot on his desk, pulled up his pant leg and yanked down the leg of thermal underwear. "They've got me canvassing the area around that Asian gal's building. I'll see if I can find someone else."

A voice startled Wally. A uniformed police officer had slipped in while they were talking and he hadn't noticed the man's presence. The cop was short and broad and had red hair. He wore a dark coat and black leather gloves.

"I'll go," said the cop. He noticed the stares, looked at Roscoe and said, "Kevin Hanratty. From the other night? I stopped by to say hello, Detective Barnes, but if I can help out, that'll work, too, eh?"

Roscoe's upper lip curled but he covered it with his hand, feigned rubbing his mustache. "Yeah," said Roscoe. "The kid's all right. In fact, he was with the FBI guy the other day, Lowell."

"That right?" asked Romar as he zipped up his coat. Hanratty nodded, so Romar said, "Cool. Let's go, man. I'll tell you what's up on the way."

Wally wadded up aluminum foil, tossed it in a wastepaper basket. He yelled to Romar as the door closed behind him and Hanratty, "Detective! I'll see you here in the morning for an early workout."

Romar nodded from the hallway and when the elevator door opened, he and Hanratty stepped inside and disappeared.

Wally turned back to Roscoe. "Tell your mom thanks for the lunch," he said. "And I don't want to see you in the gym in the morning. My ego can't take it."

1:32 P.M.

It took Wally nearly thirty minutes to drive the six and a half miles from the Area Five Police Headquarters on West Grand to River Forest. The heavy, wet snow blurred the windshield and his tires spun at every intersection. He left his seatbelt buckled until the Impala slid parallel and stopped at the curb. He buttoned his coat, slipped on his gloves and a blue stocking hat and got out of the car.

Wally walked around the only other car on the street—parked only a dozen yards from the Costa's driveway. He opened his coat, flashed his badge to the driver, buttoned his coat back up when the man nodded.

The driveway hadn't been shoveled and Wally's leather shoes slid from side to side, so he took baby steps until he reached the porch. He grabbed the black iron handrail, stepped onto the porch and knocked on the door. Moments later, the door opened and a short woman yipped at him like an angry poodle.

"Whaddaya want?"

Wally opened his coat, flashed his badge, again. "I'm Detective

Wallace Greer of the Chicago Police Department," he said. "Are you Mrs. Costa?"

A pink towel was wrapped around the woman's hair and she wore a baby blue terry cloth robe with a gold zipper. She pushed the zipper up toward the middle of her neck and shuddered. "Whaddaya want? It's freezing out there."

"I'm not with the Feds," said Wally, glancing over his shoulder at car near the driveway. He turned back to the woman and said, "Can I just come in for a moment? I need to talk to you and it's not about the charges against your husband. I want to talk to you about the man who killed Phillip Costa."

The woman's eyes narrowed but then she sighed and her shoulders fell. "Come on in. I'll give you five minutes." She stepped back and Wally entered the house. She closed the door behind him.

Wally stood on the small area rug just inside the door. The living room was off to his right and he saw a younger woman sitting on the couch. She had long, black hair and wore a brown robe and slippers. She nursed a baby and dead-eyed Wally. Her eyes said, Who gives a fuck?

"You can stand right there," said the older woman. "The snow'll melt on the rug. I'm Bernie Costa. Francis is my husband. Who killed Phillie?"

The room smelled like stale cigarettes and the old lady's face was leather and broken blood vessels. Her breath had a metallic smell to it and her hands shook at her sides.

Wally took off his gloves, put them in a coat pocket. "Look," he said. "We've got a lot of evidence that says Vitus Gorski killed a woman and her young son and ex-husband after he killed your brother-in-law and the police officer." He saw the woman's lips curl and he mistook it for scoffing so he said, "We've got a ton of evidence. I just need to find him before he hurts someone else."

"It was that scumbag," said Bernie Costa. "I knew it. Everybody else is in jail." Phlegm caught in her throat and gave her words the sound of sharp cackles, but her lungs were strong and her voice was loud. "I read about the woman and her kid in the papers. I felt sorry for them people. And we lost Phillie. He was a good man. But I don't know why you're here. I got no idea where Gorski is. If I did, I wouldn't let the G sit out front."

"I heard he and your husband were friends for a long time."

Bernie coughed. "Vitus Gorski wasn't my husband's friend. They were business associates. You don't have to like everybody you work with."

Wally gestured at the kitchen table, visible just beyond the living room. "Are you sure we can't sit down for a couple of minutes?"

"Don't let him in here!" yelled the woman on the couch. Wally glanced over at her and she sneered at him. "He's just acting nice. Where was he when Uncle Phillie was killed?"

Wally ignored her, looked down at Bernie. "I'm sorry about your brother-in-law," he said. He rubbed his chin as he felt the snow seep through his shoes and wet his socks. "But I can't figure out why Gorski would want to hurt him. After all, Gorski was friends with your husband."

"They weren't friends!" yelled Bernie. She shook her fist in the air. "I just told you. They were business associates. When Gorski came to pick up Francis, he had to wait in the car. We didn't invite him to the baby's christening," she said, gesturing at the baby nursing at the younger woman's breast. "It was a business relationship. And like all business relationships, when it's over, there are hard feelings—"

"Hard feelings?" said Wally. "The guy's murdered seven people. I'd say that was more than hard feelings." He took a deep breath, composed himself. "Listen, I talked with one of the police officers who was here Friday morning. He said it played out like some kind of charade. Like you knew they were coming . . ." Wally let it float in the air, watched for the woman's reaction.

Bernie shoved a thumb in her nose, scratched a nostril with her forefinger. She snorted. "For all I know, this place is bugged," she said.

Wally curled an eyebrow, looked at Bernie, then the woman on the couch. Both of 'em stared at him in silence. "Huh?" he said.

Bernie crossed through the living room, opened the drapes. The windows shuddered as the wind blew. Ice formed on the windowpanes. Bernie nodded out toward the street. "I can't jeopardize our deal," she said. "You want to know anything else, you can call our lawyer."

Wally stared at her, confused. "Call your lawyer? I just want to know why the Feds would come out here and make a big scene if they knew your husband wasn't here."

"She said you can call our lawyer," said the woman on the couch. When Wally looked at her, she set the baby on her knee, pulled her robe shut and tied the belt in a knot. "Grandma, get him Albert Cordell's number."

"You get it!" yelled Bernie. She crossed the room, stood next to Wally on the rug. "She sits on the couch all day, acting like feeding that kid takes a lot of effort."

"Grandma!" yelled the woman. She set the baby in the corner of the couch, got up and strode toward the dining room table, veered left. Wally heard drawers open.

"Like I said, Detective," said Bernie. "I can't jeopardize our deal. You'll have to call our lawyer." She stared at Wally like a bridge partner trying to send a signal and he stared back at her and all of a sudden found himself nodding.

"Okay," said Wally. "I'll call your lawyer. You're not gonna tell me what went on between your husband and Gorski or why Gorski would kill your brother-in-law, are you?"

Bernie shook her head. "I got nothing else to say."

Wally took out his wallet, reached in and extracted a business card. "Well, here's my card. Please call me if you think of anything you can tell me. All I'm trying to do is find this Gorski before he hurts someone else. You know," he said as he started to fidget. "I understand what you're saying. Or what you're not saying. But what I don't understand is why you're talking about Gorski's relationship with your husband like it's in the past. You said, 'were' business associates and 'worked' together."

The younger woman stomped toward him, pushed past her grandmother and handed Wally a yellow note with a name and phone number written in blue ink. He glanced at it, then put it in his pants pocket. "Thanks," he said.

"Those were just expressions," said Bernie Costa. "You know, it's hard to run a business from the pen." She took the towel from around her head and Wally saw that chunks of her white hair had been yanked out. He looked over at the younger woman, who sat down on the couch, picked up the baby and set it on her knee.

"I get it," said Wally. He buttoned his coat, put on his gloves. He opened the door and started to step out, but turned back as Bernie stepped up behind him and put a hand on the door. "But something ain't right here. Your brother-in-law got murdered, your husband is about to be indicted and you and your granddaughter are sitting around like you're waiting for your husband to come waltzing in from another day at the office. But when I ask you about your husband and Gorski, you kind of lose it. And you talk about 'em in the past tense. No, I get what you're telling me, Mrs. Costa. But it's the way you're telling it. It's like one of 'em died."

1:45 P.M.

Martin knew the case number by heart. He read the date, the first few lines: Deposition of Francis Antonio Costa. Location: Classified. Present: Raymond Denton, United States Attorney; Darren Greene, FBI Special Agent in Charge; Albert Cordell, Attorney at Law; Judith Maxon, Court Reporter. He flipped through the pages, cut to the chase.

```
DENTON:   For the purposes of this deposition, I'm
          going to ask you some general questions,
          then follow up with specifics later. I'll
          remind you that you've been sworn in.

COSTA:    I know.

DENTON:   You are the head of the Chicago criminal
          enterprise commonly known as "The Outfit,"
          correct?
```

COSTA: Yes.

DENTON: You are going to offer truthful testimony
          regarding the illegal activities of many
          known associates in return for . . .

Martin skipped ahead. Most of the testimony would support what
he'd already heard on the wire. He'd take his time, read it thoroughly,
later. He had to find the pertinent testimony, compare it to his memories, see how it would play out.

DENTON: Another known associate is Mr. Vitus Gorski,
          age seventy-five. Is that correct?

COSTA: Yeah, but I don't know how old he is.

DENTON: What is Mr. Gorski's role within your
          organization?

COSTA: He collects street tax.

DENTON: What is street tax?

COSTA: Insurance paid by a business owner to make
          sure his business operates okay.

DENTON: Charging and collecting street tax is an
          illegal activity. What else does Mr. Gorski
          do?

COSTA: He collects juice payments on loans, collects
          gambling losses. He managed a couple of
          porn shops.

DENTON: What else?

COSTA: He's an enforcer. Anyone gets out of line, Vitus takes care of 'em.

DENTON: Mr. Gorski's skills as an "enforcer" were particularly suitable for the tasks required by the Outfit, weren't they?

COSTA: He was good at his job. Some people don't have the stomach for that kind of work. Vitus was born for it.

DENTON: Mr. Costa, you will give sworn testimony here today that connects Mr. Gorski to eleven murders. Is that correct?

[CORDELL whispers to COSTA.]

COSTA: That's all I can remember.

DENTON: Mr. Costa, is it your opinion that Mr. Gorski knows nothing of our operation?

[CORDELL whispers to COSTA.]

DENTON: I asked for his opinion!

COSTA: He doesn't know anything.

DENTON: And what if he becomes unaware of your whereabouts?

COSTA: I've talked to the man every day for fifty-nine years. You better make him think anything but what's really going on.

DENTON: Because?

```
COSTA:    Because if he finds out what's really going
          on here, you'll have a shit storm on your
          hands.
```

Martin turned the pages over, stared at the wall of his office. A shit storm. Seven murders probably qualified. He wouldn't allow himself to think about the victims.

Who had brought up the idea to pull back surveillance on Costa and Gorski? He'd searched in vain the last two days, performed a Google Desktop search of all his documents and email. Nothing. Nada. Every trace had been erased.

The deposition brought it all back. Denton, Martin and Greene, they'd agreed that if they pulled back surveillance on Costa, they'd need to do the same with Gorski, so it would look like they'd treated them the same. No one could know they'd made a deal with Costa. The head of the mob turning on his own? It had to be the first time, ever.

Costa's wife and granddaughter were left at home to divert suspicion. Two FBI agents camped out in a bedroom upstairs. The brother's, Phillip's, family was in Mexico. The brother was supposed to have joined them. He claimed he wasn't part of the mob, refused protection.

Who came up with the idea? Who? Suddenly it came to him, verbatim:

```
DENTON:   Why can't we just leave the surveillance?
          We're the only ones that know he's not
          there.

GREENE:   If we're sitting outside his place but no
          one can get hold of him, it'll ring alarms.
          We need to make it look like he's just gone
          underground. Remember, we're talking about
          a short window here. Thoughts?

MARTIN:   Let's say we knew he'd picked up the
          surveillance and we didn't want to spook him
          enough to run. If we pull back surveillance
```

on the Costa home and a few others, it
will look like we simply made a tactical
decision.

DENTON: Others?! We can't afford that. We're rounding
them all up at once. We can pull back on
one other, maybe. Who is his closest ally?
Someone we can definitely say would have
spooked?

MARTIN: Lemo Brancata is his best friend. They have
lunch together every day.

DENTON: No. He's a low-level flunky. We need someone
higher up . . . Someone we could say we
definitely didn't want to lose . . .

MARTIN: How about Vitus Gorski?

Their faces were etched in his memory: Denton and Greene, eyes
gleaming. "Good, Martin. Good choice."

Good, Martin. Good choice. Email and corroborating documents
missing. Two against one. If it went down, so would he. His boss and
the state's attorney would trumpet that he'd made the decision to pull
back surveillance on Vitus Gorski.

He'd turned loose a killer.

Martin swatted the papers off his desk.

2:29 P.M.

Hanratty drove his squad car. Romar sat in the passenger seat, watched
the wind blow street signs. Bridges were ultra-slick and the River
looked frozen.

"Glad we didn't' have to take Lake Shore Drive," said Hanratty.

"Get stuck there and you're screwed." His thick red hair stood in all directions; his knit hat sat in his lap.

"We're supposed to get like thirteen inches," said Romar. "Some kinda record."

Wind pushed the car and Hanratty said, "Whoa!"

"What were you doing over here?" asked Romar.

"I met Roscoe the other night. Guy's a ball buster, but funnier 'an shit. Figured making friends with a detective can't hurt my career."

Romar tossed that around, puzzled on it. He looked at Hanratty, lifted an eyebrow. "So you drove out just to see him? You weren't doing anything else?"

Hanratty kept both hands on the steering wheel, shook his head. "No, no, no. I had a domestic violence call. Get this. Some yo smacked his old lady while he was driving. Their car got stuck in the snow and when he got out and tried to push it free, she ran him over then called it in. He's fifty-fifty. We found him in a snowdrift looking like Gumby. I cuffed her and brought her in. Figured I'd stop and see Roscoe."

Romar didn't say a word, looked at Hanratty while the guy laughed and muttered, "Some people." Romar sized him up: short on intellect and a short fuse. But, he'd help sell the serious angle to Lopes. He dressed the part: winter field jacket, cargo trousers and that knit hat.

Absentmindedly, Romar ran a hand over the Beretta at his side. "Listen man," he said. "Let me do the talking. This guy's a hard case."

"So what gives?" asked Hanratty. "Why are you so fired up on talking to him?"

"Man, we're trying to find this hit man, Vitus Gorski. You don't know where a man's at, where he's going, or what he's gonna do in a city of like ten million people? Like trying to find an ice cube in the snow. This Henry Lopes, he knows Gorski. We caught him lying about the last time he's seen him and I found out he's selling his lot and building tomorrow."

"You think he'll run?"

"I don't know, man. He's probably a cooperating witness. He's probably got some kind of deal. Wally got the original FBI press release and they was gonna pick him up. But they didn't. I'm gonna tell him how

Gorski killed that Asian girl on Friday night. That was less than a mile from here. Maybe that'll give him some incentive to help us."

Hanratty grinned. "You do the talking. You need any help with the incentive, let me know."

Romar stifled a sigh. "I don't think he's gonna get out of hand, man. But you never know."

"You never know," repeated Hanratty.

Romar saw the building from a distance, pointed at the single sign with red letters that read Auto Repair. He looked around as they entered the lot: a six-story redbrick office building to the west on the other side of Des Plaines, condos to the north. A two-story office building sat adjacent to the south and the lot was flanked to the east by another old office building. The streets were empty. Snow blew drifts as the wind howled. The city looked deserted.

Hanratty put on his knit hat, tugged it down over his ears, got out on the driver's side. Romar moved around the squad car, buttoned his coat as he walked. Wind and sleet stung his eyes. He felt the hair in his nostrils freeze. He pointed at the ground, kept pointing 'til Hanratty followed his gaze and saw the single set of tire tracks leading to the overhead garage door on the east end of the building.

Romar saw a set of footprints start in the middle of the lot, end at the front door. Another set of prints started just outside the garage door, heading north. The tracks smeared where the driver had opened the door, climbed back inside whatever vehicle he'd left in the lot, then driven inside once the overhead door had been raised. But the door was down and when Romar banged on it, nothing happened.

"Let's try the front door," said Romar. He pointed at the door under a red canopy and Hanratty followed him as he jogged toward it. When they reached the door, Romar was certain it would be locked, but to his surprise, it opened. A bell chimed as the door swung open and they entered the building.

The building was dark and when Romar reached for the light switch and flicked it, nothing happened. He looked at the counter and saw it was bare; the cash register had been removed. Damn, he thought. Man is closing tomorrow and didn't want to spend an extra penny on electricity. As if further proof was needed, he felt his wet cheeks begin to freeze.

"He's closed down," said Romar. His breath hung in the air and when Hanratty turned and looked back at him from the room beyond the convenience area, Romar remembered the heater that had been in the back room and for a moment he wished the electricity would come back on so he could turn on that heater.

His eyes adjusted to the darkness and Romar saw that the shelves of the store were empty. A sign lay on the floor and the beverage cooler door was wide open. He heard metal clang on concrete and he waved Hanratty toward the door to the garage.

Romar opened the door, stepped into the garage. Hanratty followed him. It wasn't as dark in the garage. Light came through the windows over the two overhead doors and Romar saw that there was an SUV up in the air on a rack, only a few feet off the floor. Its hood was open and a light hung over the engine. The floor was dirty, covered with spots of grease and oil and the beam from a flashlight ran over the filth and settled under the SUV, illuminating two work boots.

The roar of a generator echoed in the garage. "Mr. Lopes?" yelled Romar.

Nothing.

"Mr. Lopes?"

Whoever was under the vehicle didn't move and Romar wasn't sure they could hear him because he barely heard himself when he yelled. He stepped forward, kicked a boot. He picked up the flashlight off the floor and moved away from the lift.

Two gray pant legs suddenly appeared as the work boots slid out from under the car. The toes of the boots went straight up in the air and when the heels caught on the concrete and two knees lifted off the ground, Romar knew that the man working under the vehicle lay prone on an auto dolly. He expected the man to slide out from under the SUV, but when he didn't move, Romar called out again. "We're here for Mr. Lopes!" There was no response and Romar remembered the big Hispanic guy who had moved through the office the first time he'd met Lopes. The size of the boots had him guessing it would be that guy, 'cause they were just too big for Lopes. He remembered

Lopes talking to the guy, so he had to understand English. "Is Mr. Lopes here?"

There was no response but the figure started to move and Romar saw the man's thighs. Then the guy was out up to his waist and when Romar saw the huge hand wrapped around a wrench and the size of the man's arm, he started to take his gun out of the holster and he was glad he saw the hothead Hanratty do the same when he quickly glanced over his shoulder.

The man on the dolly pressed the hand with the wrench on the concrete floor and pulled himself out from underneath the vehicle. Romar trained the flashlight on the man, who pushed off the concrete and rose to a sitting position.

"What do you need?" asked the man, who had a full head of bushy gray hair.

Romar didn't respond. He was in shock. One second, a guy's sliding out from underneath a car on a lift and the next second, the guy they'd been looking for the past two days is sitting in front of him. And something was wrong. The guy should've been in a panic or at least startled, but he just sat there, poker-faced.

"It's Gorski!" yelled Romar. He lifted the Beretta in his right hand, took direct aim on Gorski's chest. "Do not move!" he screamed. "Do not move!"

Gorski didn't move, said, "I got no idea who you're talking about." He looked over his shoulder toward the SUV on the lift. "I got ID. Just let me—"

"Do not move!" screamed Romar, again. "Officer, get your handcuffs . . ."

Something was definitely wrong. The dead-eyed giant just stared at him, then Romar saw the man's eyes move over his shoulder. Romar took a step forward, turned his head slightly to say something to Hanratty, never taking his eyes off Gorski.

And that's when he felt the metal against the back of his skull.

The explosion sounded like a cannon in the garage. Romar fell to the floor. Blood splashed the concrete, Gorski's pants. As if on cue, the generator turned off.

"Fuck, fuck, fuck!" yelled Hanratty. "You stupid fuck! Look at what you made me do!"

Gorski stood up. He was huge. Hanratty stepped around Romar's body, pointed at Gorski. "What are you doing here?" he screamed. "What the fuck? You know *he*'s been working overtime to keep 'em off your tail. *He* is going to be pissed! What the fuck?"

"Who are you?" asked Gorski as he grabbed a greasy rag from under the SUV, wiped blood off his pants.

"I'm the guy who just saved your ass!" yelled Hanratty. He kept his SIG Sauer trained on Gorski, reached back and pulled another gun from the back of his pants. He emptied the magazine from the SIG Sauer, tossed the gun to Gorski. "There, now your prints are on it. Christ, what am I going to do?"

Hanratty paced, tried not to look at Romar's body. What the fuck, what the fuck, what the fuck? He looked at Gorski; the monster hadn't moved. "I work for the same guy you do," he yelled, pointing at Gorski, "If you think Francis Costa runs the Outfit, you're wrong! Oh, fuck," he muttered. "The only reason you are still alive is that we are all fucked if you don't kill Costa. Jesus. Fuck!"

Hanratty kept his gun trained on Gorski, ran to the other side of the room, unlocked the side door and kicked it. The door didn't budge, but when he slammed his shoulder into it, it opened. He left the door open and ran back over to Gorski.

"You have got to get out of here, now. I need to call this in. Do you know where they're holding Costa?"

"Yep," said Gorski. "The brother told me. The mouthpiece gave me the specifics."

"Good," said Hanratty. "Now get out of here." He pointed to the side door.

"I need the SUV," said Gorski. He sneered. "I can't walk from here. There's nobody on the streets today. They're bound to pick me up."

"You blew that!" yelled Hanratty. "There's one set of tire tracks coming into the garage. There can't be one coming out. If someone saw me come in, or if they see you drive out, I'm fucked. And I will not be fucked for you! Wherever it is you have to go, you can get there by walking or taking a train or a cab. But you are not leaving in that vehicle."

Gorski stared at him. He just shook his head, then said, softly, "You go ahead and leave. I'll get my coat and slip out that side door. That way, if somebody sees me leave, they'll see you heading back to your car. You can say I must've been hiding or something."

"Yeah," said Hanratty. He motioned for Gorski to step away from the vehicle. He walked over, pulled the passenger door open and looked inside. He saw the blue bag and yanked it free. He glanced inside, saw the guns and tucked the bag under his arm.

"Planning on using one of these on me?" he asked. He motioned Gorski back toward the SUV, stepped backward and stopped when he felt his hip against the door to the convenience area. "You can start walking toward that door, now. You're gonna have to figure out how to kill Costa because you're not getting these guns."

Gorski shrugged his shoulders like, So be it, and Hanratty slipped back through the shop and out the front door. He looked around, didn't see anyone, so he ran through the snowstorm to the squad car. He opened the trunk, threw the bag inside and slammed the lid shut, then raced around the car, yanked open the driver's door and jumped into the front seat.

Hanratty's hands trembled as he slipped the gun between his legs. Think, think, think. What to do? What to do?

He stared at his radio, and instead reached into his coat pocket, pulled out his cell phone and dialed. He cupped the phone to his right ear, listened to it ring as he looked across the lot, tried to make sense of all the footprints in the snow. How would they see it? Could anyone tell he'd gone in, then out? He'd have to go back in, mess up the tracks.

He heard a loud noise and when he looked to his left, he saw the overhead door open and Gorski step outside. Gorski wore a heavy black coat, but no gloves and he walked straight toward the squad car.

What the fuck? What was the giant doing?

Hanratty felt his blood begin to boil. He dropped his cell phone in the passenger seat, ignored the voice that said, "Hello?" He looked out at Gorski, thought about plugging him, then thought about the hell he'd have to pay if they knew he'd killed him.

When Gorski got about five feet from the squad car, Hanratty rolled down the window, stifled a yell and said, "What the fuck?"

Gorski stepped forward, opened his hand. There was something inside it. It looked like a handful of ice chips but Gorski threw it in his face. The shards caught in his eyes and he screamed. Oh, my God! Jesus, the pain! He flailed at his eyes with his palms, tried to rub the stuff out of his eyes, but blood and tears covered his cheeks and hands. Then he felt the hand on his waist, then in his lap. He tore his hands from his eyes, grabbed the huge arm in his lap, tried to yank it away, but the arm went rigid. He felt the muscles in Gorski's arms flex as the monster's hand wrapped around the gun and the arm broke free and Hanratty felt himself scrambling, kicking, frantically trying to get to the other side of the car and out the passenger door. But a voice cut through the howling wind, cut off Hanratty's scream.

"You forgot to say goodbye."

2:54 P.M.

Wally drove, lost in thought. It hadn't gone that bad with the old lady. She'd said that the business between her husband and Gorski was over. She'd told him she couldn't risk their deal—flat out told him they *had* a deal. One of the few reasons anyone ever got a deal was in return for testimony so now it was all starting to make sense. If Costa was set to testify against Gorski or any of the others, it wouldn't be all that surprising if Gorski wanted to find and kill him. But the other victims? That was beyond reason. But, for guys like Gorski, there didn't need to be any reason.

His watch read a bit before 3 p.m., so Wally figured he had time to stop at Butch's for a beer. He needed to think about how his conversation with Theresa would go, play it all out in his head, predict her questions and plan his answers. Moving her sister to Chicago was something that required thought and commitment. He doubted his brother-in-law would go along with it, but he also knew Theresa—she wouldn't give up until her sister was there.

Time. Theresa's sister, Maria, would require time and he didn't feel like he had much to spare. His job wasn't an eight-to-fiver, nor was it five days a week. No, working as a homicide detective was a calling and once you were in, you were on call 24/7. On top of that, he was finishing his book on homicide investigation, with the goal of using it to teach a course that summer. And Theresa? She taught at Anixter Center five days a week and spent a couple evenings each week with Lou Lou. If he was short on time, Theresa was flat out of it.

Wally turned off the Drive, cruised south until he hit Division and headed west. He idled at a stoplight. Snow blew across the intersection like tumbleweeds in a deserted Wild West town.

Commitment. Maria would need commitment. There was no "getting better" but there was sure going to be a lot of "getting worse." He remembered visiting his grandfather on the farm—the old man going from pulling weeds to eating them. His mind had gone quickly, and although his grandfather had been a lot older than Maria, Wally had read that early onset Alzheimer's was quicker and more savage than what people used to call senility.

Time and commitment. How much would Theresa want? His wife was like him—all in or all out. If she was tortured thinking of her sister languishing at home, literally babysat by a teenager while her husband was at work, how would Theresa act if her sister was nearby? She'd want to spend time at the assisted living home or bring her sister to their place for the weekends. And while he was glad to help, thrilled that he'd married such a kind woman, he was also a realist. It was going to be a drain on his time, their time. But, there was no turning back. Theresa was committed, so he'd have to commit. They'd just have to figure it out.

The light turned green. Wally stepped on the gas, moved forward. He saw the sign, Butch's was on his right, when he heard the call on the radio: "10-1, officer down. Patrolman on site, no apparent suspects visible. Ambulances on the way."

He gripped the wheel, hit the gas. The tires spun as he shot west on Division. When he turned south on Clybourn, the car slid through the intersection, nearly crashed. He'd heard the address, but now it echoed loud and clear.

The address in the call, where an officer was down, was Henry

Lopes's place. Henry Lopes—the man Romar had been on his way to see.

Romar.

Wally pushed the gas pedal toward the floor.

Please, God, no. Please, no.

The speedometer hit seventy-five.

Not again.

2:59 P.M.

Vitus Gorski went west on Congress. He drove like an old man, but he had to do it. If he got pulled over for speeding or some stupid maneuver it would be all over. Then, again, in Chicago, you practically had to drive through a building to get a ticket.

Some asshole cut him off; he fought the urge to force him off the road. Easy, easy. No time to lose it. He had one shot at Frank and all it required was a cold night and some careful planning. He calmed himself, thought about the last few minutes: No loss leaving the guns—that fucking guy across the street had screamed when he shot the cop, forced him to forget about looking for the bag, hustle back into the garage, get the SUV and drive. The bag was gone and he'd emptied that dirty cop's other gun into the cop's head. That gun had gone out the window a couple of minutes ago. No, no, no. Relax. It was all going fine. By the next morning, Frank would be dead and then he could leave. Now, it was gonna be a long, cold night in the same stinking clothes he'd worn for days. But, it would be worth it. It would most fucking definitely be worth it.

3:03 P.M.

Wally's legs shook like he'd stepped on a live wire. He slid into the car into the lot, stopped a few feet from the squad car at the perimeter.

Visibility was nil—they were a few flakes short of a whiteout—and when Wally scanned the lot, he saw the other police car, a uniformed cop and not much else.

The car door nearly blew shut when Wally opened it, but when he grabbed it, it wasn't to push it closed so much as to keep his balance. Adrenaline coursed through his body like he'd mainlined it. He half ran, half slid the twenty feet between his car and the squad car and when he made it there, the cop stopped him with a hand.

"Hold, on, sir. This is an active crime scene," said the cop. The hat and heavy coat hid the cop's age, but to Wally, he was just a kid. The cop's eyes darted and he held his hand in the air like he was waiting for Wally to give him permission to put it down.

Wally took out his badge. "I'm Detective Wallace Greer. This is now my crime scene!" He raced past the cop, toward the familiar sight of a white Ford Crown Vic with a light blue stripe and the words *Chicago Police* below the stripe in bold red letters. He stopped a foot shy of the car, peered in the open window and saw the body of Kevin Hanratty. Frozen streaks of blood slashed across the windshield. Hanratty's face and hair looked frozen. His mouth was wide open, as was his left eye.

Wally turned back toward the cop, who had stepped in behind him. "Where is Detective Jones?"

"Huh?" responded the cop. "Me and Mike were the first ones on the scene. There's no one else but you."

"What else have we got here, Officer?" yelled Wally. He turned to look at the building and saw that the overhead door to the garage was open. He squinted, but the blowing snow blocked his view of the interior of the garage.

"The location is secure, sir," said the cop. "There's another body in there." He turned and pointed toward the garage.

Wally rammed the cop's shoulder as he blew by him, raced for the garage. His feet slipped out from underneath him halfway there, but when he fell onto the snowy concrete, he ignored the pain in his knees, hoisted himself to his feet and ran inside.

The second uniformed cop was also young and he stood facing the street as Wally nearly careered into him. "Sir," yelled the cop, but Wally pushed him out of the way.

Wally stopped when he saw the pool of blood, crumpled body. It took him a moment to put it all together—the man lying on his stomach on the concrete, light blue shirttail exposed, gray pant legs straight, arms under the body. The skin of the neck and the hair on the portion of the head that remained told him all he needed to know and when recognition washed over him, he fell to his knees, out of breath.

"Oh, God. No. No. Romar! No. No. No." He leaned forward, reached for the body, but left his hand remained in the air, suspended with his disbelief. "No. Oh, God, partner. No."

Wally covered his face with his hands, heard his breath as he gulped cold air. He took his hands from his face and felt the moisture around his eyes begin to freeze. One of the young cops stepped up behind him, placed a hand on his shoulder and said something.

Wally didn't move. He tried to bark the orders, knew they came out like a long, dry scream: "Start a log. Start it with your names and badge numbers. I need yellow barrier tape at the lot lines and red barrier tape ten feet outside the deceased officer's car. Start a scene sup . . ."

He heard the cops talk to one another, then move. He stared at Romar. He wanted to fall on the body, hold him until he was alive again. It couldn't be. Just a few hours ago, they'd been eating and laughing. And now. Now. Oh, Jesus, this could not be happening. *It could not be happening.*

He heard the sirens. Tires slid on snow. Doors slammed. Voices grew near. He raised himself, stood and turned. As he walked through the garage, he heard it like a faint whisper. "Billy."

He said his brother's name, again, to himself as he stepped into the blinding snow.

3:20 P.M.

"Take the Ike," said Vitus Gorski.

The cabdriver didn't give him a glance. It was a common place for a pickup; the guy couldn't care less about another old man driving from the backseat. It was risky, but the only other way would've been on the Red Line and quick math showed the cab was the way to go.

They drove in silence for fifteen minutes, got off at Congress. "Take Lower Wacker over to Randolph and Wells," said Gorski. Again, the driver nodded, didn't speak.

A few minutes later, they exited Lower Wacker, took Post Place south, then turned right on Franklin. Gorski gave the guy a twenty, told him to keep the extra buck. The man snorted and Gorski slammed the door when he exited.

Gorski stood in front of the entrance to the office building until the cab pulled away, then walked south back to Lake, took a left, then went north on Post Place. When he got to Lower Wacker Drive, he cut behind a straight truck, walked past the first few docks, fought the stiffness in his legs. It didn't take much searching and when he saw it, he walked over to the dock, grabbed the metal rail and put one foot on the concrete step.

His legs ached as he took the steps, one at a time. When he stood on the dock, he gathered himself, waited to get his balance. He'd run out of medicine the day before so when it came to keeping his balance, he was on his own.

Gorski shrugged at the thought. He was always on his own. Frank had only reinforced it. That motherfucker had . . .

The sound of a diesel engine snapped him back. Air brakes hissed. He took a deep breath, fought off the thought and looked across the dock. Nothing. He walked over to two Dumpsters that stood, nearly side-by-side, saw the cardboard and tattered green blanket and breathed a sigh of relief. The blanket was wadded up and rested near one Dumpster, so Gorski shuffled around, sat down between the two Dumpsters. The concrete was cold and he smelled himself and he thought that he'd give his left foot for that thermos of coffee. But then, he thought of Frank and popping his eyes out and the thought comforted him, made the shit more tolerable. He pulled his legs toward his chest, leaned back into the Dumpster. The position hurt like hell, his knees were too swollen. So, he stood up, took two plastic bags full of trash from one of the Dumpsters, sat back down and pulled them around him.

It was gonna be one long fucking night.

3:27 P.M.

Wally stood by his car, arms pulled to his chest. He knew he had to fight off shock. He'd learned it early: The mind is a file cabinet. It stores things in different drawers. He closed the drawer on emotion. It was time to think like a detective.

A crime scene didn't stagnate. It constantly evolved. The snow provided clues and its state was changing, deteriorating. He was glad to see Fred Pence already on the scene, camera in hand, snapping photographs. Time was their enemy.

Wally stared at the snow, tried to make sense.

Reverse chronology: Fresh tire tracks in the snow from the first responders' vehicle. Two sets of footprints from their vehicle—one set led to the garage, the other to Hanratty's squad car. Only one set returned to their vehicle, the one from Hanratty's car. Mike must've stayed in the garage with Romar's body.

The remaining tracks weren't as distinct. Snow blew, blurred. The clearest set came out of the building from near the entrance to the convenience shop. It looked like two sets went from Hanratty's car into the shop, but only the one set returned. That set went around back, toward the street, circled the car, then ended near the driver's side door.

Next, there were faint tire tracks leading into the garage and a more recent set out from the garage and into the street. One set of footprints led from the clearest spot in the lot (where the vehicle must have sat) to the garage, then near the building toward the convenience shop entrance. Another set led straight from the garage to Hanratty's car and back to the garage.

Footprints in snow: Heels leave a smaller track than the base of the foot, toe of the shoe. That showed direction. But it could be wrong—all wrong. Wind pushed the snow around, whipped it through the air, turned distinct prints into faint hopes. They weren't footprints so much as paths.

Still . . . It looked like: Someone drove a car into the shop (Henry Lopes?). Then, Romar and Hanratty showed. They entered through the convenience shop. They'd been surprised. Someone shot Romar. Hanratty had gone back out. Through the convenience shop? It didn't make sense. Had Hanratty been behind Romar, run out when Romar was shot? Had the killer run out through the garage?

No. If the garage door had been open, Romar and Hanratty wouldn't have gone in through the convenience shop. They'd have entered through the garage. But they didn't enter through the garage; their footprints were still visible leading from their car to the door of the shop. So, why? What happened?

Wally stared at the footprints in the snow, tried to see the picture through the tracks. He followed the freshest set from the shop to the back of the squad car. The tracks went around the passenger side, stopped at the rear of the car, where snow had been pushed around like it had been shoveled away. Then, they led back to the driver's-side door. *Someone had left the building, gone to the car and accessed the trunk. But why? For what?*

Wally looked at the group of cops standing to his left, deference offered in their stances. He waved at Delia Grant, motioned for the others to get to work. Delia strode up beside him.

"Glad you got your gloves on already. I need you to lean inside the officer's squad car and pop the trunk. I'm too big and awkward. Can you do that without violating the scene?"

Wally watched her nod and when he turned and walked back to the car, she followed him. When they got to the car, she leaned through the open driver's-side window, craned her neck around the steering wheel and reached inside. Wally saw her reach under the A.M./F.M. radio knob and hit the trunk release button.

Wally turned, started to walk toward the back of the car, thought better of it. "Freddie," he yelled, looking at Fred Pence. "You get pics of the snow around here?"

"Yeah!" yelled Pence. "Got the entire lot. I'm heading inside."

Wally turned back to Delia. "Someone opened that trunk. Let's see why."

Wally walked to the back of the car. The trunk had been released, but hadn't popped open—it was frozen in place. He slipped a gloved hand under the trunk lid, lifted it free and when the lid sprang high, he gasped.

Wally glared at the blue bag, nudged it with his glove so that the writing was clearly visible. He read it out loud. "Lindbergh Hardware." Delia stared at him, uncomprehending. Wally looked past her, toward the garage where his partner lay, dead. "Gorski," he muttered. "It's Vitus Gorski."

5:01 P.M.

Portable lights had been set up. The lot glowed. Chicago's Finest worked the crime scene. The lot was swarming with cops. They lined the perimeter, refused to let news crews anywhere near. Delia Grant had crime lab technicians working Hanratty's car, the garage, lot. Fred Pence took pictures from every angle, of everyone and everything. Nothing at the crime scene would go unnoticed.

Roscoe Barnes had gone bat-shit, yelled 'til his lungs hurt. His rage made the storm seem mild. The other detectives scattered when Roscoe hit the lot—they canvassed the neighborhood, interviewed the man who'd called it in and per the man's comments, searched the streets for a black SUV. Roscoe had taken a post next to Wally until Wally had assured him he was okay, convinced him to lead the search for the SUV. "I should've been with him," Roscoe had muttered as he left. Wally nodded, shared the thought, grief. If only . . .

Delia Grant corralled Wally in the lot. She wore a parka and gloves, but her face was beet red. Snot ran from her nose and she wiped it away with the sleeve of her coat. Her teeth chattered.

"Let's go inside," said Wally. He looked past her, dreaded heading back into the garage.

"No," said Delia. "I need to tell you something alone."

Wally motioned toward his car. He used the remote starter and when they slipped inside, the heater was already blowing. Wally sat in the driver's seat, Delia in the passenger seat. He slipped off his gloves, rested his hand on the laptop that sat where the arm rest would've been in a regular car.

"You okay?" asked Delia.

Wally turned to look at her. At the moment, the lines around her eyes and mouth made her look twenty years older than her forty years. The rims of her eyes were raw and Wally figured she'd taken a few moments and cried. He could relate. The palms of his gloves were sopped. "No," said Wally. "I'm far from okay. But someone's got to do this."

"Uh huh," said Delia. She held her hands in front of the heater, closed her eyes. "Principal, I've got to tell you something. I've been thinking. I know that's a dangerous habit to get into . . ." She smiled, tried to lighten the situation, but realized it was fruitless. She spit it out. "The shells on the scene are from two different weapons."

"And," said Wally.

"I found a .40 caliber cartridge in the garage. Whoever shot Romar didn't bother to look for it. Then, we found a smaller cartridge in the squad car, probably .32 caliber. That's the kind of shell casing you find from a smaller weapon, like a Tomcat."

"Okay," said Wally. He knew he was missing something. He thought about what she said. Something about two different bullet sizes. Two different guns. "Did he get Romar's weapon?"

"No," said Delia. She twisted in the seat, stared at Wally. "That's just it. We found his Beretta under the lift. The lift was set down on it."

"So, the lift was in the air when he was shot?"

"No doubt about it. You couldn't wedge it underneath. It probably slid over there when he was shot and then the lift was set down on it afterward."

"Jesus."

"But, Wally. That's not the most important thing. Romar was shot with a gun that fires .40 caliber bullets. Hanratty was shot with a pocket pistol. Romar's weapon was never fired and the Tomcat is missing. Something's not adding up. One bad guy and two good guys and the good guys are shot with two different guns . . ."

Wally covered his eyes with his hands, rubbed his forehead. The skin on his face burned. "Delia," he said. "What size cartridge does a SIG Sauer take?"

"Depends what kind. 9 millimeter, 357, .40 caliber . . ."

It hit Wally full force: Romar shot from behind. The single set of tracks from the shop to the trunk of the car. The blue bag. Hanratty shot in the car. "Jesus, almighty," said Wally.

"What?" asked Delia.

It couldn't be. A cop shot Romar? Just couldn't be. Wally rubbed his eyes, cracked his knuckles and stared through the windshield into the snowstorm. He had to gnaw on it, digest it. It wasn't something a guy just threw out there. He had to be certain. But he remembered, distinctly, seeing Hanratty's gun when he had entered the station earlier that day: a SIG Sauer.

"Wally? Wally?"

"Jesus, Delia," he whispered. "What's happening here?"

Delia reached over, touched his arm. "What? What are you thinking?"

Wally gathered himself, sat up and took a deep breath. "I think you'd better do a gunshot residue test on Hanratty."

"I was thinking the same thing. But Wally, how could . . . ?"

Wally raised an eyebrow. "Perform the test. The evidence is going to tell us what happened." He reached into the pocket inside his coat and took out his cell phone. "I'll check back with you soon. But, right now, I'd better call my wife. I don't want her finding out some other way. She and Romar—"

"Oh, shit," said Delia. "I'm so sorry." She zipped up her coat, pulled on her gloves, dropped her gaze. "I'm here 'til we're done."

"Thanks," said Wally as Delia got out the passenger door. She turned and looked back at him before she crossed the lot, walked back into the garage.

Wally held the cell phone in the palm of his hand, punched in the phone number with his thumb. When he heard it start to ring, he lifted it to his ear.

"Hey, hon!" said Theresa when she answered. "Are you on your way home?"

"Theresa," he stammered. He tried to speak but his voice betrayed him. "Honey . . ."

"Wallace?" said Theresa. "What's wrong, honey?" Her voice shot high. "Wallace, are you okay?"

"Babe, it's Romar. He was shot. He's gone . . ."

He couldn't complete the sentence. Her scream came through like she was in the seat Delia had just vacated, and it was all Wally could do to keep it together. Her words were jumbled and came gushing out, and he let her go on for what seemed like an eternity before he interrupted. "Babe," he said. "Babe, I need you to go to Lou Lou. The department will send someone over but she can't be alone. She needs you there. I'd go but I can't."

Wally held the phone in his lap, listened to Theresa sob. She screamed his name until she was short of breath, gulped for air. "Wallace!" she yelled. "Wallace! Just come home. Come home, Wallace. Come home!"

He stared at the phone, unable to speak. He wanted to rush home to her, hold her in his arms and cry until his body was dry. But there was work to do. Someone had to do it and that someone was him. It was his job. His calling. And tonight, it called.

"Wallace! Come home! Wallace, please. Please, come home!"

He raised the phone, again, took a deep breath.

"I can't."

6:00 P.M.

"I hope this makes you happy baby. You've been so distant lately. You know, with this thing coming up, we won't have a lot of time together. Let's make it count. Maybe we should go to Lake Geneva for the weekend and snowmobile . . . I think I missed the turn . . . Jesus, I've got to turn around in someone's driveway. I think I just scared the shit out of some old man. Maybe he was growing medicinal weed . . . Ha, ha, ha. Okay. I'm here. I'll call you when we leave. I love you! Oh, I can't believe I left that on your phone. But it's true. I love you, Martin!"

There was a call on the other line. Martin let the message end, didn't want to risk losing it. He waited a moment, took the call.

"Hello."

"Martin." It was the director.

"I'm in my office, sir."

"This will do. The connection's fine. I wanted to call you personally. I just hung up with Deputy Superintendent Allen Yates of the Chicago Police Department. It appears Vitus Gorski has murdered two police officers."

"Oh, my God."

"They were going to interview a witness of ours, Henry Lopes. Is Mr. Lopes accounted for?"

Martin spat it: "How would I know. Greene pulled me off."

"Fair enough. Are you prepared for tomorrow?"

"Prepared? I have been and will be. I've lived this case. Christ, are our men looking for Gorski?"

He heard the director tap at computer keys. "Yes," said the director. "We're working with the CPD in preparation for tomorrow. They'll stake out the route to the courtroom as well as other known haunts, for lack of a better term. Their belief, at this point, is that Gorski is going to try to kill Francis Costa."

"Never happen. I can assure you of that. That will never happen."

The director said, "The CPD thinks he's after Francis Costa, but have you ever given any thought that he might be after you?"

Martin said, "No. He's not after me. I met him once. I ran into him at Al's Beef. He said, 'Excuse me, Special Agent,' then squirted mustard on my sleeve. Then, he said, 'I'm sorry, G.' He thinks I'm a peon."

The voice came through the cell phone, again. "Martin, is he coming for you?"

Martin hit end, waited until the phone number disappeared, then went back to his voice messages. He hit the symbol for the message to play, leaned back in his chair, closed his eyes and lifted the phone to his ear.

"I hope this makes you happy, baby . . ."

6:15 P.M.

Theresa sat in the front seat of her car, outside the apartment building.

She was still in shock; she wore sweats underneath her winter coat. She also wore flats; her feet were freezing cold. She stared at the steering wheel, wondered what she would say.

How do you tell a young girl that the only relative in her life that is there for her and loves her is dead? How do you tell anyone that? And how can you brace yourself for the scream, anguish? The loss. The unbearable loss.

Wallace. Pangs of guilt riddled her because he kept popping into her head. *Wallace.* She couldn't lose him. They'd been together nearly fifteen years and her plan didn't include anything that ended with "do us part." No, no, no. He had to come home.

Fifteen years ago: Humboldt Park for the Puerto Rican Day parade. She'd gone with her older sister. She saw him by one of the rides, talking to a group of kids. A big man in his uniform. Ruddy complexion, barrel chested, thick and powerful, but with a huge grin and eyes that laughed. He'd spotted her from a distance, followed her and her sister for half an hour—at a distance and with a knowing smile. When he'd finally worked up the courage to talk to her, he'd flirted like mad. He was kind of corny; she expected him to punctuate a sentence with "Gee willikers!" But he was nice, and there was something about him.

He'd introduced himself as Officer Wallace Greer. When she told him they were headed to a street festival, he offered them a ride. They accepted and rode with him and when she got out, he offered her his card. A week later, she called him. They went out. She told him about being beaten, raped. He told her about losing his girlfriend, his brother. They were *intimate* before they were intimate. Ten months later, they were married.

Fifteen years later and Theresa had never told him she'd left her car in Humboldt Park to take him up on his offer of a ride. There was something about him . . . Fifteen years later she sat in front of Lou Lou's apartment building. She wanted to get out, but she was afraid. She was afraid of losing Wallace. She was afraid that one day, someone would sit outside her house, afraid to come in and face her.

Theresa wiped a tear from her cheek. The wind whistled through the rusted hole in the passenger-side door of the car she'd never sell. A street lamp flickered. Headlights appeared in the rearview mirror; she saw the first squad car approach and park ten yards behind her.

Her flats slid across the icy pavement when Theresa got out of her car. She caught herself, regained her balance and started for the sidewalk. When she looked back at the squad car, she saw another and another fill in and park behind it. By the time she reached the revolving door, five Chicago Police cars had parked on the street, headlights on, motors running. A tall man got out of the passenger side of one of the cars and, as he approached her, she recognized Don Haskins.

"Theresa," said Haskins as he stepped over the curb, onto the sidewalk.

"Don. Are you here to . . . ?"

Haskins shook his head, absentmindedly stroked his mustache. "No," he said, softly. "We're here to take you home. Take your time with Lou Lou and when you're ready, we'll escort you."

Theresa felt her brow furrow. "Are we in danger, Don? Is something going on?"

"No," said Haskins. He reached over and put an arm around her, started to walk her toward the door. Two uniformed cops rushed past them. One got the door. The other entered, stood in the lobby, waited for Theresa and Haskins to enter the building. When they did, the two cops stood on either side of them as Theresa walked up to the guard's desk and asked to be buzzed in to see Lou Lou Jones.

The doorman's eyebrows rose as he picked up the phone, dialed, then asked who he should say was visiting.

"Theresa. Tell her I need to come up."

The doorman talked into the phone, then nodded at Theresa, pushed a button. When Theresa heard the buzzer and saw the door release, her stomach filled with acid. She felt her hands shake, so she stuffed them in her pockets.

"Are you . . . ?" she started to ask Don Haskins.

"Not unless you want me to," he said. "We'll wait right here and when you're ready, we can go."

"Are you sure we're safe? You're not here for our protection?"

"No," said Haskins. He smiled, soft. "No," he said, again. "This is for family, Theresa. She's family."

Theresa turned so he wouldn't see her eyes well with tears. She looked out through the glass lobby walls, saw the headlights from the cop cars, lined up, waiting. She imagined them leading her, two in front of her car, two behind, as they wound their way across Ohio Street, slid north, then drove west on Ontario. It would be like a funeral procession. And she knew, as she turned, walked through the lobby door and toward the elevator, that's exactly what it was.

7:03 P.M.

Charlie walked down the stairs from Michigan Avenue. He gripped the handrail hard, took the steps one at a time. His hands felt frozen; he'd lost his gloves somewhere, some time ago. He didn't really remember, but he wished he still had them.

It hadn't been a bad day, though. It was too cold for most people to be out and the ones that were shopping or going to work or something had been kind of nice. He'd made a few bucks and the people at the Starbucks across from the *Tribune* building hadn't hassled him when he drank a cup of coffee inside. And someone had bought him two bananas, too. One of the people that worked there had just set them on the table in front of him and smiled. That had been nice.

Charlie passed the Billy Goat, kept going. A few minutes later, he saw the traffic shooting under the city and he was glad he'd be at his place soon. No one ever bothered him there, and he would be out of the wind. It would be cold, but nowhere near as cold as it would be if stayed up top somewhere. And darn it, it wasn't just his gloves, but his hat was gone, too. No wonder his ears burned. Maybe it hadn't been a good day, after all.

It seemed like forever before there was a break in the traffic and he could make his way across Lower Wacker Drive. Car tires splashed slush as they whizzed by and he wondered where all the people were going on a Sunday night. Weren't they like him, where they wanted to get some rest before Monday morning? He shook his head, thought about how crazy people could act. Night like tonight, a man shouldn't go anywhere or do anything but find somewhere warm to sleep.

Charlie moved up the steps onto the dock quicker than he'd come down the stairs from Michigan Avenue. The steps to the dock weren't covered with snow. They were dry and they led to the dock and the Dumpster and his spot and . . . There was someone else on the dock.

His breath caught in his throat as Charlie made out the figure in his spot. It had to be a man. He wore a long black coat and even though he was all curled up, Charlie could see he had on gloves, too. There were two trash bags on either side of him, but at least he'd left Charlie's blanket alone. It sat, a couple of feet from the man, in a wad.

"Hey!" yelled Charlie. He hadn't meant to yell, but this was his spot on his dock. No one ever slept there but him and sometimes Mary, but this sure wasn't Mary. It had to be a man because it was just too big for a woman. And suddenly, the man rolled over and sat up.

The dock light was on, but it was still dark and Charlie couldn't really see the man until the man took out a cigarette and lit it. The man's face looked red in the glow from the match. And his eyes were like fish eyes—that's the way Charlie thought of 'em—eyes that were dark and didn't move. And the man didn't move, at least not very fast. He just looked at Charlie, puffed on his cigarette and when a cloud of smoke curled around his head, he said, "Want one?"

Charlie ignored the question. He didn't want any trouble. He'd found that it paid to be nice to people, but this was *his* dock and *his* place. "What are you doing here?" asked Charlie, again, louder than he wanted. "This is my place!"

"No problem, friend," said the man. He took another puff on his cigarette, said, "Are you sure you don't want one?" When Charlie shook his head, the man said, "I just don't have anywhere else to go . . . and it's cold."

"You're not going to try to take something from me, are you?" asked Charlie.

The man shook his head, stubbed out the cigarette on the concrete. "Friend, you don't look like you've got anything worth taking. No. I just want somewhere to sleep tonight."

Charlie looked at the man again. He was big, even bigger than

Charlie, himself, but his clothes were dirty and his boots had some kind of red oil on the soles. And the man looked tired. He sat with his back against the Dumpster. His legs were spread and Charlie remembered that when the man had rolled over, he'd grunted, so it probably hurt, which meant he was old and tired. Charlie heard himself say, "I sleep there. They stack flat boxes on that other dock over there, so if you want to get some, you can sleep under 'em, but on the other side of the Dumpster, okay? 'Cause you're in my spot."

The man nodded and, as he crawled to his feet, Charlie heard him grunt again, and when he walked, his steps were kind of slow and funny. Charlie figured he'd watch the man for a while, make sure he didn't try to take anything from him and if he didn't, maybe he'd give the man one of the bananas. After all, the man had just called him "friend."

8:30 P.M.

The crime scene was still active. The chief medical examiner himself had pronounced the deaths. Wally sat in his car, heater blowing, tried to make sense of it all. He opened his little notebook, scanned five and a half hours of notes.

Romar's phone was in a bag in the passenger seat; the only calls were to and from Lou Lou and to a payphone at Stateville.

Hanratty's phone was on its way to the Chicago Regional Computer Forensics Lab. They'd extract every number, image, bit of evidence and put it all on a CD. But Wally had looked at the calls, noted the times, scrawled them in his book.

Hanratty's recent calls: black for incoming and outgoing, red for missed. An outgoing call at 2:48 p.m., duration: five minutes.

Notes, times:

- The neighbor's call was received at 2:57 p.m.
- OEMC broadcast at 2:59

- An outgoing call on Hanratty's phone from 2:48 through 2:53

Suppositions:

- Hanratty was killed between 2:53 and 2:57; the neighbor said he'd called 911 within two or three minutes of seeing the blood bomb in the squad car.

- Hanratty made a call after Romar was killed. To who? Why?

- *Hanratty shot Romar.* Was it friendly fire? Did he panic, run to the car, try to call for help?

You're forgetting: He accessed the trunk, threw in Gorski's bag of guns. He called someone after he shot Romar, but from his personal cell phone. He didn't call an ambulance. He didn't call it in. Instead, he had called someone from his cell phone. And that phone number is right there in fresh ink on that page of the little notebook.

Wally took out his cell phone, dialed *67 and the 312 number. He heard a ring. It rang again and again. It kept ringing. He turned off the heater so he could hear better; he could see his breath inside the car. He held the phone close to his ear, felt the cold metal in his hand and was about to hang up when a voice answered.

"Hello?" Husky, with some background noise. A few loud voices, a cavernous echo.

"Who's this?" asked Wally.

"This is Mr. Robinson, but this ain't my phone."

"Whose phone is it?"

"Dunno. Just heard it buzzing when I was about to empty the trash."

Wally said, "Excuse me? I'm not following you."

"Whoever you're calling must've lost his phone. I just found it in the trash can."

Wally lifted the veil. "Mr. Robinson, this is Detective Wallace Greer of the Chicago Police Department. Where are you, sir?"

"I'm at the United Center. The Bulls game just got over. They moved it for ESPN."

"Sir, did you see the person that dropped that phone in the trash can?"

"No. I didn't see nothing. If I hadn't heard it buzzing, I would've walked right past it. What's this all about, anyway?"

"Mr. Robinson, please stay right where you're at. A detective will be there shortly to pick up that phone and take your statement. We'll make it quick, sir."

"I'm all right. Just come in the main entrance and tell 'em you need to see Rhino Robinson. Everybody knows me. And hey . . ."

"Yes?"

"You never asked me! The Bulls won!"

Wally sighed. "That's great, Mr. Robinson. We'll see you soon." He hung up the phone, jotted the name Rhino Robinson in his notebook. He looked out at the lot, saw Dan Shepherd, the First Watch dick he'd seen on Friday. Shepherd was a good man—he'd pick up the phone, take Rhino's statement.

Wally started to get out of the car, turned when he heard another vehicle enter the lot. He recognized 'em right away. The body snatchers were there. It was time. He closed the car door, raced toward Dan Shepherd.

The wind picked up. His shoes slipped in the snow. Everything was a blur. He tried to slam the file cabinet door shut, but it hung open in the night. He couldn't believe it! It was time. And he had to go with them: The body snatchers were there . . . for Romar.

9:48 P.M.

He heard the snarling beast roar in the dark. Its bark echoed under the city. Charlie hugged himself tight, tried to wedge himself under the Dumpster. He pulled his blanket up under his chin. He felt the animal's hot breath and the gnash of its teeth. He smelled the dog, awoke in the darkness with a scream.

Charlie rolled over, saw the German shepherd lunge at him. Its head snapped back as the leash caught. He felt its breath again, saw the saliva drip from its open mouth.

"That him?"

"Can't tell. Officer Lee sure thinks so."

Two men in army fatigues stood behind the dog. They both looked young, strong. The shorter one held the dog back by a leash. He held a pistol in his other hand. The taller one had a flashlight in his left hand and an assault rifle in his right.

Charlie screamed, pulled his knees to his chest, leaned back against the Dumpster. "Don't hurt me!"

"Easy," said the one with the dog. "He won't hurt you. Put your hands in the air. Cook County Sherriff's Department."

Charlie put his hands in the air. The man with the flashlight aimed it at his face. He couldn't see! What was going on? Why was the army after him? Was something happening in the city? He should've known. The wind, cold. Night had fallen earlier than usual, of that he was sure. And that wasn't just a dog. It was some kind of ferocious animal. He could see its eyes glow through the dark. "I haven't done anything!" yelled Charlie. "I'm an American!"

"Search him," said the shorter one.

The taller man handed the assault rifle to the shorter man, who tucked it under his arm. The taller one stepped forward, patted Charlie under his arms. The man lifted him to his feet, patted his pockets, pulled out his papers. The man stepped back, shined the flashlight beam onto Charlie's rubber-banded papers.

"Some cash, a black and white picture of a woman and a State of Illinois Identification Card. There's a paper from some shelter, folded up behind the card." The man read the card. "Says his name is Charles Mumford."

"Could be a fake. He looks about the same size. Gray hair, too."

Charlie stared at the dog. It seemed to be looking right through him. "I'm Charlie," he stammered. "Everyone knows me. I work by River Center. Sometimes the Boeing Building."

"Work? You're a beggar. That ain't work."

"I'm there!" yelled Charlie. "I'm there every day. But today is Sunday, so I was on Michigan Avenue."

The tall one looked at Charlie. He was scared. Charlie could see it! "Take your coat off, Mr. Mumford."

"Why?" asked Charlie.

The man yelled, "Just do it!"

Charlie took off his coat. He held it under his arm as he started to shake in the cold.

"He's not two-seventy," said the one with the dog. He let the dog nearer. It sniffed Charlie, then calmly sat down.

"Since when can you weigh a guy with your eyes?"

"He's no more than two-twenty, tops. It's obvious."

"Maybe he lost weight."

They talked to each other like he wasn't even there. The tall one looked at his ID, then pointed the flashlight at Charlie's face. The light blinded Charlie again and he reared back.

"Not him. The suspect's got brown eyes. This guy's are blue." The man wrapped the rubber band around Charlie's stuff, handed it back to him.

Then the dog began to bark again. It leaped forward, dragging its handler as it made its way toward the Dumpster. It began sniffing the flattened cardboard boxes piled by the Dumpster.

"Bumford! Is there someone here with you?"

Charlie stared at the men. He looked at the cardboard boxes. The man had been there earlier, but he was gone.

"Hey, Sinatra," said the taller one. "I'm talking to you. Is there someone in that Dumpster? Someone here before?" The man took the butt of his assault rifle, beat on the side of the Dumpster. The sound came back muffled, not the hollow sound of an empty Dumpster. A rat scurried out from underneath the cardboard. The dog leaped at it.

The cop with the leash started to laugh. "Jesus, you had me going for a minute, there." He yanked on the leash. "Easy, Officer, easy. Check it out, Mims. We better be sure."

The other man glared at him. "For Christ's sake, you gotta be kidding me." He waited a minute, didn't get a response. He sighed, set the rifle on the concrete, put his hands on the edge of the Dumpster and did a quick chin up. "Trash!" he yelled. He let himself back down, brushed off the front of his coat. "That ain't the only rat feasting in there. Disgusting."

The two men and the dog made their way off the dock. "Call us on your iPhone if you see anyone that looks like you, Charles!" yelled one of them. Their laughter echoed, then grew faint.

In the old days, he'd have been mad. But not now. They'd been afraid. People do strange things when they're afraid.

He couldn't see 'em anymore. He barely heard the dog's barks, then there was silence. There was no traffic. He put his coat back on, sat down, back against the Dumpster. He put his hands in his pockets, tried to warm up.

His eyelids started to fall. Maybe it had all been a nightmare. There was no man. No army men. No dog.

He slid to his left, hit the concrete shoulder-first. He took his left hand out of his pocket, pressed his hand on the concrete to push himself up. Seated, upright, he lifted his hand toward his pocket and as his fingertips moved across the concrete, they brushed the cigarette butt.

11:53 P.M.

Wally sat in front of his locker. He'd dressed after his shower but hadn't got past his boxers, socks, blue slacks and dress shoes. His shirt still hung in his locker.

He couldn't stop sweating. He dabbed at his skin with the towel. He just couldn't get over it! Romar's stuff was in his locker and his body was on a slab at the medical examiner's office, but where was Romar? How could the man have laughed with him over lunch, then just disappeared?

Reel it in. Reel it in. Focus. Focus. This isn't doing any good. Focus. Focus.

You've got pieces of the puzzle, but no outline. Be creative. See what you've got. Figure out what's missing.

Go upstairs and create a ledger. On one side, put down the facts as we know 'em. On the other side, put down the questions. We know Gorski killed the Costa brother and cop. But why? We know Gorski didn't leave town. But why? What's he going to do?

It could go on all night. It *would* go on all night. He was going to go upstairs, fire up his computer, get on iClear and read everything he could find on Gorski, the Outfit, the trial. He'd file his report, scour his earlier reports, decipher what was missing. And he had phone calls to make, and he didn't care if it was nearly midnight. He was going to call them all.

Wally stood, took the fresh white shirt from his locker, slipped it on, buttoned it up. He tucked the shirt into his pants, stepped to the end of the row to look in the mirror and saw two men standing at the end of the rows of lockers, between him and the door. Barry Brooks and Allen Yates. Two of the top cops.

"Detective," said Yates. "I don't know what to say. I'm very sorry."

Brooks repeated the condolences, reached for Wally's hand, clasped it in his own. The remorse was genuine. And Yates had gone overboard at the crime scene, making sure everything had been done properly and that the press had been cordoned off as much as possible.

"I just can't believe it," said Wally. "Just this afternoon—"

Yates interrupted. "Detect . . . Wally. You need to go home, get some rest. You've been working a lot of hours. This thing is almost over. I talked with the FBI a short while ago. Francis Costa is set to testify against the other members of the Outfit. This will be the end of the mob in Chicago. This Gorski character seems to have gone mad and apparently thinks he can kill Mr. Costa. We'll have Mr. Costa well protected and if Gorski tries anything, we'll apprehend him or kill him."

Wally stared at Yates. He gathered his composure, took a deep breath. "It would've been nice if they'd have told us that earlier. As it so happens, I've already figured that out. But it's not almost over. It's just beginning. You'll read it in my report, but it appears that Officer Hanratty shot Romar. He also placed a cell phone call after he shot Detective Jones!" Wally's voice grew. "Mr. Costa will be well protected? Well, you can bet my sweet Scottish fanny he'll be well protected because if that is where Gorski is going to be, that's where I'm going to be! The man shot my partner! I will apprehend him! And I will get to the bottom of this!"

Wally fought his rage. He took a deep breath, stopped himself from beating the lockers. Instead, he cracked his knuckles, waited for either man to speak.

"Detective," said Brooks. "We've heard. Delia Grant reached the same conclusion. She's testing Hanratty's hands, postmortem. We've already got people looking into Hanratty. Jesus, this thing is going to blow up, isn't it?"

Wally didn't answer. Instead, he asked, "What are we doing about Gorski?"

"We've set up a joint task force with the FBI and the marshal's service," said Yates. "We're going to man the route from the Metropolitan Correction Center to court in the morning. Security at the courthouse will be beefed up. Other than that, I'm assuming we're following the leads. Once you've got some rest, you can pick up where you left off."

"I don't need any rest," said Wally. "I'm going to be downtown as soon as they start lining up. Right now, I'm going to go finish my report and get it to Commander Brooks. But I need something from you two."

"What is that?" asked Yates.

Wally took a step closer, looked Yates straight in the eye. "I need you to get me in front of FBI Special Agent Martin Lowell, and I need you to get me time with Francis Costa. This isn't a request, sir."

Yates returned Wally's stare. "Done. We may work differently, Detective, but we're on the same side. This monster has killed members of our family and he's going to pay for it."

Wally walked back, closed his locker, spun the dial. He strode back to the two men in suits, reached a hand out toward Yates and grasped the man's hand when it was extended. "I'm glad to hear you say that, sir. Let's go get him."

Monday

12:07 A.M.

Martin lay on his back, on top of the covers. His bedroom was dark, but city light streamed in through a crack in the shades, played a Rorschach test on the ceiling. He saw his father's deep-set, dark eyes. Dead at sixty-two, a year shy of retirement. A lifelong FBI agent; he never got his due. His career had peaked early; he worked with super-cop Gus Carson, stopped the poisoning of the city's water supply. Carson had liked his dad, gave him his pearl-handled revolver. His father had given it to him on his first birthday. Guilt ate Martin—he'd put Carson on a pedestal, caused trouble for his father. Age taught him the lesson: Carson was dirty and mean. His father was a hero. But four years after the father's death, the son announces he's about to crush Chicago's Outfit and who does he laud in the press conference? Dirty Gus.

The voice from his messages mocked his attempt at sleep. The words were garbled. He rolled over, pulled the covers up, but the voice became clear.

A near whisper: "We won't have a lot of time together."

Martin put the pillow over his head, pulled it around his ears. He rolled onto his back, started to think of names, dates. He anticipated questions, gave his answers. He made statements. He pontificated. He screamed.

The voice taunted him, louder. "Let's make it count."

He sat up. Sweat beaded on his forehead. This was ridiculous. Nerves? He had nothing to worry about. He knew his case up, down and sideways. And it was a simple arraignment; he'd do nothing until the press conference afterward. Make it count? Of course, he'd make it count.

Martin got out of bed, walked down the hall, stepped into bathroom. He brushed his teeth, took a lukewarm shower, then returned to his room. He picked out a tasteful but understated dark blue wool suit, white shirt and red tie. He got dressed, tightened the tie around his neck, stepped in front of the dresser mirror. He had to look good— he was representing his father, as well as the Federal Bureau of Investigation. And he did look good. He had eye drops at the office to get rid of the red eyes; other than that, he looked ready for battle. But there was something missing. He thought about it, fidgeted, then opened the dresser drawer and took out the pearl-handled revolver. He took off his jacket, tucked the pistol into a shoulder holster, slipped it on, then slid back into the jacket. One last look: Not bad.

He glanced at the clock: 12:52 a.m. The day had started. The first day of his life. The last day of his life. Who knew what the future held?

3:32 A.M.

Wally: shirtsleeves rolled up, elbows propped on his desk, eyes on the computer screen. It was hard to concentrate and impossible to explain. He had energy but no energy. It was like adrenaline coursed through his body but it was false, dangerous. It was the kind of energy that could lead to a slipup, or worse. He'd been on the telephone for the past three hours, and it wasn't busy work, but playing a hunch, covering the bases. Calls, emails and faxes: The "work" part of his job. *The cows don't milk themselves.*

He took another sip of black coffee. His mind wandered. Every time he took a corner, focused on a thought, he forced the wheel, confronted another:

What would Lou Lou do?

Who was Hanratty?

Why did Hanratty kill Romar?

Why hadn't *he* gone with Romar?

A screeching halt: He hadn't gone with Romar because he had gone to see the Costa woman. What had that accomplished? Nothing, save giving him a head's up on info the top brass had just shared: Costa had cut a deal, turned on the Outfit and now Gorski was intent on killing Costa. Or was he? That conclusion was based on conjecture, circumstance. It might prove right, but hadn't been proven. Something was still missing. Some things.

A buzz. Another. The desktop vibrated. What in the . . . ? Wally looked to his right, saw the screen inside the plastic bag—Romar's phone. He reached over, unzipped the bag and took out the phone.

Wally clicked the button to turn the screen on, slid the arrow right to unlock it. He tapped the green message icon and the list of text messages showed. The most recent was from a 773 phone number. He tapped the number and the message appeared.

"It's Kristie. From the club. I'm sorry I didn't send this to you yesterday. I went out after work. Like I did tonight, too! J It was industry night (I work at a bar, too). Anyway, here's the only picture I have of that girl. She was beautiful! That's the guy I know, Dave, on her left. We're just friends. I don't know any of the others but when he comes in, I can have him call u. K? Call me some time. If you're up and wanna cum over now, call me. Kristie J"

Wally tapped the picture underneath the message. It filled the screen. The picture was of a group of people, all appeared to be in their late twenties or early thirties. Each wore running shorts, T-shirts and a Chicago Marathon bib with a number. His gaze went directly to Officer Rodriguez. The girl had understated it: she was a knockout. He glanced at the guy to her left, long hair and a goofy grin. He glanced at the guy to her right, did a double-take. He tapped the picture, clicked the arrow inside the box in the upper right-hand corner, then hit the email icon, typed in his email address and hit send.

The email appeared in his inbox and he opened it, then the attachment. He blew up the picture until it was perfectly clear.

He stared at it. He'd be able to check the runner's number, but he'd seen enough pictures of her to know, for certain, that the beautiful woman was definitely Officer Rodriguez. And he was certain about the man to her right, who wore a white T-shirt, blue shorts and red running shoes. The man whose left hand, hidden from the rest of the group, pressed against Officer Rodriguez's right hand. The man who he'd just told his superiors he had to see, as soon as possible.

Wally hit the file button, then the print command, sent the picture to the color printer. He walked over, picked it up. He stared at it again, tried to understand the significance of the picture of a young, beautiful and now deceased Chicago Police officer, standing next to, and touching the hand of, Martin Lowell.

5:08 A.M.

Cops milled in the lobby. They wore sidearms, shoulder holsters and bulletproof vests. Some carried assault rifles. A buzz echoed. The words *Hanratty, Romar* and *Detective Jones* punctuated conversations.

Most of the First Watch detectives had already trickled into the office. Wally sat at his desk; the only time he'd left it in the past hour and a half had been to fill his coffee cup. He'd played the Lowell-Rodriguez angle over and over, had come up with nothing. He'd researched Martin and Rodriguez, and still nothing. The only references to Martin outside the Bureau came from newspapers that covered college races. The only references to Officer Rodriguez were on her Facebook page. Martin wasn't tagged in any of her photos, but he stood in the background at a boat party: Martin in a suit and tie—the only one not in swimwear.

Wally couldn't figure it, but since Martin hadn't divulged it, he could be played. Wally didn't like the thought, but Martin sure hadn't been forthcoming and, at this point, that just couldn't be tolerated. They were all going to work together, or get worked. He disliked the thought of strong-arming Martin, but worse was the thought of not getting cooperation. That just wouldn't do.

A pile of paper and a map sat on the corner of Wally's desk. Roscoe Barnes sidled over, picked up one of the sheets of paper, looked at the picture of the young boy Wally had printed earlier in the night.

"Jesus, you been to bed, yet?" asked Roscoe.

"No. I wouldn't have been able to sleep, anyway," responded Wally.

"I got a bottle of vodka on the nightstand. I used to get up for a glass and some ice. A few chugs and it's like Nyquil." Roscoe looked over the picture. "Who's the kid?"

"I have no idea," said Wally. "That's just one of the many things that don't make any sense. Gorski texted that from Ling Lee's phone to someone. Obviously, it's some kind of threat. Could be a witness's kid or something. I'm gonna take those copies down to the courthouse in a while and distribute 'em."

"Let me make some more copies," said Roscoe. "I'll do the same thing." He lingered, waited 'til Wally looked him in the eye. "Listen, about Hanratty . . . Did he really kill Romar?"

Wally sighed. "Looks that way. Red and Jacintha took over. They're still out there. So's Delia."

"Jesus," said Roscoe. "I . . . I shoulda said something. I had kind of a run in with him the other night. He was with Freddie Pence. The guy was all for show."

"Internal Affairs is already on it," said Wally. He shook his head slowly. "They're trying to figure out who he was calling, who he might've been working for or what was up. It doesn't peg as an accident."

"I talked to Freddie," said Roscoe. "Turns out he barely knew the guy. You know Freddie's not the most secure guy in the world—always cracking jokes . . . Hanratty met him on the street, told him he recognized him and buddied up to him. Hanratty used Freddie to get to us. Like he used me to get to Romar."

Wally lifted an eyebrow, leaned back in his chair and sighed again. "I could've gone with him, too, Roscoe. We didn't know."

"You never know," said Roscoe.

"You never know," replied Wally.

Roscoe folded the paper, tucked it in his left hand. "So, you said you're going down to the courthouse soon?"

"Yeah. I'm standing my point. If the SOB did all this to get a shot at Costa, he's not getting it on my watch."

"I hear ya," said Roscoe. He turned to walk away, paused. "Wally, I'm sorry."

"Me too, Roscoe. Me, too."

5:40 A.M.

It hadn't been a dream. Charlie smelled smoke, woke to the man's face, inches away, a cigarette dangling from his lip. The man squatted in front of Charlie. "Wake up," he said.

The dock lights were on, as were the lamps that hung from the concrete above Lower Wacker, but other than that, it was still pitch dark outside. The brightest light came from the tip of the man's cigarette. When he puffed on the cigarette, the tip glowed, showed his bushy gray eyebrows and the squint of his black eyes.

"Wake up," said the man, again. He nudged Charlie. "I've got a warm place for us to go."

Charlie pulled his blanket around him, sat up. "Where?"

"You know those small redbrick buildings over near the river, down by the railroad tracks?"

Charlie nodded. He used to pass 'em on the way to work, every day, 'til he started walking the lower streets.

"Well," said the man. "I've got a key to one. A buddy of mine works for the Federal Transit. He lets me stay there."

Something inside him told Charlie to say no, but instead, he said, "Why were the police after you?"

The man stubbed out the cigarette on the concrete. "Police? After me? Really?"

Charlie was confused. "Didn't you hear 'em? You slept in that big construction Dumpster, right?"

The man laughed. His laugh was loud and wet. He wheezed at the end of it. "I have no idea what you're talking about." The man snapped his fingers. "I'll bet they were after me for staying on Federal Transit property. My buddy told me that could happen. But it's no big deal. They'd just chase me away. Anyway, I left some food and booze at this place. Let's go check it out, warm up. Whaddaya say?"

"Why didn't you stay there last night?" asked Charlie.

"I forgot about it," said the man. "Sometimes I forget things."

That, Charlie could understand. Just look around. Where were his gloves? He had the blanket and after he ran a hand over his pocket, knew he had his money and identification, too. But the man was right. It was easy to forget things. And it was so darn cold. Colder even than the night before.

"Where's this place at?"

The man stood up. "Off Lake Street, right by the river. We can be there in about ten minutes. I don't know about you, but I'm cold and hungry and God damn could I use a drink."

Charlie stood up, pulled the blanket around his shoulders. Lake and the river was on his way to work, so at least he could warm up a little before the day started. There was no traffic on Lower Wacker Drive and it wasn't light yet, so he figured he had some time before the trains came in and people started to go to work.

"Okay," said Charlie. The man turned and started to walk and Charlie followed him. Part of him didn't want to go, wanted to tell the man that he didn't drink alcohol and that he'd get some food from some of the regulars later in the morning. But another part of him was afraid of how the man would react if he said no. So, instead, he trailed behind the man, tried to make some conversation. "So, what's your name?" he asked.

The man didn't turn around, muttered over his shoulder. "Charlie."

Charlie's face lit up. "Mine, too!"

"Imagine that," said the man. "We're both Charlie."

6:02 A.M.

Wally was just about out the door when the phone rang. He stared at it, momentarily thought about letting it continue to ring, then picked up the receiver. "Hello," he said.

"Detective Greer?"

"Yes."

The voice was soft, weak. "This is Elbert Winslow. My daughter's Julie Patterson. We met the other day . . . We haven't heard from anyone."

He recognized the voice, remembered his weathered, grief-stricken face. "I'm sorry, Mr. Winslow. Things have been really hectic here. But, we should have called you. I should have called you."

"Have you found out anything?"

No use in beating around the bush. "We're pretty certain we know the perpetrator. We haven't apprehended him, but we're in pursuit."

"What do you mean?" asked the voice on the other end of the phone. "What do you mean by 'We're in pursuit'? Do you know where he's at?"

"We believe he's still in Chicago. He's left a trail."

"If you know who he is, how come you can't find him?"

"It's not that simple, Mr. Winslow. If you've read anything on the Internet or seen the news or a newspaper, you know that we're after a man named Vitus Gorski. He's a mobster."

"Oh, my God. What does he have to do with my daughter? She wasn't mixed up in anything—"

"No," said Wally. He exhaled, loud. "I'm afraid your daughter and her son and ex-husband were just in the wrong place at the wrong time. This man is twisted. He's killed others."

"Others?"

"Two other young women, and two men."

"I still don't understand, Detective," said Winslow. His voice wavered, fell to a near hush. "If you know who he is, why can't you find him?"

"He fled. He's hiding out in the city, waiting to do something. Every law enforcement officer in the city is looking for him. He killed a police officer. And my partner's dead."

"My Lord. I'm sorry," said Winslow. There was a long silence. Wally knew Winslow was digesting the information. Midwest etiquette left questions in the man's gut, rather than on his lips. Finally, Winslow spoke. "So, he just keeps killing people until he gets what he's after?"

"Not if I can find him," said Wally.

Winslow's voice rose. "Detective Greer, when a coyote sneaks onto a farm and gets a calf or lamb or some chickens and gets away, it keeps coming back for more. You can try to scare it off, or put out watchdogs or try all sorts of crazy things. But, in the end, you just gotta stop it. Do you hear what I'm telling you, Detective? You're not gonna be able to catch him. You're gonna have to kill him."

6:15 A.M.

They stayed on Lake, crossed Wacker Drive. Charlie was glad they'd walked on Lake rather than Wacker. He'd heard lots of people say that the coldest corner in Chicago is at Michigan and Wacker, but he thought it was on Randolph, just south of Wacker. That's where the wind blew the hardest, it seemed to him. It was probably on account of the river, but he didn't know much about that. All he knew was it got cold and boy was it a cold morning.

The wooden bridge felt slick as they crossed it. Charlie heard the man's footsteps on the bridge, watched as he turned his head, looked over each shoulder. It was like he was looking for someone, but Charlie looked around, too, and saw that it was just them. In fact, there was no one else on the streets at all. It was just too cold and windy.

They stopped at a rusty metal gate. On the other side of the gate, a set of concrete stairs led to the ground near the bank of the Chicago River. Charlie looked down toward the riverbank. It was still dark out, but the light from the streetlights and bridges gave him a hazy view of the area. There were a few trees but there were no leaves on their branches. About ten yards from the bottom of the steps was a redbrick building. It was small, looked like it had two white doors, but there was a chimney and some kind of red clay tile roof, so it was probably warm. The railroad tracks ran just to the left of the building and on the other side of the tracks was a dirty white shed and a white trailer. There were four steps leading up to the trailer and when the wind howled and blew through his coat, Charlie hoped the man would enter the brick building and not the trailer.

"C'mon," said the other Charlie. He swung the gate open, walked down the steps and Charlie followed. "Let's clean up first."

Charlie stopped when he got to the bottom of the steps. He watched as the man walked past the building, moved toward the river.

"What are you doing?" yelled Charlie.

The man must not have heard him because he walked through the snow, stopped near the edge of the water. The river looked frozen, but when Charlie looked out, toward the buildings on the other side of the river, he saw the bridge lights glisten on the water. The man dropped to his knees, near the water's edge. Charlie was about to tell him to be careful not to fall in, when the man leaned forward and dunked his head in the water.

What was happening? Charlie started to move from under the bridge, saw the man pull his head out of the water, straighten up and scream. "Aaaah!" The man rose to his knees, threw his head back and water gushed off his hair and onto the back of his coat. He turned toward Charlie and Charlie could've sworn he saw the wind freeze the man's hair and eyebrows. The man looked at him, eyes wide, as if he was in a rage, but, suddenly, he leaned forward and dunked his head in the water again!

Why was he doing it? Why? The man stood up. He wobbled, took a step backward but regained his footing and quickly turned to face Charlie. Charlie looked up at the stairs, felt himself backing up underneath the bridge.

The man's face looked yellow. His eyes were nearly closed and his frozen hair stood like icicles springing from his scalp. When the wind howled and the man started toward him, Charlie tried to move, but there was no strength in his legs and he felt his body start to shake.

Why did the man do that? Why?

And why was he picking up that rock?

6:25 A.M.

Wally, wired on nervous energy, pulled on his bulletproof vest. Fatigue hadn't set in, yet. The nervous energy, deep anger fought it off. To Serve and Protect. He didn't get to choose who he served or protected and he was going to protect Francis Costa. He had to see it through—for Romar.

Just twenty three hours ago, he'd been lifting weights with Romar. Now Romar was gone. His mind raced. Would Gorski be crazy enough to try to kill Costa on his way to the Dirksen building? The streets would be lined with cops. The transport vehicles were armored. If he tried anything, it would likely be inside the building; the route had been secured and security at the building was impenetrable.

Gorski had a plan. He'd gone through so much effort to work his way downtown; the bodies marked his path. No, it wasn't haphazard. He had a plan.

Why had Gorski been at Lopes's garage? Tracks showed that a large vehicle had entered and exited through the overhead door. The lift had been set down on Romar's weapon, meaning the lift had been in the air when Romar entered the garage. It was likely Gorski had been working on his vehicle, which meant he had a vehicle. Maybe he'd done whatever it was he'd hoped to do and had simply driven away.

Wally let out a deep sigh. His detective's intuition gave it to him straight: Gorski was going to try to kill Francis Costa. If not today, then soon. Who knew how much time would pass between the arraignment and the trial? But, after today, Costa would be locked up, impossible to hit before the trial. No, today was the day and Wally wasn't going to let it happen. No matter what, he was going to serve and protect one man today, even if that man was the head of Chicago's Outfit.

Wally fastened his flex cuffs, holstered his Glock. He picked up his coat and gloves and as he walked toward the door, he thought about the last couple of days, realized the Mr. Winslow had been right: Gorski was an animal. He'd committed murder, got away and was coming back. Wally stepped back to his desk, opened a drawer. He took out an extra clip and slipped it into his waistband at the small of his back.

6:35 A.M.

Commuters spilled out of Ogilvie like waves of puke. They gushed out in a spasm, then there was a shitty, awful stillness, but he knew the next wave was coming, and as he teetered, tried to hold his balance, they scurried past him.

He thought back to Friday morning, remembered how the bum had nearly sang to the crowd, "Good morning, young man. Good morning, young lady. Good morning, old man . . ." But he didn't give a thought to trying to mimic the voice. One thing he knew, a guy could change his clothes, looks. But his voice? That stayed with him forever. So no, he didn't say a word, just stood there, kept his head down, waited.

It was probably ten minutes and four groups of commuters crossing at the light later before he heard the sweet sound. "Charlie?"

He kept his hands in the pockets of the burnt orange coat, head near his chest. He wore the guy's fucking stocking hat, didn't look up when people slowed, expecting him to ask for money.

"Charlie?"

He lifted an eye, saw a bald guy in a heavy winter topcoat staring at him. The guy pushed through the crowd as they headed north by the CVS. When the guy got a few steps from him, he toppled to his left, hit the concrete with his left shoulder. He pulled his legs up toward his chest, turned his head away from the guy.

"Charlie!" yelled the man. Suddenly, the guy was on top of him, screaming, "Call 911!"

He tried to keep his eyes closed but they fluttered when the guy rolled him over, screamed, "Stay with me, Charlie!"

He stayed with the man, closed his eyes again as the guy muttered to himself or someone in the crowd that had started to gather. "Jesus, what's the world come to? I see this man every day, but if it wasn't for his clothes, I might not even have recognized him."

7:30 A.M.

Wally stood on the street behind the Metropolitan Correctional Center. He grabbed two uniformed cops, pointed them toward the surface parking lot east of the building.

"Check every car in that lot. Assume there's someone in every car. Be careful, but be thorough."

The cops trotted toward the lot. Wally turned and walked north on Federal. Uniformed cops stood every ten yards, eyes focused on pedestrians, vehicles and the street. There were cops on every fire escape, Rock River Arms at their sides.

Cars were parked on both sides of Federal; Wally saw two detectives working their way south, peering into each car.

The wind gusted. Peopled scurried up and down the sidewalks. Businessmen in heavy winter coats hustled into the Union League Club. Wally saw Dan Shepherd just inside the door. Wally stepped inside, handed Dan a copy of the picture of the kid.

"Who is he?" asked Shepherd.

"That's what we want to find out," said Wally. "Gorski texted this picture to someone. I'm gonna hand out copies at the courthouse but figured you'd want one."

"Yep," said Shepherd.

Wally clapped Shepherd on the shoulder, turned and stepped back outside. The cold kept him awake. He walked north, turned right on Jackson. He stopped at the light at Dearborn, glanced at the blue newspaper vending machines to his right. Both the *Tribune* and *Sun-Times* had pictures of Gorski on the front page. The *Sun-Times's* headline read Mob Butcher on the Loose.

Wally crossed Dearborn, walked east until the saw the concrete ramp at the south end of the Dirksen building. He stared down the ramp. If the U.S. Marshal's Service vehicles made it down the ramp into the underground parking garage, the odds on Gorski getting a shot at Costa increased to a thousand to one; it was nearly impossible for someone to get inside the building without credentials. Security was tight and the glass façade meant that even the cops on the street could see everyone who entered the building. The security wasn't just for show.

Wally knew it was a long shot that Gorski would try to hit Costa on the route to the U.S. District Court. That simply didn't jibe with his modus operandi. But then, a lot of people had died because they'd underestimated their foe and had failed to prepare. Wally wouldn't make that mistake.

Wally looked back toward the intersection of Jackson and Federal, took a quick count. Probably fifty cops. Practically a gauntlet. It wasn't likely that Gorski could get through that wall of force, do any harm. But he could hear Romar say, "You never know." He walked west, turned north toward the building's entrance, made a mental note to put more cops near the steps leading down to the trains. He repeated Romar's mantra as he handed a picture of the kid to another group of cops. "You never know."

8:50 A.M.

Martin got out of the cab on Dearborn, was hit by a gaggle of reporters before he made it to the entrance of the building.

"Special Agent Lowell, Special Agent Lowell!"

Martin walked past the group. "No comment."

A silver-haired veteran reporter stepped in front of him, microphone held high. "Special Agent Lowell, is it true that Vitus Gorski has murdered seven, or possibly, eight people over the past few days after slipping FBI surveillance?"

Martin's gut went tight. "No comment." He ducked his head, put a hand out in front and started toward the entrance. The reporter stepped in front of him and when Martin turned to his left to avoid the man, he saw the detective he'd met on Saturday; he stood off to the side, a stack of papers in his hand. When the man recognized Martin, he nodded and waved him over. "Excuse me, official business," said Martin as he avoided the reporter.

There was a roar from the reporters and when Martin looked over his shoulder, he saw a black Town Car stop in front of the building. He heard the name Denton and watched as the reporters rushed toward the car. Martin stepped toward the detective and looked down at the papers he was holding.

"This is a picture that Vitus Gorski text messaged to someone," said the detective. "Do you recognize the young man?"

"No," said Martin.

"It could be the son of one of your witnesses or someone working the case."

Martin took one of the photocopies, studied it, then folded it and slipped it into his coat pocket. "Sorry, I can't help you, Detective. Frankly, I just used you as an excuse to slip away from those reporters."

The man held out his hand. "Detective Wallace Greer. Wally. We met Friday."

Martin accepted Wally's hand. "I remember."

Wally shuffled his feet, looked down at the ground, then met Martin's gaze. "I'm sorry for your loss, Martin."

"Excuse me?" said Martin. The wind howled and he assumed he'd misheard the man. "My loss?"

"You've got to be hurting, Martin." Wally took a page from the bottom of the stack, handed it to Martin. Martin took the paper, glanced at it. The marathon. Him and Anna. Christ, he hadn't even allowed himself to think her name . . . He felt her breath on his cheek and he trembled.

"It was an accident," said Martin. "She—"

"It was no accident," said Wally. His voice was firm but Martin didn't detect outrage. The man was simply correcting him. "She was tortured and murdered. We need to talk about what she was doing there. Listen, this Gorski murdered my partner yesterday so I know what you're going through. You haven't been open with me and I need your cooperation. Now."

Martin started to answer, but felt his bottom lip quiver. He bit his lip, searched for words, but then heard his name over the crowd. He glanced toward the building and saw Elizabeth Hughes charging toward him. "Excuse me," said Martin. He turned to meet Elizabeth when he heard Wally say, "In this day and age, haven't you people learned to cooperate?"

"I'll be right back," Martin shouted to Wally. He held a finger high. "Right back."

Ten steps away, Elizabeth Hughes stood, eyes on fire. When Martin reached her, she didn't bother with pleasantries. "You made this hard for us, Martin. You didn't email her and her cell phone is missing. Her cell phone records don't show any calls between the two of you, so you must have called her on a disposable cell phone. But, you know what did you in? Her fingerprints were on the package of facial wipes I found in your bathroom." She sighed. "Christ did you fuck this up, Martin. All those years of work down the drain because you wanted to give your girlfriend a present? Was it to help her career?"

"It wasn't like that," whispered Martin. "She—"

"Save it. We win the trial, it was an error in judgment, a blip on the radar. Lose and your career is over." Elizabeth spun back toward the entrance, stopped and looked back at him. "What a man will do for a fuck."

Martin's head sank. "I loved her," he muttered. He stood there as Elizabeth strode back into the building. He saw her greet Denton just inside the door. She pointed outside, toward him, and Martin watched as Denton and two of his cronies shook their heads. He saw Elizabeth turn her back toward him and it reminded him of her leaving his room the day before, giving him that "What are you doing?" look. And he'd whispered after her, "Mourning."

Martin felt a hand on his shoulder. He looked up to see Wally, brow creased, eyes narrow. "We're not done here, Martin."

"I know," said Martin. "I'll meet you right here after the arraignment. I'll tell you everything."

10:00 A.M.

Wally stood on the southeast corner of Federal and Jackson. He looked into the distance, saw the first black SUV coming north. He signaled the traffic cop, heard the shrill whistle and suddenly all vehicular traffic was stopped. The intersections at both Federal and Jackson and Dearborn and Jackson were clear.

The convoy of five SUVs made its way north on Federal. Some pedestrians stopped to watch. Most seemed to be irritated that they couldn't cross the street or puzzled as to what was happening.

As the SUVs drove by, each uniformed cop turned and watched them pass, like they were drug along in the slipstream. Wally saw Roscoe Barnes break from the ranks, run up alongside the first SUV. Another, then another detective did the same thing, and soon uniformed cops ran alongside their brethren. When the entourage moved past him, Wally stepped into the street and jogged with them. After they passed the intersection at Dearborn and Jackson, the SUVs turned north, then disappeared down the long concrete ramp. The cops gathered at the top of the ramp, eyes on the streets.

Pedestrians stood on each corner, stared at the cops. Some pulled out cell phones and took pictures. Wally recognized a newspaper photographer, watched him position himself on the south side of Jackson, snap pictures.

Wally caught his breath, walked around the building to the main entrance. His heart continued to pound. There had been no attempt on their prisoner's life. But it had been a show of force. The Chicago Police Department was on duty.

The entire trip had taken less than four minutes.

11:20 A.M.

The courtroom was jammed. Martin sat in the row behind Denton, his colleagues and Elizabeth. He'd already received and earful from Greene: his voice, but the director's words, "It's all about perception. The media is going to jump on the romance angle, whether Officer Rodriguez was there of her own volition, as you claim, or otherwise. She was there. The perception will be that if it was a more senior, skilled officer or agent, then none of this would have happened. The murders are a direct result of this investigation and this trial! If Gorski is apprehended or killed, it may fade away. If not, the take-away will be that your pillow talk led to the murders of Ms. Rodriguez, Mr. Costa, the Pattersons, Ms. Lee and the two police officers. You've opened the department up to serious litigation and the media is going to have a field day with this!"

> Directive: Immediately after the arraignment, meet back at FBI headquarters.

> Directive: Only work on the case and testimony. Prepare for the trial.

> Directive: Do *not* speak to the media.

> Directive: Work from the office only. "You are not fit for fieldwork."

Martin had listened, but the words had no effect. It had been like trimming the branches of a hollow tree.

The call had come in early Friday morning. They'd alerted him to the death of Phillip Costa. He'd moved in a trance, felt nothing, felt *everything*. Standing over her body, he'd grabbed Anna's cell phone from the right pocket of her pants. It had been a defense mechanism; shame ate at him.

He'd gone through the motions on Friday—the "raid" on Costa's home, meeting with the cops—Wally Greer had walked in and he'd nearly admitted everything to him. His prevailing thought was: I must protect the case. She must not have died in vain. But a creaky voiced whisper played constantly in his head: This cannot be happening!

Reality set in. It wouldn't look like he'd been protecting the case. It would look like he'd been protecting his ass. But that wasn't it. She'd wanted to help him. She could convince anyone to do anything. She wanted to convince Phillip Costa to accept the FBI's offer of witness protection. She wanted to bring him in. She was Anna Rodriguez, the only woman he'd ever loved.

Martin rose, bumped into Greene as he slipped out. "Can't you hold it?" croaked Greene. "They're starting any minute!"

Martin ignored him, moved through the throng of attorneys. He felt the mobsters' eyes on him. He ignored them, too, as he pushed open the heavy door and left the courtroom.

11:30 A.M.

Wally rolled up the last picture with the glove on his right hand. He tapped it in the air, absentmindedly, as he watched two uniformed cops stop people as they entered or exited the subway at street level. They slowed down the commuters, made sure they got a good look at the men. Wally was about to go help them when he heard his name. He turned and saw Martin Lowell leaving the building, buttoning his overcoat as he strode across the plaza.

"Quickest arraignment ever," said Wally.

Martin responded, "It hasn't started. I'm not staying." His breath hung in the air. "I need to talk to you about Vitus Gorski. I'm going from out of the loop to out of commission."

Wally felt a tap on his shoulder and turned to see a Chicago cop, blue jacket and hat, holding a picture of the kid in his hand.

"Sorry to interrupt, Principal," said the cop.

Wally put a hand on Martin's shoulder as if to say, "You're not going anywhere." He looked at the cop. "What is it?"

"I know the kid in this picture," said the cop. He was thin and had black hair and dark eyes and his face was red from the cold. "That's Mickey Cordell. He plays on my son's baseball team. His dad's an attorney."

Martin interjected, "Albert Cordell? He's Francis Costa's attorney."

Wally looked from the cop to Martin, then back toward the cop. "Are you sure?"

"Yeah, Albert Cordell. I coached for years and that asshole of a dad never responded to my calls or emails. I probably gave Mickey a ride home every other game or practice. No doubt about it, sir, it's him."

Wally asked Martin: "Is Cordell here?"

"I didn't see him," said Martin. He took out his cell phone. "I'll try his office."

Wally stared at Martin, waited for him to say something. Instead, Martin just shook his head, then tapped at his phone.

"No answer," said Martin. "I'm texting Elizabeth Hughes. She's inside, working for the prosecution."

Barely a minute went by, then Martin held his phone up to Wally. Wally read the exchange:

"Is Albert Cordell in there?"

"No. Where the fuck are you?"

Wally grabbed the cop by the sleeve. "You know where this Cordell lives?"

"Yeah," said the cop. "Over near where Daley used to live. By Soldier Field."

"Get your squad car and meet us at the rear entrance to the MCC."

The cop nodded, trotted off. Wally looked at Martin, "My car's a couple of blocks away. Let's go. Mind driving?" He didn't wait for Martin's answer before he turned and started to jog toward Federal.

11:50 A.M.

The ride was uncomfortable. Wally looked tired and wired. He just stared out the window.

Martin drove, riddled with guilt. Three days of holding it in his gut had him dazed, in shock. He heard Wally speak to him, but didn't answer. Instead, he turned the steering wheel, followed the squad car south onto Michigan Avenue.

"I asked what the hell is going on," said Wally.

Martin bobbed. "We'll find out at Cordell's place. If he's there, I can get him to tell you. If not, we've got an even bigger problem."

The squad car turned left on Indiana, then took another turn and stopped in front of a series of redbrick townhouses. The cop got out of the car, pointed a forefinger at Cordell's home. Martin pulled in behind the squad car, and he and Wally climbed out of the vehicle.

Martin pulled back, let Wally take charge. He saw Wally look at the black gate in front of the townhouse, then followed his gaze as he looked to the south end of the townhouse and saw another gate that led to the development's courtyard.

"Think you can make it over that gate?" Wally asked the cop.

"Yes sir," came the rapid response.

"This is Cordell's unit on the end, right?" asked Wally. The cop nodded, so Wally continued. "Then get over that fence and go around back to the garage. Engage your weapon. We're trying the front door, but be ready if someone tries to get out through the garage. It's happened before."

Martin watched as the cop jogged across the small patch of grass that constituted the front lawn, then put a foot on the bottom of the iron gate and two hands on top of it and quickly hoisted himself over the top. When he landed on the other side, turned and gave them a thumb's up.

Wally took the glove off his right hand, unholstered his Glock, motioned for Martin to do the same. When Martin pulled out the pearl-handled revolver, he saw Wally smile. But, instantly, Wally was all business.

"For all we know, Cordell is sleeping one off and will answer the door in his pajamas," said Wally. "But we'd better be safe than sorry."

They walked up the short sidewalk and Wally turned the knob on the black gate, and when it opened, he held it for a moment so Martin could follow. A few steps later they stood in front of the door, and Wally didn't hesitate to hit the doorbell. Martin heard it ring, but a minute later no one had come to the door, so Wally took his gloved left hand and pounded on it.

"We're going in," said Wally, over his shoulder. He tried the doorknob, but when it didn't turn, he leaned back, lifted a leg and kicked the door just underneath the doorknob. There was a loud bang as the door splintered and flew open.

They entered the home, Wally first. Wally yelled Cordell's name, and when there was no answer, they stepped across the marble entryway. They looked to their left at the front room at nearly the same time and when Wally said, "Looks like we've got a problem," Martin knew it was true. The carpet was bloodstained.

"I've got to secure the scene," said Wally. He moved forwarded, headed up the stairs.

"Right behind you," said Martin. He followed Wally up the stairs. They stopped on the second floor, checked the bathroom, living room. They made their way up to the next level, checked two bedrooms and an office and finally to the top floor. Empty. They moved back down to the ground floor and Martin followed Wally out through the back door and into the garage. Wally turned on the light and Martin immediately saw the dark smear stains on the concrete toward the back end of the vehicle parked in the garage.

Wally reached over toward the wall, hit a button and the garage door opened. Light streamed in and the cop who had led them to the house stood, transfixed, weapon drawn. When he saw it was just the two of them, he lowered the weapon.

Martin heard Wally sigh, watched as he opened the driver's-side door, leaned inside. The trunk of the car opened and the cop outside screamed, "Shit!"

Martin followed Wally to the back of the car, stared into the trunk and saw the rigid body of Albert Cordell. He heard Wally yell for the cop to call in the homicide squad and secure the scene with barrier tape.

Martin felt his hands begin to shake as he holstered his revolver. "Wally," he said. Wally must not have heard him because he continued to yell orders to the cop. "Wally!" said Martin, louder, and this time Wally turned. "We've got to move!"

Martin turned, sprinted through the house. He heard Wally behind him.

"Where are we going?" yelled Wally.

Martin burst out the front door, through the gate. He had already opened the car door before he answered. "To the hospital!"

12:20 P.M.

The nurse was a guy, bald, short, skinny and black. He wore light-blue hospital scrubs and talked slow, like he was mumbling to himself. And his voice was weird—sounded like an old lady who smoked. And talked to herself.

Gorski leaned back in the tub, stared at the ceiling. The nurse filled a bowl with hot water and held it above Gorski's face.

"The water temperature is 104 degrees Fahrenheit," said the guy in that weird voice. "You may feel a severe burning sensation, but that's normal. It's the blood returning to your skin. Your skin may swell and change color, but it won't be long before it returns to normal."

Gorski clenched his teeth as the guy poured the hot water over his face. Christ did it hurt! He wanted to grab the guy by the neck, but instead he made two fists in the water, tried to stop from kicking the end of the tub with his feet. Fuck!

"Now, that couldn't hurt a big man like you," said the nurse. "And you don't have to thank me now, but I put you into the tub for this treatment so you could get a bath, because goodness knows you needed one."

The guy stood up, kept talking as he crossed the small room. "The frostbite was contained to your face and ears, like you slept face down in the snow. Your face is all red now. Let's just hope it doesn't blister. The doctor said you've also got mild hypothermia, but I don't see that. I think you were just cold. No, all you needed was a hat and scarf and you'd have been just like all the other transients that come here—a little cold but in no medical danger."

The little fucker walked back over to the tub, handed Gorski a towel. He set a hospital gown over the back of the rolling chair he'd sat on when he'd poured the water over Gorski's head. "Dry yourself off and put on your gown and I'll wheel you back to the room—hospital regulations," he said as he turned and left the room.

Gorski stood up, stepped out of the metal tub, dried himself off and put on the gown. He thought about taking a quick walk down the hall, but the little fucker showed back up a moment later, pushing a wheelchair in from the hall.

"Sit down and I'll take you back to your room. You can enjoy a lunch on Cook County while we finish that paperwork."

Gorski turned around, sat down in the wheelchair. The nurse pushed him out the door, into the hall. They stopped and Gorski heard the nurse muttering to himself, then saying, "You can just come with me. It won't take a moment."

The nurse pushed the wheelchair down the hall and when they stopped in front of the nurses' station, the man locked the brake on the chair's wheels and disappeared into a back room.

Gorski stared down the hall. He felt his leg start to shake when he saw the guy in the uniform—obviously a U.S. marshal. He counted doors on the left side of the hall; the marshal stood in front of the fifth door. Then, he felt a jerk on the chair and the little fucker released the brakes, spun him around and started to push him back toward the elevator. He gauged the distance as the nurse muttered to himself, then dropped a clipboard in his lap. "You can start looking this over so when we get to your room we can finish it. That paperwork ain't gonna fill itself out, Mr. Mumford, and I am in need of a smoke break."

Gorski barely heard him. When they stopped in front of the door to his room and turned, he thought, Just off the elevator. Forty yards. Only forty yards.

12:48 P.M.

Wally and Martin stood outside the hospital room door, which was open. Two FBI agents stood inside, on either side of the bed, facing the door. A deputy U.S. marshal stood outside the room, his left shoulder pressed against the door jamb.

They'd spent ten minutes in the administrator's office, alerting the hospital rep to the danger posed by Vitus Gorski. Wally had pulled up several pictures of Gorski on the administrator's computer, asked him to print 'em and distribute them among his staff. He didn't need to be pushed; he called in his administrative assistant and told her to print copies of each picture and personally hand them out to the staff. Since the hospital had nearly five hundred beds, Wally knew there could be anywhere between fifteen hundred and two thousand people in the building, including staff, patients and visitors. Alerting them all was a daunting task, if not flat-out impossible.

Wally peered into the room. Francis Costa laid on his back, bed-covers pulled up to his waist. He wore a faded green V-neck pajama top and the thin hair on his head was gray, limp and matted to his skull. His skin was jaundiced and he was slack jawed. His lips were covered with a white film and his eyes were wide open but vacant.

It was like he saw a spider slowly descending from the ceiling, but couldn't avert his gaze or move before it dropped into his open mouth.

Wally took the winter coat from Martin's hand, threw it over his own coat, stepped into the room and hung them up in Costa's closet. The room smelled of antiseptic—not clean, but a warning signal for disease and decay. As he stepped back into the hall, he saw the two FBI agents trail his movements, but the old man in the bed never flinched. Wally closed the door behind him.

Wally peered down the long hallway. The sandstone-colored concrete walls appeared endless. Noises bounced off the walls, filled his ears, overwhelmed him—the wheels on a nurse's cart, two custodians jabbering, a man with a bouquet of flowers asking for a room number. Martin inched next to him.

"Francis Costa turned himself in," said Martin. He's been cooperating with us for the past few months. We'd meet a few times a week, take his testimony. He's got nothing to lose but everything to gain for his family. In return for his testimony, we won't prosecute him or go after his family or anything they own. See, he's got stomach cancer. It's advanced and took a really bad turn for the worse last week. So, we had to check him into the hospital, speed everything up. He's been giving us testimony every waking moment. Today is the first day we haven't been questioning him with a court reporter present."

Wally sighed. "All those cops and all that manpower and he wasn't even in the vehicle we just escorted to Dirksen. We were just part of the show." He let his voice trail off, digested it. "What have you got from him?"

"He's implicated all the others. Until the other day, when he started to go downhill, he gave us names, dates . . . The others that have been indicted will go down. I'm not worried about them. We want the rest—the crooked politicians, cops, maybe even FBI agents. We've got enough evidence to crush the Outfit, once and for all."

Wally leaned against the wall, jammed a hand in his pocket. His eyes felt like someone had scratched them with needles. "Why didn't you pick up Gorski when Costa turned himself in?"

"We planned on picking them all up at once," said Martin. "If we grabbed Gorski first, the others would've scattered. It's a complicated operation." He sighed. "But, Costa is the one that convinced us to pull back surveillance on Gorski. He said if Gorski saw us and was tipped off, he'd flee and we'd never find him. It's obvious, now, that he really wanted us to leave Gorski alone so he could send Dragone in to kill him. You see how that worked out."

"Why kill him?"

"One of the truest statements that Costa's made is that he's afraid of Gorski. He describes the guy like he's the devil incarnate. Costa's holding one last ace. He claims that there's one man, sitting above it all, running the Outfit. He told us he'll give us that name when we get Gorski—one way or another. And if Costa dies before we get Gorski, he's left instructions with his attorney to turn over the name, along with a ledger detailing payoffs, skims . . ."

"His attorney's dead," said Wally.

"Well, Costa's still alive. I've seen him look a lot worse, then straighten up and order a Chicago dog."

Wally rubbed his eyes, stood up straight. "You messed up. We both know that. But how did Officer Rodriguez get to the scene?"

Martin shuffled his feet, stared at the floor a moment and then answered. "Costa wanted us to take his brother, Phillip, under protection. We'd been watching Frank's wife and granddaughter ever since he turned himself in, but the brother refused protection. Said he wasn't part of the Outfit and had nothing to do with it. Guilt by association. I told Anna about it. It was a stupid, stupid breach. I looked at her as an officer of the law, so I was a lot more open than I should have been. But I did not tell her to go there."

"You were in love with her," said Wally. He saw Martin jerk, like he'd been stuck with a pin. "Sometimes you share too much with the ones you love. Other times, you don't share enough."

"It was stupid," said Martin. "If I hadn't told her, she'd be alive. She went over there to convince Phillip Costa to turn himself in for protection. Gorski must've shown up after she got there."

Wally nudged Martin away from the door, stopped when Martin's back was against the hallway wall. "With all of this, what have you done to find Gorski? Why haven't you been looking?"

Martin nearly exploded, shouted a whisper: "Are you kidding me? They shut me down right away! They're basically going to say I'm responsible for him being on the loose and all of these murders! If I dropped everything to look for him, it would look even worse. You're on it, my colleagues at the FBI are on it. There's nothing I can do."

"Martin, you've been investigating him. You know his habits."

"I turned over all my files on Gorski to the other agents. There's nothing I know about him that hasn't been shared with my fellow FBI agents."

It was Wally's turn to explode. "But you didn't share it with us! When will you people learn? We're in this together!"

Martin stepped away from the wall. "I'm going to ignore that. There's a bigger picture here. This will bring down the Outfit. Not just hurt it—kill it. There will be no more organized crime in Chicago." He jabbed a finger in the air. "None! That man in there is giving us details on a life of crime. And we're protecting him. Phillip Costa, Anna, none of them will have died in vain. No one is getting to Costa. He's going to finish this testimony and we will win that trial."

Wally looked at Martin. The man looked as tired as Wally felt. He saw Martin slip a hand into his pants pocket, noted the pocket shake as his hand trembled. The guy had been through the wringer. Wally dropped his voice, lost the tone of rebuke. "You should move him. There are private hospitals . . ."

"We thought of it, but we'd have to have his family's permission. We can't get it."

"I know the wife a bit," said Wally. "I could give it a shot."

Martin sighed. "We've tried. They rejected us and they'd reject you. I'm not convinced Gorski's coming, but if he is, we'll capture or kill him right here."

"So, you've got twenty-four-hour guards here, right?" asked Wally. "You heard me call the station on the way here. We've got cops covering all points of entrance and exit, but if you need more up here, I'll call 'em in."

Martin let out a deep breath. "Thanks. No. We've got our two agents in the room and the deputy from the U.S. Marshal's Service here in the hall." He nodded toward the marshal on the other side of the door, who quickly glanced at them, then up and down the hallway. "The only time this procedure changes is from five p.m. until six p.m. daily, when Costa's attorney shows up. Then, it's just the officer at the door. Costa and his attorney get the room to themselves, attorney-client privilege. Now I know why Cordell didn't show up last night."

Wally stepped closer, gave Martin a somber look. "I've been doing this a long time. There's a pattern to what Gorski's been doing. He kills and moves, kills and moves. He's not moving randomly. He's got a destination. You know why I think he killed Phillip Costa and Albert Cordell? Information. He wanted to know where he could find Francis Costa—exactly where he could find him."

Martin shrugged. "He's not getting near Costa. This place is sealed off, and pretty soon, everyone here will know what he looks like. You're wrong. It'll never happen. He's on his way out of town or he's holed up somewhere and, eventually, we'll find him. Things are fine here. The best thing that you and I can do is go back to our respective offices and work. Or, in your case, get some sleep and then work."

"I'm not going anywhere!" snarled Wally. "Have you heard a word I said? This is it! If Gorski is going to try and kill Costa, it's here and now!"

"No," said Martin. "You were convinced it was today because you thought he would try to kill him on the way to Dirksen. You thought it was his one shot. Well, it's not just a one shot opportunity. We will have guards here 24/7. But think about it, if Cordell told him that Costa's in the hospital, he also told him he's dying of stomach cancer. My guess is that once he found that out, he took off. You and I need to put our heads together, investigate this thoroughly, find him and prosecute him."

Wally snorted. He didn't have time for nonsense. His gut told him. "Martin. I'm here to tell you, you're wrong. It's going to happen. He's coming."

1:12 P.M.

The little fucker finished rubbing salve into the skin of Gorski's face, lifted the back of his head. "Just lean forward a bit, Mr. Mumford."

Gorski pushed his chin toward his chest. He glanced to his right, saw the guy in the other bed roll over, heard him blast a fart.

"Christ," muttered Gorski.

"Don't you worry about your roommate. He just got a little indigestion. I think there was some garlic in that rice dish you men had for lunch." The nurse took a long strip of gauze, began to wrap it around Groski's head. "The salve will help with the blisters. The doctor told me to wrap this gauze around your face, which I'll do, but I certainly don't agree with it. The skin is an organ. It needs to breathe."

Gorski grunted. The nurse finished wrapping the gauze around his head, snipped the gauze with a pair of scissors. He set the scissors on the end table next to the bed, touched Gorski's forehead and motioned toward the pillow. "You can lie back, now Mr. Mumford."

Gorski set his head back on the pillow. He could see through a slit in the gauze wrapping over his eyes. His clothes were piled on the counter to his left. His boots were in the opposite corner of the room. The shades were drawn and the light in the room was dim. He saw his roommate roll over again; the man's head lolled to the side and Gorski saw no recognition in the man's eyes; one eyeball was transfixed on the floor, the other rolled back in his head.

Gorski heard the little fucker mutter and when he looked up, the nurse stared down at him. He mumbled something, then wandered off. Gorski trailed him with his eyes, gripped the sides of the bed. So far, Cordell's information had been right; the room number jibed. Now, all he had to do was wait it out until five o'clock and there would be only one man between him and Costa. He was sure of it; he could take out the marshal. No way the man would be suspicious of a wounded, wandering patient . . . He'd move past the guy, cause him to follow him into the room and then kill him. Then, it was Frank's turn. Then . . . He put the kibosh on the excitement, let the voice in his head repeat one word, over and over: Patience. Patience. Patience.

1:30 P.M.

Theresa hung up the phone. Their neighbor, Carol, had agreed to come over and watch Lou Lou that evening. Although she didn't think that it would be more than a few hours, Theresa struggled with guilt. She didn't want to leave Lou Lou for even a moment during such an awful time. But, she also didn't want to desert her students on a night that meant so much to them. If she decided not to attend, the other teachers and staff would obviously understand, but many of the students wouldn't—and not because they weren't sympathetic, loving people, but simply because they wouldn't be able to comprehend her absence.

She walked over to the sink and turned on the faucet. She took a glass from the cupboard and pushed it under the stream of cold water. As the glass filled, so did her eyes.

How could it happen? Romar! He was such a good man. Wallace loved him and she loved him. And Lou Lou loved him.

What would happen to the girl? She was so beautiful and had such a wonderful smile, but it was as if her soul had been ripped from her body. She hadn't wanted to leave her apartment; she wanted to wait for Romar. But after Theresa finally convinced her they needed to leave, she'd simply wilted. Since Theresa brought her home, Lou Lou hadn't left the spare bed. And whenever Theresa checked on her, the pillow was sopped and the skin around her eyes was raw from the constant stream of salty tears.

Theresa thought about the worst moment of her life, when she didn't think she could continue. And she'd questioned God. But what had he had in store for her? Wallace. So, maybe this was another one of God's mysteries. Maybe she could help. Maybe . . .

Theresa felt cold on her hand and looked down to see the water running over the sides of the glass and her hand and down into the sink. She reached over, turned off the faucet and as she took a drink, she glanced at her watch.

She set the glass down on the counter, walked over the kitchen table and picked up her cell phone. She typed a text message to Wallace, hit send and then set the phone back down on the table.

The Literacy Showcase would be starting soon. She realized she had to start getting ready.

Theresa only had a few hours.

3:00 P.M.

Truce: They would stay until the new shift came on at six o'clock. Martin had agreed to appease Wally; the detective leaned against the wall in the hall, out on his feet.

Martin had called Greene, scotched the directive to return to headquarters. He'd stressed cooperating with the police, reminded Greene it could be a year before the trial began. Greene had acquiesced; the message: Martin was about to be swept under the rug. He'd been told to stay at work and study the case—punished like a child sentenced to summer school. His first assignment: Tutor the cops on Gorski.

What did he really know about Gorski? The facts had been laid out. The man was the face of evil: cold-blooded, no human emotions. It appeared he'd slaughtered his way downtown, bent on revenge. It wasn't just that Costa had testified against him: His old boss had ordered his murder. But Gorski had intercepted his killer, murdered the man and fed him to his dog. And what the man had done to Phillip Costa, Anna and the others? Gorski was a sick, sick animal.

Martin tucked his hand inside his suit coat. There was no way the man would try to get inside the hospital, was there? No one in his right mind would . . . No one. In his right mind.

Martin brushed his hand over the handle of his revolver, was relieved when he heard Wally's voice. He looked at the detective, saw him lift both eyelids, rub his eyes.

"Something else, isn't it? First time I've ever waited inside a secured facility, waiting for someone to break in. Who'd ever have thought it? Who'd have ever thought any of it?"

3:30 P.M.

Time for a test run: Gorski swung his legs over the edge of the bed, stood up. He took the blanket off the bed, sat down in the wheelchair the nurse had left in the room. He draped the blanket over his legs. He moved forward in the chair, folded his legs back underneath the seat so the top of his toes touched the floor. His height masked, he bent forward in the chair, put a hand on each wheel and rolled out into the hall.

It wasn't tough to play sick—he was bone tired from the few hours of shitty sleep he'd had the night before. He wheeled slow, eyes cast down the hallway. Nice and easy, let 'em get used to seeing him rolling up and down the hall. Nothing special here, just another guy in a wheelchair, face mummy-taped.

It took him five minutes to reach the elevator, but when he pressed the button, the door opened right away. The car was empty. He wheeled inside, turned around and pressed the button next to Hematology and Oncology. Moments later, the door opened and he wheeled out and to the nurses' station. The marshal was in full view. There was a uniformed cop standing next to the marshal in front of the door to Frank's room. Gorski squinted through the slits in the gauze, saw two more men in the hall—that asshole Lowell from the FBI and some fucknut in a sport coat. He glanced to his right, down another hall and watched as two uniformed cops queried people as they approached from the other side of the building. Another cop walked past him, tugging at his zipper and stationed himself in front of the elevator.

He looked back toward Frank's room and at that moment the man in the sport coat turned. He was stocky, looked kind of square. His silver hair looked like it was Brylcreemed. But the guy was staring at him, straight at him, like he knew him. But how the fuck? There was no way the guy could know! He was about to turn around when he heard Lowell yell to the guy, "Wally. Detective Greer!"

Detective Wallace Greer. The asshole that had called him deranged. Gorski sat in place, waited for the motherfucker to turn back around, stare at him again.

"Oh, there you are!"

Gorski nearly jumped out of the chair. It was that fucking nurse, loud enough to nearly give him a heart attack. Fuck!

"Why are you wandering out here?" asked the nurse. He didn't wait for Gorski to respond. "I'll bet you were on your way back to that tub. Sorry, but you've had your bath for the day."

The nurse grabbed the handles of the wheelchair and as he was spun around, Gorski saw the detective down the hall give him one last glance, then look away.

"Say, Mr. Mumford," continued the nurse, yammering again. "When you checked in, you had a picture of a lovely woman in your pocket. Who is she?"

"My mother," muttered Gorski.

"Really," said the nurse. He stopped in front of the elevator, said, "Thank you, Officer," when the door opened and the cop pressed his hand against the elevator door as the nurse rolled Gorski inside. The nurse was silent as they rode the elevator back to Gorski's floor, but when the door opened and he pushed Gorski back toward his room, he said, "You know, I like the old movies and your mother is an exact double for Rita Hayworth. Did anyone ever tell you that? In fact, she could be Rita Hayworth."

The nurse pushed the chair back into the room, tapped Gorski on the shoulder and pointed to the bed. Gorski stood up, blanket in hand and climbed back onto the bed.

The nurse folded up the wheelchair, pushed it into the corner of the room. He glanced at the guy in the other bed, shook his head, walked back over to Gorski's bed and stared down at him again. "That picture was torn from a magazine." He tucked the sheet under the mattress. "It's not like I don't have feelings, you know. I could have treated you and released you, but I put you in a room. I didn't do it to raise our admissions, either."

The nurse started to walk out of the room, stopped in the doorway and looked back at Gorski. "They start rounding the transients up in the lobby at 5:15. They have vans that will take you back to the shelters. I suggest you enjoy that nice bed. You only have about an hour and a half left, Mr. Mumford."

4:18 P.M.

Wally looked at the text from Theresa: "I have the Literacy Showcase at Anixter Center tonight. Carol is watching Lou Lou. You need to come home tonight, Wallace. We need you. I love you. T."

He *had* to stay through the shift change. The administrator had put the kibosh on a room-by-room search, said they had to care for sick people and couldn't tolerate the interference. Wally had nearly told him it was easier than caring for dead people. Instead, he'd reminded him to tell his staff to be on their toes for any sighting of Gorski.

Wally knew there was ample precedent for a revenge killing. He knew of plenty of guys released from prison who wasted no time in killing the one they thought sent them there—and thus set the stage for their return to lockup. He thought about mobsters who had killed over a slight insult, a girl or a show of disrespect. And he thought about Gorski, tight with Costa for fifty-nine years, only to be betrayed. The rage had to be overwhelming, but Gorski had quelled it enough to act deliberately. Place by place, person by person, he'd made his way downtown. Of that, Wally was certain.

If they made it through the shift change, thought Wally, he'd go sleep, come back on Tuesday to interview Costa, get information on where to find Gorski. But first, he had to sleep. He needed to be sharp. Jiminy, he'd seen a patient in the wheelchair earlier, apparently the victim of some kind of accident, his face wrapped in gauze and all Wally could think was that it was Gorski, hidden but in the open, ready to pounce. But then, the nurse came up and grabbed the wheelchair, and Wally saw he couldn't have been as tall as Gorski and it hit him: his nerves were frayed by the lack of sleep and the loss. He was filled with too much adrenaline, caffeine. He was overcompensating, pushing too hard. He reached for any explanation. Except the one he knew was true: He was afraid.

4:20 P.M.

Martin stared at the floor in the hall. He felt the dampness under his arms; steam seemed to rise past the collar of his suit coat. He stood straight, leg-locked, rigid. His posture reflected his attitude; shame replaced by conviction. He'd find Gorski, put him on trial, lock him away. He'd spend the time before the trial dotting every *i* and crossing every *t*. He'd make sure that anyone connected with the Outfit went away, forever. He'd avenge Anna. He'd . . .

A shoulder tap knocked Martin out of his thoughts. He looked up, saw Wally's tired, solemn face.

"I just got the call," said Wally. "It's time."

4:57 P.M.

It was time. Gorski rose, gathered his clothes, took off his gown and got dressed. He took the covers off the bed, pulled the scissors from underneath the pillow.

He stepped over to the bed where the other man in the room laid, eyes fixed on the ceiling. On cue, the man's eyes dropped toward Gorski and his lips began to move, in silence.

Gorski tossed the covers over the man's body, slipped a hand over his mouth; his eyes bugged. Gorski plunged the scissors through the blanket, into the man's chest. A current of air blew through Gorski's fingers as the man exhaled. Gorski muffled the scream. The blanket filled with blood. He waited until the man stared off into the big nowhere, then yanked out the scissors, pulled the covers over his face.

Gorski checked himself in the mirror, saw no blood. He turned on the faucet, ran cold water over the scissors, then turned off the faucet. He slipped the hospital gown back on, over his clothes, then sat down in the wheelchair and slowly rolled into the hall, closing the door behind him. He sat for a moment, watched as a nurse from the next room scurried by, smiled at him as he nodded. He waited until she was out of sight, then turned and began to roll toward the elevator. He made it undisturbed and was relieved when the elevator door opened moments later and the two men standing there in hospital scrubs barely gave him a glance as they stepped to the side, let him roll inside. One of the men asked which floor he needed and when Gorski grunted the answer, the man leaned forward and hit the button. Moments later, the elevator stopped, the door opened and Gorski wheeled himself out of the car and back onto the hospital floor.

The number of yards to Frank's room descended in his head. Forty, thirty-nine, thirty-eight. He rehearsed in his mind:

"A man just came into my room and stabbed the guy in the other bed."

It would set off a chain reaction: The nurse would be skeptical, question him, but he'd answer with hysteria, plant the word. *"It's murder! Murder!"* The nurse would run down the hall, hit the stairs or an elevator and ultimately see the scene, scream the word, *"Murder! Murder!"* Word would spread, quickly and the FBI agent, Lowell, and that detective, Greer, would run toward the elevator like firefighters to a fire—they wouldn't be able to help it. He'd watch them go, wheel to Frank's room, ask the marshal a question in a quiet voice and when he leaned down to answer, he'd bury the scissors in his neck, drag him into the room. Then, he'd step over, say hello to Frank, make sure he knew it was him. He'd leave the scissors in Frank's throat, climb back into the chair and wheel to the elevator. In all the confusion, the cops wouldn't bother to check the patient they'd seen earlier in the day, the poor guy with his face wrapped in gauze who was on his way out . . .

Twenty-three, twenty-two, twenty-one . . . He stopped at the nurses' station. Perfect. The guy nurse stood at the station, alone, eyes on the counter. Gorski looked at him, then glanced down the hall. He blinked, looked again.

The hall was empty.

"Yes?" That fucking mutter.

Gorski looked at the nurse, gripped the arms of the wheelchair. He tried to hold his composure. "Where's the marshal?"

"Excuse me? It's time for you to catch your van."

Gorski paused, thought. "I know. But something's happened.

Where's the marshal, those guys that were by that room?" He nodded his head toward Frank's room.

The nurse sighed. "That's none of your concern. What are you doing on this floor, anyway?"

Gorski's voice rose. "Where's the marshal?"

The nurse looked back down at the counter. "He's gone."

Gorski's gut filled with acid. "Gone? Why? Did they move the man in that room?"

"You're full of questions," said the nurse, talking to him like he was some kind of piece of shit.

"Where the fuck is he?" yelled Gorski. He barely stopped himself from leaping out of his chair, beating the man senseless.

The nurse's voice rose to match Gorski's. "I don't appreciate your tone. The world doesn't revolve around you, Mr. Mumford. The man in that room died. And I don't know why you're so interested in that marshal or anyone else, but I do think you should be interested in your van driver. He might decide to leave soon. The elevators are right around the corner and I suggest you leave the wheelchair right here. We both know you don't need it." Gorski heard a notebook slap shut as the nurse crossed his arms, looked over the counter. "I can see you're dressed and you're wearing your boots, so you can leave the gown in the chair and be on your way. Now, is there anything else?"

"Yeah," said Gorski. He waited until the nurse leaned over the counter, gave him that "I'm waiting" look. "Go fuck yourself."

5:07 P.M.

Gorski rolled the wheelchair over by the elevators. He was in a state of shock. It was impossible to gather his thoughts, but when he looked at the elevators, it hit him: The cop who had been guarding the elevators was gone. And the marshal was gone. And that FBI asshole and dickhead detective were gone.

And Frank was dead.

Gorski yelled, "Fuck!" as the elevator door opened and he stepped inside.

5:11 P.M.

Wally sat in a fake leather overstuffed chair inside the hospital room that had previously been occupied by Francis Costa. He was afraid he might not be able to get up. His bones ached and his eyelids drooped and the chair was warm and comfortable. He looked over at the only other person in the room, Martin, who sat in the other chair, legs crossed, leaning back so far that his back nearly rested on the seat of the chair.

"So," said Wally. "We don't release official word of his death, yet. But, we let it trickle out. We buy some time, start putting some real detective work into finding this Gorski. You know, I feel like some kind of ambulance chaser right now. We just get a call after he's killed someone, then show up and hope we find something that will help us nab him. So far, that's got us a big helping of zilch."

Martin shrugged. "You know that's real life, Columbo. You follow the trail, questioning people, searching for evidence and more often than not, the perp does something so stupid they get caught."

"Not this guy," said Wally. "He doesn't have the ties. Usually, it's a friend or colleague that turns a guy in. This Gorski, he doesn't have to worry about that. But we'll get him."

Wally started to get up. He shook his head as he looked down at Martin, who had dark circles under his eyes. He'd just made it to his feet when he heard the scream, saw a security guard sprint past the door. At first, he thought he'd heard it wrong, but when Martin leaped to his feet and they both ran toward the door, they heard the scream again.

"Oh, my God! Murder!"

5:13 P.M.

A doctor stood over the man, searched for a pulse. He shook his head, stepped away from the bed. "He's been murdered!" yelled the doctor. "My God, who did this?"

Wally barked at the nurse. "What happened? Exactly!"

"I don't know!" shrieked the nurse. "The other man that was in this room came down to tell me something happened. I asked him what it was, but he just kept asking me about the marshal and you men."

"Who was the other man in the room?" asked Wally.

The doctor cut the nurse off. "Severe frostbite. A transient."

The nurse stammered. "Mr. Mumford. He was the other patient. He came to get me. He wanted to know why you were gone. When I told him the man in that room was dead, he told me to go fuck myself and left." The nurse put a hand over his heart. "And after the way I took care of him . . ."

Martin interrupted. "Mr. Mumford?"

The nurse's voice cracked. "The big man with the bandage over his face. I treated him for frostbite and mild hypothermia. But—"

Wally started to tremble, grabbed the nurse by the shoulder. "I saw him in his wheelchair!" he yelled. "He wasn't a big guy—"

"He was slouching!" yelled the nurse. "Please." He pushed Wally's hand off his shoulder. "He tucked his legs under his chair. I think he wanted to look more ill than he was. You know, a warm bed and free meals."

"How long ago did he leave?" asked Martin.

The nurse said, "I don't know. A few minutes ago. But why would Mr. Mumford . . . ?"

Wally reached into his pocket, took out one of the pictures of Gorski the hospital administrator had run off. He pushed the picture in front of the nurse's face. "Is this the man who was in this room?"

"It might be. His face was discolored and swollen, it was starting to blister. But he had identification. His name was Mumford."

Wally took his radio off his belt, shouted, "Suspect seen leaving seventh floor of the hospital. Possible that his face is wrapped in bandages. Consider him armed and dangerous. Apprehend anyone vaguely resembling Vitus Gorski!"

"Don't let anyone in this room until I give you the word!" Wally yelled to the doctor and nurse. He sprinted down the hall and skipped the elevators. He hit the emergency exit and rumbled down the seven flights of stairs, heard Martin close behind. When he hit the first floor, he burst through the door, ran down the hall past the admissions counter. People in the lobby stopped and stared as Wally ran by them, past the gift shop and coffee counter, then out into driveway in front of the building.

It was already dark outside, but the overhead lights in the loading and unloading zone in front of the hospital gave Wally a clear shot of the three patient transport vans that sat, idling, exhaust spouting from tailpipes. Squad cars were parked in front of the lead van and behind the last van. Four cops stood behind the vehicles, arms at their sides. Wally heard the purr of the engines and he watched Martin stepped toward the first van and motion for Wally to take the last one. Wally nodded, then stepped forward and tapped on the passenger window of the van.

The window slid down but Wally couldn't see inside the vehicle. "Turn on your dome light," he yelled. "Everyone out of the van!"

The driver yelled something, but when Wally flashed his badge, the man turned on the dome light, the passenger doors opened and people started to get out of the van. Wally stepped back, hand on his Glock and watched. To his right, he saw Martin standing by the next van, a similar scene playing out.

Nine men exited the van. All were thin, with ragged clothes and dull, uninterested gazes. It was obvious that being stopped was old hat for them. None were Gorski's size and when Wally glanced at Martin, he saw Martin shake his head no.

"What's up, Officer?" asked the van driver as he rounded the front of the van.

Wally handed him the picture of Gorski. "Did you see this man?"

The van driver shook his head. Wally motioned for him to pass the picture around, but no one remembered having seen Gorski. Wally took the picture from the last man, then said, "He may have had his face wrapped, like he's been injured."

"Like a mummy?" asked one man.

"Yes," said Wally. "Did you see him?"

"No," said the man. "But I know what a mummy looks like. I've seen 'em in movies."

Wally told the driver he could go, then walked over and showed the picture to the men standing by the next van. He struck out again, then handed the picture to Martin, who took it to the van at the front of the line. When Martin looked back and shook his head, Wally sighed.

The three vans drove off as Martin joined Wally in the drive near the front door of the hospital. A stream of squad cars pulled into the parking lot, sirens blaring. They formed a convoy as they beelined toward the front door. Wally stared at them, thought about how he'd disburse the men. He had to man the parking lot exits, convince the administrator to let them perform a room-by-room search. He'd . . .

A car door slammed. Roscoe Barnes stepped away from a Crown Vic, waved as he made his way across the icy concrete toward Wally. Two other men in blue Chicago Police Department winter coats followed Roscoe. Wally breathed a sigh of relief as the help arrived.

Wally felt a tug at his sleeve, turned to face Martin but then followed Martin's gaze as the FBI man stared at something in the parking lot, pointed with his right index finger. Wally looked across the drive, into the snowy lot and, at first, he didn't note anything. Then, the wind kicked up and he saw it through the light from a street lamp. A long piece of white gauze had been snagged by a slat on a brown metal trashcan. It flittered in the wind, pointing across the parking like a trail of cotton smoke left in Vitus Gorski's wake.

5:32 P.M.

The SUV reeked. He should've dumped Lopes's body the day before, but he hadn't had the chance. He'd planned on doing it after he'd fixed the engine, but those stupid fucking cops had shown up and that plan had gone to shit. He'd stashed the SUV in the hospital parking lot and hopped a cab to meet his mark, his unlucky look-alike, Mr. Mumford.

Christ. He couldn't believe everything had gone so perfectly after the ass-fucking of a lifetime. Once he'd found out about Frank's betrayal and butchered that talentless fuck Dragone, things had kind of fallen into place.

First, his visit to Phillie told him Frank was sick and in the hospital. Phillie hadn't known exactly where—that dentist knew pain, but turned out to have near zero tolerance. But that lady cop? She was one tough bitch. She may have stumbled onto the scene, but he'd never know why. The only thing she'd told him was, "He'll get you." But she wouldn't even tell him who "he" was or why she was there. Yeah, tough bitch.

Next, a nice warm place to stay after he'd found that woman in the grocery store. Her son and the guy the next morning were stumbling blocks, but they wouldn't get him caught. And the look on that long hair's face when he ran him over in the driveway? Now, that was funny.

No, even the Asian girl's apartment and car had turned out to be okay. Then, that traitor Henry had saved him a trip and, finally, the coup de grâce: Cordell giving him the room number and laying out the timing.

But now? Now, Frank was gone. He'd shit away fifty-nine years of business and friendship. And for what? A clean conscience before he died? "Safety from prosecution" for his family? That fucking idiot. Did he really think he could escape? He might be gone, but someone would have to pay. Maybe Bernie and that whore granddaughter. Maybe Cordell's son, too—'cause that hadn't worked out the way he'd planned.

Gorski took a deep breath, stared at the dash, which he'd beat nearly to death with his fists. The radio knobs hung by wires and the dash lights were out. He shook his head at his own fuckup; if he couldn't gauge his speed on the way to Louisville, he might get pulled over. That would be one major fuckup. Louisville meant a charter flight to Atlanta and then to Costa Rica, which meant freedom. He'd sit there at some bar on the beach, warm weather, Ticas and plenty of time to think.

The thought made him anxious, so he opened the glove compartment, took out the cell phone he'd been carrying in his coat. He'd only used the phone once before and the guy would recognize the number.

He punched in area code 507 and then the number and listened to it ring before a soft voice with a slow southern drawl answered.

"Hey Low."

"It's me. I'm probably five hours away. Be ready to go. Get me some beer for the flight."

"Sir," said the man on the other end of the phone. "I don't know how much time you've got, but I know two things: It's not my problem, and I don't need to get you any beer."

"What the fuck are you talking about?"

There was a pause. "I know your name, but I don't feel any need to use it. You won't be my passenger tonight, or ever, for that matter."

"You son of a bitch! If you screw me, I will kill you! I've paid you for that flight, good money. I'm meeting you in five hours and if you're not there, you know I will hunt you down."

The man whistled. "Well, hell yeah, that's what I expected you to say. But I'm not in Kentucky, and you'll never find me. Now, listen. I gave you the courtesy of accepting your phone call and I didn't tell the authorities about you. You see, you're in some mighty deep shit now, Mr. Gorski. Oh, shit, I said it. Well, anyway, I got a call this morning from a buddy of mine at the airfield we was gonna use. He told me he got a personal telephone call and a facsimile picture of you. Now, he didn't know you was flying with me, but he knew I'd registered myself and one passenger, so he was just lettin' me know."

Gorski fought rage, tried to keep the plan in order. "There's more than one airfield in Kentucky. Pick another and I can meet you there."

"Now, you see, that's just it. There are over eighty airports in Kentucky, a fact you might find hard to believe. But what's even harder to believe is that one Chicago Police Officer called 'em all and sent 'em that picture of you. A Detective Wallace Greer. How the hell he knew you were flying out of Kentucky, we'll probably never know, but I'm telling you, you ain't flying out of here anymore. And although I'll admit to being scared of ya, I can bide my time until they catch ya."

"Catch me," muttered Gorski, trying to stifle his rage. He lost the battle, screamed, "What makes you think they'll catch me?"

"A man takes the time to call every airport in the state of Kentucky?

I can't even imagine what he's doing in the state of Illinois to find you. Sir, you can take this to the bank. He's coming for you."

The line went dead. Gorski stared at the phone. He punched in the number again but didn't hear a ring. He tried it again and nothing happened. He tried it one last time before he crushed the phone in his hand. He screamed, then looked back toward the hospital. It was only a couple of hundred yards down the street from where he'd parallel parked near the curb and he could still make out the parking lot.

Cop cars blocked the entrance to the parking lot. The sight made him want to puke—or maybe it was Lopes—but the rage started to return. They'd stolen his life! Fucking cops! Someone was seriously going to have to pay. They weren't getting away with it! He was about to start beating the dash again, when an unmarked cop car stopped at the exit and a guy got out and started giving orders. A car turned into the lot just then, and the guy got caught in the high beam. It was that fucking detective. The one who'd made a fucking mess of his plan. Greer.

5:43 P.M.

Gorski waited until Greer got back into his car and it rolled away. Quickly, he jumped out of the SUV, opened the trunk and yanked Lopes's body out of the vehicle. He tossed it next to the curb, near the gutter. He closed the trunk, hopped back into the driver's seat and took off. Two blocks away, he made the car.

5:49 P.M.

Wally had told 'em to check every vehicle that entered or exited the parking lot. He told 'em that if he returned, he expected to be stopped and questioned, but one young cop had missed the point, yelled, "C'mon, we know you, Principal!" Wally had snapped, told the cop that if his own mother showed up with a box of cookies, he'd better search the car.

Wally had been up for thirty-six hours. He didn't trust himself behind the wheel. He looked at Martin, in the driver's seat. "Mind if we make a quick stop on the way? My wife's at Anixter Center. She just sent me a text. She'll be leaving soon. I haven't seen her since Romar." His voice cracked. "I have to see her."

"No problem," said Martin. "But you might think about getting some sleep."

"Not yet," said Wally. "Soon, but not yet."

They drove in silence. North on Clybourn. Shops and bars. It had turned into a big shopping corridor, especially around North Avenue. There was plenty of vehicular traffic but not many pedestrians out on a cold winter night.

They passed a few bars on the west side of the street. Wally looked in one window, saw a group of people standing around a table, laughing. "Laugh all you can," he said, to himself.

"What?" asked Martin.

"Nothing," said Wally. He looked north, saw the block-long, three-story brick building. He pointed. "Take a left on Magnolia and park in the back. I'm not sure if the back door or front door's open."

Martin passed a strip center, turned left at the light. He saw a battered fence with no gate but a vacant section that signified the entrance to the paved lot. A sign on the fence said, "Private Property."

Martin pulled into the lot. Wally saw Theresa's car, two vans and a white bus, but that was it. He looked at Martin, patted his arm. "Give me a few minutes," he said.

"I'll give you whatever you want," replied Martin. "We passed a Dunkin' Donuts a block ago. I'll walk back and get some coffee. Pick me up whenever you're ready—and then I'll drive. Hey, want a coffee?"

Wally opened the passenger door and got out of the car as Martin exited the driver's side. The wind gusted so much Wally had to shout as Martin walked around the front of the car and sidled up next to hm. "No. No more coffee for me, thanks."

Wally zipped up his coat, looked toward the entrance to the lot. He could've sworn he'd heard a car engine, tires sliding in the snow. But there was nothing.

Two headlights appeared.

5:57 P.M.

Gorski gunned the engine. The SUV's tires spun in the snow so he didn't get the speed he wanted, but it worked. He caught Greer head on—he saw the man thrust out his hands at the last moment, but the force sent him back ten feet. The cop landed on his ass, flipped over and Gorski saw the back of his head bounce off the frozen pavement.

Lowell was hit by the left side of the front bumper. He spun, banked off the Impala and crumpled near the front tire.

Gorski stomped on the brakes, fishtailed to a stop. He leaped from the SUV, ran over to Lowell. He bent over him, saw recognition in the FBI prick's eyes. "Are you okay, pal?" asked Gorski. He pulled the scissors from inside his coat and plunged them into Lowell's chest. The guy blew air like a belch of chimney smoke.

Gorski yanked on the scissors, but they wouldn't budge. He figured they were stuck in a rib, said, "Fuck it," and got to his feet.

The other son of a bitch, Greer, lay flat on his back, arms at his sides. Gorski walked over to him, leaned over, saw his eyes were shut. He unzipped Greer's coat, took the Glock from the shoulder holster. He reached down, took the radio off the cop's belt and smashed it against the cement. He heard vibrating and reached inside Greer's sport coat and pulled out his cell phone. The message icon was illuminated in the dark.

Gorski opened the phone, clicked on the message icon, looked at the last message, then followed the message trail for "Theresa." The next-to-last message read, "I have the Literacy Showcase at Anixter Center tonight. Carol is watching Lou Lou. You need to come home tonight, Wallace. We need you. I love you. T."

He read the last message, again. "Are you coming?"

Gorski laughed out loud as he punched Greer in the jaw, for good measure, said, "Oh yeah. I'm coming."

6:12 P.M.

The cold air snapped Wally awake. There was a pounding in his head. His vision was blurred. He rolled over, felt pain from his tailbone to the top of his head. The nausea came from nowhere, but it came quickly. He tossed his head to the side, threw up in dirty snow.

What was he doing? Why was he lying outside in a snowy parking lot?

It came back to him the moment he saw Martin.

Wally slapped his hands on the icy pavement, tried to get to his feet, but he stumbled forward, lurched and fell next to Martin.

"Jesus! Martin!" he yelled.

Martin's eyelids flickered. His coat was soaked in blood. Wally saw the scissors, thought better of trying to yank them free. Instead, he took off his coat, molded it around the scissors. "Can you hold this in place?" he asked. Martin nodded, so Wally said, "Good. Keep pressure on it."

Wally reached for his radio. Gone. He reached for his cell phone. When he realized it was gone, too, he fought to stave off panic.

"Martin, do you have your cell phone?"

Martin looked up at him, wheezed. "No. I felt around for it. It must've been knocked from my pocket. Wally. It was him!"

Wally was confused. "Him? The guy who hit us?"

"I saw him when he stabbed me. It's Gorski!"

Wally bolted upright, yelled, "Theresa!" He looked down at Martin. "Hang in there. I've got to get my wife. I'll get to a phone—"

"He's in there," said Martin. "Look. The SUV's still here. I saw him walk around the building."

Wally lifted a knee, got one foot underneath himself. He braced his hands against the car, got to his feet. "Hold on," he said to Martin as he stumbled away, ran toward the building.

6:16 P.M.

The back door was locked. Wally ran back toward Magnolia, east around the building, then north. Clybourn was full of cars but he didn't have time to stop and flag someone down. Instead, he sprinted toward the blue awning.

Wally jerked open the front door. It was dark inside but the exit sign gave off just enough light. To his right was a reception window; to his left, an elevator and a set of concrete stairs. He heard a wail from the stairwell and a man stumbled down the steps and into the lobby.

"That man laughed at me!" he said. He was crying. He was short and had on dark pants and a thick sweater. He wore thick glasses and his thin hair was wet with sweat. Wally recognized him. He was one of Theresa's students.

Wally's heart pounded. "What man was laughing at you?"

The man wailed, again. "The big man! He laughed at me!"

Wally stepped forward, offered his hand. The man took it, tentatively. "I'm Theresa's husband, Wally. Do you remember me?"

"Yes," said the man. "I'm Clifford. Do you remember me?"

"Yes, Clifford. Now, where is Theresa?"

"The big man took her!" yelled Clifford. "I told him not to, but he just laughed at me. He hit Theresa when she screamed."

Wally gulped. He tried to keep his voice calm. "Where did he take her?"

"Up the stairs. I wanted to go after them, but the man told me he would hurt Theresa if I did."

Wally looked at the stairs. The second floor was mostly open space, a work area full of racks, where they did packaging. The classrooms were on the third floor.

"Clifford, can you count to ten?"

"Yes."

"Then I want you to start counting to ten. When you reach ten, I want you to start yelling, 'Help!' as loud as you can. When you've yelled 'Help' ten times, I want you to go outside and keep yelling 'Help' until someone comes. But Clifford, if the big man comes outside, I want you to run. That's very important. If you see him, run!"

Clifford sniffled. "When do I start counting, Wally?"

Wally took off in a sprint. "Now!"

6:21 P.M.

"Help!"

"Help!"

Clifford's cries rang out as Wally made it to the second floor. He ran through the packaging area, stopped briefly to listen, but heard only the heating system and creaks from the building.

"Help!"

There's a freight elevator on the far end of the building, a set of stairs nearby. The classrooms are on the north end of the building. There's a computer center . . . If I can make it onto that floor, I can find them. Please, God! Keep her alive!

Wally kicked off his shoes as he heard Clifford's loud, "Help!" Then he heard it again, the sound was muffled, but clear: "Help."

Clifford was outside.

6:23 P.M.

It was an old-fashioned freight elevator, deep and dark with wood slats and control buttons on the inside. Wally lowered the gate, tried to reach inside through the slats to touch the controls, but his arm was too big. He gripped the sides of one of the slats, pulled and broke it off at the top, then the bottom. Then, he pushed the broken slat through the gap in the gate and touched the button for the third floor. When the elevator started to rise, he turned and ran toward the stairs.

The pain in his back and legs nearly dropped him when he reached the first step, so Wally used the wood slat like a crutch. He steadied himself with the makeshift crutch, then grabbed the handrail with his right hand. The stairwell was pitch dark. The only sounds other than his breathing were the freight elevator and the old building's constant hum.

Nothing came from the top of the stairs. No light. No sound. He could be up there, standing on the top step, thought Wally, with my Glock or some other kind of weapon. Or he could just step out of the darkness, push me, watch as I plummet down the stairs.

Wally stared up into the darkness. His eyes didn't adjust. He couldn't see a thing. He'd have to feel his way to the stop of the stairs, find the door. And who knew what would be waiting.

But he was certain of two things. Theresa was up there, somewhere. And so was Vitus Gorski.

6:24 P.M.

Martin's lips smacked with each breath, made an odd, popping sound. He was cold. The blood in his coat had frozen. He rose up on his left elbow, slipped his right hand into the sleeve of Wally's coat, then grabbed the scissor blades. When he yanked them free, he felt a spurt of warm blood gush down his stomach. He dropped the scissors, rolled onto his stomach, then rose up on his elbows and slowly pulled his knees underneath him. When he reached an upright position, he fell forward, slapped the car with his palms and dug his fingers inside the frame by the passenger window. His arms and legs trembled as he lifted himself to a standing position. When he finally stood, he turned, but nearly fell.

His head swam as he looked at the corner of the building. It was twenty yards away but looked like twenty miles. But he had to make it. Wally and his wife needed him. They were inside. With the man who had killed Anna.

Martin untucked his shirt, rolled up the bottom half and pressed it against his wound. Then, he did what he'd been doing his entire life.

He ran.

6:25 P.M.

Wally made it to the top step. He stopped, lifted the piece of wood like a baseball bat. Light peeked under the doorframe. He opened the door, slowly stepped into the hall, wood cocked.

The hallway was empty. He craned his neck, listened. No voices. Nothing. He stepped across the hall, into the north-south hall and waited. Seconds later, the freight elevator jolted to a stop. Wally flattened himself against the concrete wall and waited. And waited. No one came.

Wally slid along the wall. His eyes were beginning to adjust and although he couldn't make out anything clearly, the light from the streetlights that snuck in through the windows allowed him to make out the doorways. The doors were closed, probably a sign that the rooms had been cleaned. He walked east, across the hall, paused in front of each door. Still no light and no sound.

As Wally neared the windows facing Clybourn, he heard Clifford's muffled screams. And if Gorski was there, he thought, he'd hear them, too. And someone would stop, investigate. Gorski had to know that! So he'd leave. Or . . . he'd finish what he'd entered the building to do. It hit Wally like a shot of pure adrenaline. He had to find Theresa, now!

He was running out of time.

6:27 P.M.

The last classroom on the north end of the building. The door was only half shut. An interior office. Please, God, let her be here. I've never been to the other side of the building. I don't know where to look and soon . . . Oh, God, he'll kill her.

It was like Clifford's muzzle had been removed because his yell of "Help!" was louder than his previous screams. But, just as suddenly, the cries grew faint again.

Wally stepped toward the door. He gently placed his hand on the knob, slowly pushed the door open.

The room was completely dark, but as the door opened, the soft light from the hall showed several small rectangular tables situated in a square. Two metal framed chairs with plastic seats and backs were positioned in front of each table. The edges of the room were still dark and Wally was about to leave when he heard a noise. He lifted the wood slat into the air when he heard it again. It was a whimper. A low, weak whimper.

Wally knew it could be a trap. But maybe Gorski had left when he'd heard Clifford's screams or the elevator. Either way, time was up. He waved his left hand against the wall, found the light switch and flipped it up.

Theresa sat in a chair in the back corner of the room. Her arms were tied behind her back. Her legs were taped to the chair and her eyes and mouth were covered with duct tape. Wally yelled, "Honey!" and rushed toward her.

Wally stopped in front of her and when he touched her shoulder, she began to thrash and rock violently, side to side. Wally found one end of the duct tape behind her left ear and pulled on it. Skin tore and the tape ripped off most of her eyebrow as Wally unspooled it from around her head. But when one of her eyes was clear, he stared straight into it. "Honey, I'm going to get you out of here!" he said as he bent over and pried at the tape around her legs.

Suddenly, Wally heard the ring of a cell phone.

His cell phone.

The shot caught him just as he turned. It blew into the left side of his chest, toppled him over one of the classroom tables. He landed on his hip against the far wall, about five feet from his wife. He slumped to the floor as Gorski stepped into the room and closed the door behind him.

"You should have stayed out of my way," said Gorski. There was no anger. It was matter of fact. "I wouldn't have hurt any of you if you'd have stayed out of my way."

Blood pooled around his pants as Wally fought to stay conscious. He felt useless. His body wasn't responding. He pushed his back against the wall and tried to stand, but Gorski took four steps across the room and knocked him back to the floor with a punch to the jaw.

Wally stared in horror as Gorski leaned forward, said, "Stay put." His face looked like a yellow rubber mask. A huge blister grew on his right cheek and the skin above his eyebrows had split. Spider veins in his cheeks appeared to throb.

Gorski stood and moved slowly, methodically. He crossed the room, stopped in front of a black supply cabinet and opened the door. A few seconds later, he turned, two pencils in his hand.

What was he doing? Didn't he realize the place would be swarming with cops soon? Someone would hear Clifford's screams, stop to check it out.

Or would they? Would they listen to someone who was mentally challenged or dismiss him?

Focus. Concentrate!

"When it's your time, it's your time," said Gorski. He inserted one of the pencils into an electric sharpener. He kept talking while the device noisily ground the pencil. "It was Frank's time. And because you stopped me from helping him go, it's your time. And your wife's too."

Time. Buy time!

Wally leaned forward. Theresa screamed through the tape. The guttural scream and the sound of the sharpener forced Wally to yell. "It wasn't his time! Francis Costa is alive!"

The pencil sharpener went silent. Gorski stepped across the room, swatted Theresa on the side of her head with his palm. The chair fell toward Wally, Theresa out cold.

"You son of a bitch!" yelled Wally. He lunged forward, but Gorski stepped around Theresa, put a foot on Wally's shoulder and forced him down. He held the sharp tip of the pencil high, stared down at Wally, emotionless.

"You won't believe the damage it will do. I'll start with her eye . . . So, what did you say?"

Wally took a deep breath. There was a wet, gurgling sound as he inhaled. He threw his head back, then slowly let it fall forward until he stared Gorski in the eyes.

"Francis Costa is alive. I called his wife and got permission to move him. We got the administrator to approve it, then lied to the hospital staff. The body snatchers moved him to a private hospital."

Gorski stared at him, absentmindedly moved his fingers over the sharp tip of the pencil. He leaned over, grabbed Wally and flung him over a table. Gorski roared as Wally hit the floor. "You're lying!"

Wally lifted his head, looked up at Gorski. "I'm not! I was on my way there!"

"There's no way," said Gorski. He tossed the table out of the way, stepped over Wally. "Cordell told me they wouldn't move him. He said Bernie wouldn't allow it. And believe me, he wouldn't lie to me. You're just making up this shit."

"I'm not," said Wally. "You made a mistake! I knew it, so I played you!"

"You did not! You're making this shit up . . ."

Gorski paused, like he wanted to hear more. Wally seized the opening.

"You tortured Phillip Costa for information. You found out where Francis Costa was, but you needed to get to him. You had nowhere to go, so you followed that poor Patterson woman home and killed her. And that's when you made your mistake. You banged her head on that banister, moved her over the sink in the bathroom, slung her around the room and then wrapped her hand around the telephone. The evidence showed it and I know it. You wanted to make it look like an accident. And why? Not because you were afraid of getting caught—you already had two murders on your hands." Wally stopped, struggled for breath. "No, because you knew we'd connect the three murders and you didn't want us to do that, because you didn't want us to know you'd stayed."

Gorski shook his head. "You don't have any idea what you're talking about."

"Don't I?" asked Wally. "Once I saw that you'd staged that scene, I knew it. You were staying. You killed that little boy and his father, then took the train downtown. The conductor saw you, reported it. You killed that young woman in her condo—the building has a security camera and I saw you on the tapes. You were there when Hanratty killed my partner and then you killed him. I found your bag in the trunk of the police car. Lindbergh Hardware? They remember you. Then, you killed Albert Cordell. You threatened to harm his son. We'll probably find a body—a Mr. Mumford. You killed him to get into the hospital. And that man at the hospital . . . Jesus, he was a diversion."

Gorski stared at him. He didn't speak.

Time. Time!

"Did I miss anything?"

Gorski tossed the pencil at him. "Henry Lopes. They sent him to kill me."

"Who's they?"

"Who knows? That one was probably just Cordell. But who told that dirty cop to look out for me? I don't know. That stupid fucking cop thought I did, but I don't. But, I'll figure it out. I'll have plenty of time."

"No, you won't," cried Wally. He had to buy more time! "You're going to jail. You screwed up. If you'd have fled when the FBI pulled back surveillance, you'd probably be okay. And if you hadn't killed Mrs. Patterson, they probably would have assumed you fled. But Mrs. Patterson and all those other people? They're the ones who led us to you. You think you've been making your way downtown to kill Francis Costa. But all this time, we've been in pursuit. That's why you'll be brought to justice!"

Gorski laughed. "Is that what you think? 'All this time'? Well, it's over." Gorski pulled Wally's Glock from his waistband and turned back toward Theresa. But then he stopped, looked at Wally. "Tell me one last thing. What made you call the airports in Kentucky?"

"It was a guess," said Wally. "It was a hunch. Lopes told us about your trip there, said it was the only time you'd been outside Illinois."

Gorski nodded slightly, muttered, "Not bad." He lifted the gun, shook his head as he focused on Theresa. "Time's up."

"No!" yelled Wally.

There was a thud at the door. Gorski stopped, raised the Glock and pointed it at the door. The doorknob moved slightly, stopped, then moved again. The door slowly swung open and Martin Lowell pitched forward, fell to the floor.

Gorski laughed as he strode across the room. He stopped, rested a boot on Martin's head, then slipped it under Martin's shoulder and kicked him over.

Wally pleaded. "No, no, no!"

Gorski stood over Martin, who lay on his back, right hand inside his blood-filled coat. Gorski laughed again, said, "Fucking FBI," as he leaned over, opened Martin's coat.

Wally saw Gorski's eyes go wide, heard him mutter, "Oh, shit," as the gunshot exploded in the room.

6:31 P.M.

The pearl-handled revolver fell from Martin's hand as the shot tore through Gorski's shoulder. Wally's Glock flew from Gorski's hand, clattered on the floor as he screamed, "Motherfucker!"

The shot had knocked Gorski over two chairs. Wally's eyes darted around the room: Theresa, on her side, fastened to the chair, awake, one eye bugging, a few feet to his left. Martin, near dead, on his back, gaze fixed on the ceiling. Wally's Glock, ten feet to his right, nestled against the wall. Could he reach it in time? He weighed his chances, gasped when Gorski rose to his feet.

The monster's right arm hung at his side, useless, but he stood, staggered, made his way across the room, toward the gun.

Time. He didn't have much time! Wally gathered himself, fell forward, pushed off from the wall. He rammed his knees and elbows into the floor, frantically crawled toward Theresa. With one final heave, he flung himself over her, covering her body as he felt Gorski above him.

Time.

Fleeting.

Ending.

A loud thump. Wood splintered. Wally lifted his head from Theresa's side, looked at the door as the steel-toed boot blew through the doorframe. Roscoe Barnes stepped into the room, sawed-off shotgun pressed to his shoulder.

Another explosion. Wally saw Vitus Gorski's body fall, cleaved at the neck.

The sounds were distant thunder. His heartbeat fell. The drops of blood that followed each pump of his heart grew smaller and smaller.

The noise grew faint. The room fell dark. Martin tried to form the words. He wasn't sure he could find the breath.

"I hope this makes you happy baby. You've been so distant lately. You know, with this thing coming up, we won't have a lot of time together. Let's make it count. Maybe we should go to Lake Geneva for the weekend and snowmobile . . . I think I missed the turn . . . Jesus, I've got to turn around in someone's driveway. I think I just scared the shit out of some old man. Maybe he was growing medicinal weed . . . Ha, ha, ha. Okay. I'm here. I'll call you when we leave. I love you! Oh, I can't believe I left that on your phone. But it's true. I love you, Martin!"

He found the breath.

"I love you, too, Anna."

Three Months Later

Wally parked on Division. Walking was still difficult. His hip had been shattered; he'd probably use a cane for another six months. But he considered himself lucky; the bullet from his own gun had lodged in his left pectoral muscle. The doctor told him weight-lifting had saved his life. He'd wished Romar would've been around to hear that one.

Recovery had been awful, but he felt guilty. He certainly had it better than Martin Lowell. Martin was still bed-ridden. He'd nearly bled to death. The silver lining? The Bureau had flip-flopped, pegged Martin as a hero. They'd promoted him from his bed: Melvin Purvis status awaited.

It was just before five o'clock in the evening when he stepped into Butch's. Typical Chicago: Seventy-five degrees in the midst of a string of forty-degree days. The south window was open and a group of construction workers sat in front of the rail by the window, guzzled mugs of beer.

The doorman recognized him, nodded toward the bar. He saw Stacy before she saw him, but when she did, she shut off the tap, left a pitcher half full and sprinted around the bar. He raised his right hand to offer her a soft hug and protect his left arm, which was still in a sling. She slipped under his arm, threw her arms around him. He winced as she squeezed him, then said, gently, "Hey, easy. Easy."

Stacy stepped back. Her dark eyes were red-rimmed. She wiped her eyes with the bottom of her green apron. "I read about . . . I'm so sorry," she said. Her eyes filled with tears again and this time, when she moved into Wally's arm, he held her, patted her back and said, "It's okay. It's okay."

Wally tapped his cane on the floor. "Let's sit down," he said.

Stacy started toward the back of the bar, across from the jukebox, but Wally touched her shoulder, pointed to the side room and said, "Let's go over there. It'll be more quiet."

They moved into the side room, sat down at a high-top table. They sat for a moment, in silence.

It was her eyes. Always her eyes. He stared into them and she stared back, not afraid to let him in, somehow comfortable, trusting.

"I'm so sorry about Romar," said Stacy. Her lower lip quivered. "I really liked him."

"So did I."

Wally looked over her shoulder, back into the main bar. A green Santa Claus hung from the ceiling. Behind the bar, a stocky bartender poured a draught of Guinness.

Time. It was all about time. Not timing, but time. There was here and now and nothing else was guaranteed, ever. He took a deep breath, leaned over the table and took her left hand with his right hand. He was relieved when she gave him a warm, soft smile.

"Life sure changes in an instant," said Wally. "Romar's gone. His niece is living with us." He let go of her hand, rubbed his thumb and forefinger over his eyebrows. "I'm not sure what . . ." He stopped. That wasn't why he was there. He took her hand again and this time he saw that she was apprehensive. It was like she suddenly knew he wasn't there just to recount what had happened or to reassure her. He looked into her eyes, started: "The one thing I've learned—the one thing I know—is that you can't live in the past or future. There's here and now and nothing else. God willing, you have your memories and you've got to plan for the future, but if there's something you need to do now, do it. Because, you might not get another chance."

Stacy stared at him, puzzled. He saw that she gripped the side of the table with her right hand. But, he had her attention—all of it.

"Remember that story I told you about my girlfriend and brother?"

She nodded.

"That was nearly thirty years ago. Sometimes, it seems like a long time ago. Other times, it feels like yesterday. It's lingered with me, haunted me. What were they doing? I had all sorts of ideas, but one day, it hit me: It didn't matter. They're gone and I loved them both, but I've got a life to live." He sighed, shook his head. "And that would have been it, but last year, I got a letter from my brother's girlfriend's sister. Remember, I told you my brother's girlfriend took off after he died?"

Stacy nodded, again. "Yes."

"Well, she moved to a small town in Nebraska."

Stacy's hand started to tremble. Wally squeezed it.

"And it turns out, she was pregnant. She had a little girl . . . I never knew." Wally choked up. He gulped, regained his composure. "I never knew, or I'd have been there for them. My brother's girlfriend, Rachel, died last year. Her sister told me in the letter. She thought I should know."

Stacy gasped. She tried to jerk her hand away, but Wally squeezed it, harder.

"All we have in this world is the people we surround ourselves with and our short time together. Surround yourself with the right people and they'll be there for you when you need 'em. The wrong people, and you'll fight stuff alone." His eyes welled. He lowered his head, spoke soft. "I had to know, honey. I had that mug I took from here the first time I met you. Remember, you tried my Old Style? I had it tested. But I really didn't need the results. I already knew. The first time I saw you, I saw him."

Wally choked up again. He struggled to his feet, moved around the table. He was worried that he might frighten her, but he couldn't help himself.

"You've got his eyes."

Stacy's eyes filled with tears as she leaped to her feet, threw her arms around him and sobbed.

"Honey, I'm your Uncle Wally."

CPSIA information can be obtained
at www.ICGtesting.com
Printed in the USA
FSOW01n0137130815
9677FS